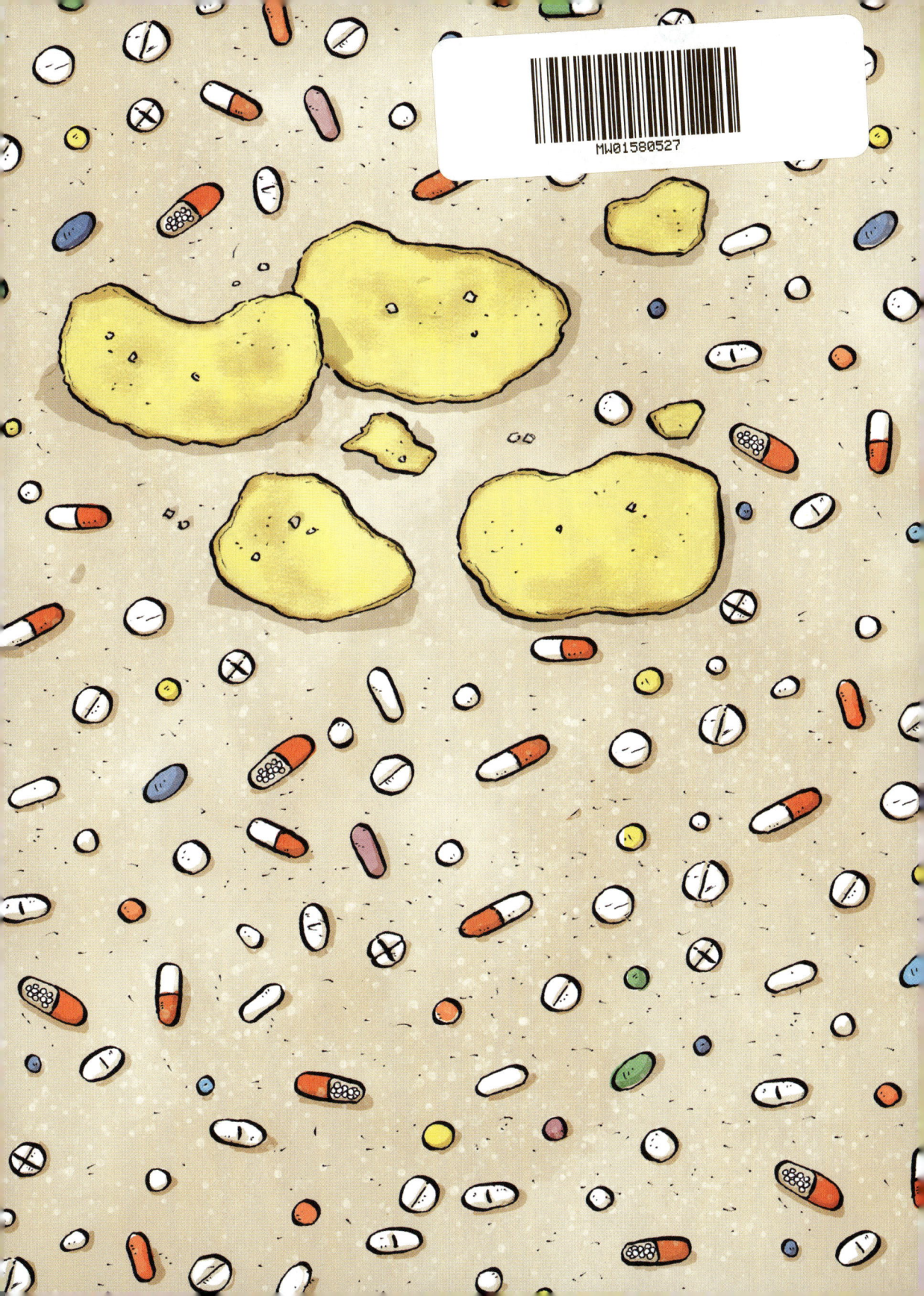

HELVETIQ publishing has been supported by
the Swiss Federal Office of Culture with a structural grant
for the years 2021–2025.

My Trip with Drip
A Graphic Novel

Originally published as:
Trip mit Tropf
© Josephine Mark 2022
© Kibitz Verlag for the original German edition
Translation made in arrangement with Am-Book (www.am-book.com)

Translation from German: Andrew Shields

ISBN: 978-3-03964-107-9
First edition: 2025
Printed in the Czech Republic

All rights reserved.

© 2025 HELVETIQ SA
Mittlere Strasse 4
4056 Basel
Switzerland

helvetiq.com

Josephine Mark

Translated by Andrew Shields

My Trip with Drip

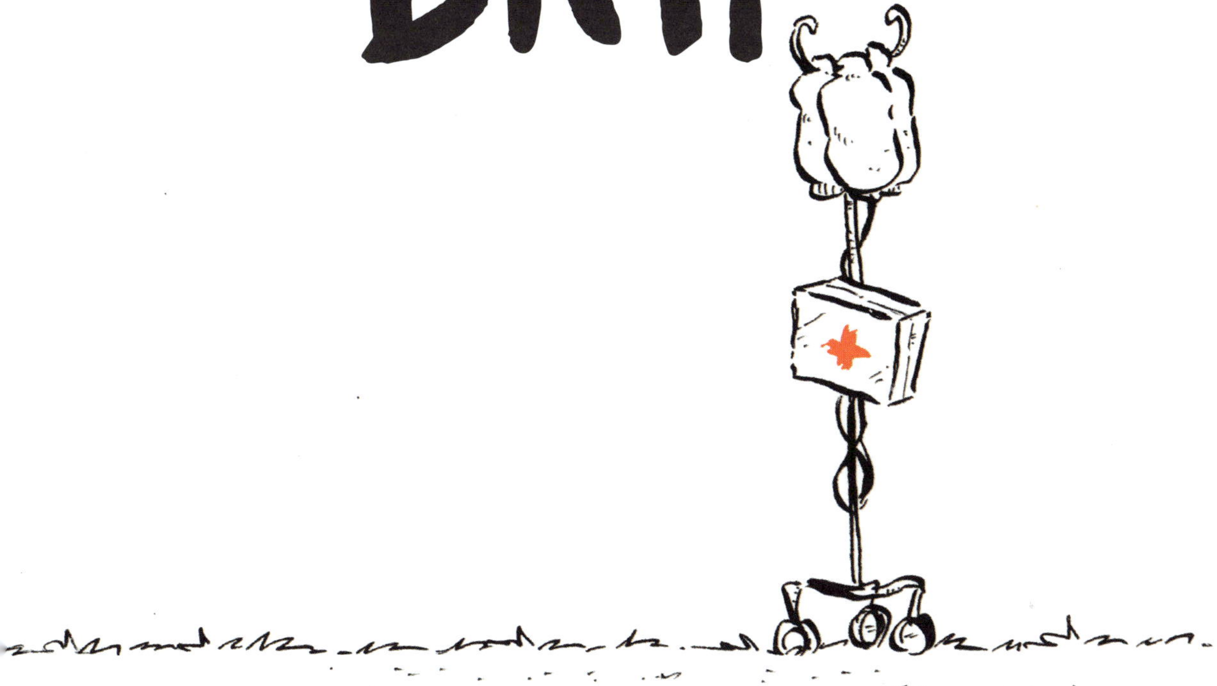

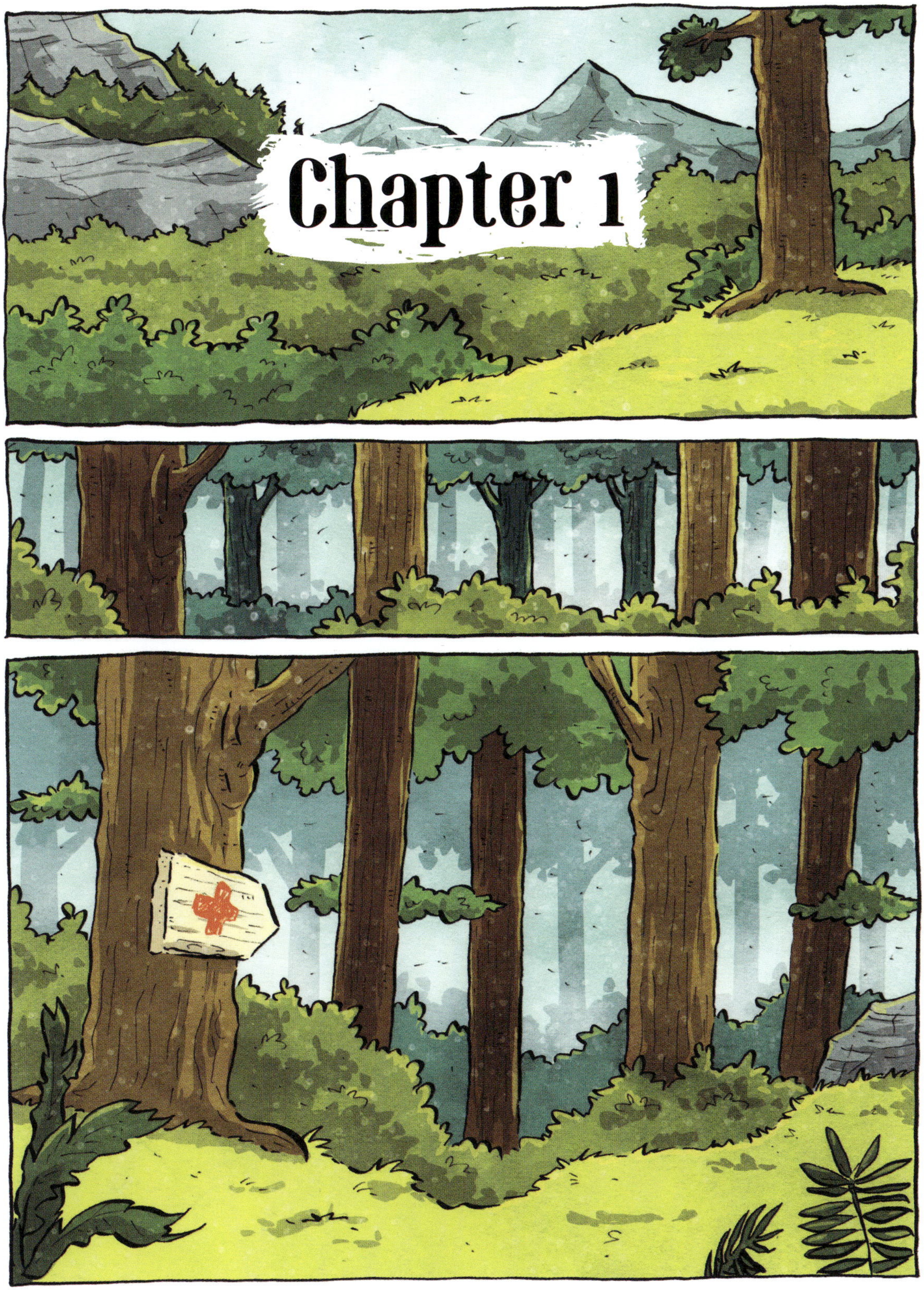
Chapter 1

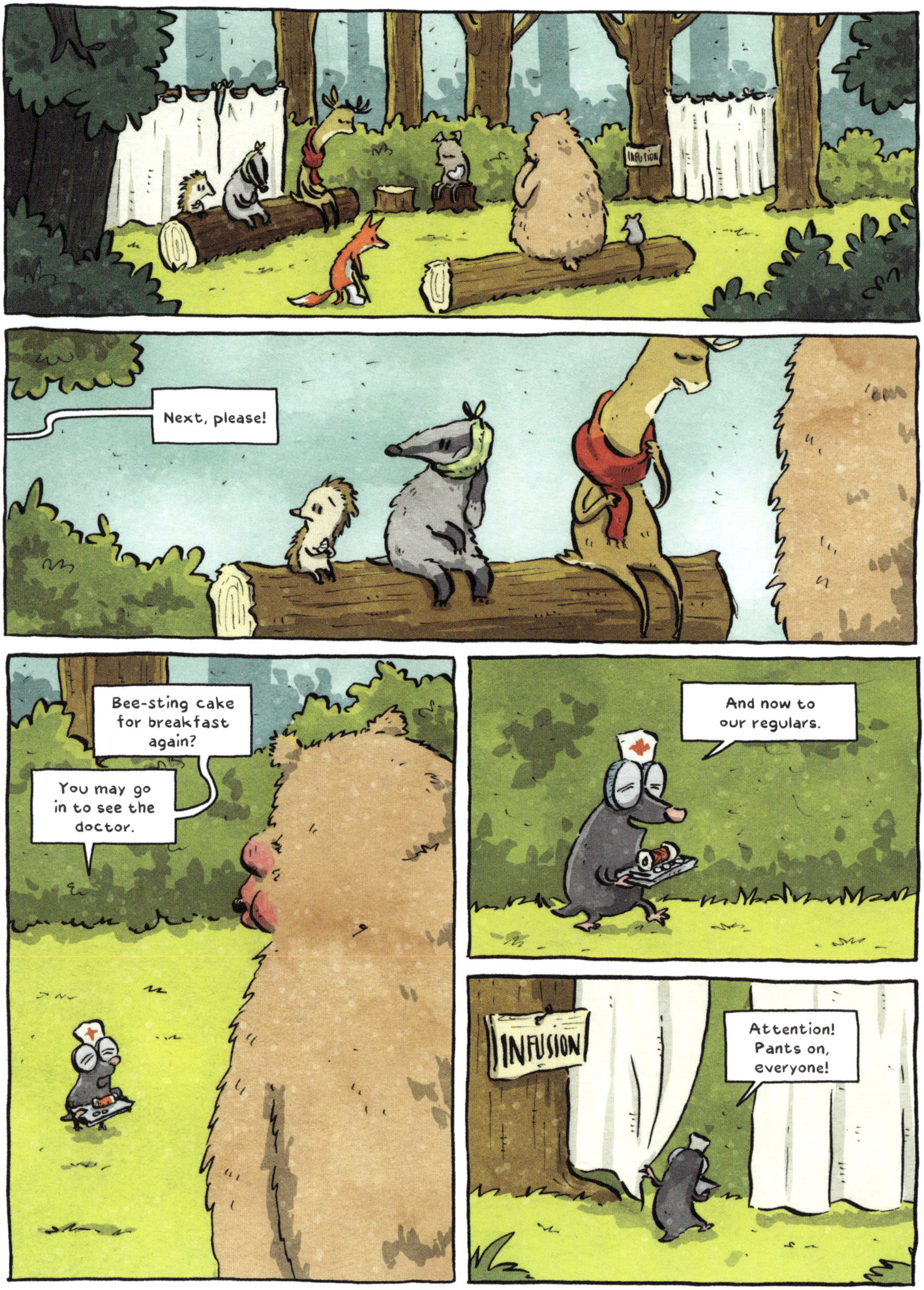
INFUSION
Next, please!
Bee-sting cake for breakfast again?
You may go in to see the doctor.
And now to our regulars.
INFUSION
Attention! Pants on, everyone!

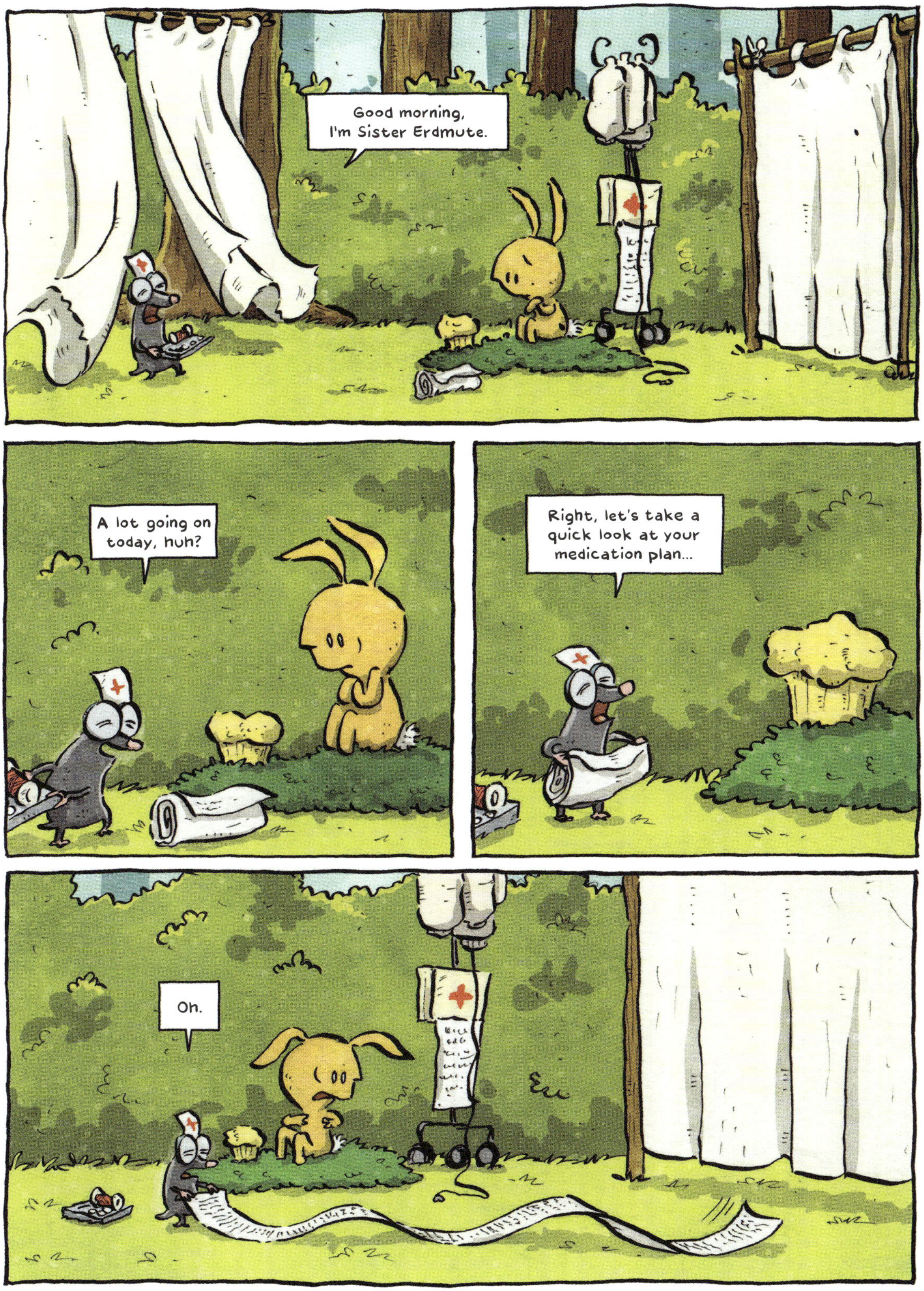
Good morning, I'm Sister Erdmute.
A lot going on today, huh?
Right, let's take a quick look at your medication plan...
Oh.

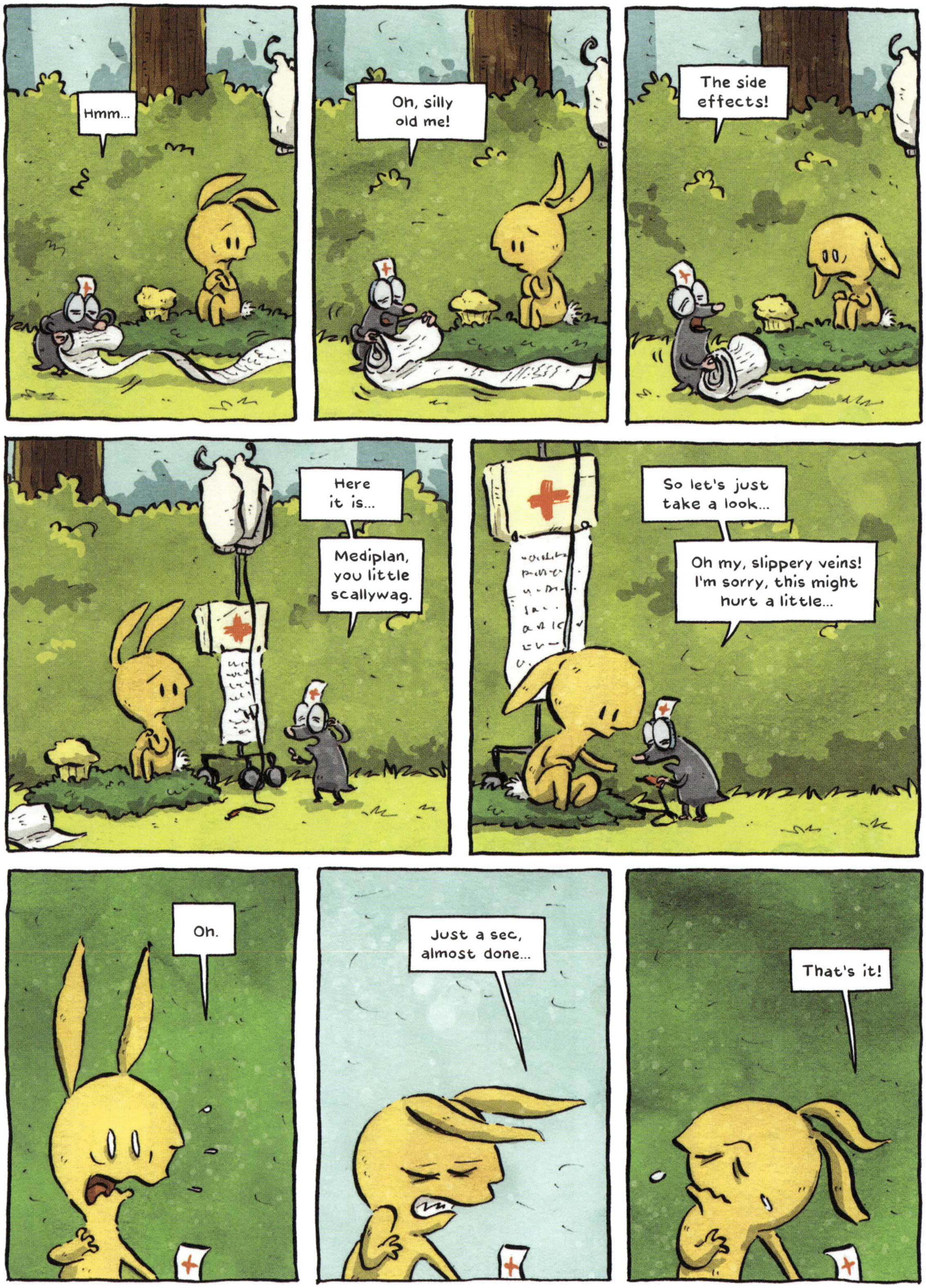
Hmm...
Oh, silly old me!
The side effects!
Here it is...
Mediplan, you little scallywag.
So let's just take a look...
Oh my, slippery veins! I'm sorry, this might hurt a little...
Oh.
Just a sec, almost done...
That's it!

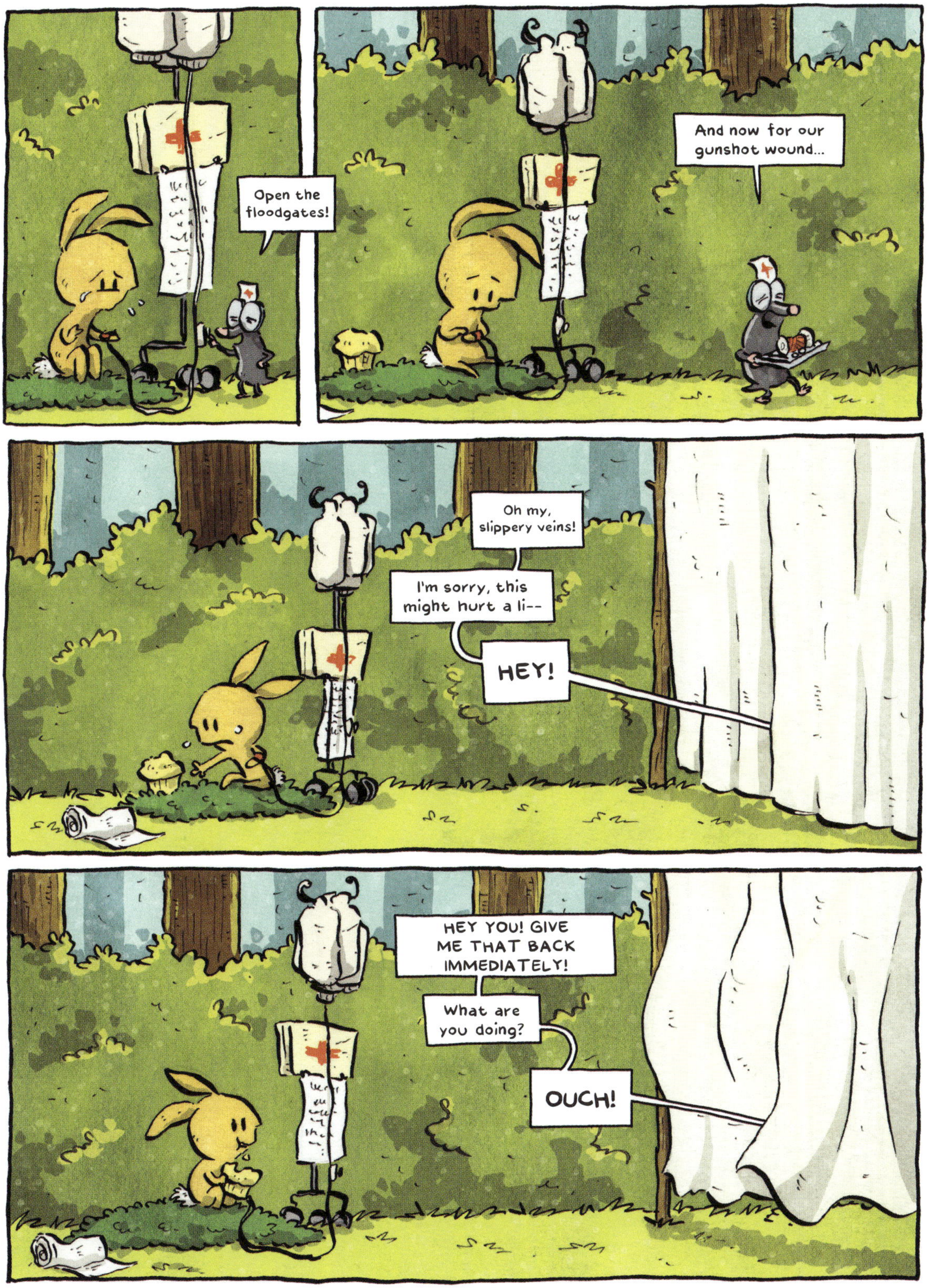

Open the floodgates!
And now for our gunshot wound...
Oh my, slippery veins!
I'm sorry, this might hurt a li--
HEY!
HEY YOU! GIVE ME THAT BACK IMMEDIATELY!
What are you doing?
OUCH!

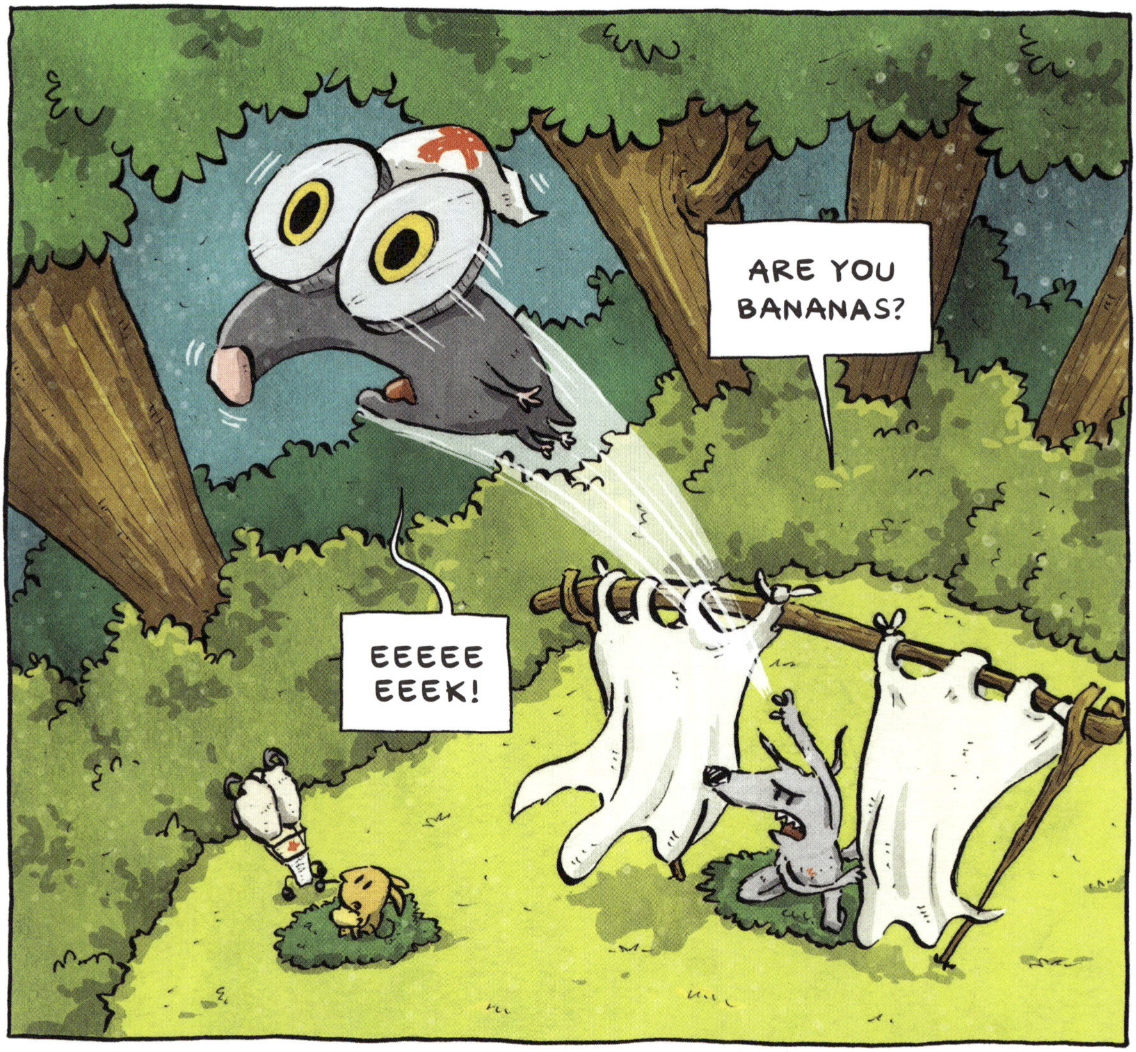
EEEEE EEEK!
ARE YOU BANANAS?

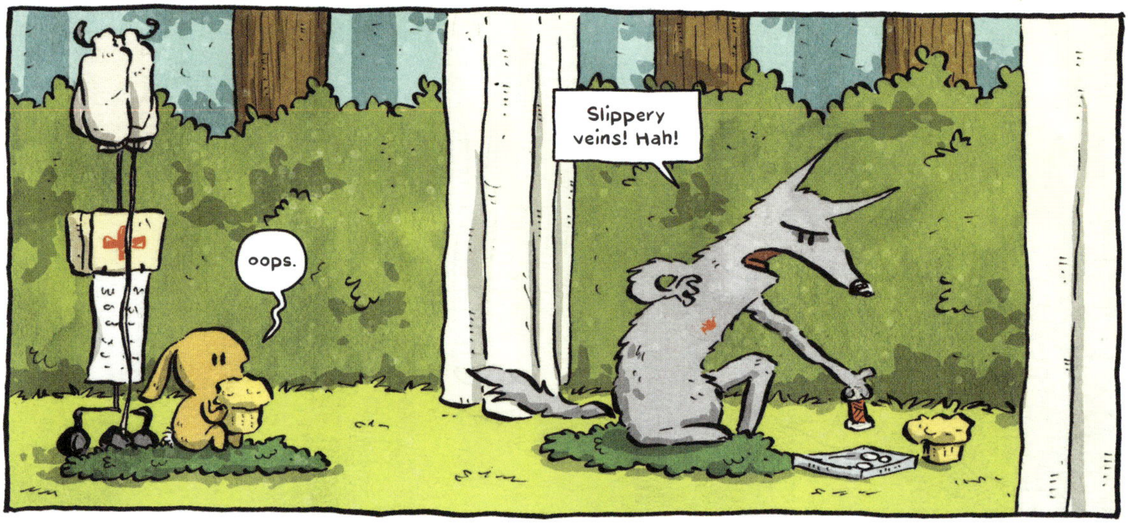
oops.
Slippery veins! Hah!

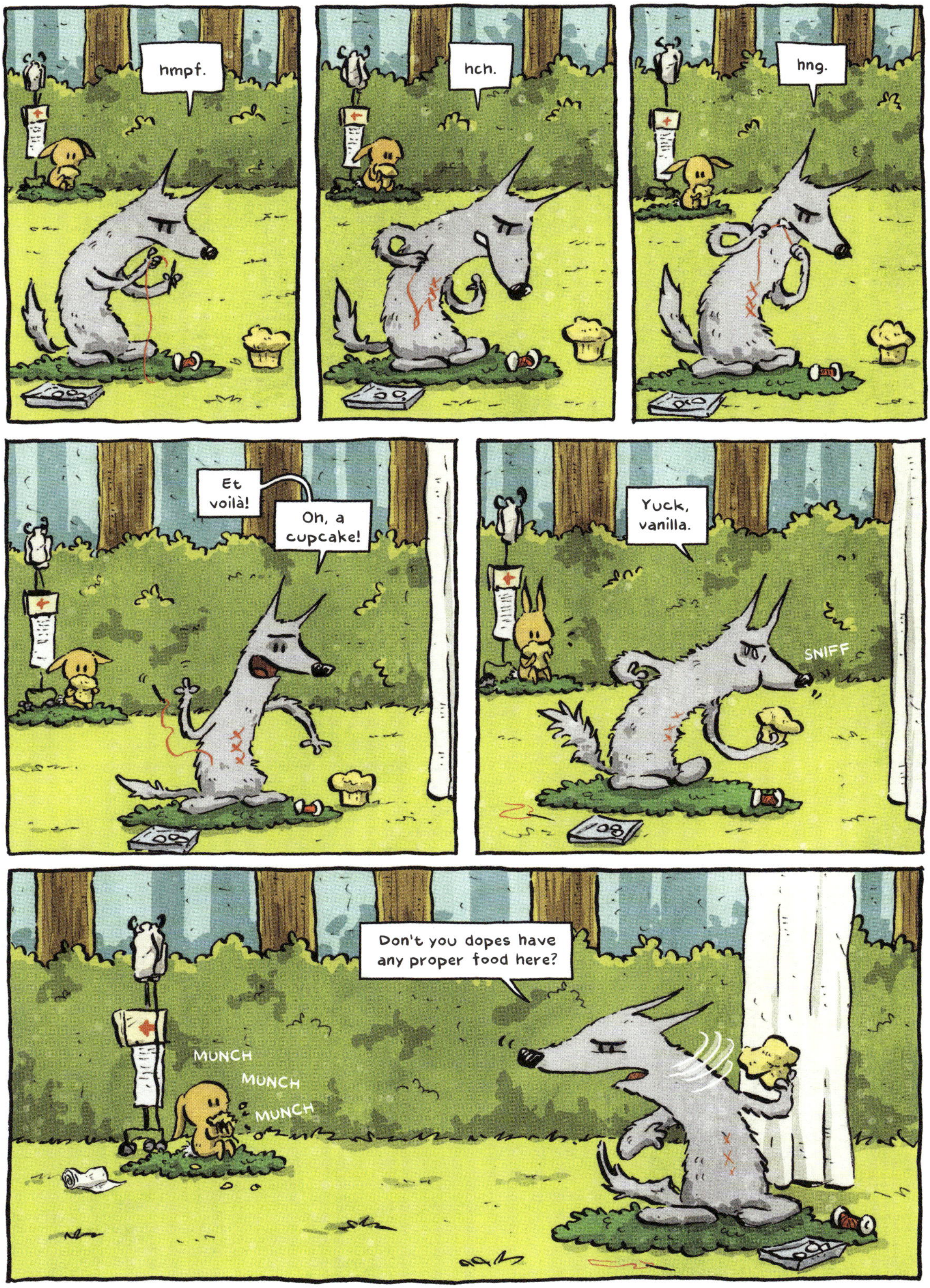
hmpf.
hch.
hng.
Et voilà!
Oh, a cupcake!
Yuck, vanilla.
SNIFF
Don't you dopes have any proper food here?
MUNCH
MUNCH
MUNCH

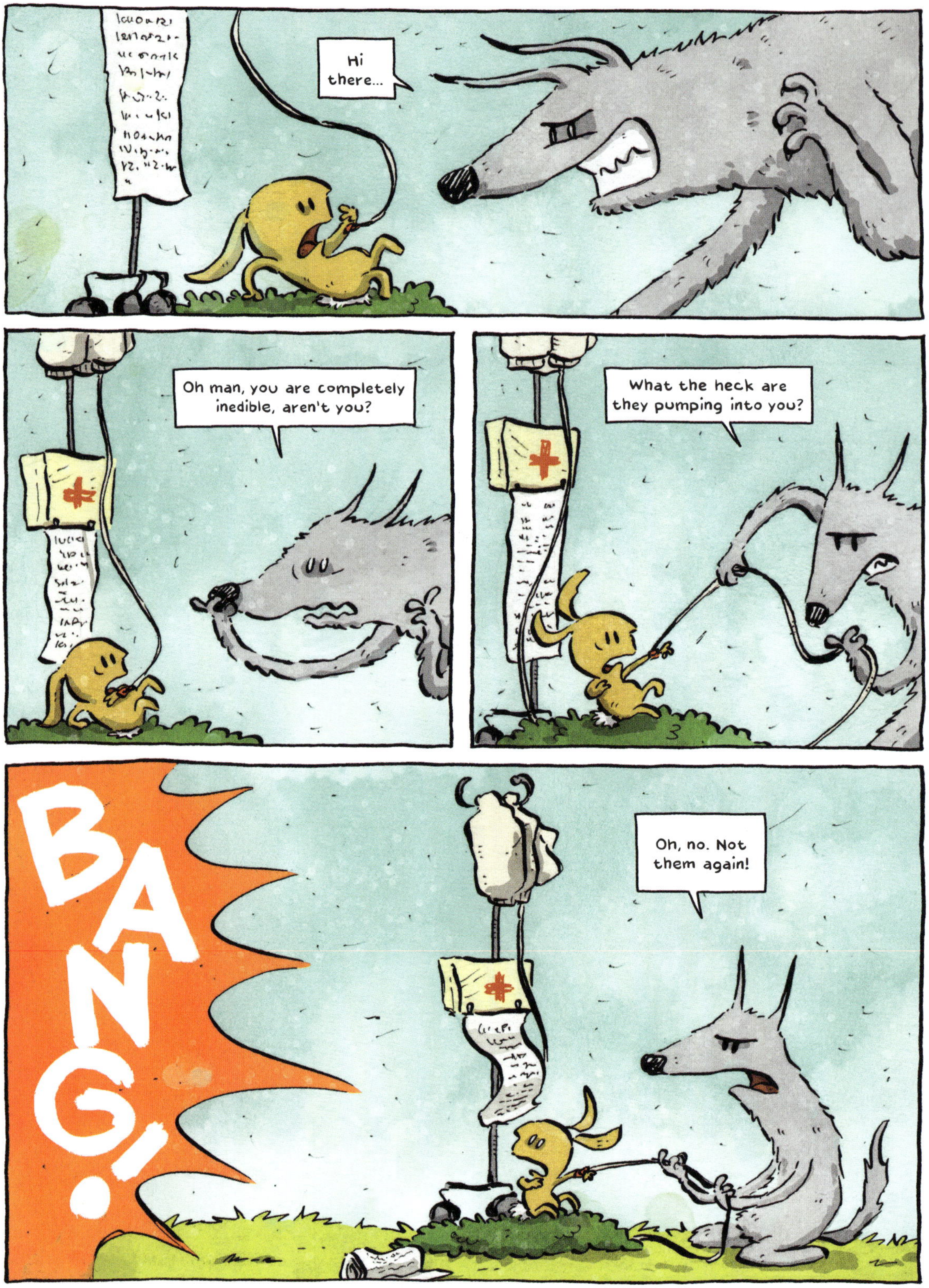
Hi there...
Oh man, you are completely inedible, aren't you?
What the heck are they pumping into you?
BANG!
Oh, no. Not them again!

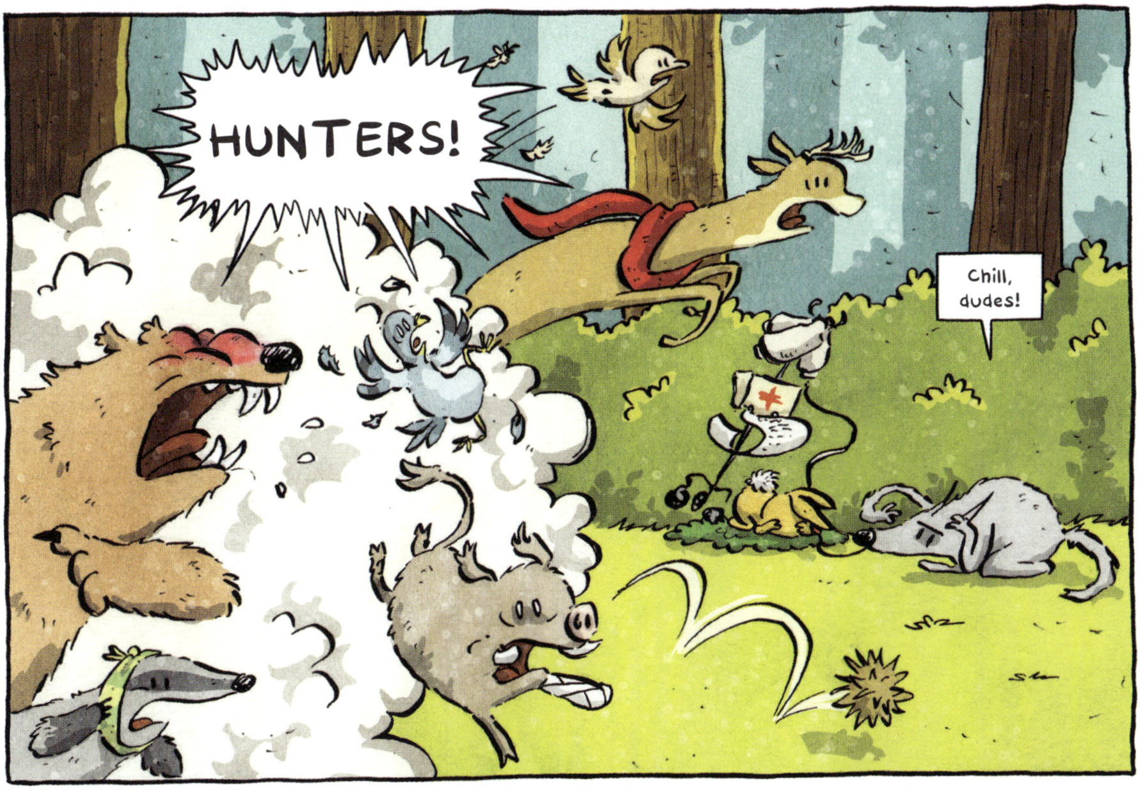
HUNTERS!
Chill, dudes!

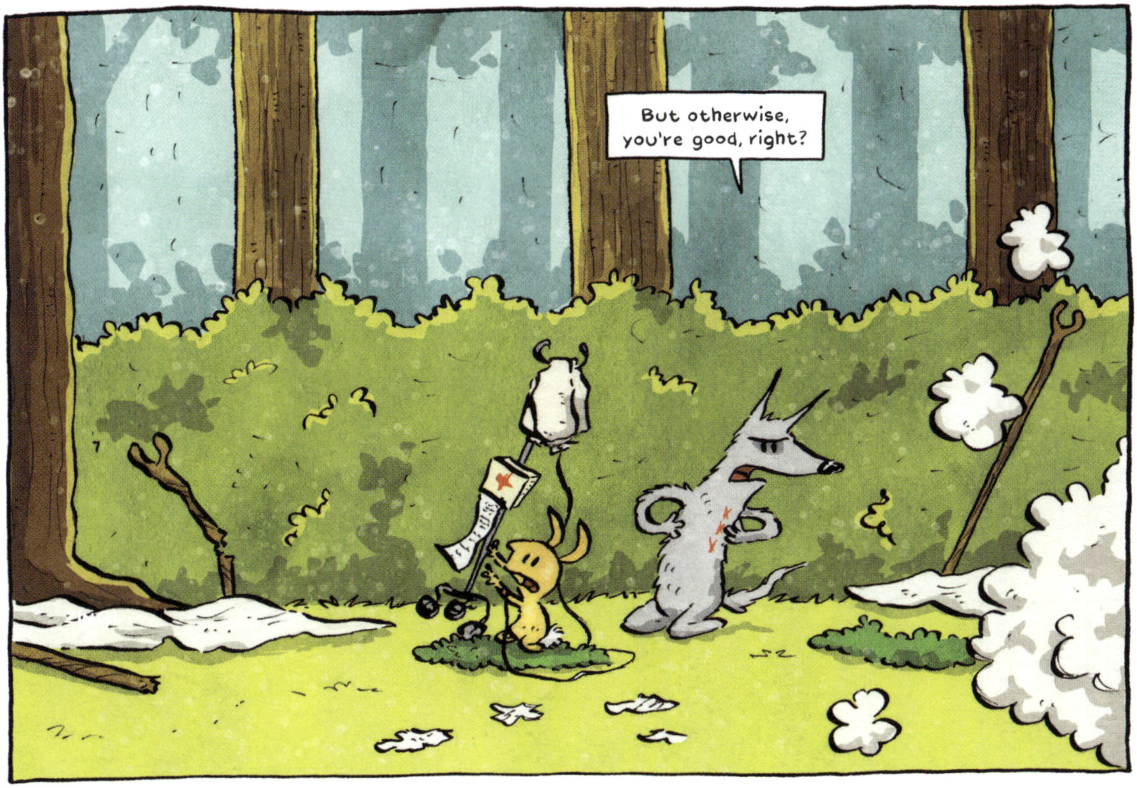
But otherwise, you're good, right?

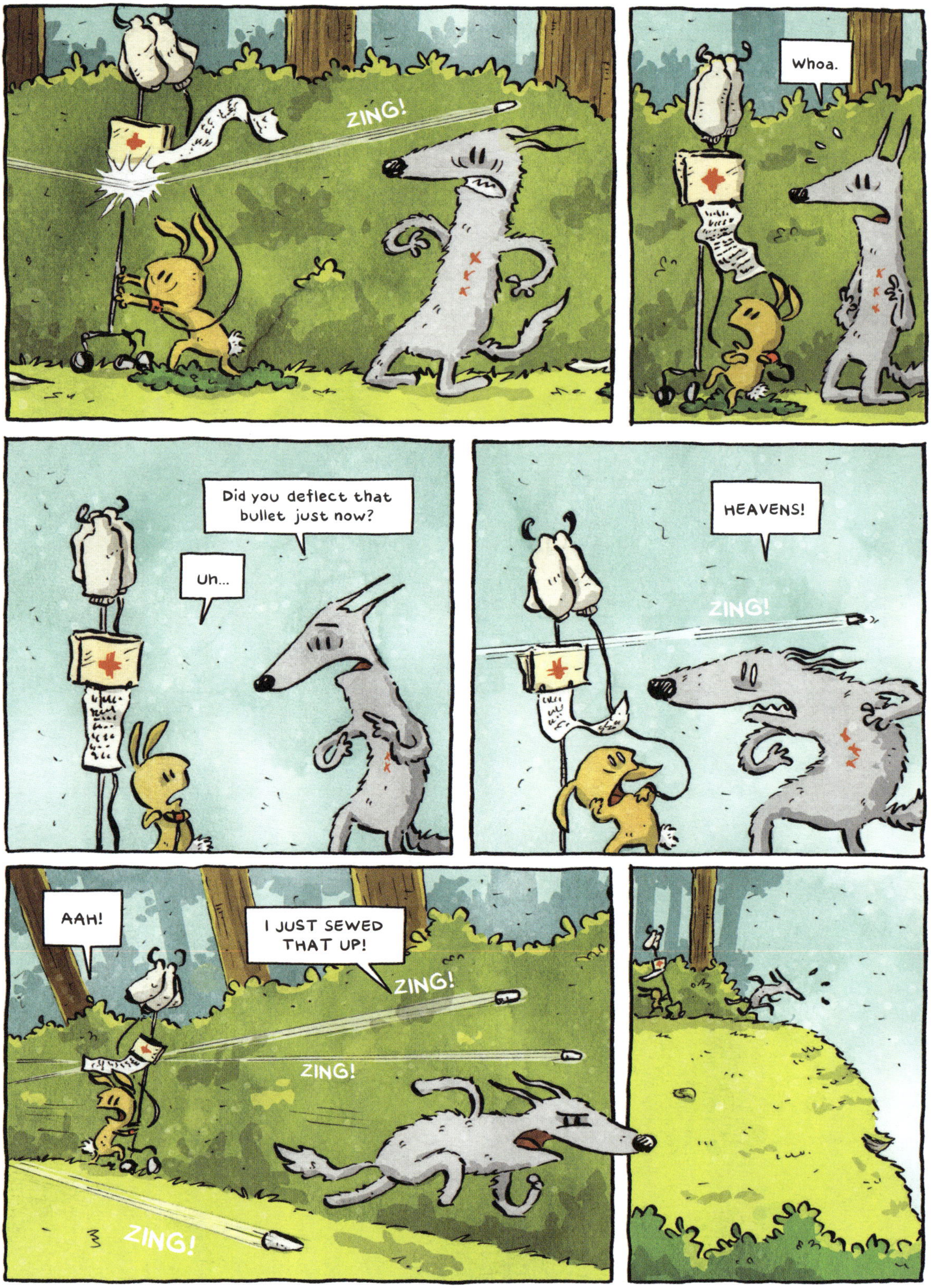
ZING!
Whoa.
Did you deflect that bullet just now?
Uh...
HEAVENS!
ZING!
AAH!
I JUST SEWED THAT UP!
ZING!
ZING!
ZING!

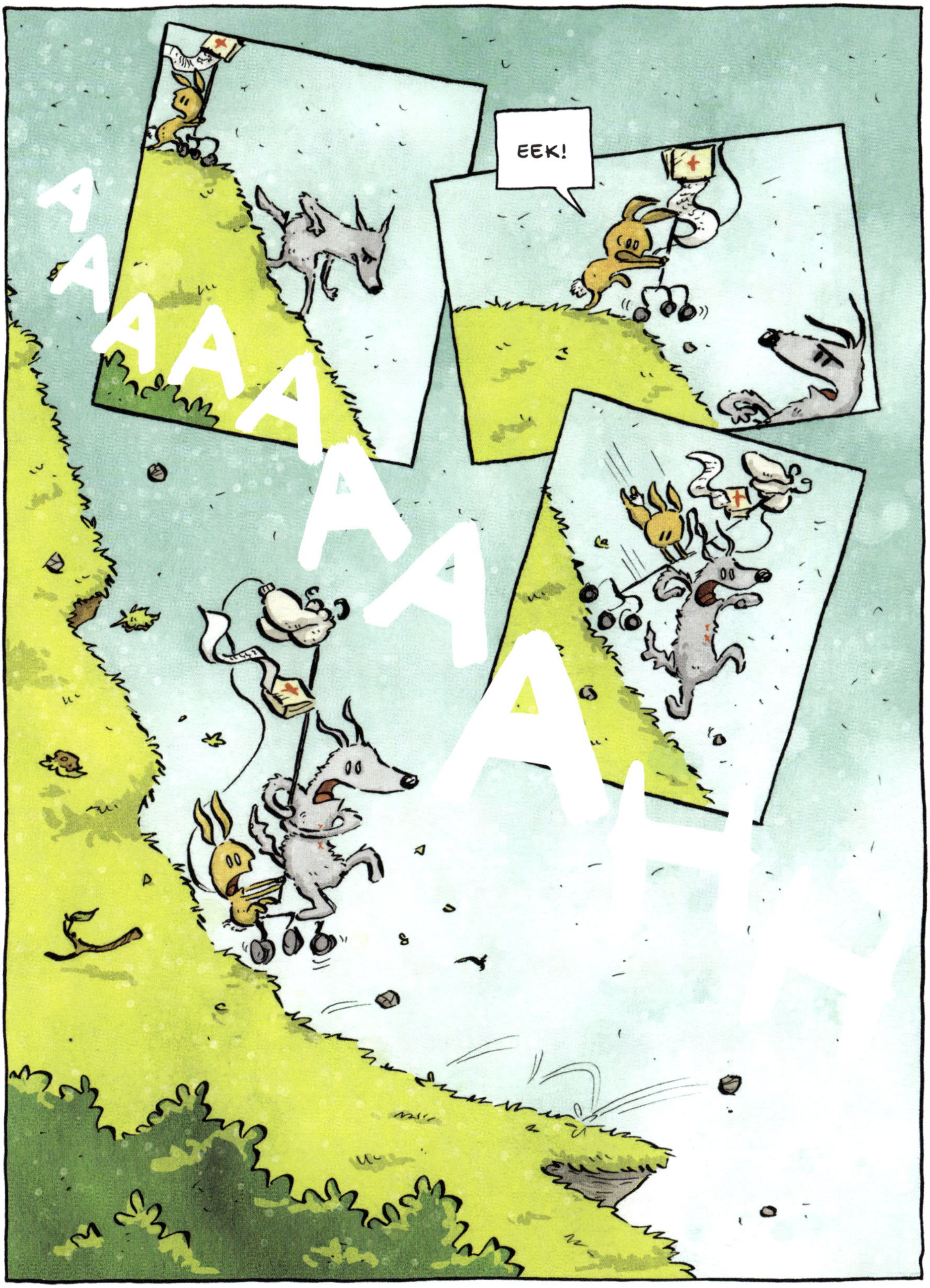
AAAAAAAAH
EEK!

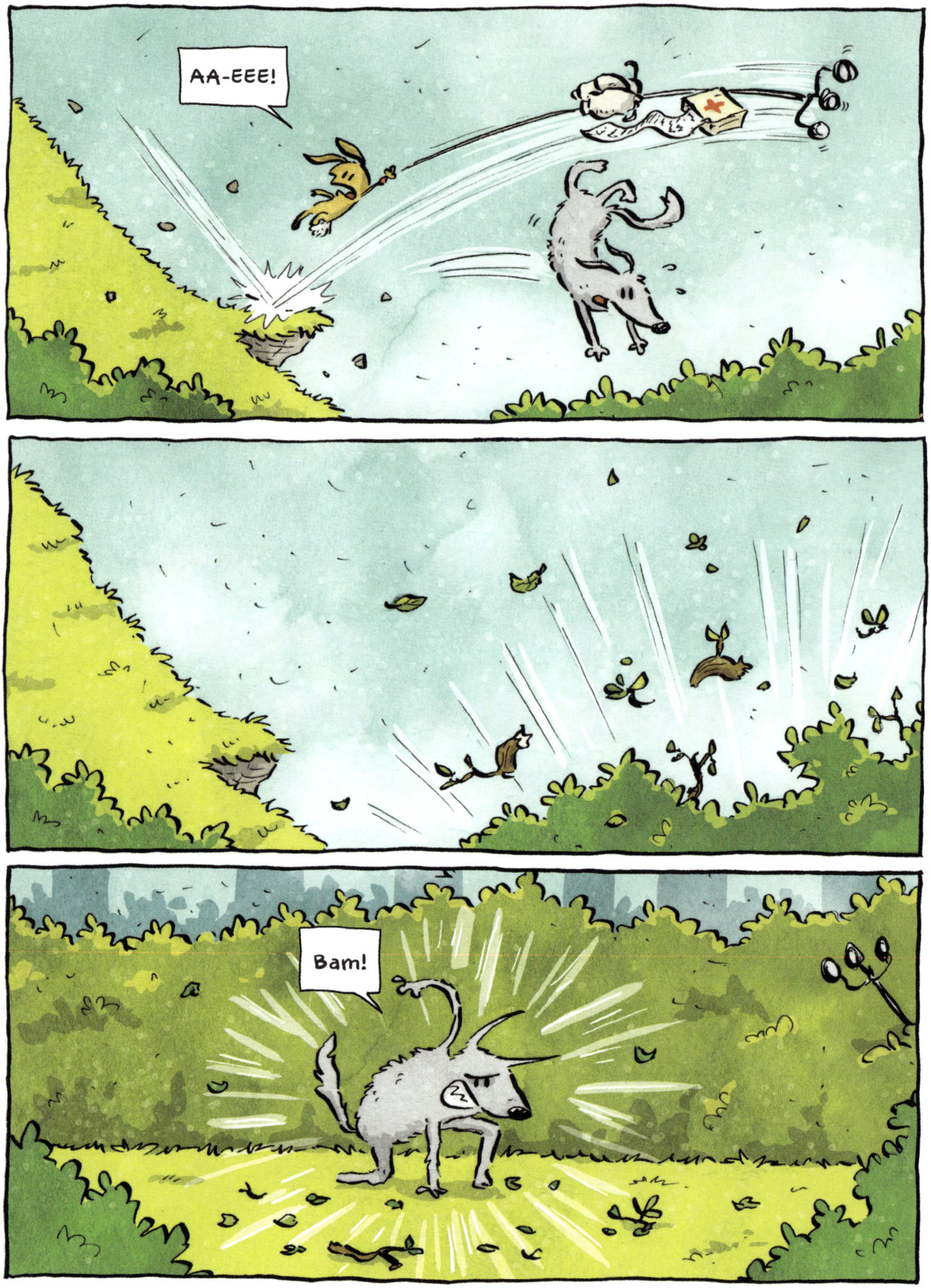
AA-EEE!
Bam!

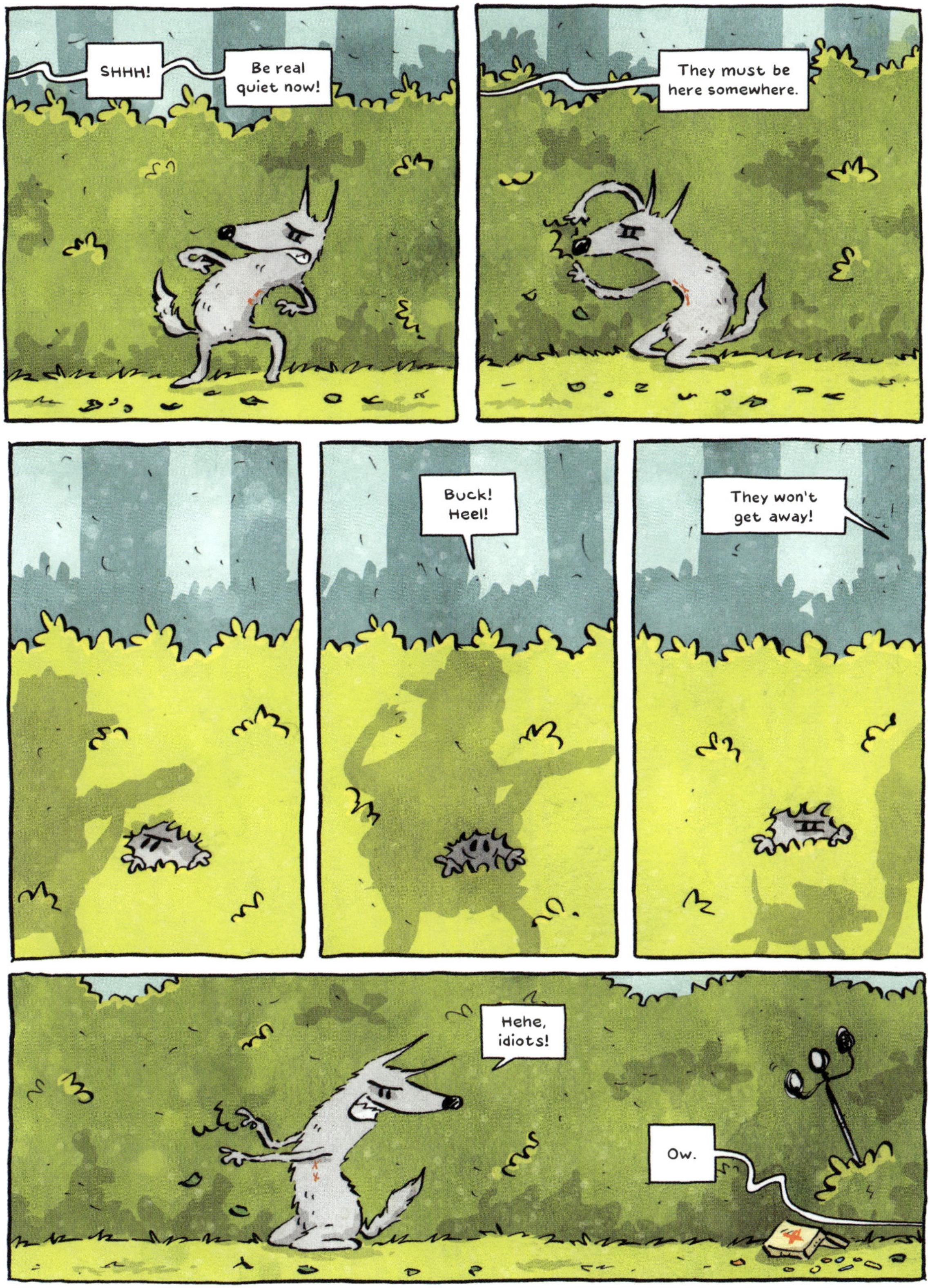
SHHH!
Be real quiet now!
They must be here somewhere.
Buck! Heel!
They won't get away!
Hehe, idiots!
Ow.

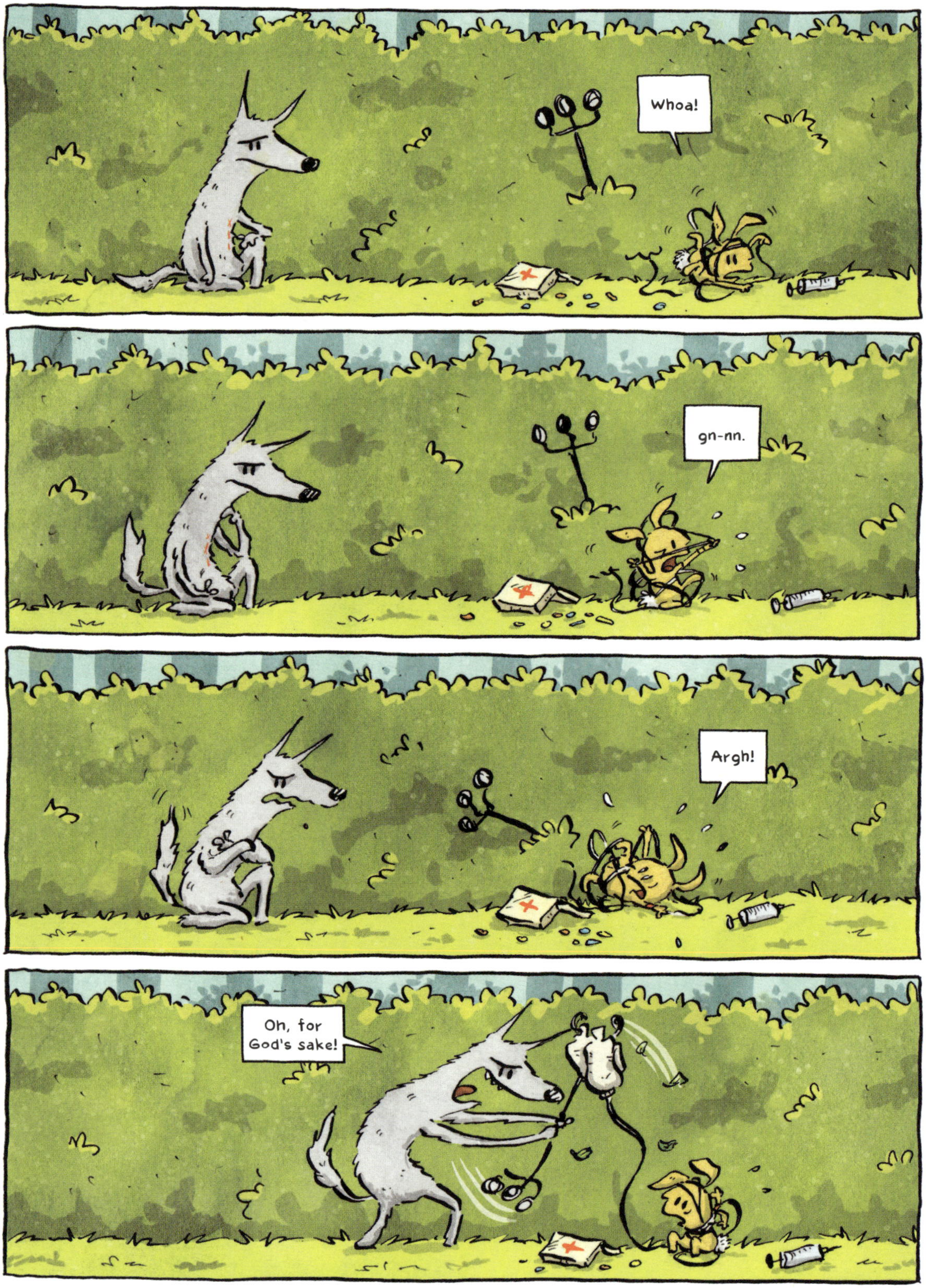
Whoa!
gn-nn.
Argh!
Oh, for God's sake!

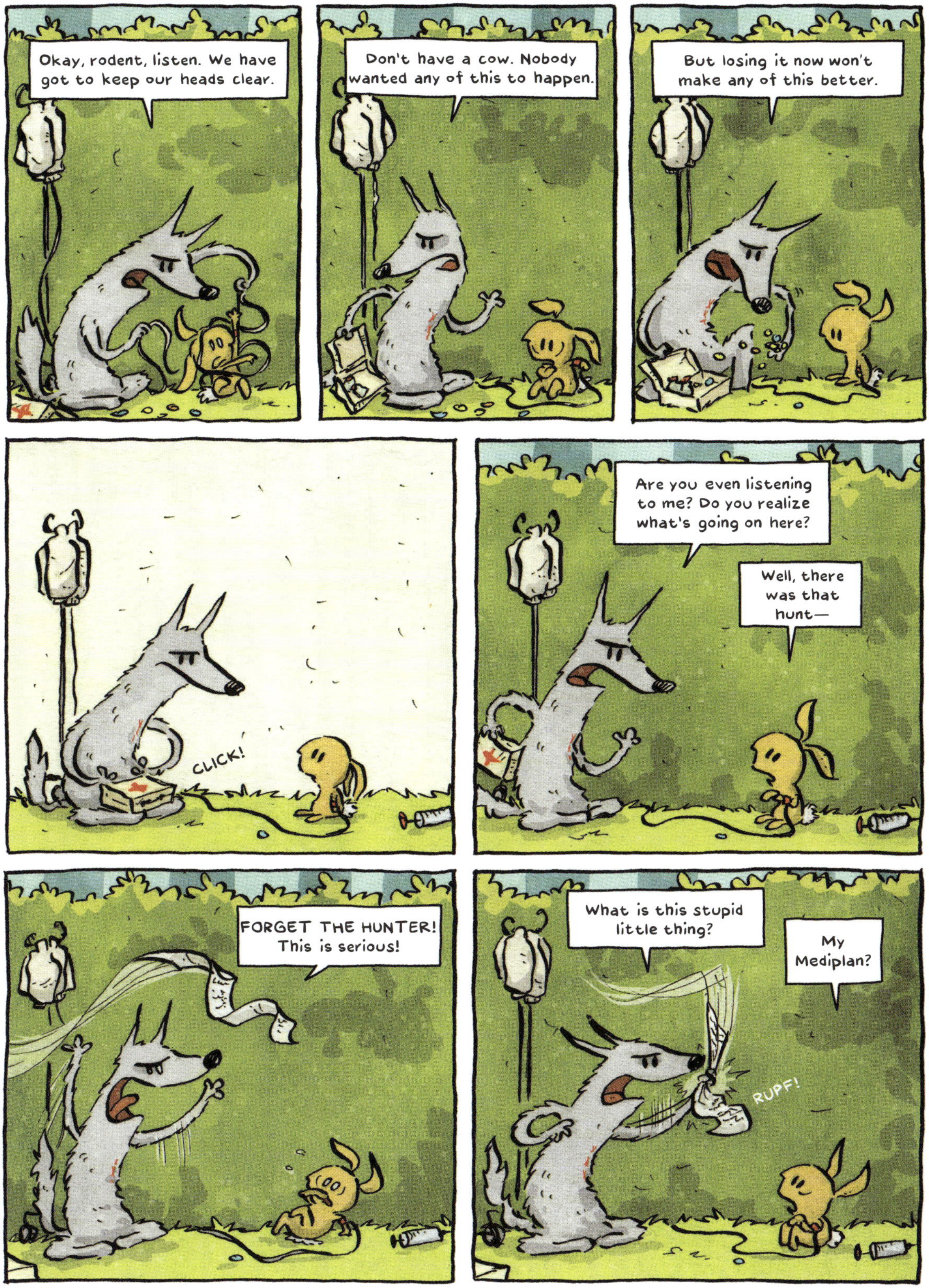
Okay, rodent, listen. We have got to keep our heads clear.
Don't have a cow. Nobody wanted any of this to happen.
But losing it now won't make any of this better.
CLICK!
Are you even listening to me? Do you realize what's going on here?
Well, there was that hunt—
FORGET THE HUNTER! This is serious!
What is this stupid little thing?
My Mediplan?
RUPF!

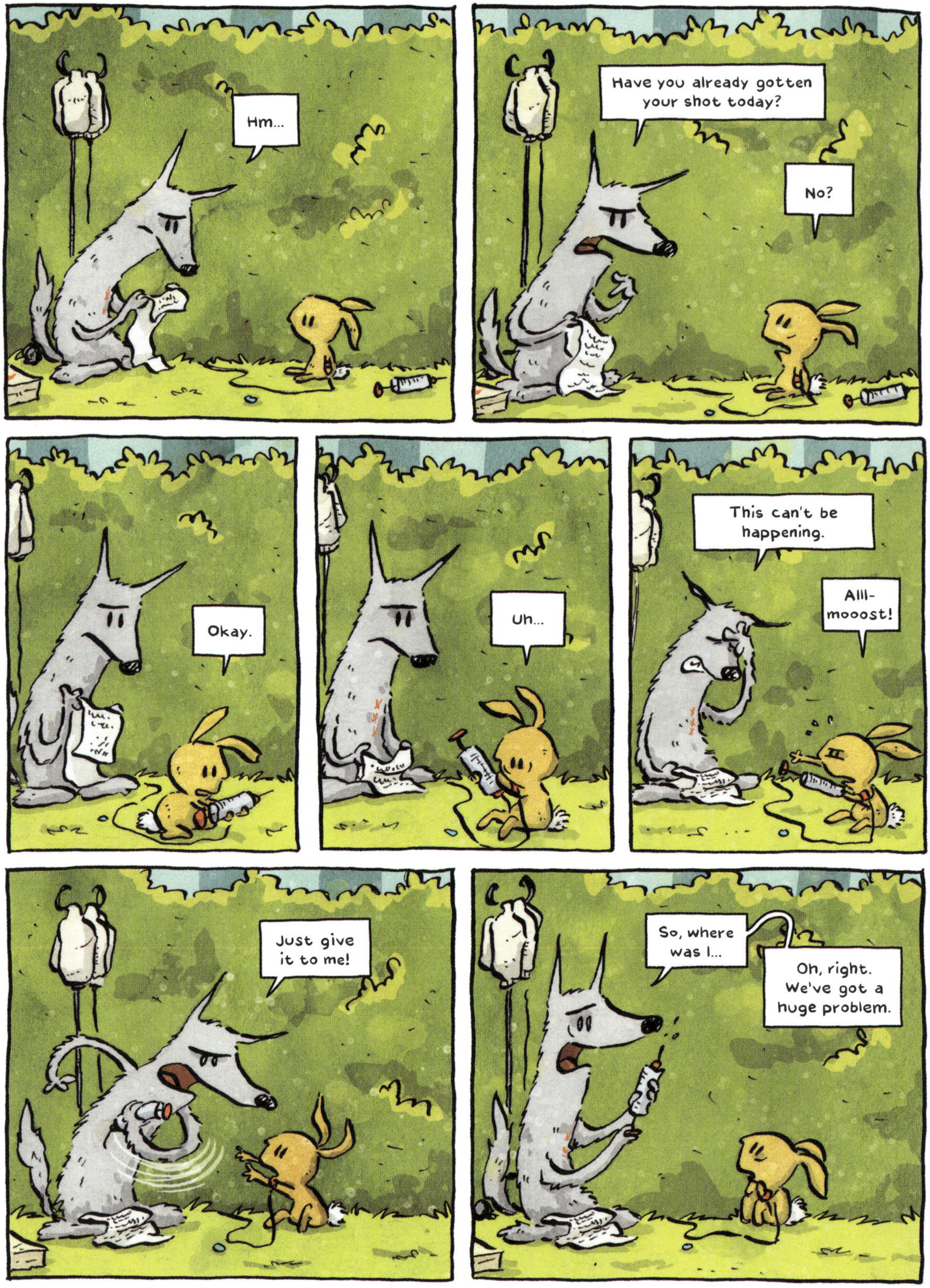
Hm...
Have you already gotten your shot today?
No?
Okay.
Uh...
This can't be happening.
Alll-mooost!
Just give it to me!
So, where was I...
Oh, right. We've got a huge problem.

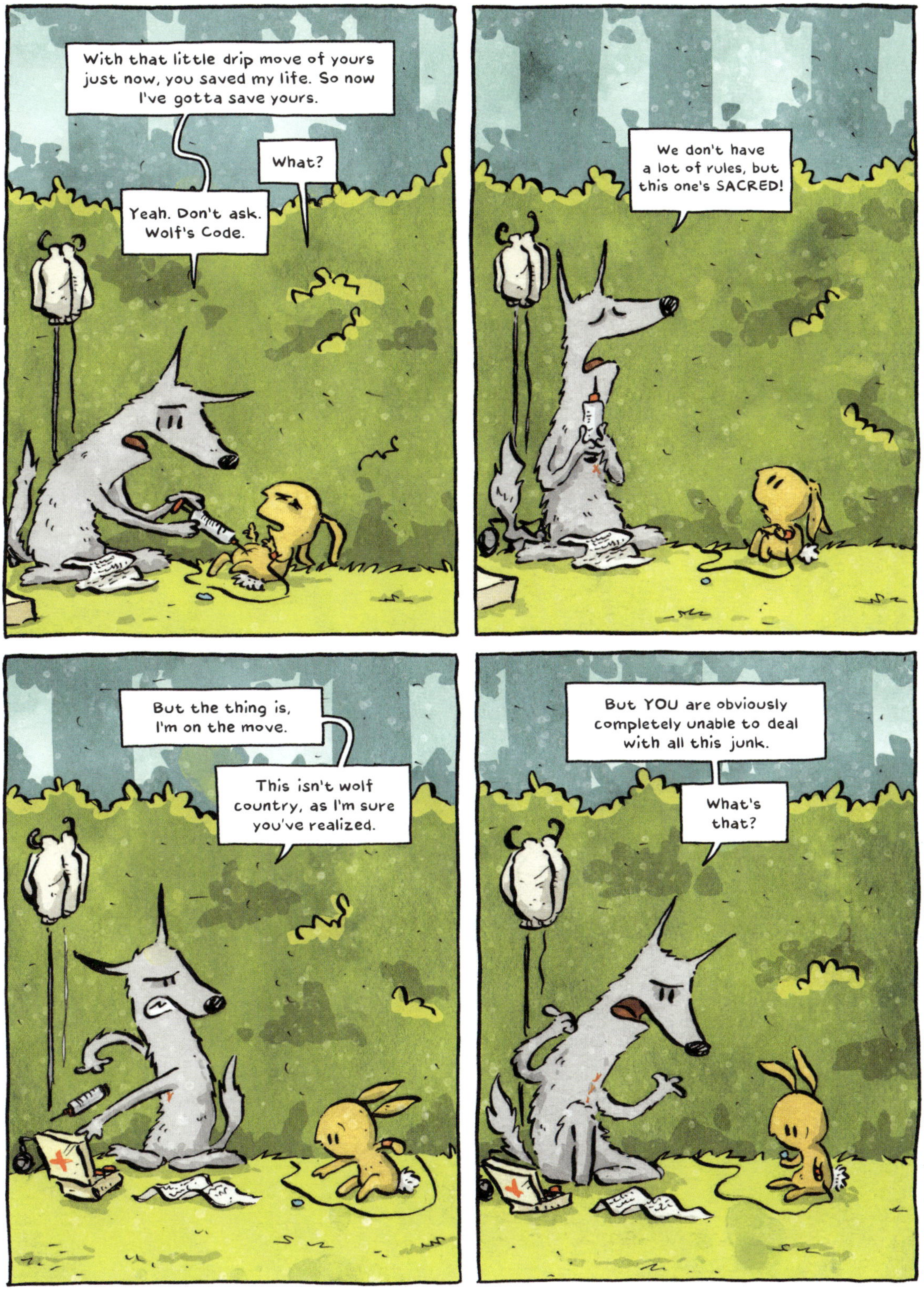
With that little drip move of yours just now, you saved my life. So now I've gotta save yours.
What?
Yeah. Don't ask. Wolf's Code.
We don't have a lot of rules, but this one's SACRED!
But the thing is, I'm on the move.
This isn't wolf country, as I'm sure you've realized.
But YOU are obviously completely unable to deal with all this junk.
What's that?

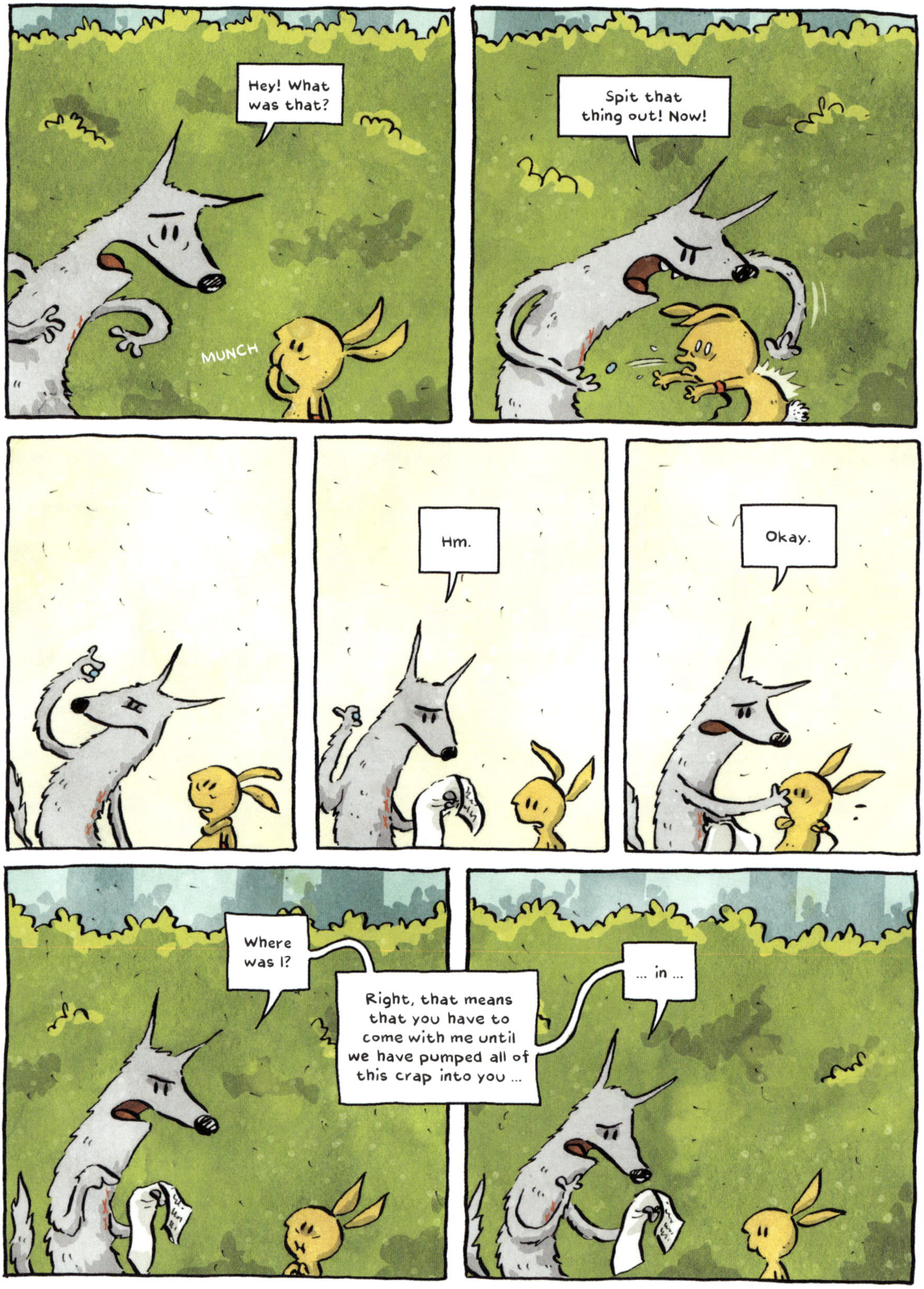
Hey! What was that?
MUNCH
Spit that thing out! Now!
Hm.
Okay.
Where was I?
Right, that means that you have to come with me until we have pumped all of this crap into you ...
... in ...

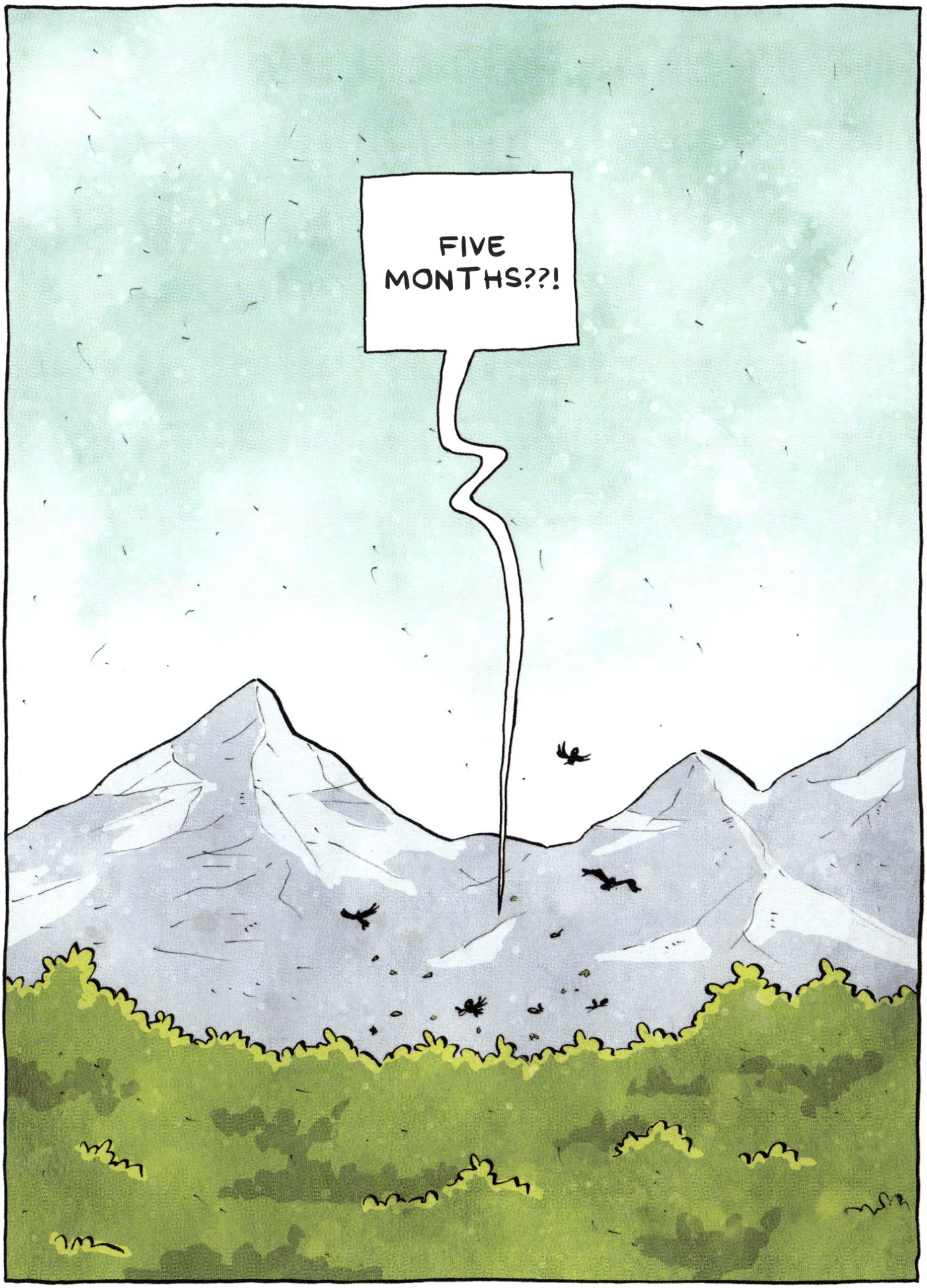
FIVE MONTHS??!

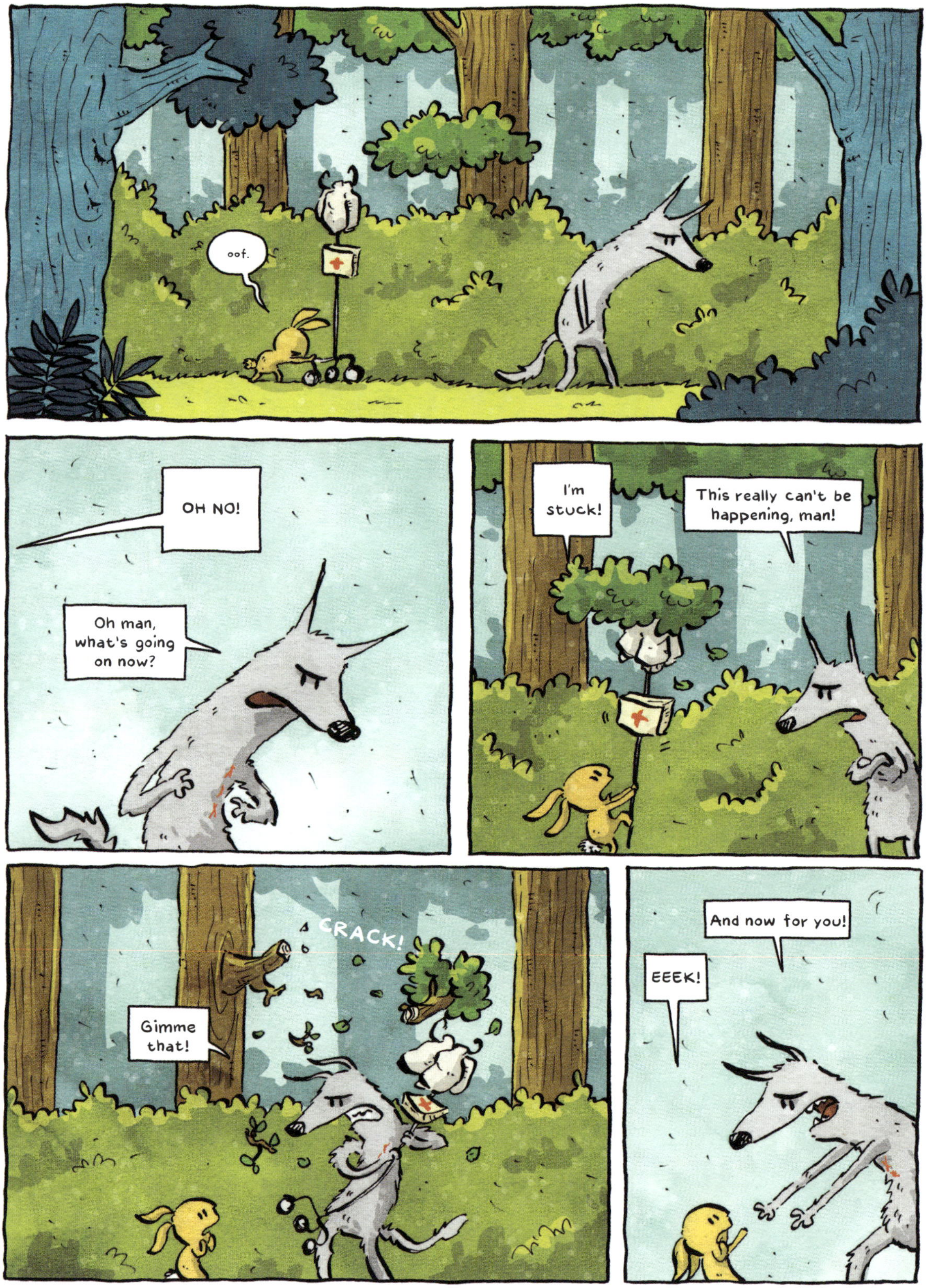
oof.
OH NO!
Oh man, what's going on now?
I'm stuck!
This really can't be happening, man!
CRACK!
Gimme that!
And now for you!
EEEK!

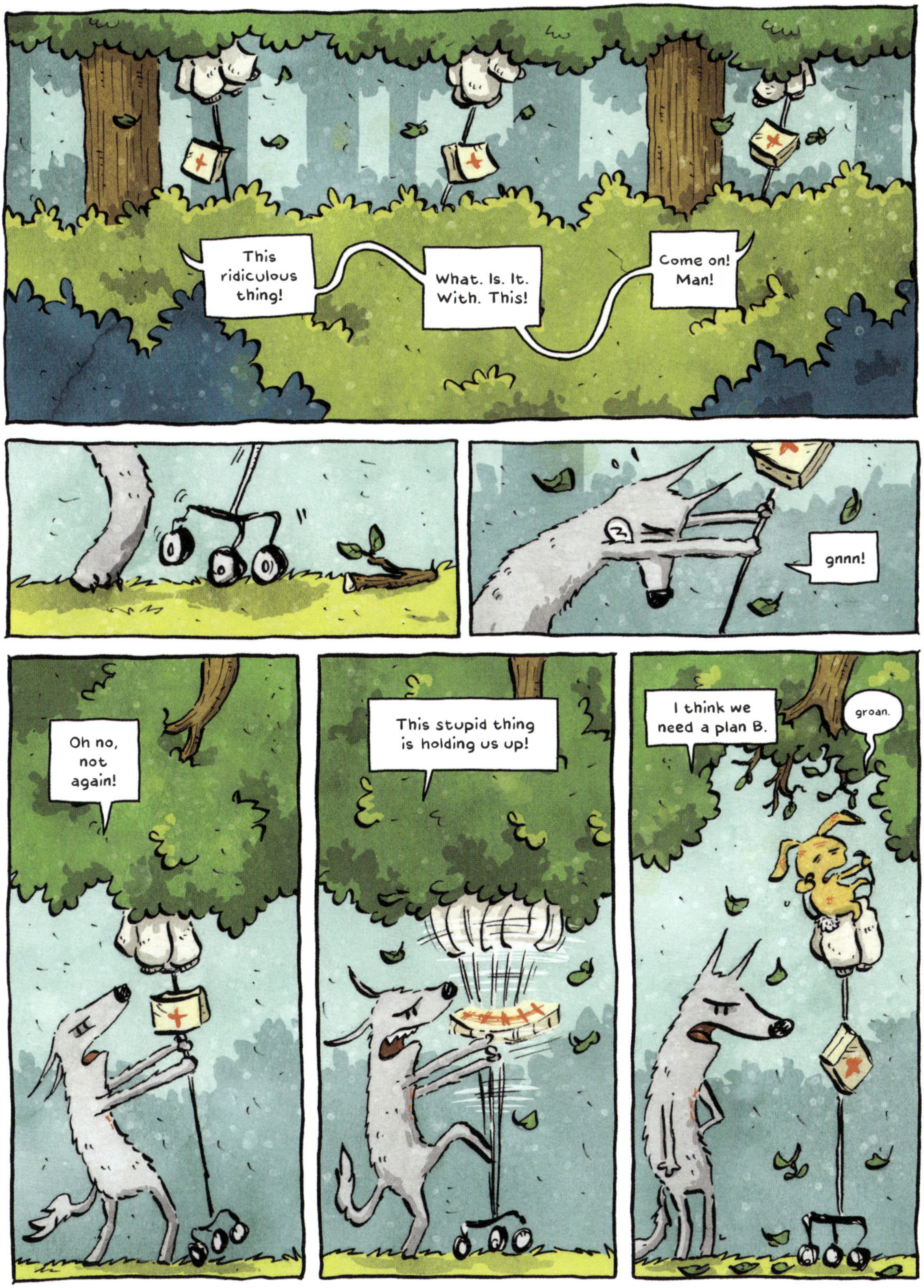
This ridiculous thing!
What. Is. It. With. This!
Come on! Man!
gnnn!
Oh no, not again!
This stupid thing is holding us up!
I think we need a plan B.
groan.

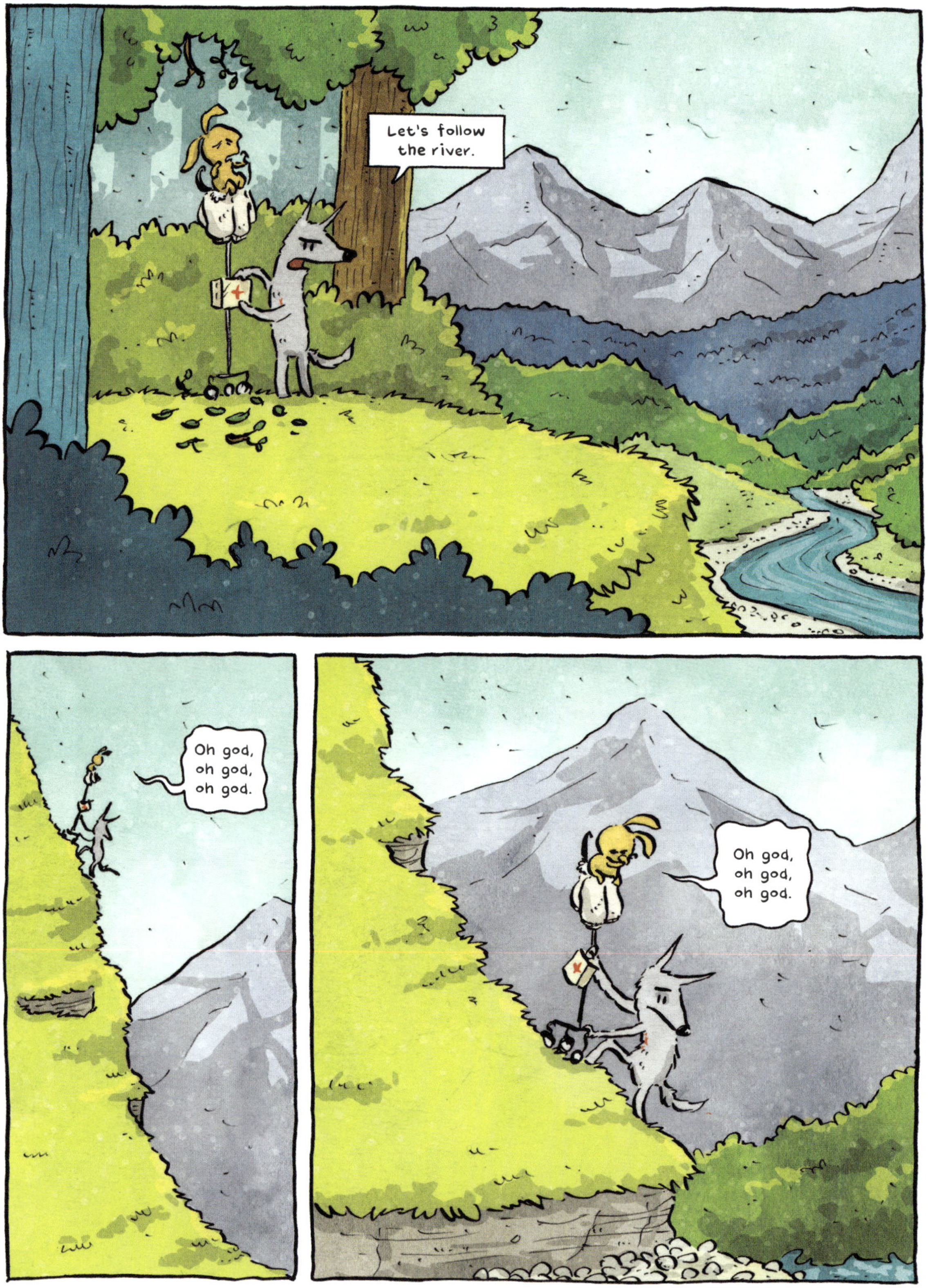
Let's follow the river.
Oh god, oh god, oh god.
Oh god, oh god, oh god.

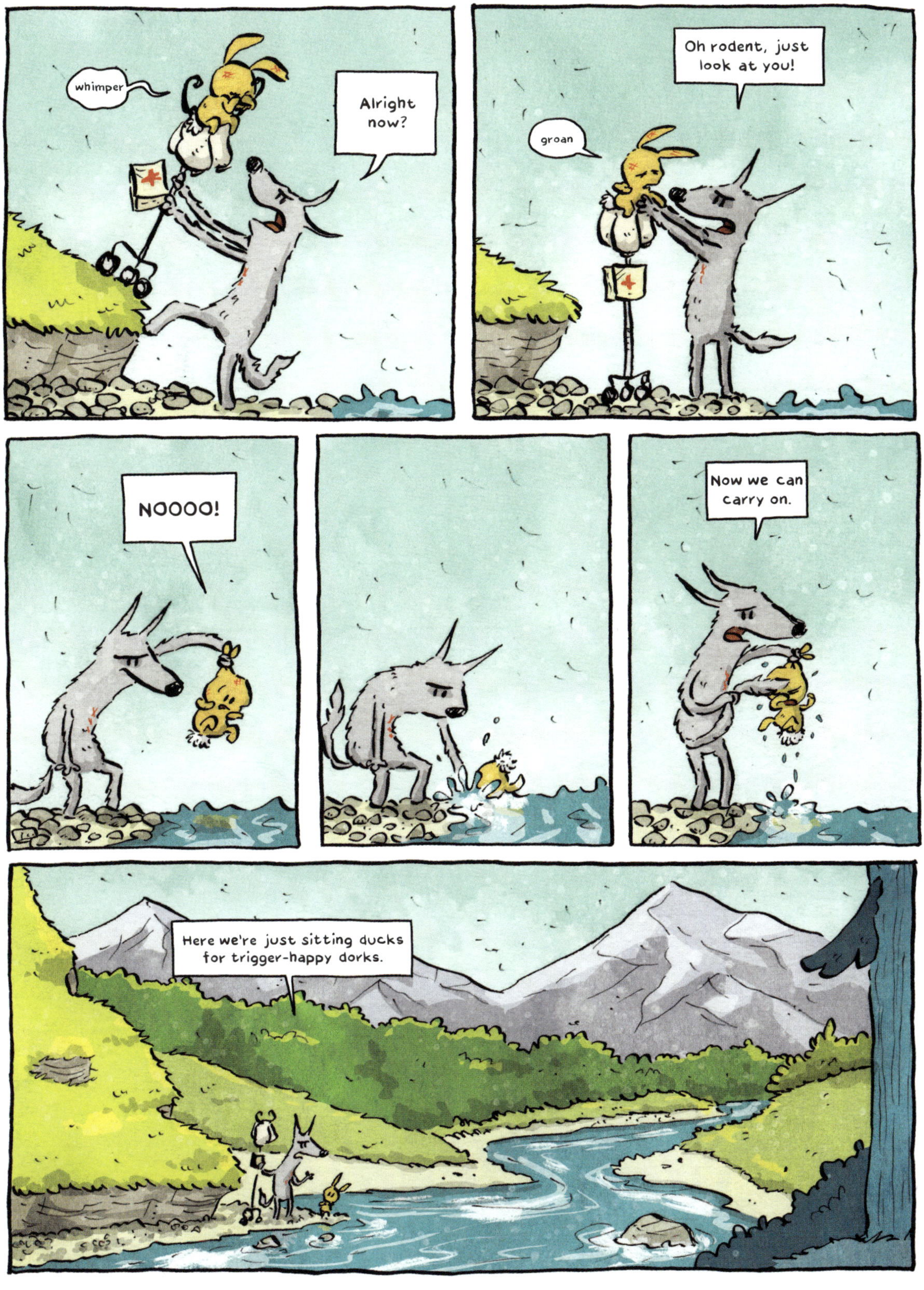
whimper
Alright now?
groan
Oh rodent, just look at you!
NOOOO!
Now we can carry on.
Here we're just sitting ducks for trigger-happy dorks.

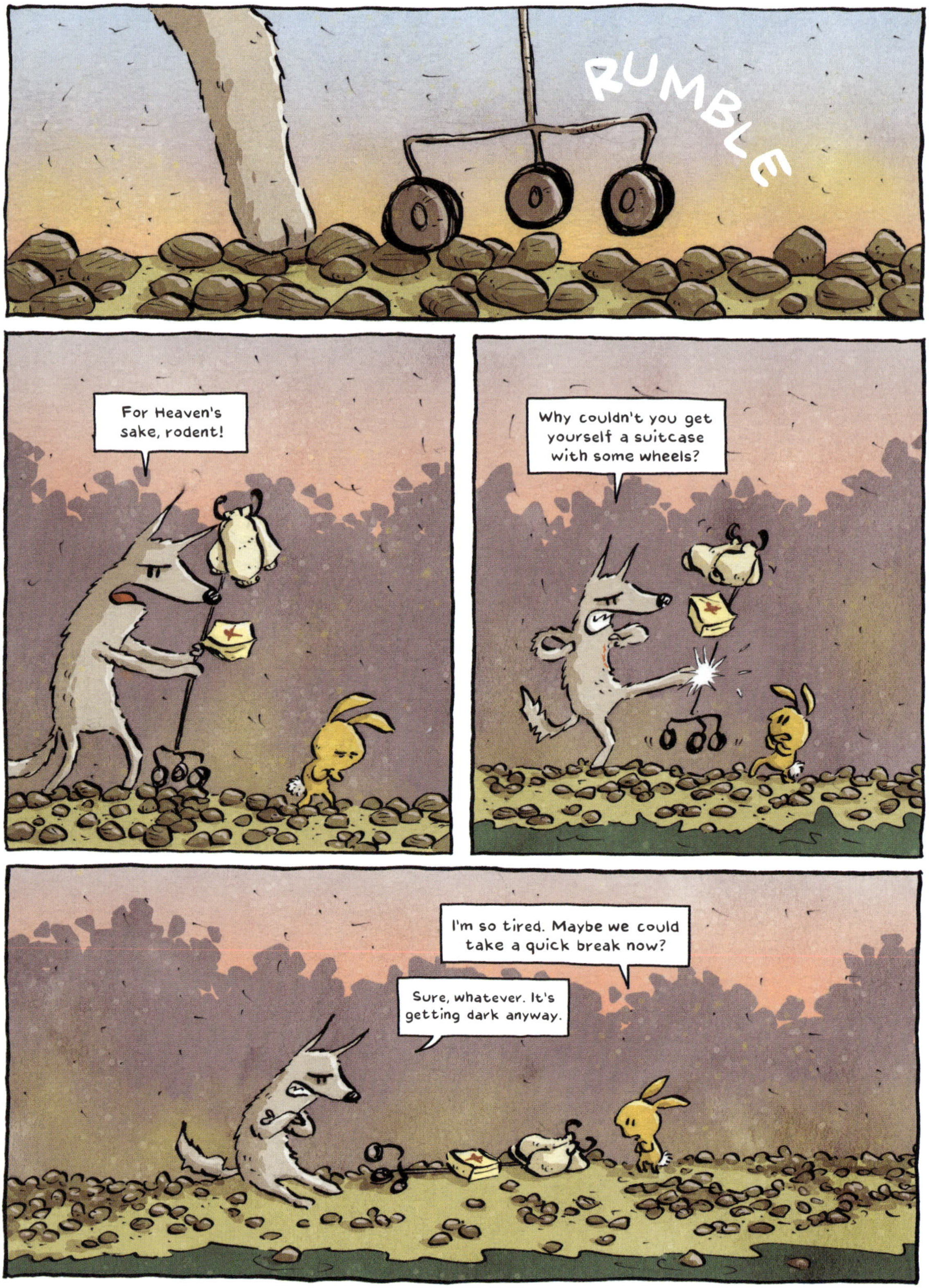
RUMBLE
For Heaven's sake, rodent!
Why couldn't you get yourself a suitcase with some wheels?
I'm so tired. Maybe we could take a quick break now?
Sure, whatever. It's getting dark anyway.

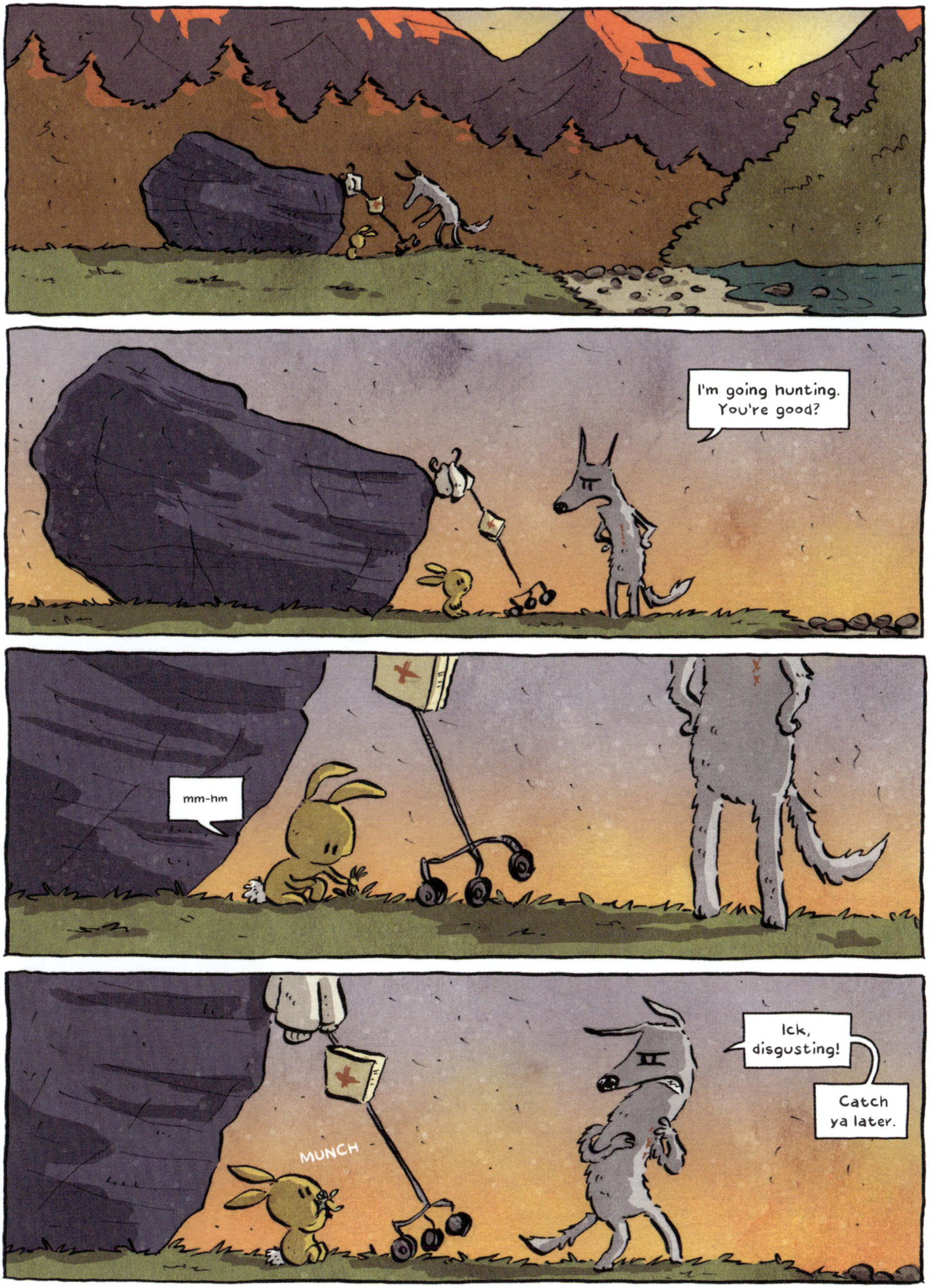
I'm going hunting. You're good?
mm-hm
MUNCH
Ick, disgusting!
Catch ya later.

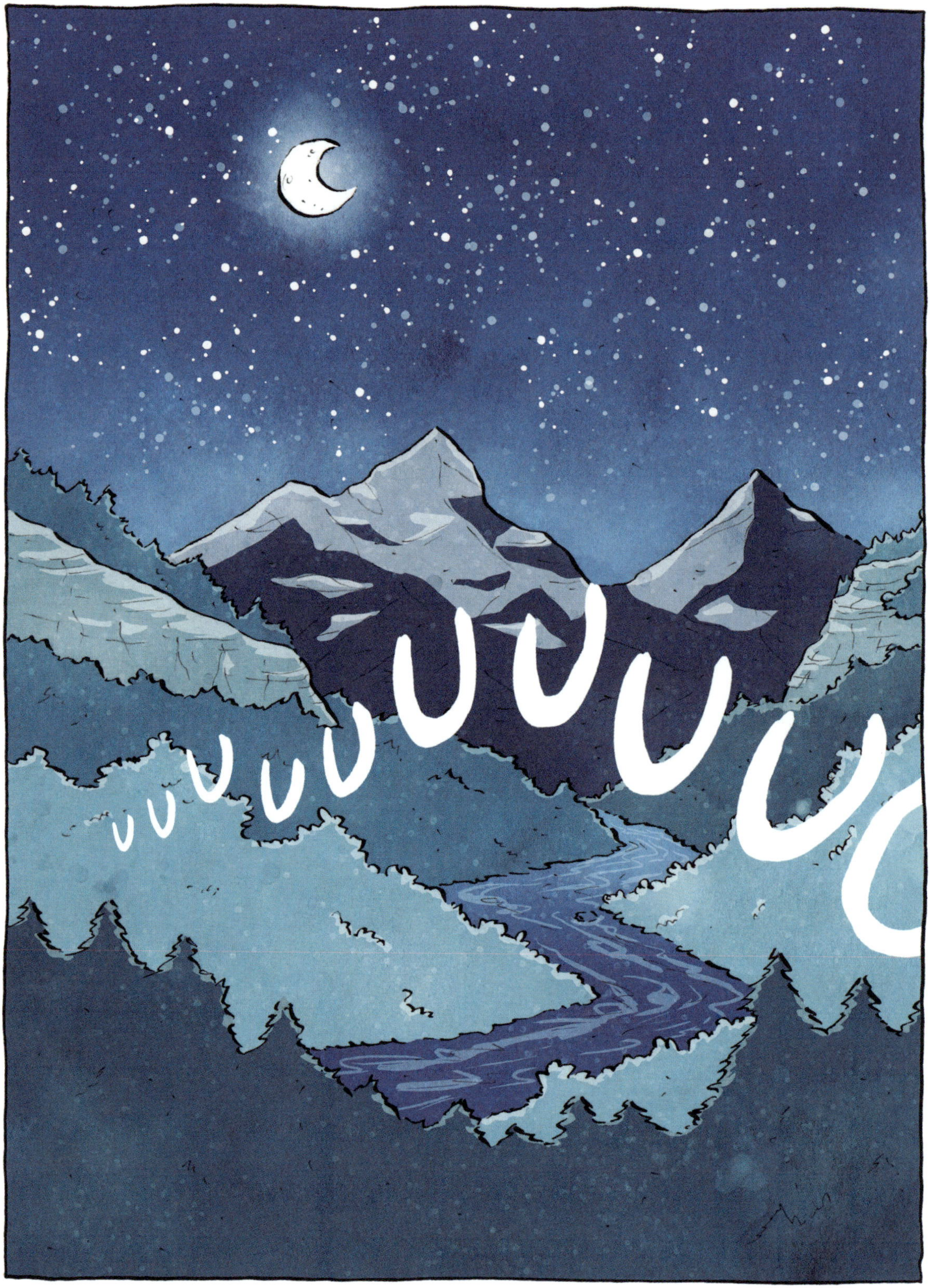

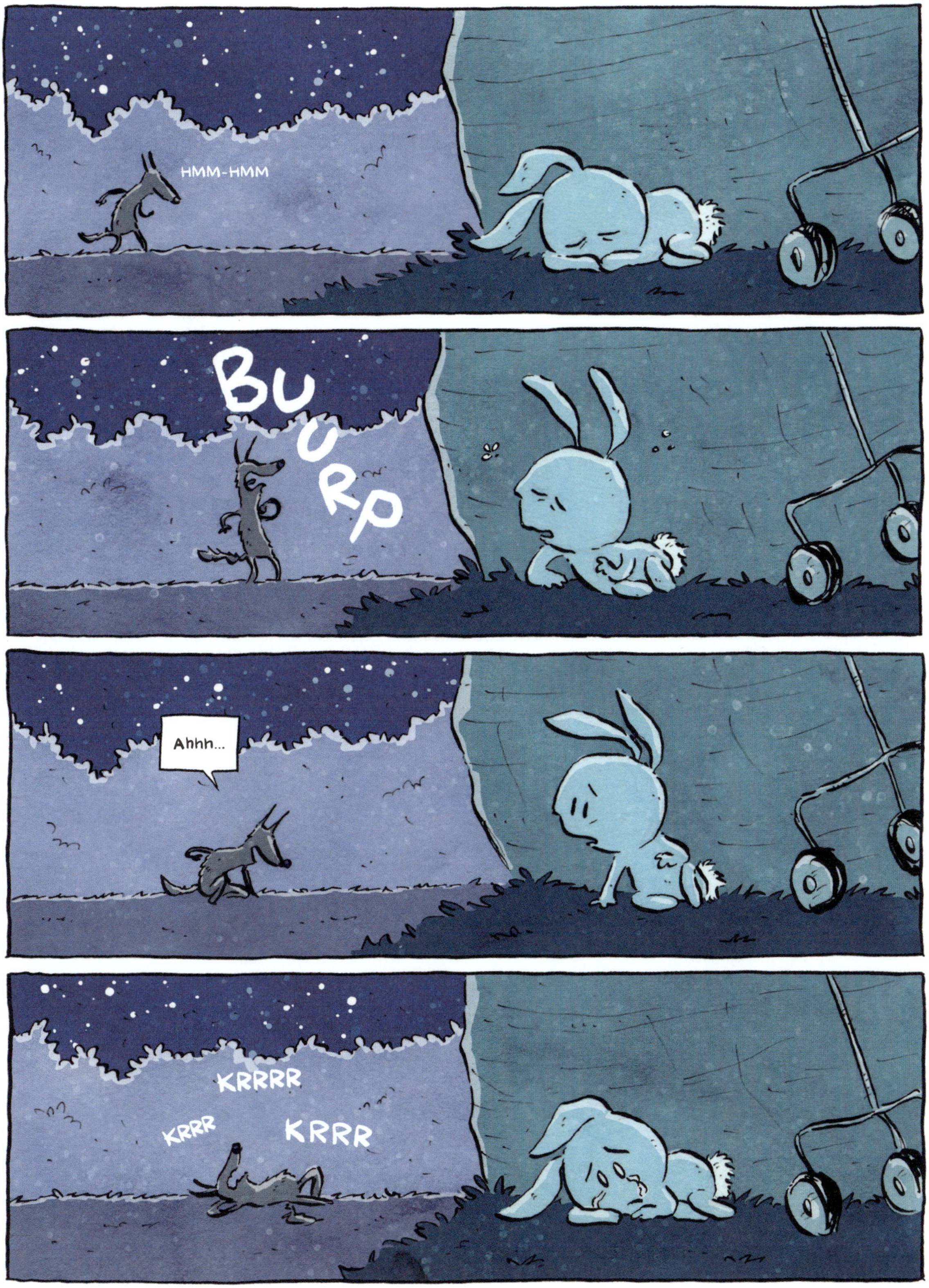
HMM-HMM
BUURP
Ahhh...
KRRRR
KRRR
KRRR

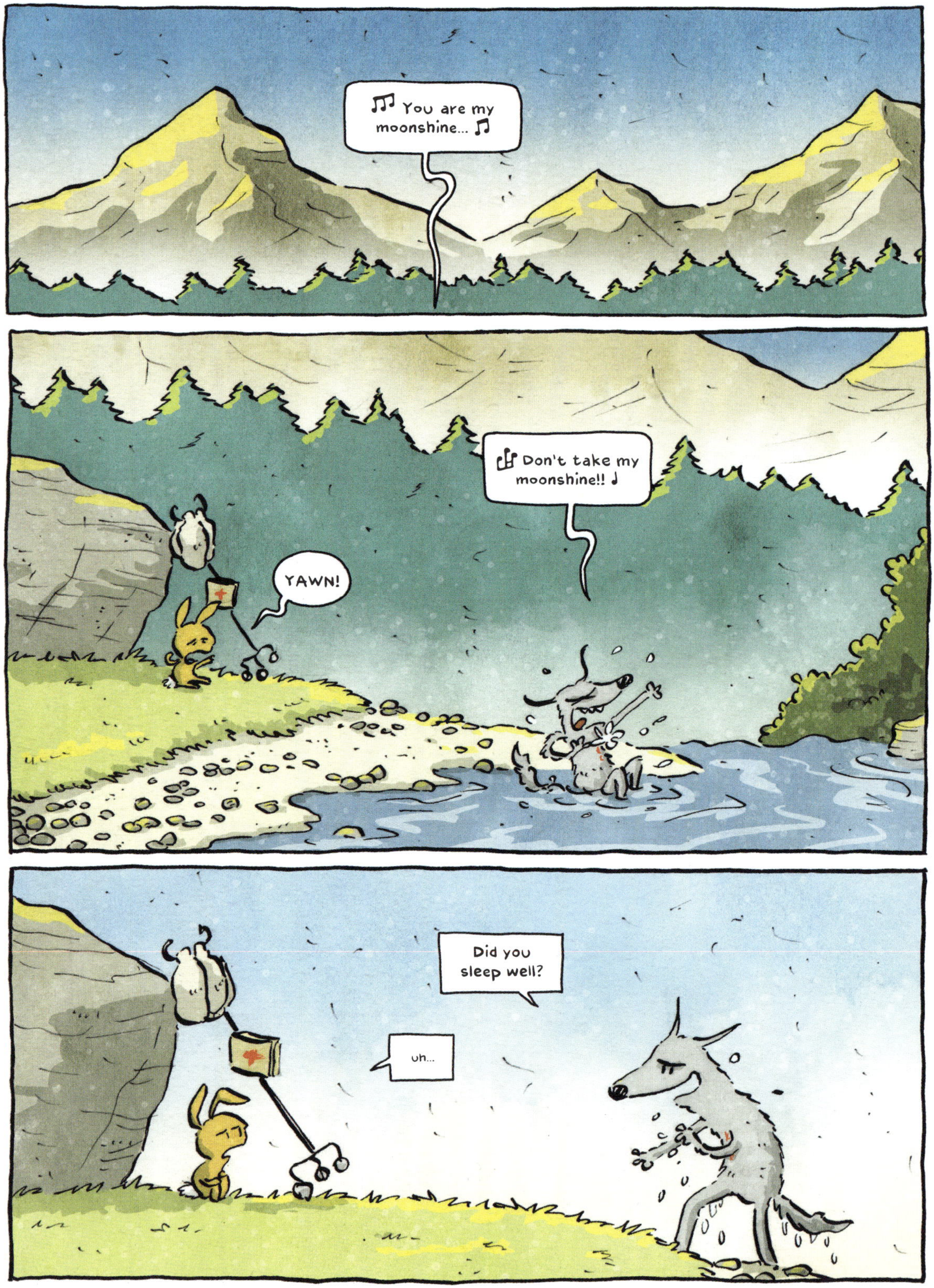
♫ You are my moonshine... ♫
♫ Don't take my moonshine!! ♩
YAWN!
Did you sleep well?
uh...

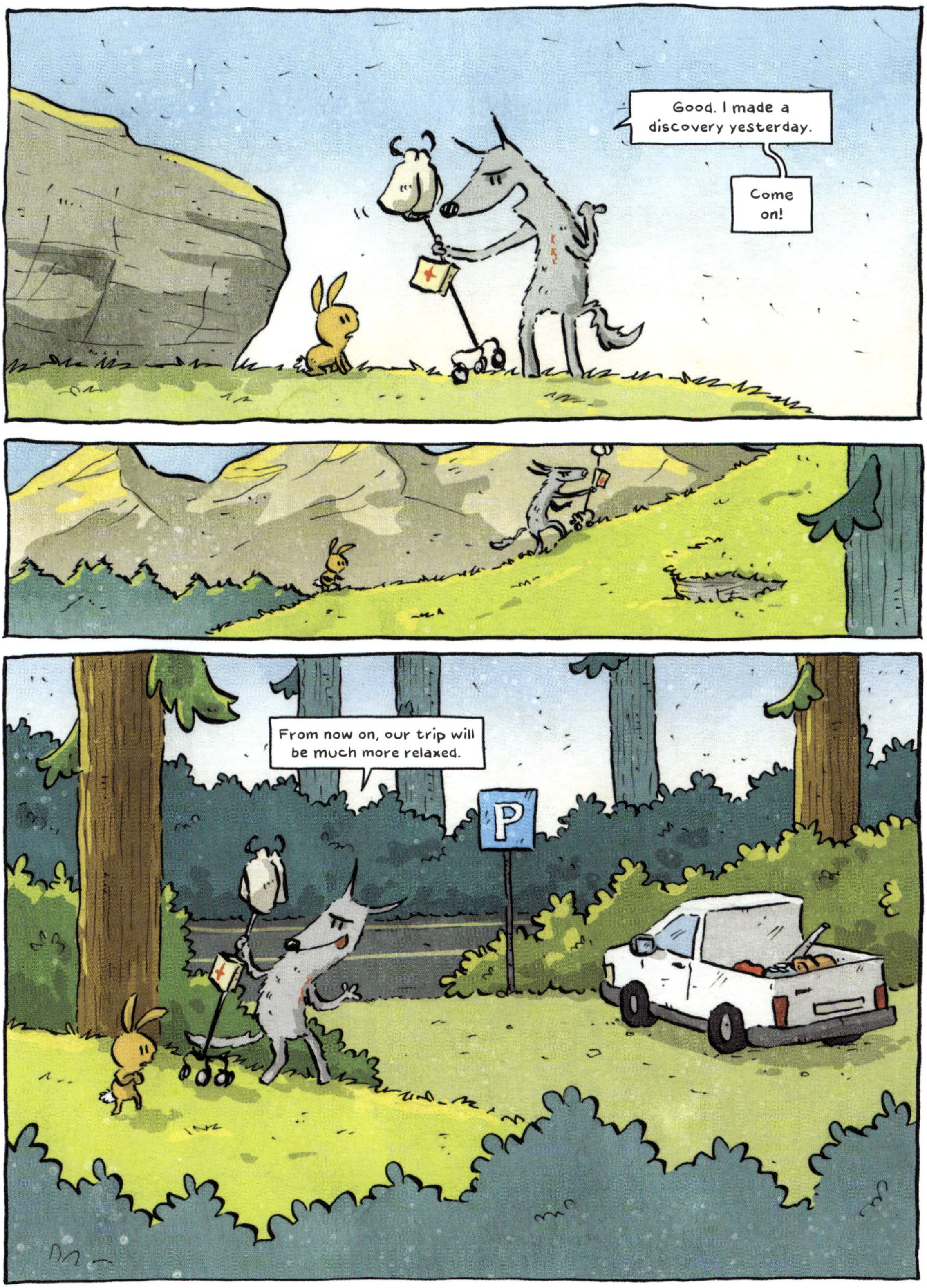
Good. I made a discovery yesterday.
Come on!
From now on, our trip will be much more relaxed.
P

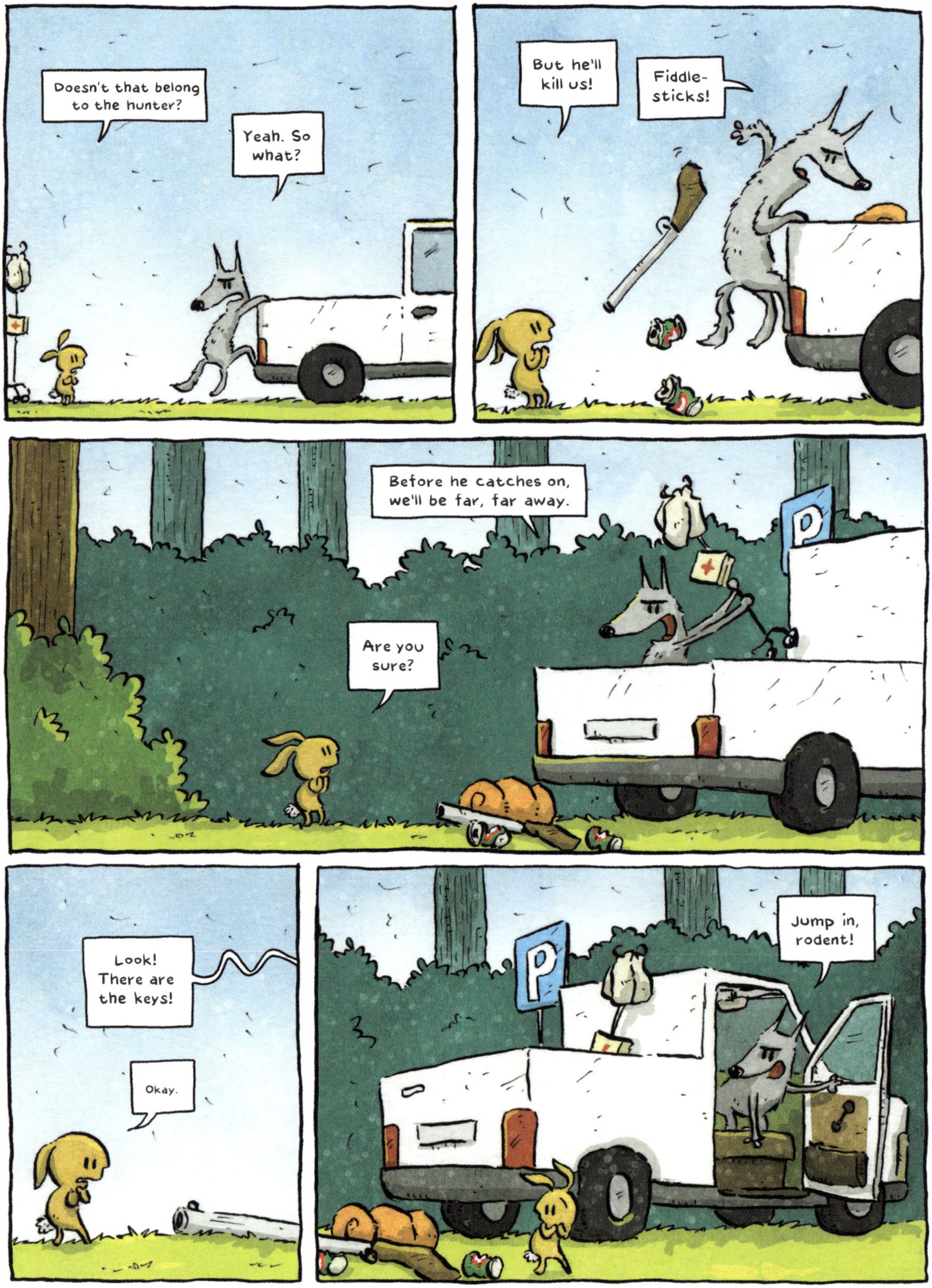
Doesn't that belong to the hunter?
Yeah. So what?
But he'll kill us!
Fiddle-sticks!
Before he catches on, we'll be far, far away.
Are you sure?
Look! There are the keys!
Okay.
Jump in, rodent!

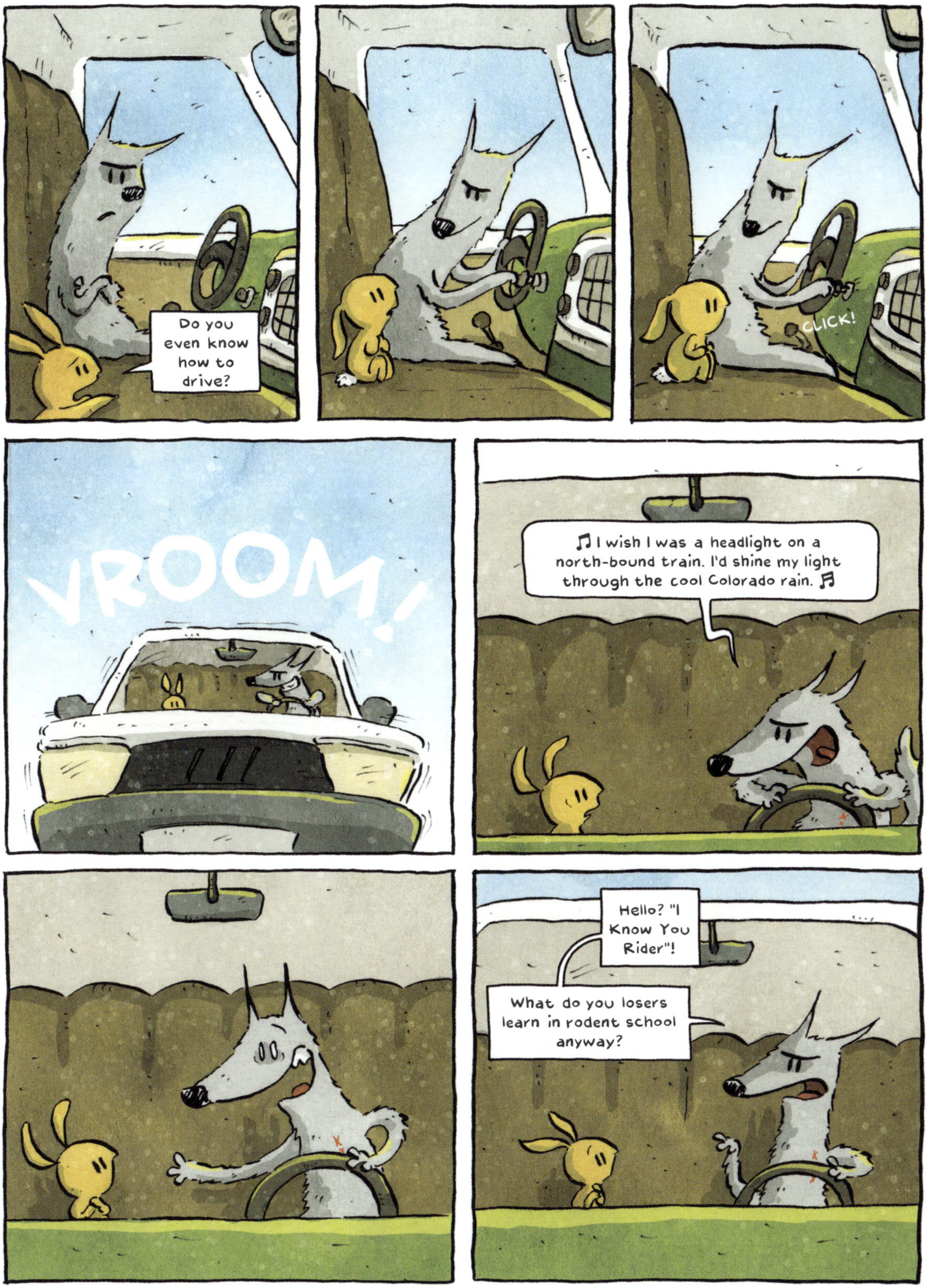
Do you even know how to drive?
CLICK!
VROOM!
♫ I wish I was a headlight on a north-bound train. I'd shine my light through the cool Colorado rain. ♫
Hello? "I Know You Rider"!
What do you losers learn in rodent school anyway?

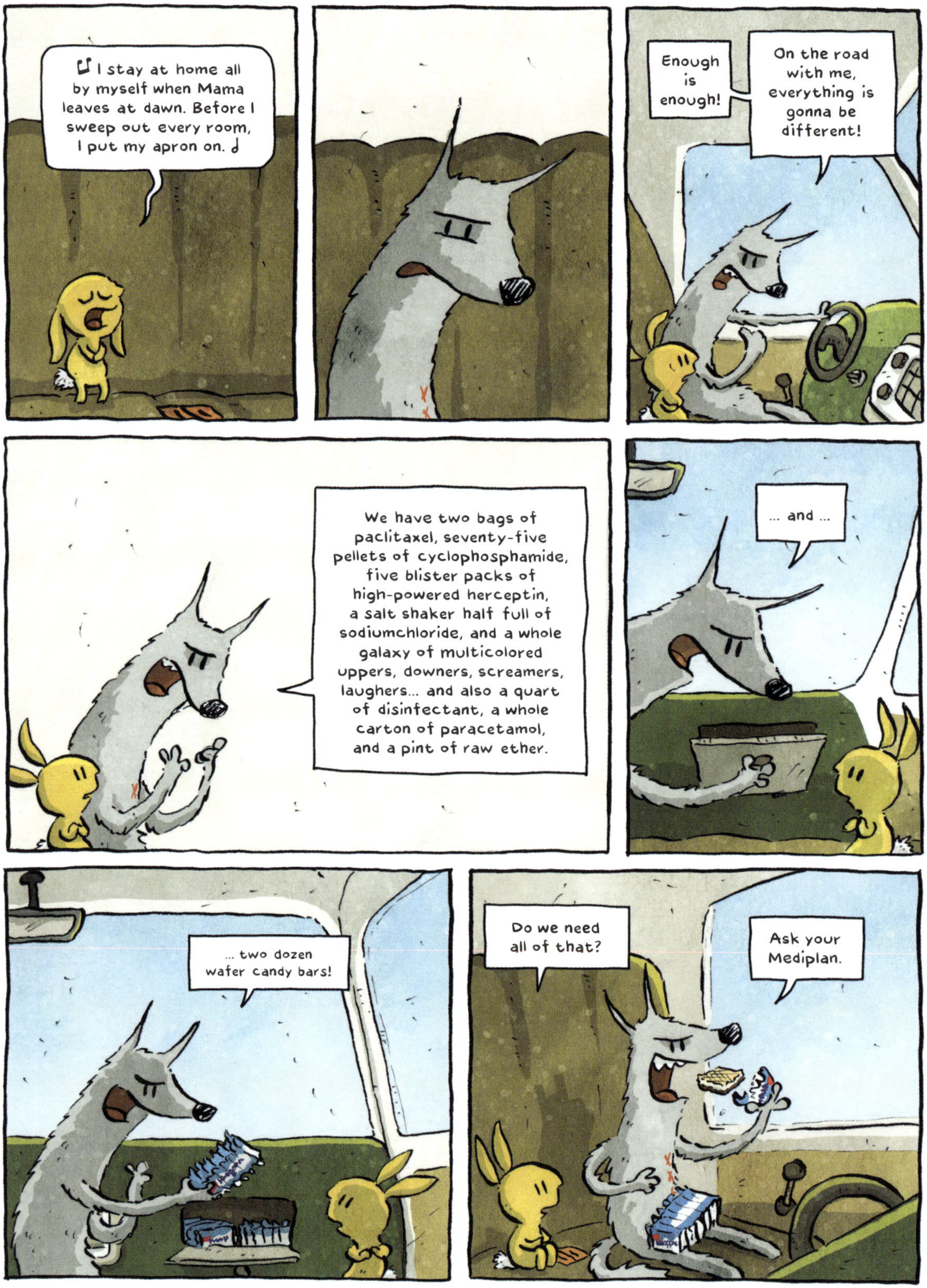
I stay at home all by myself when Mama leaves at dawn. Before I sweep out every room, I put my apron on.
Enough is enough!
On the road with me, everything is gonna be different!
We have two bags of paclitaxel, seventy-five pellets of cyclophosphamide, five blister packs of high-powered herceptin, a salt shaker half full of sodiumchloride, and a whole galaxy of multicolored uppers, downers, screamers, laughers... and also a quart of disinfectant, a whole carton of paracetamol, and a pint of raw ether.
... and ...
... two dozen wafer candy bars!
Do we need all of that?
Ask your Mediplan.

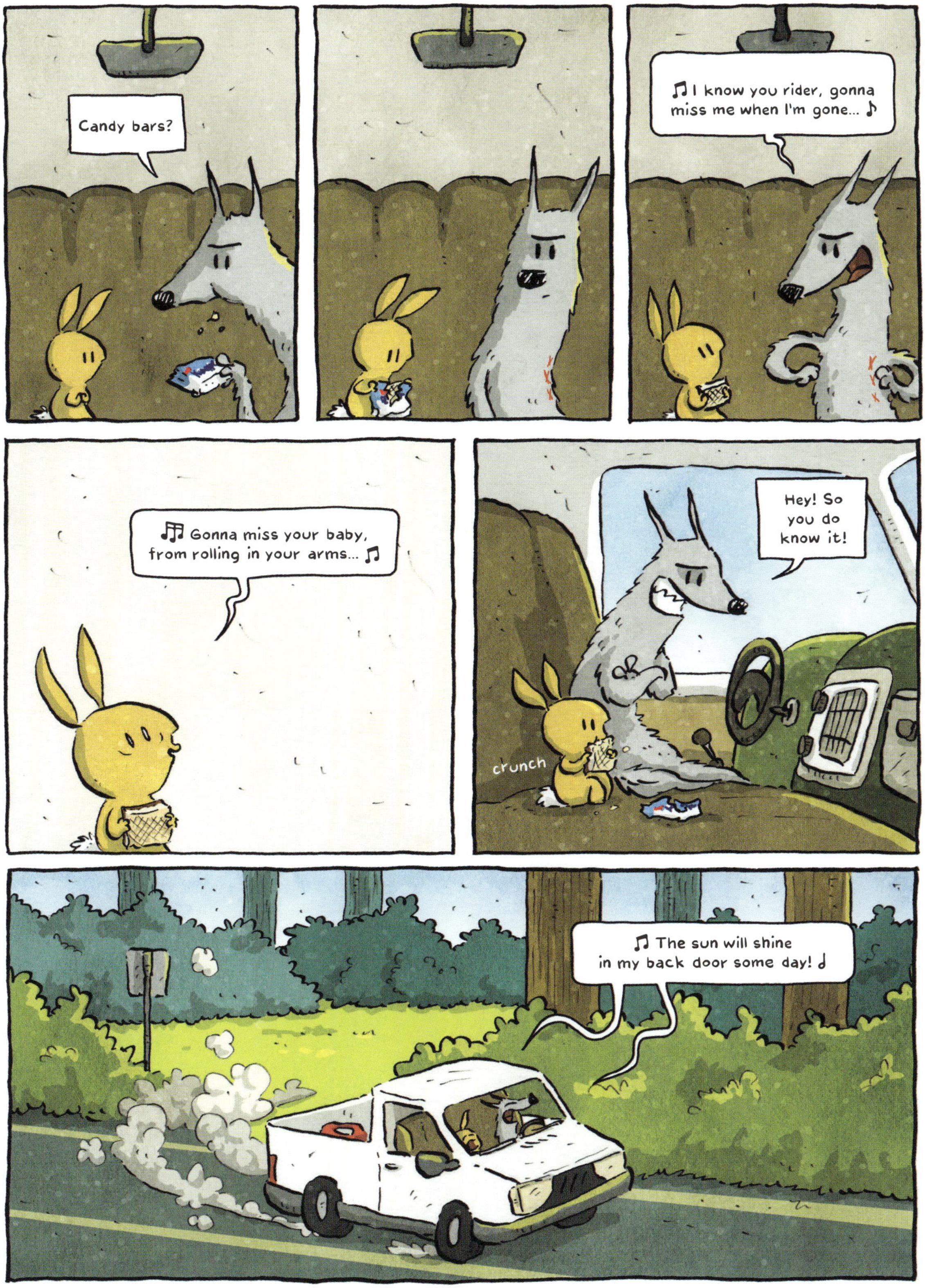

Candy bars?
♫ I know you rider, gonna miss me when I'm gone... ♪
♫ Gonna miss your baby, from rolling in your arms... ♫
Hey! So you do know it!
crunch
♫ The sun will shine in my back door some day! ♩

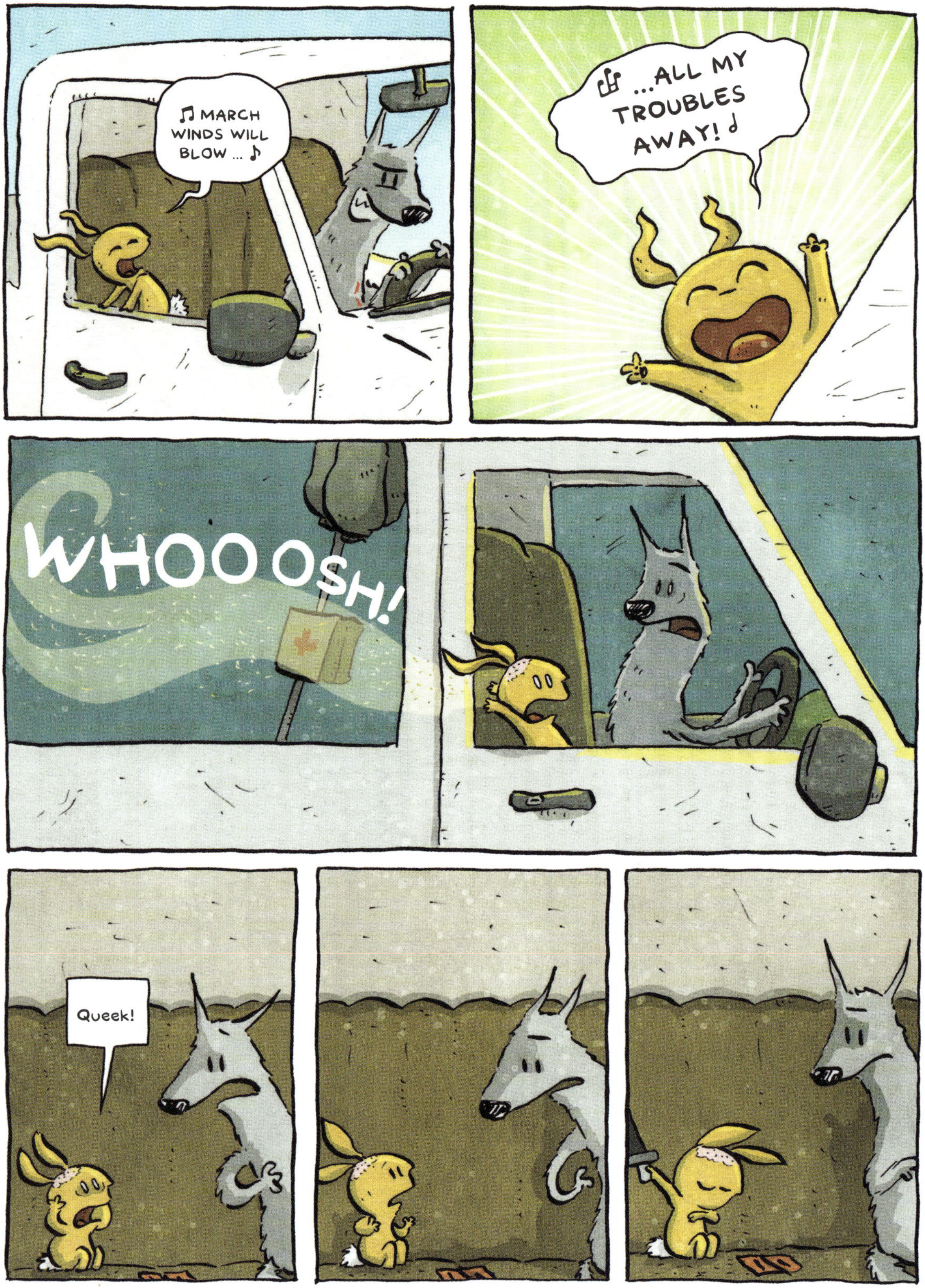
♫ MARCH WINDS WILL BLOW ... ♪
♫ ...ALL MY TROUBLES AWAY! ♩
WHOOOSH!
Queek!

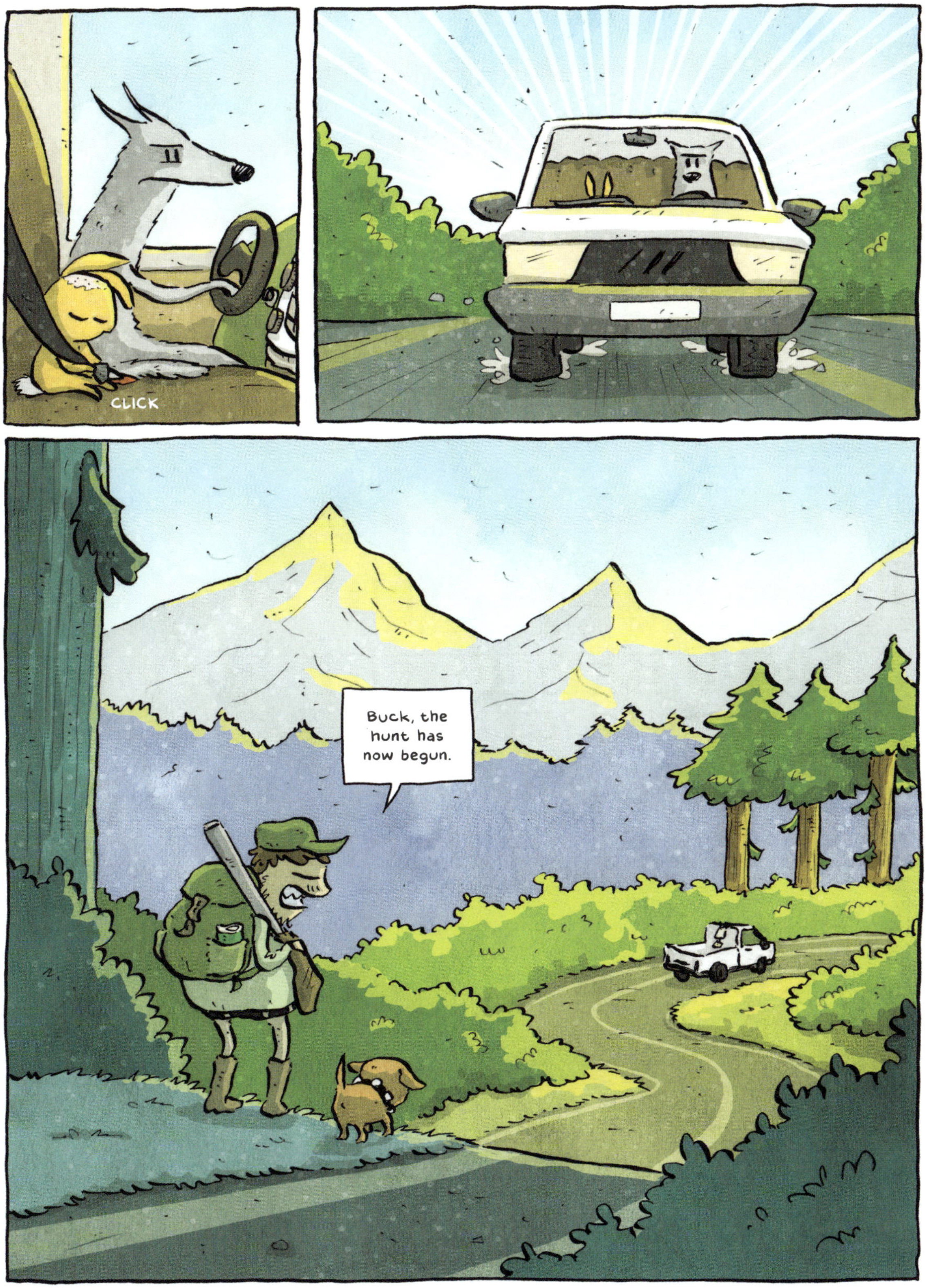
CLICK
Buck, the hunt has now begun.

Chapter 2

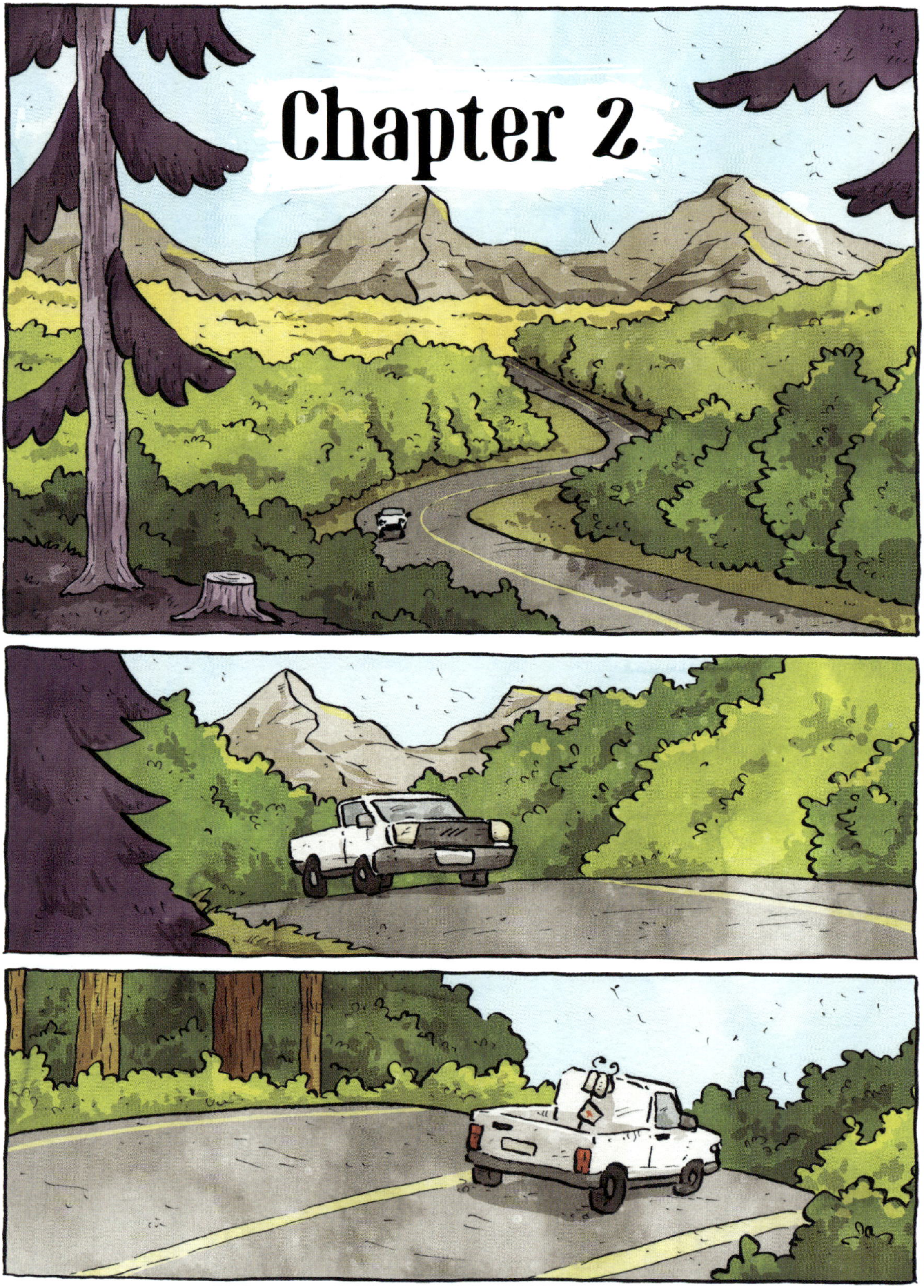

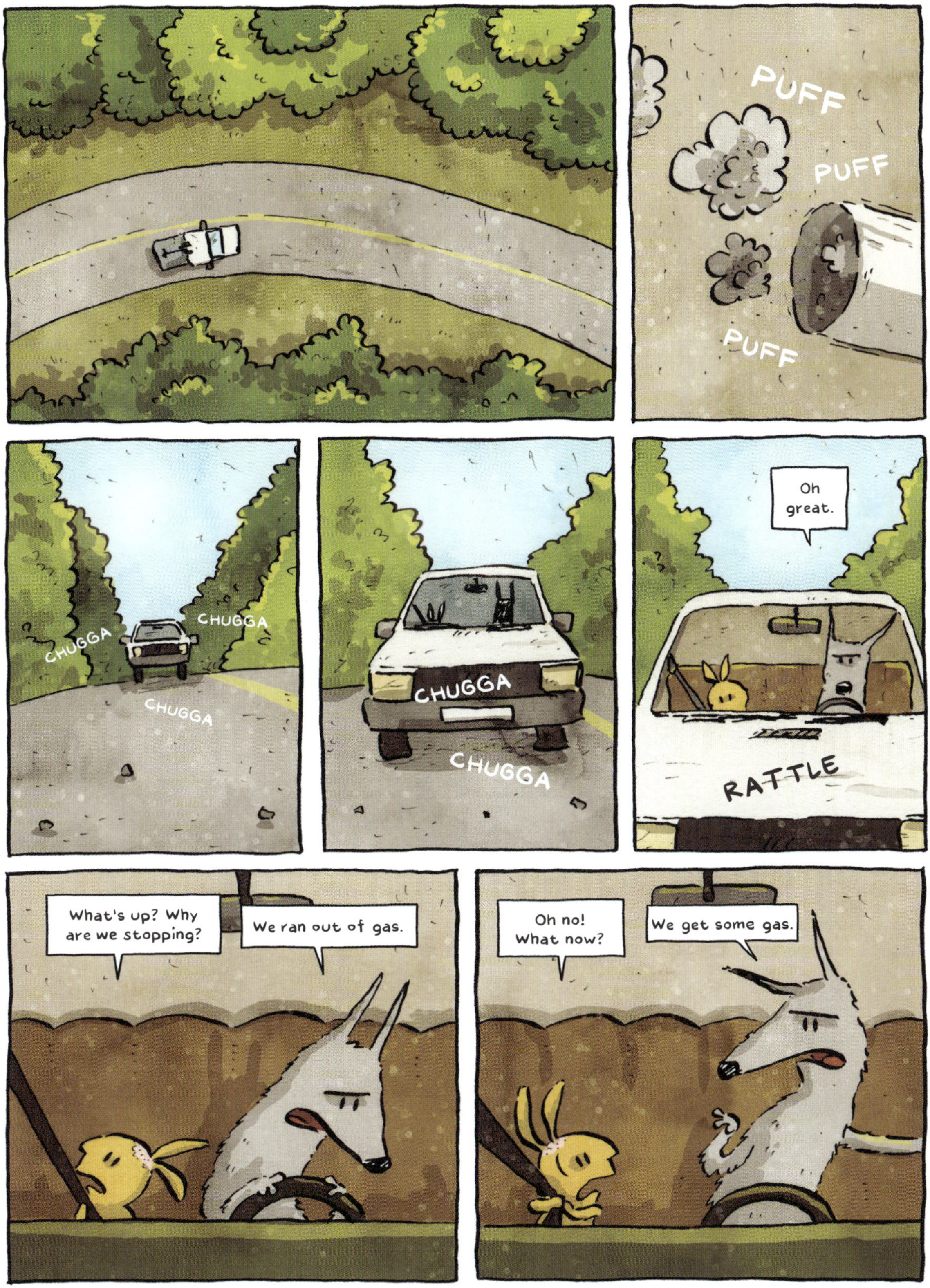
PUFF
PUFF
PUFF
CHUGGA
CHUGGA
CHUGGA
CHUGGA
CHUGGA
Oh great.
RATTLE
What's up? Why are we stopping?
We ran out of gas.
Oh no! What now?
We get some gas.

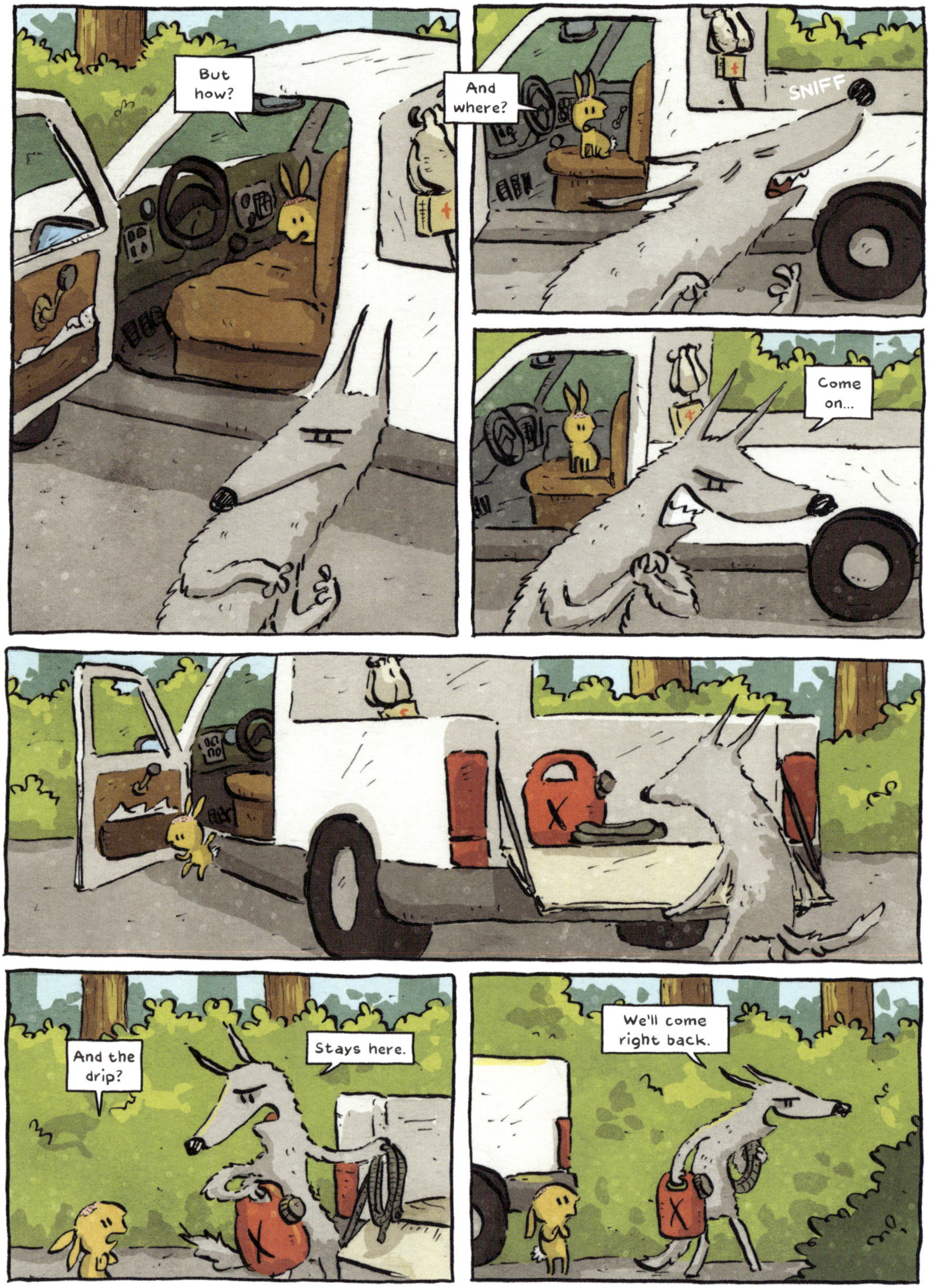
But how?
And where?
SNIFF
Come on...
And the drip?
Stays here.
We'll come right back.

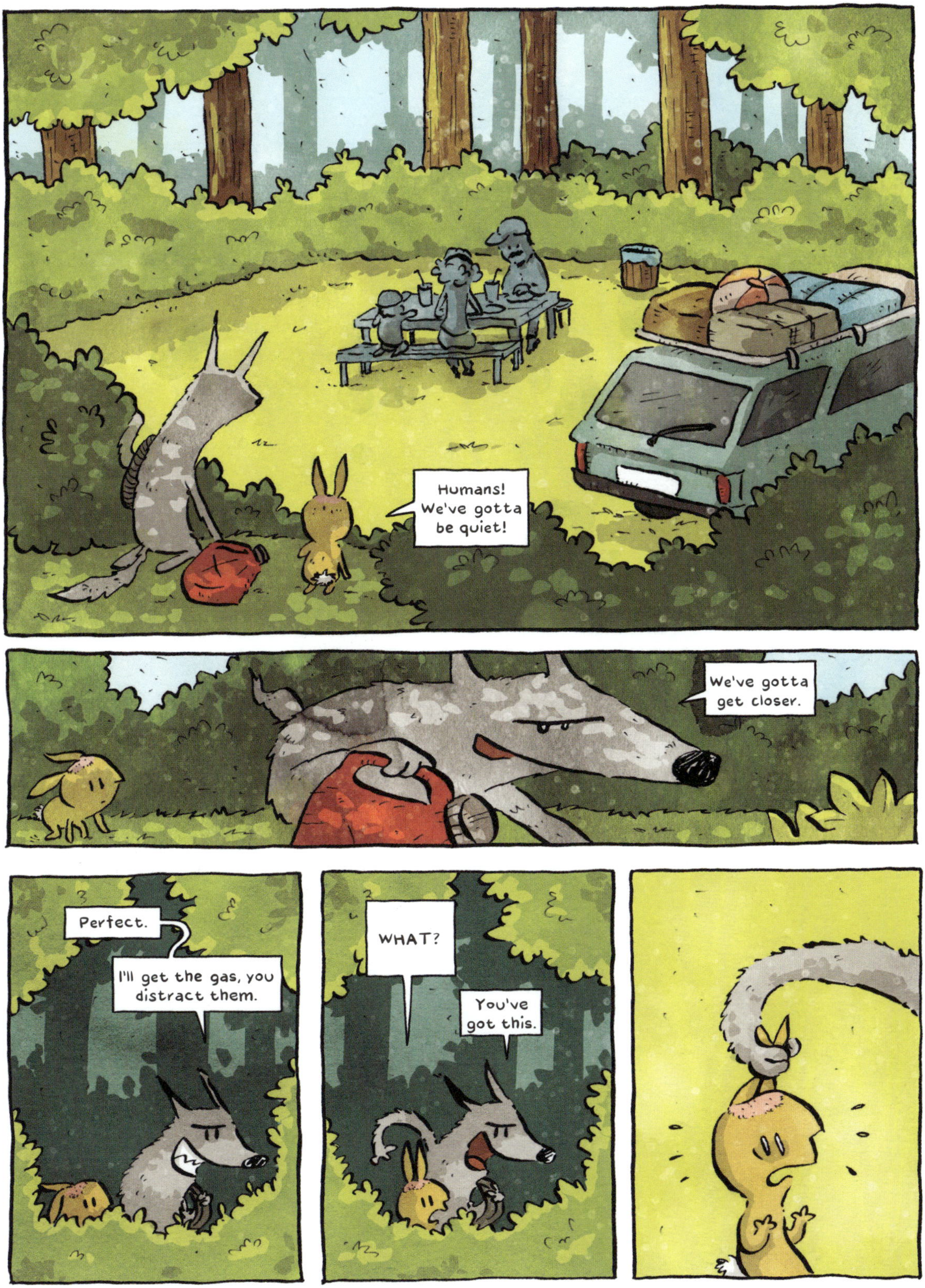
Humans! We've gotta be quiet!
We've gotta get closer.
Perfect.
I'll get the gas, you distract them.
WHAT?
You've got this.

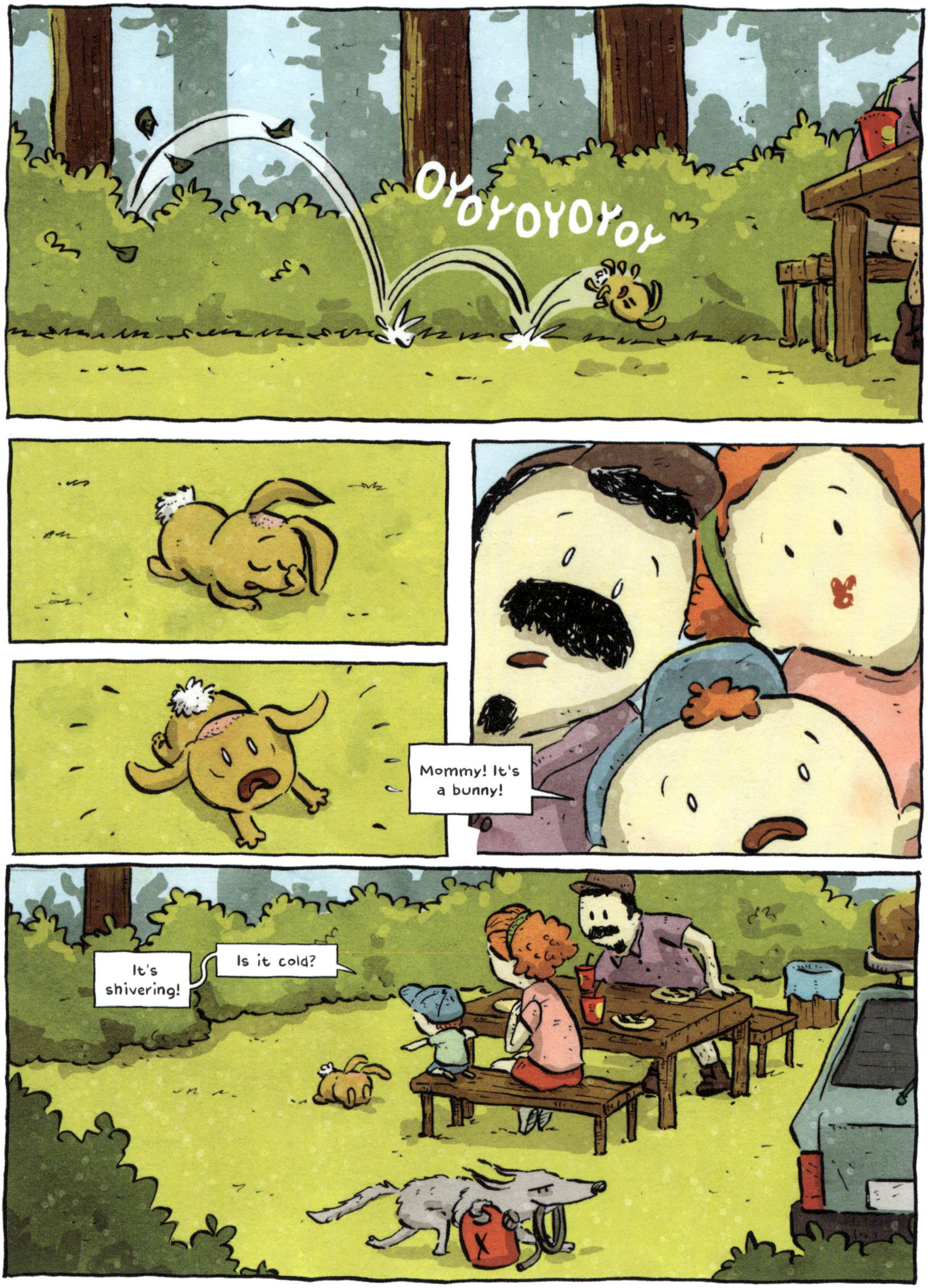
OYOYOYOYOYOY
Mommy! It's a bunny!
It's shivering!
Is it cold?

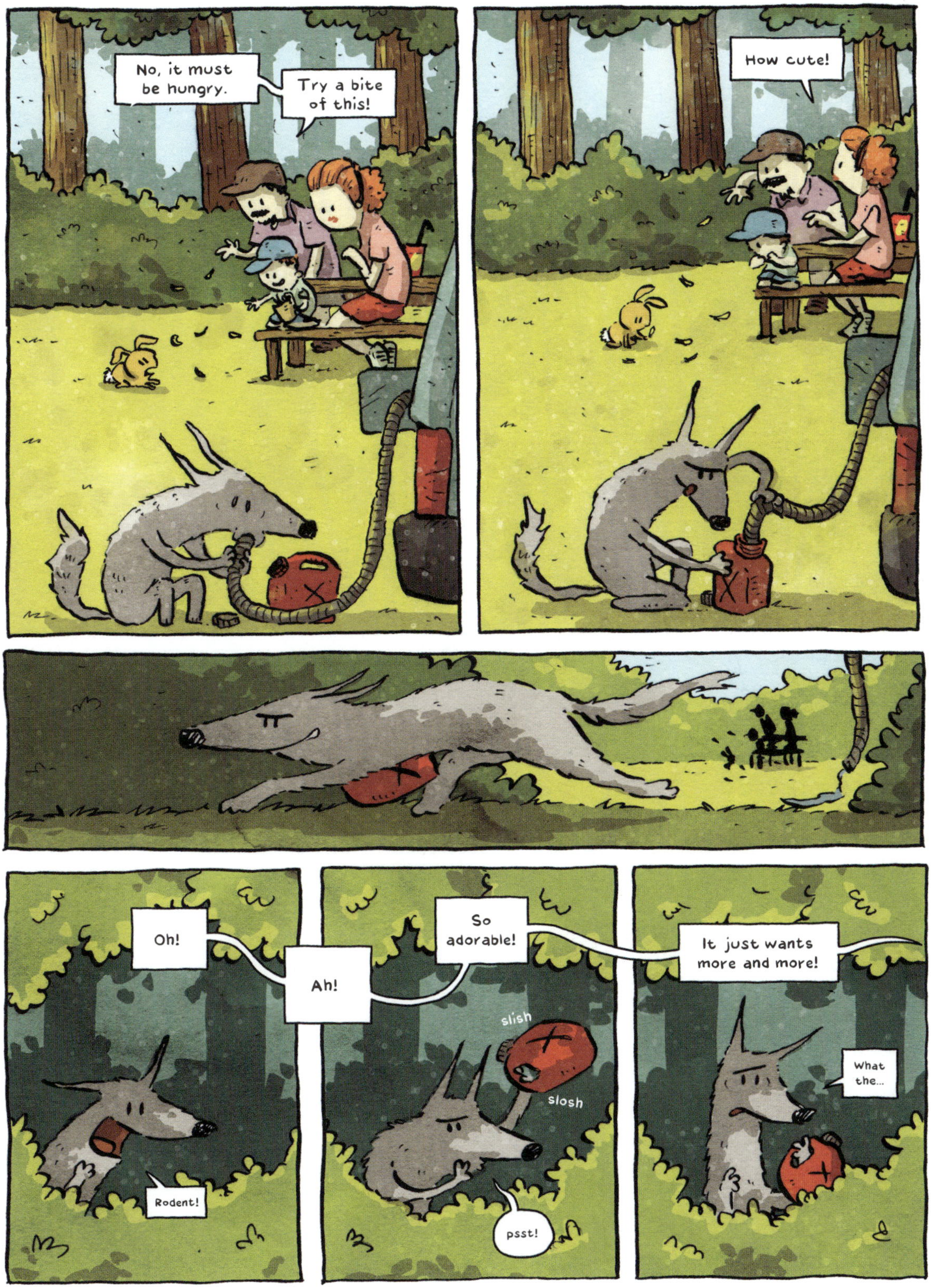
No, it must be hungry.
Try a bite of this!
How cute!
Oh!
Rodent!
Ah!
So adorable!
slish
slosh
psst!
It just wants more and more!
What the...

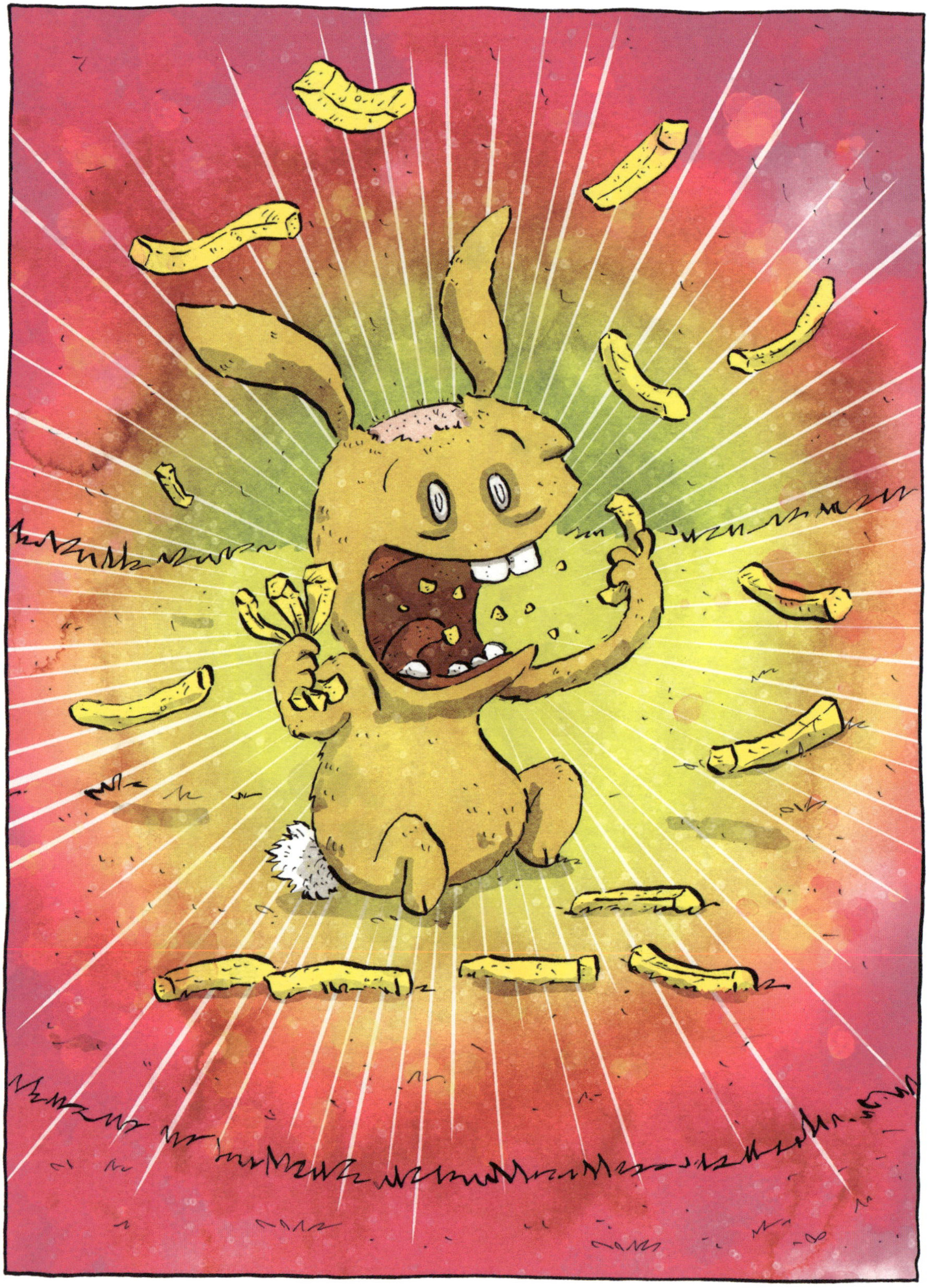

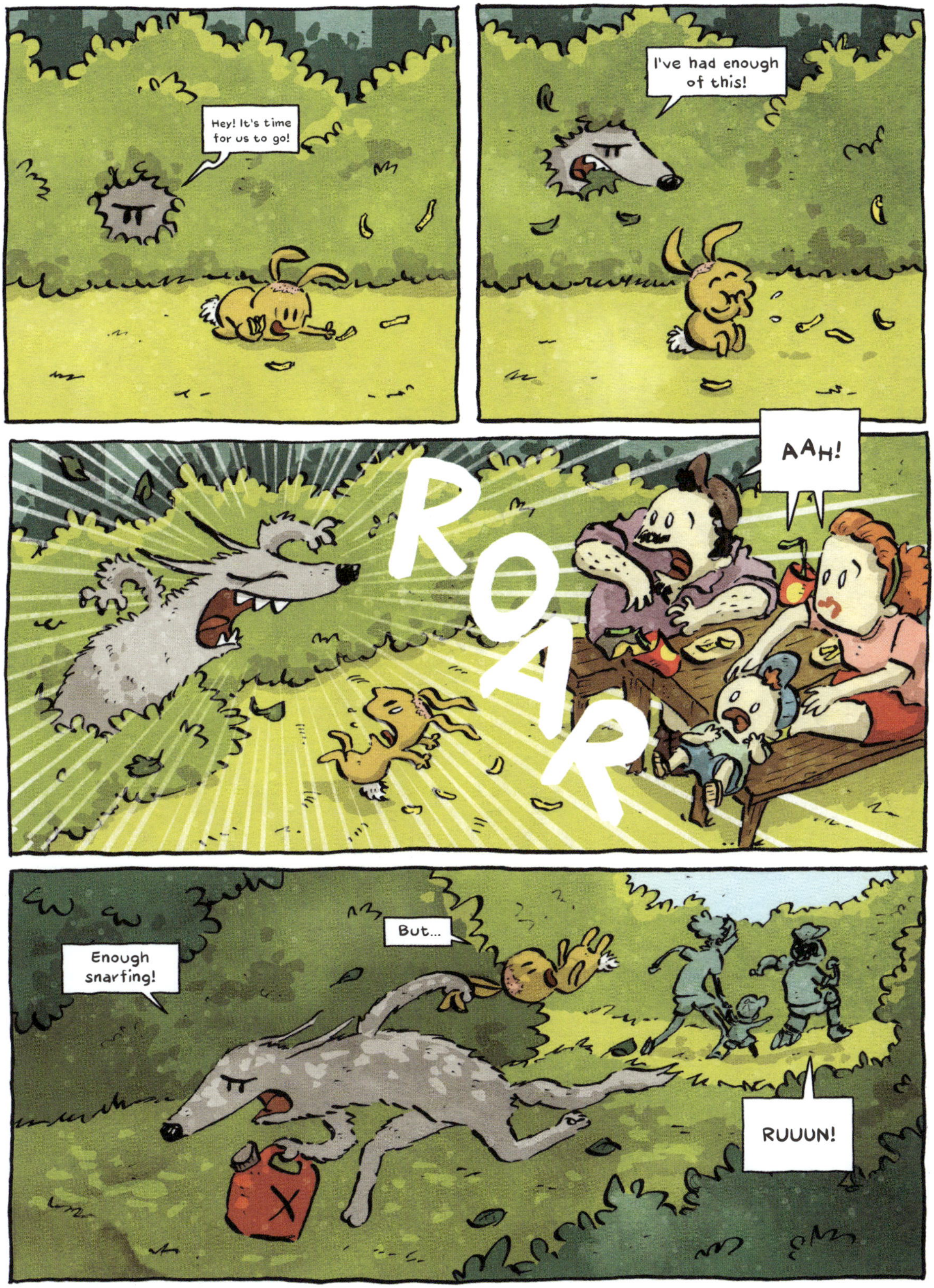
Hey! It's time for us to go!
I've had enough of this!
ROAR
AAH!
Enough snarfing!
But...
RUUUN!

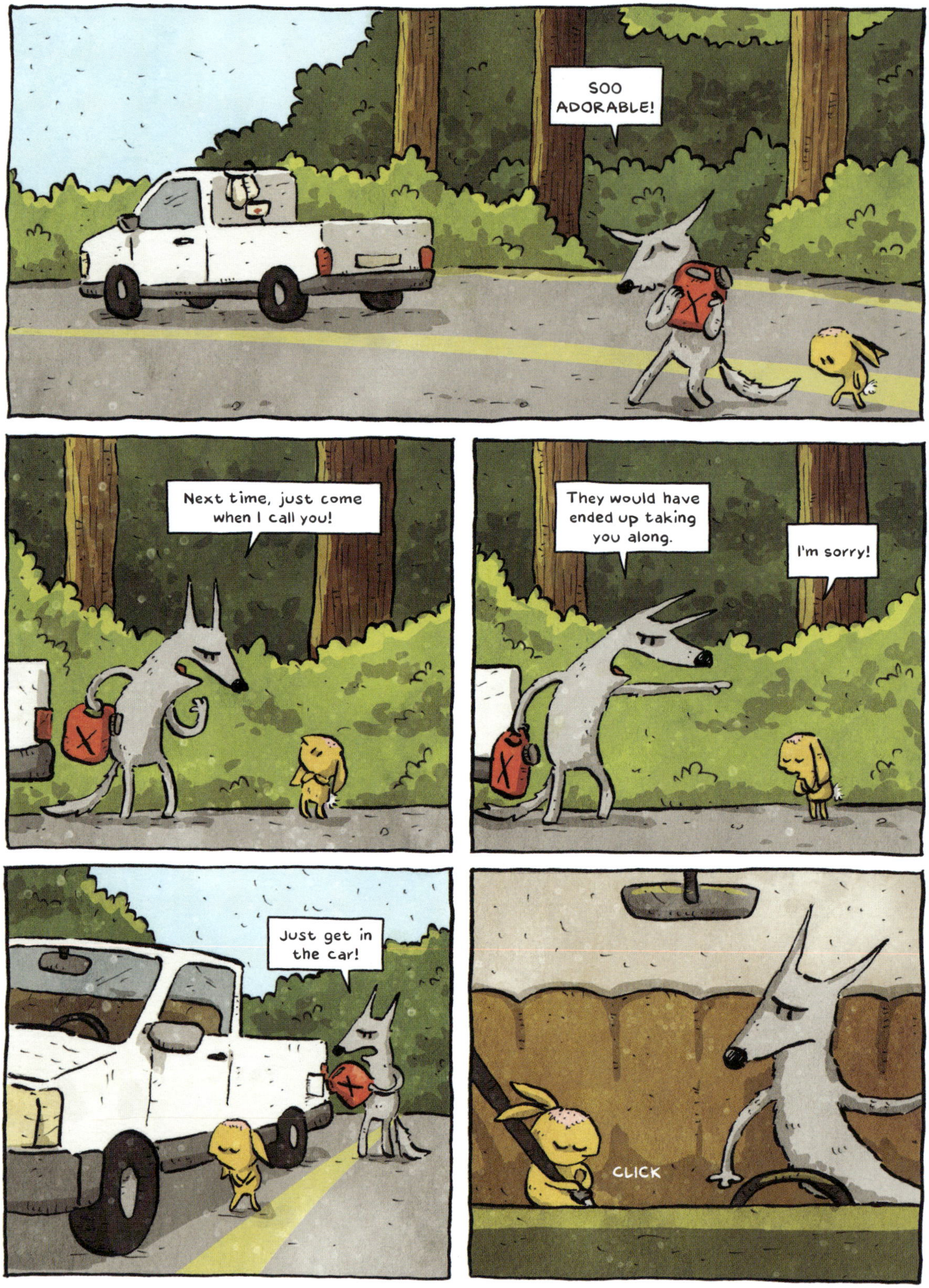

SOO ADORABLE!
Next time, just come when I call you!
They would have ended up taking you along.
I'm sorry!
Just get in the car!
CLICK

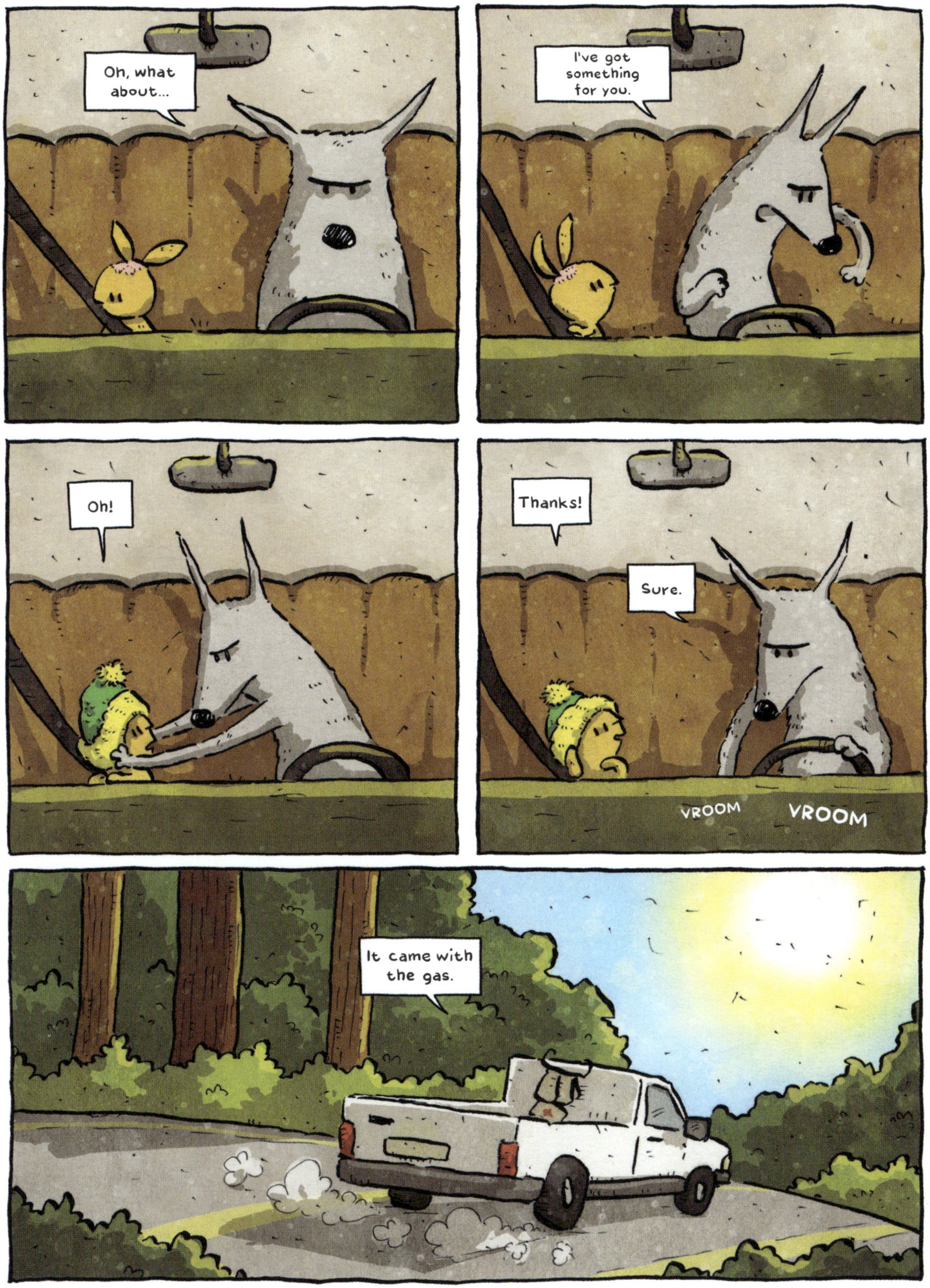
Oh, what about...
I've got something for you.
Oh!
Thanks!
Sure.
VROOM
VROOM
It came with the gas.

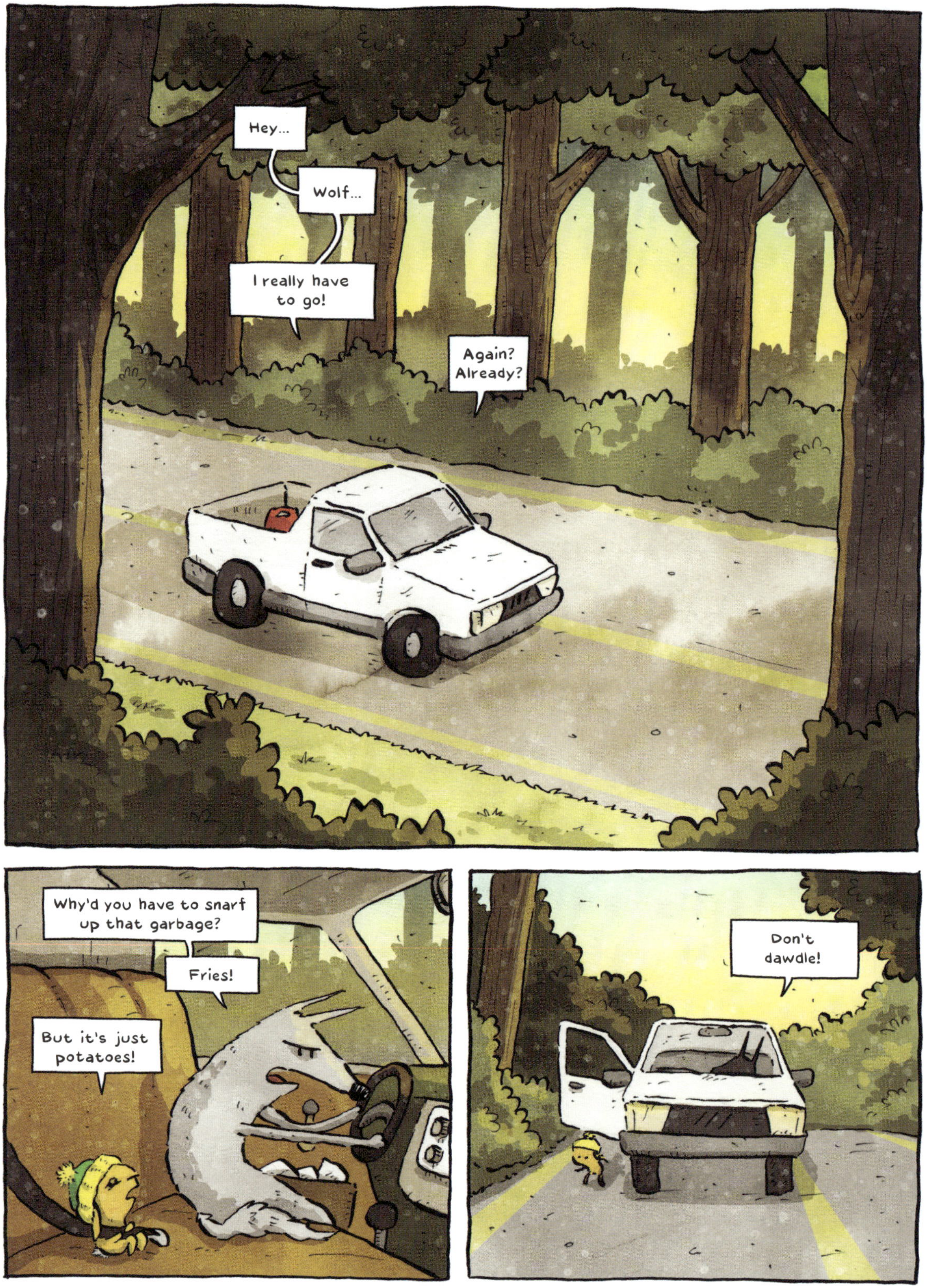
Hey...
Wolf...
I really have to go!
Again? Already?
Why'd you have to snarf up that garbage?
Fries!
But it's just potatoes!
Don't dawdle!

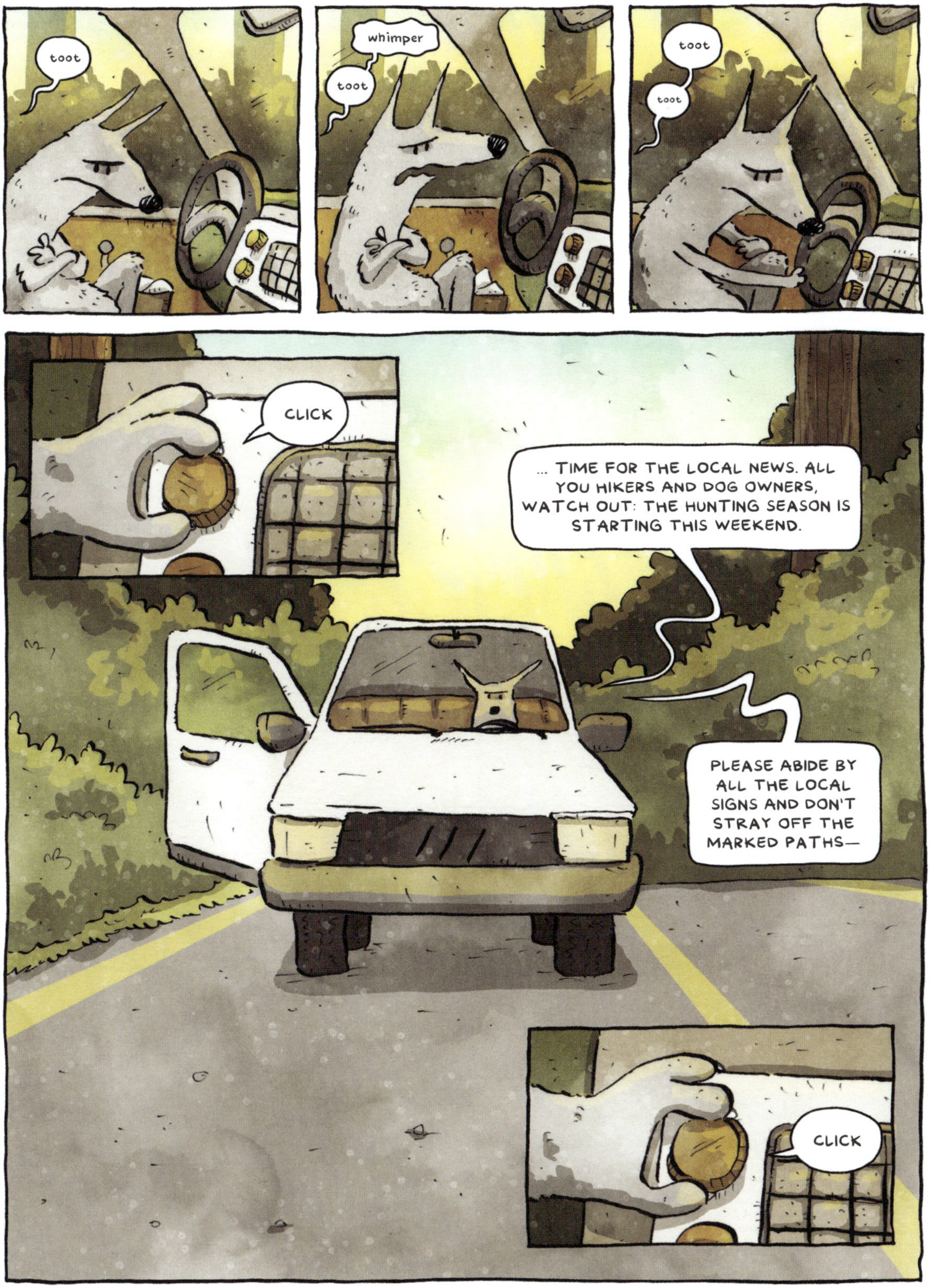
toot
whimper
toot
toot
toot
CLICK
... TIME FOR THE LOCAL NEWS. ALL YOU HIKERS AND DOG OWNERS, WATCH OUT: THE HUNTING SEASON IS STARTING THIS WEEKEND.
PLEASE ABIDE BY ALL THE LOCAL SIGNS AND DON'T STRAY OFF THE MARKED PATHS—
CLICK

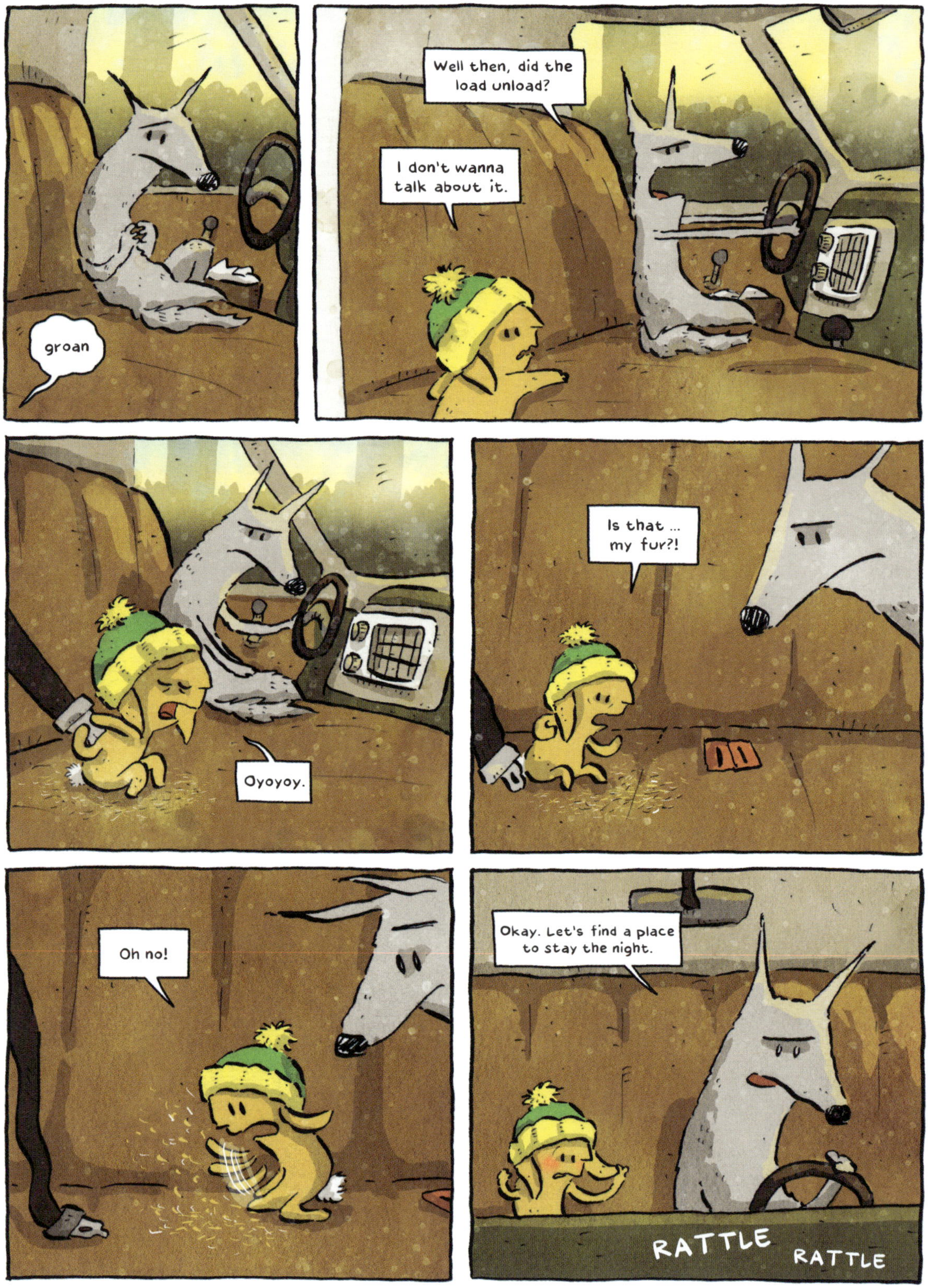
groan
Well then, did the load unload?
I don't wanna talk about it.
Oyoyoy.
Is that ... my fur?!
Oh no!
Okay. Let's find a place to stay the night.
RATTLE
RATTLE

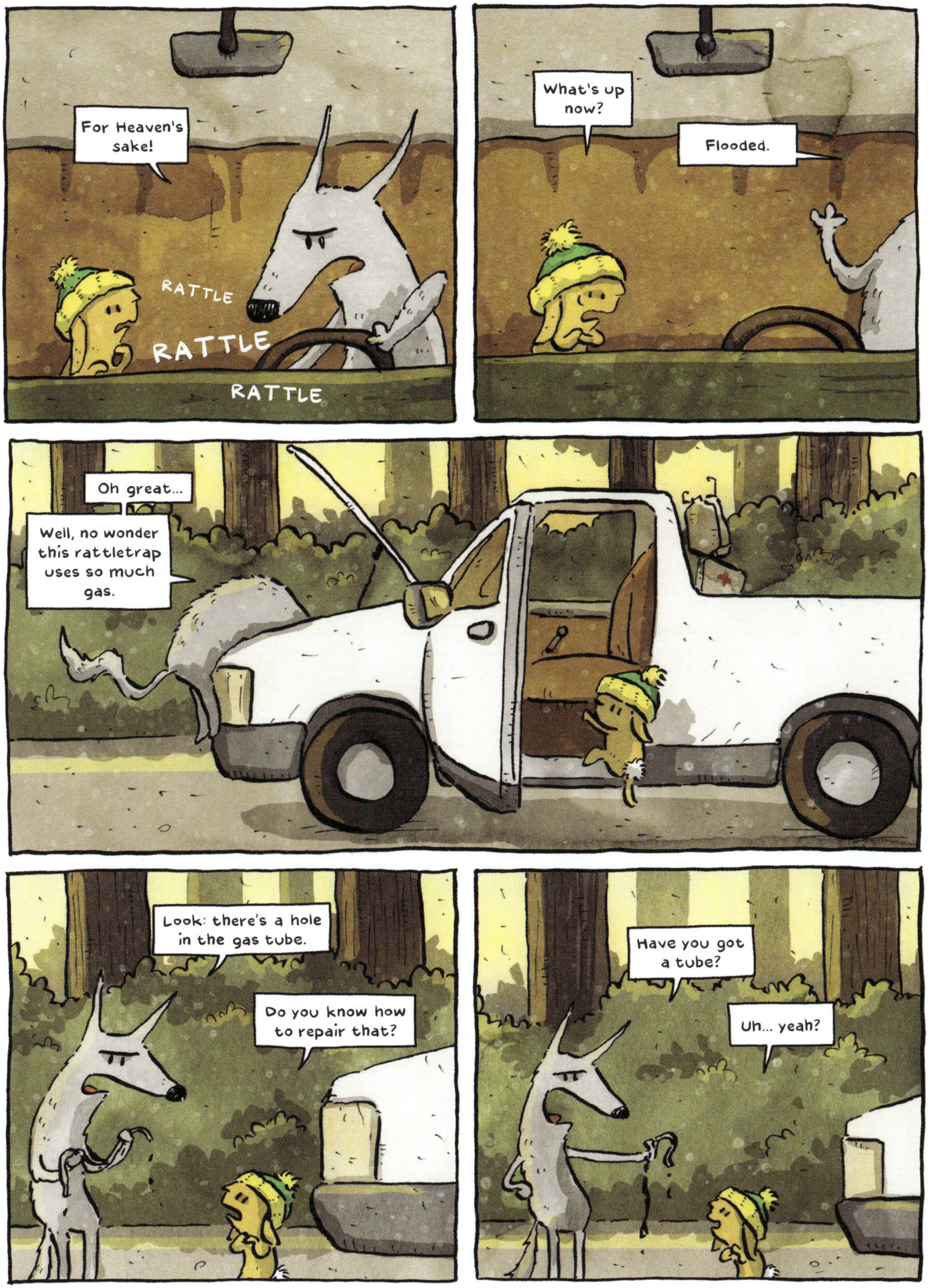
For Heaven's sake!
RATTLE
RATTLE
RATTLE
What's up now?
Flooded.
Oh great...
Well, no wonder this rattletrap uses so much gas.
Look: there's a hole in the gas tube.
Do you know how to repair that?
Have you got a tube?
Uh... yeah?

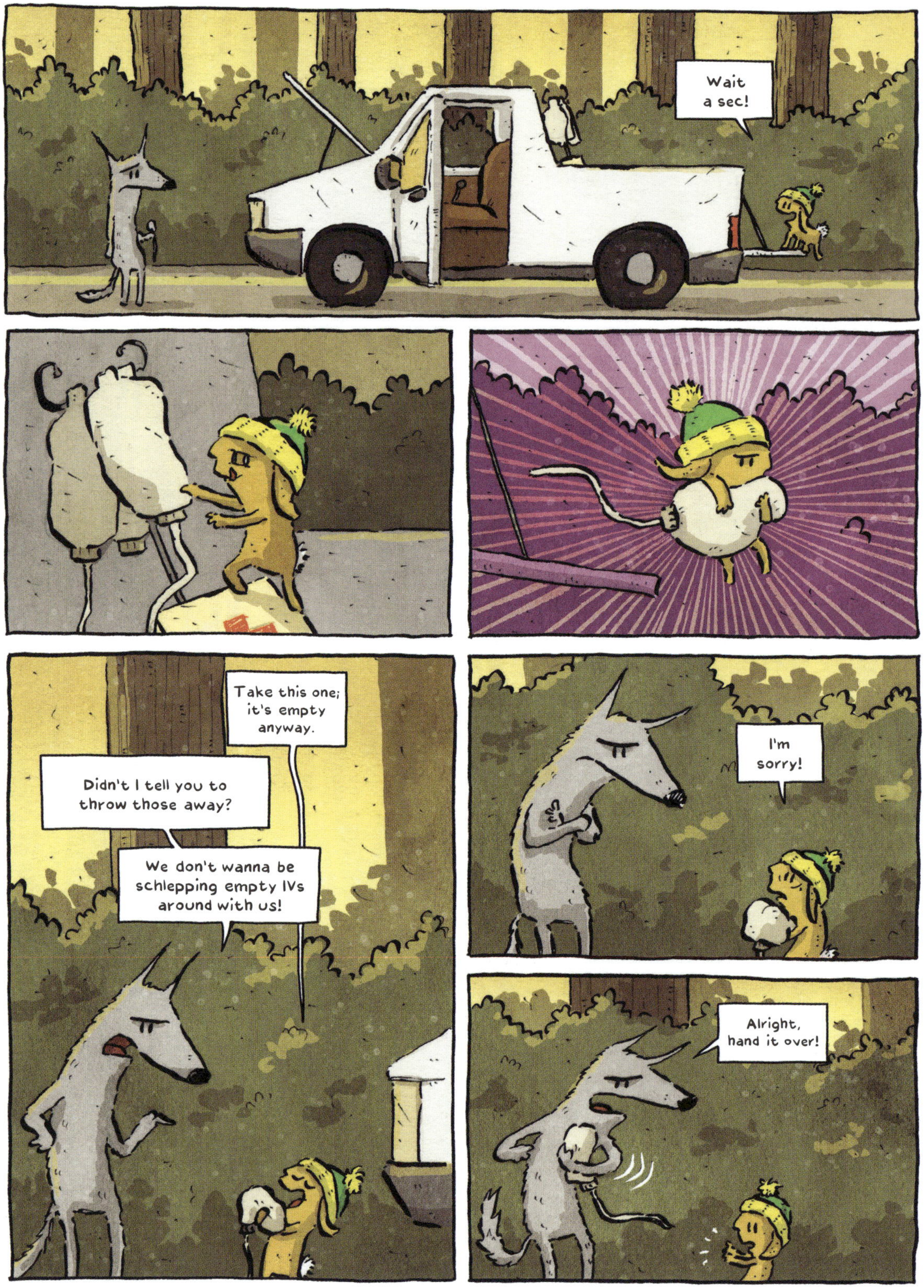
Wait a sec!
Take this one; it's empty anyway.
Didn't I tell you to throw those away?
We don't wanna be schlepping empty IVs around with us!
I'm sorry!
Alright, hand it over!

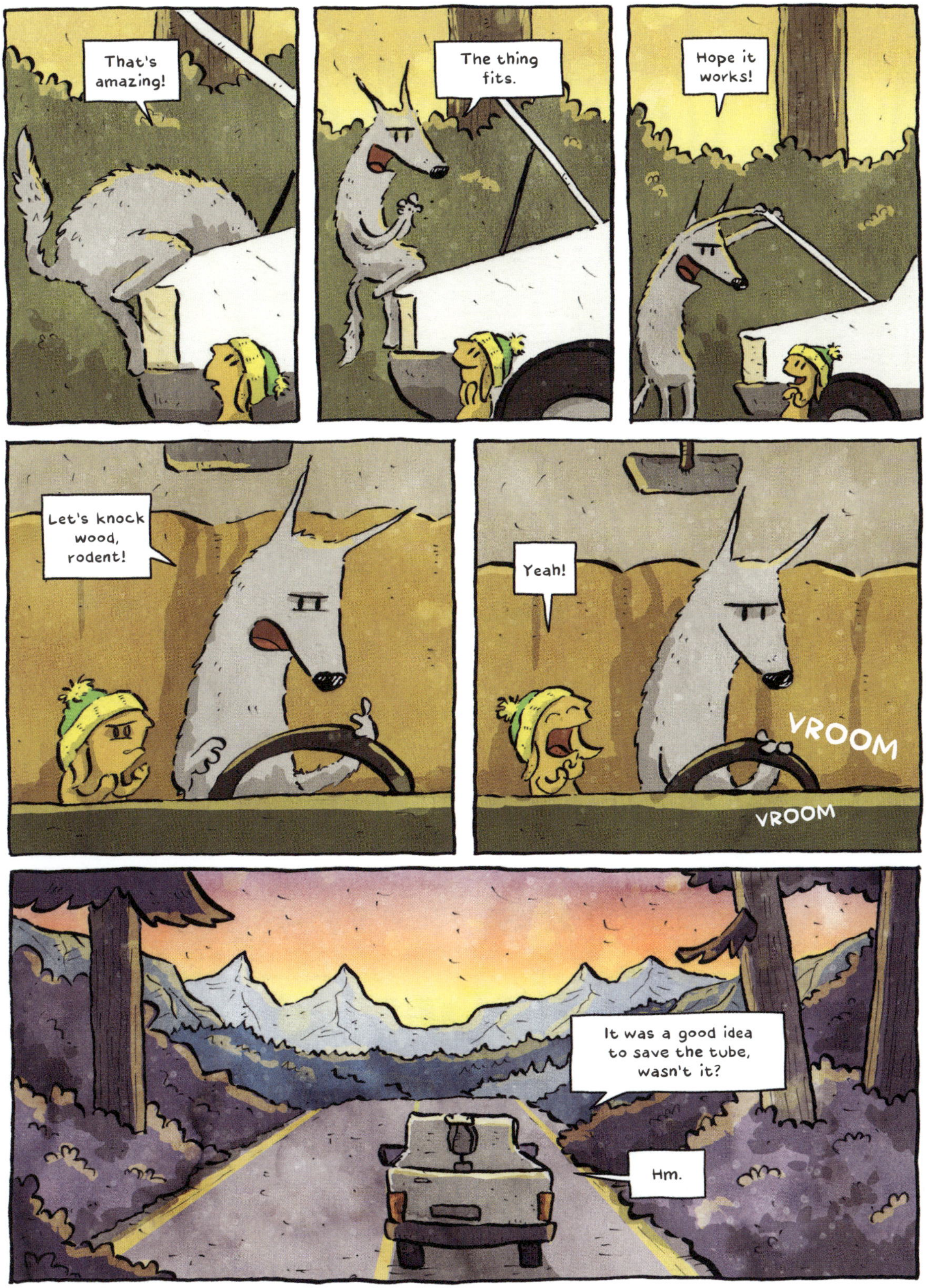
That's amazing!
The thing fits.
Hope it works!
Let's knock wood, rodent!
Yeah!
VROOM
VROOM
It was a good idea to save the tube, wasn't it?
Hm.

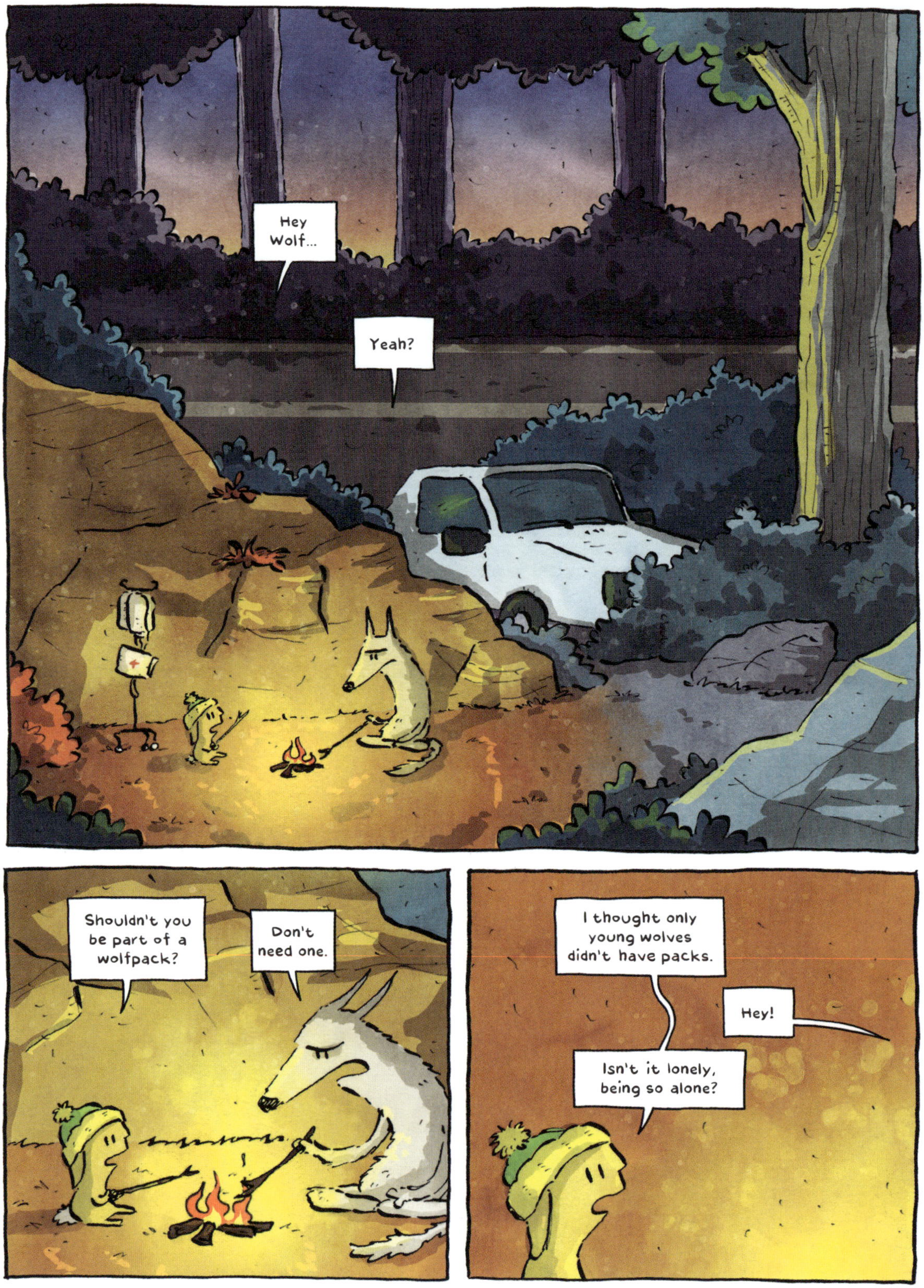
Hey Wolf...
Yeah?
Shouldn't you be part of a wolfpack?
Don't need one.
I thought only young wolves didn't have packs.
Hey!
Isn't it lonely, being so alone?

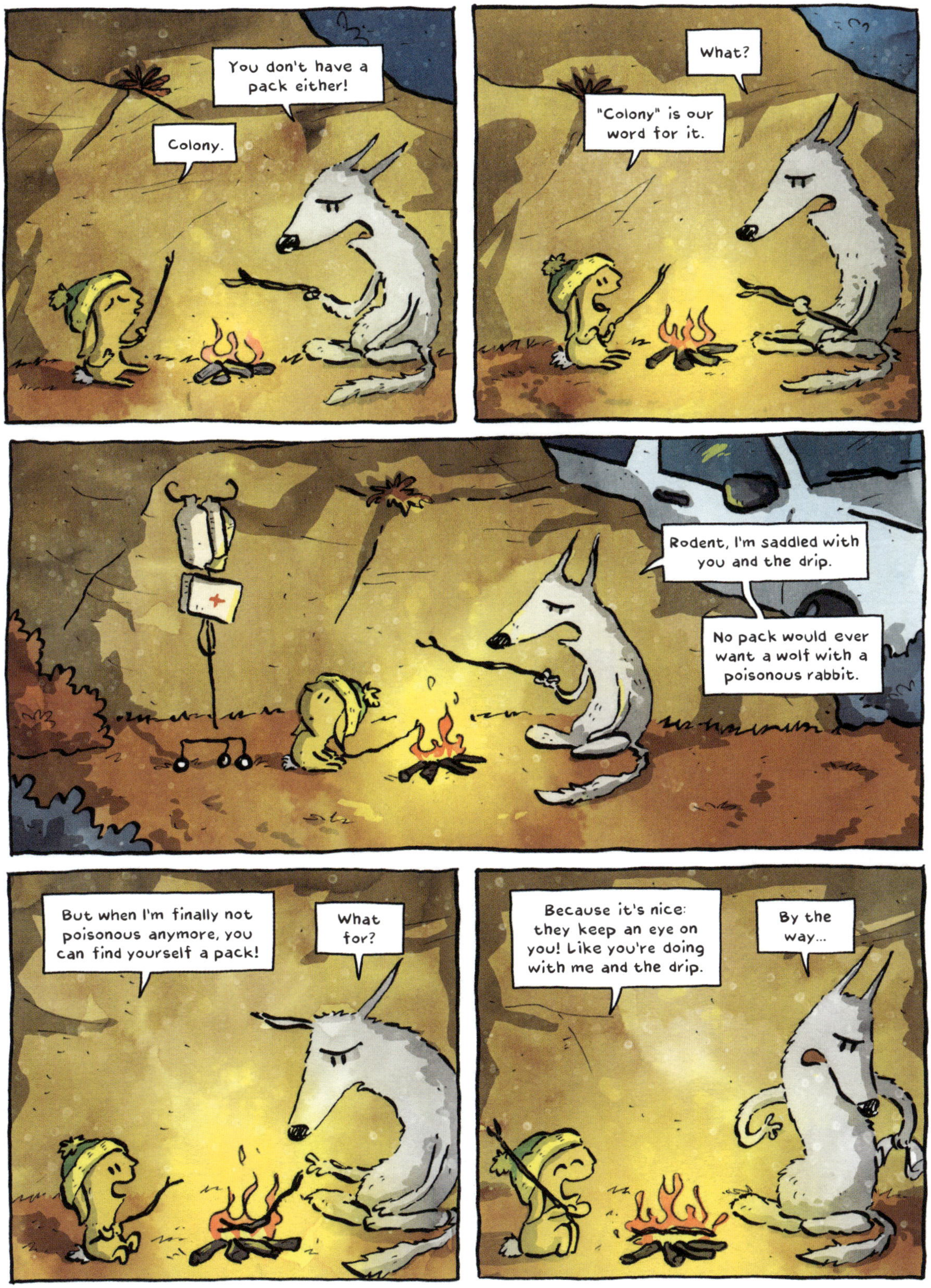
You don't have a pack either!
Colony.
What?
"Colony" is our word for it.
Rodent, I'm saddled with you and the drip.
No pack would ever want a wolf with a poisonous rabbit.
But when I'm finally not poisonous anymore, you can find yourself a pack!
What for?
Because it's nice: they keep an eye on you! Like you're doing with me and the drip.
By the way...

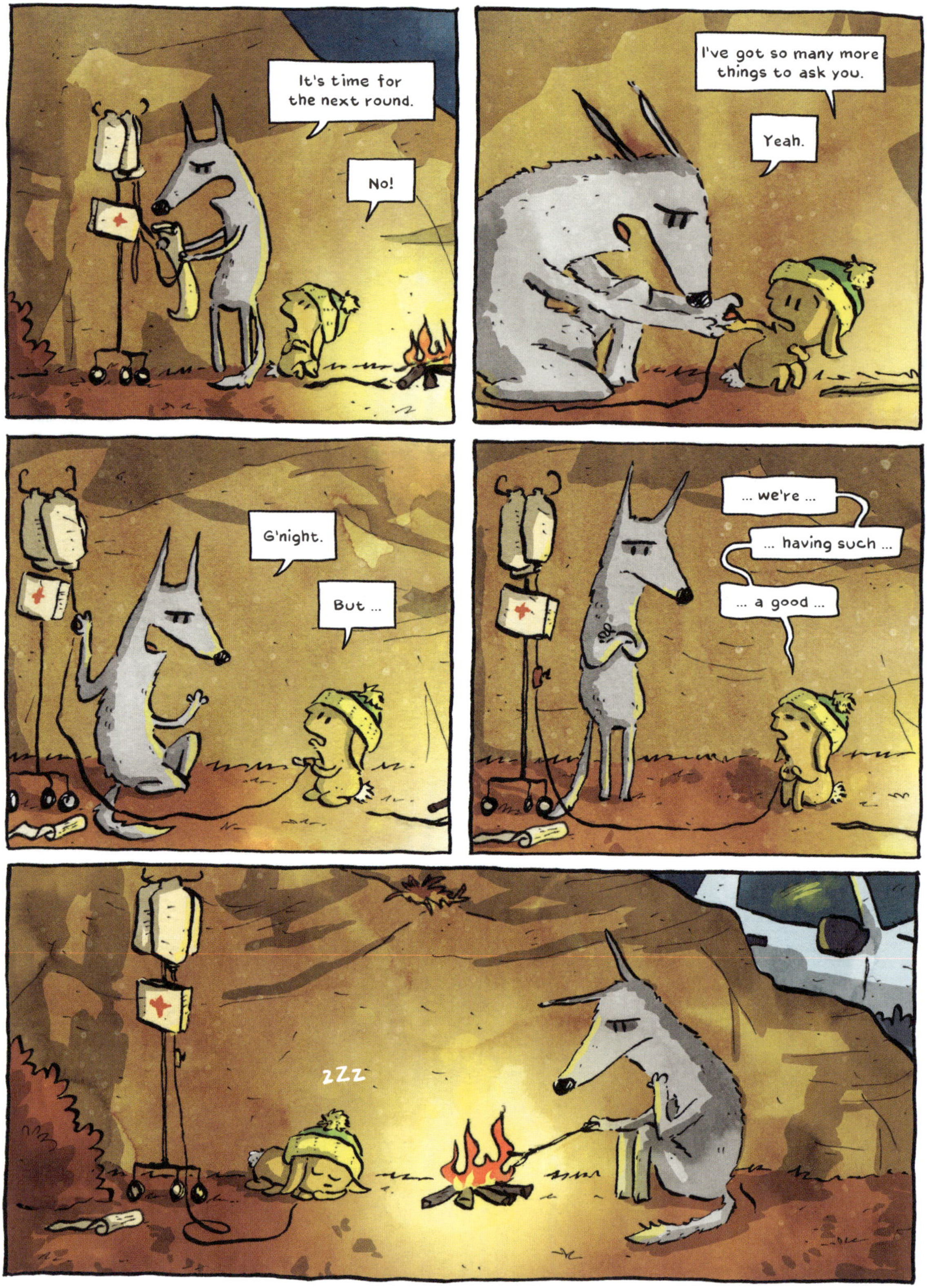
It's time for the next round.
No!
I've got so many more things to ask you.
Yeah.
G'night.
But ...
... we're ...
... having such ...
... a good ...
ZZZ

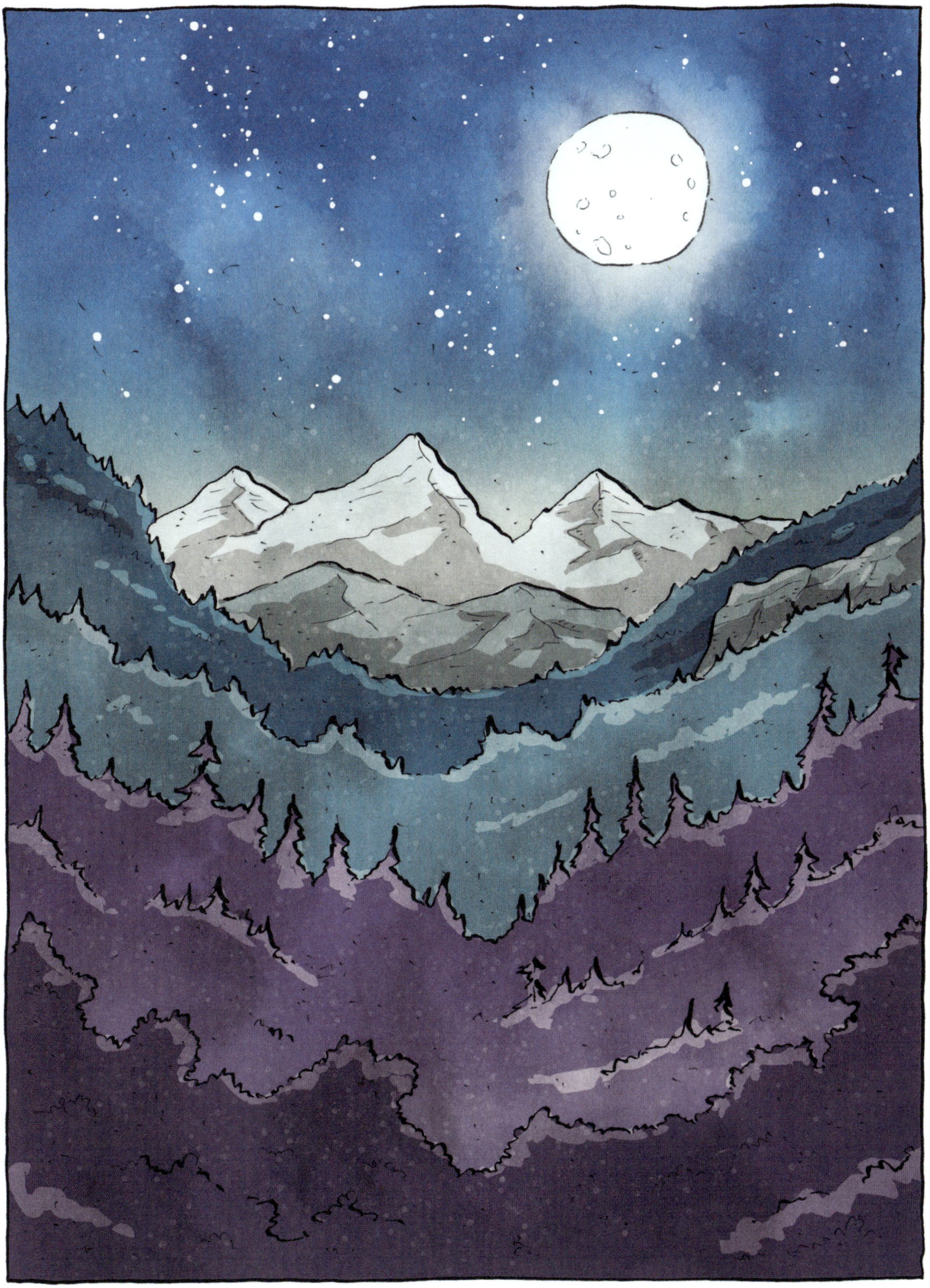

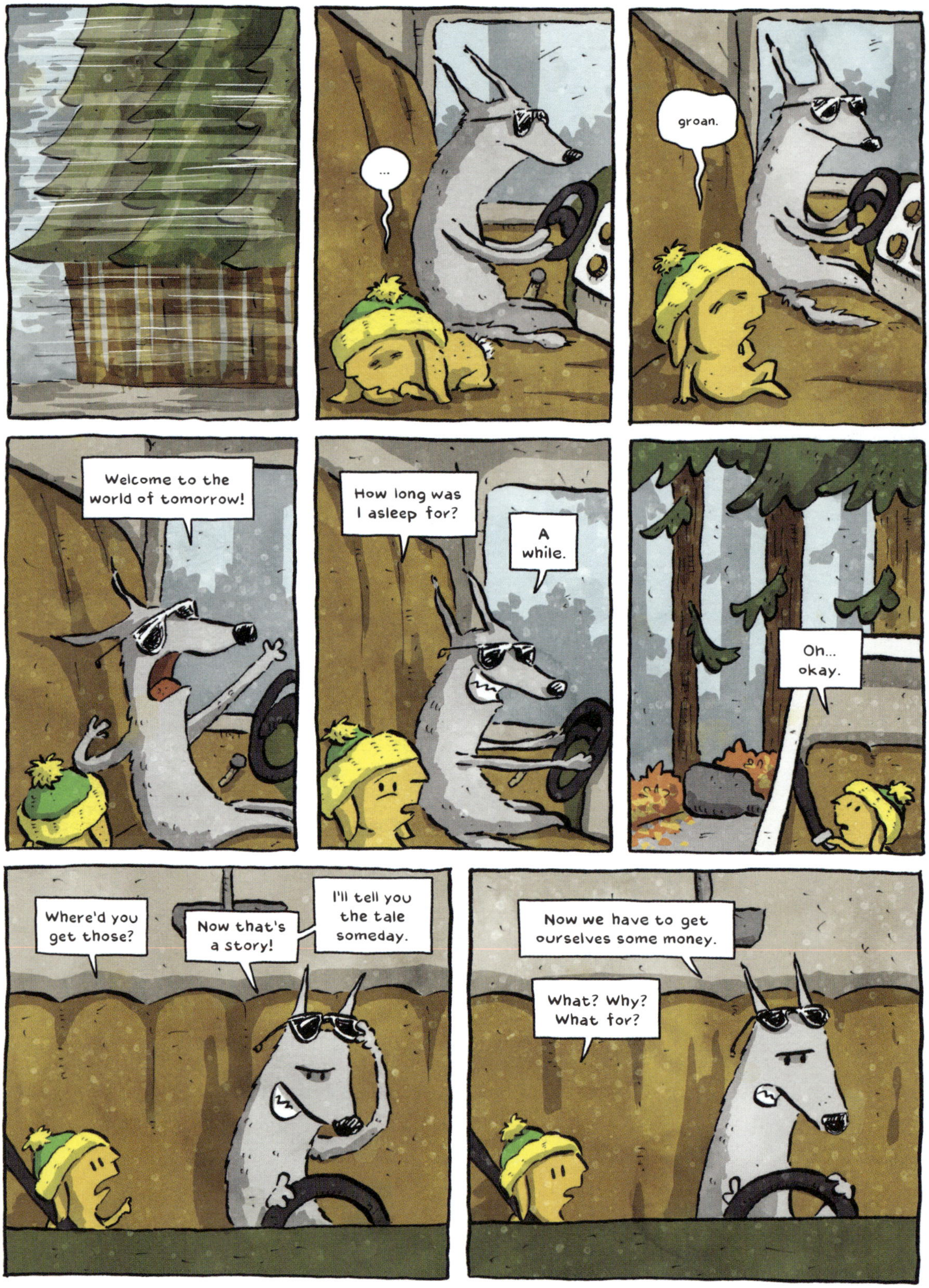
...
groan.
Welcome to the world of tomorrow!
How long was I asleep for?
A while.
Oh... okay.
Where'd you get those?
Now that's a story!
I'll tell you the tale someday.
Now we have to get ourselves some money.
What? Why? What for?

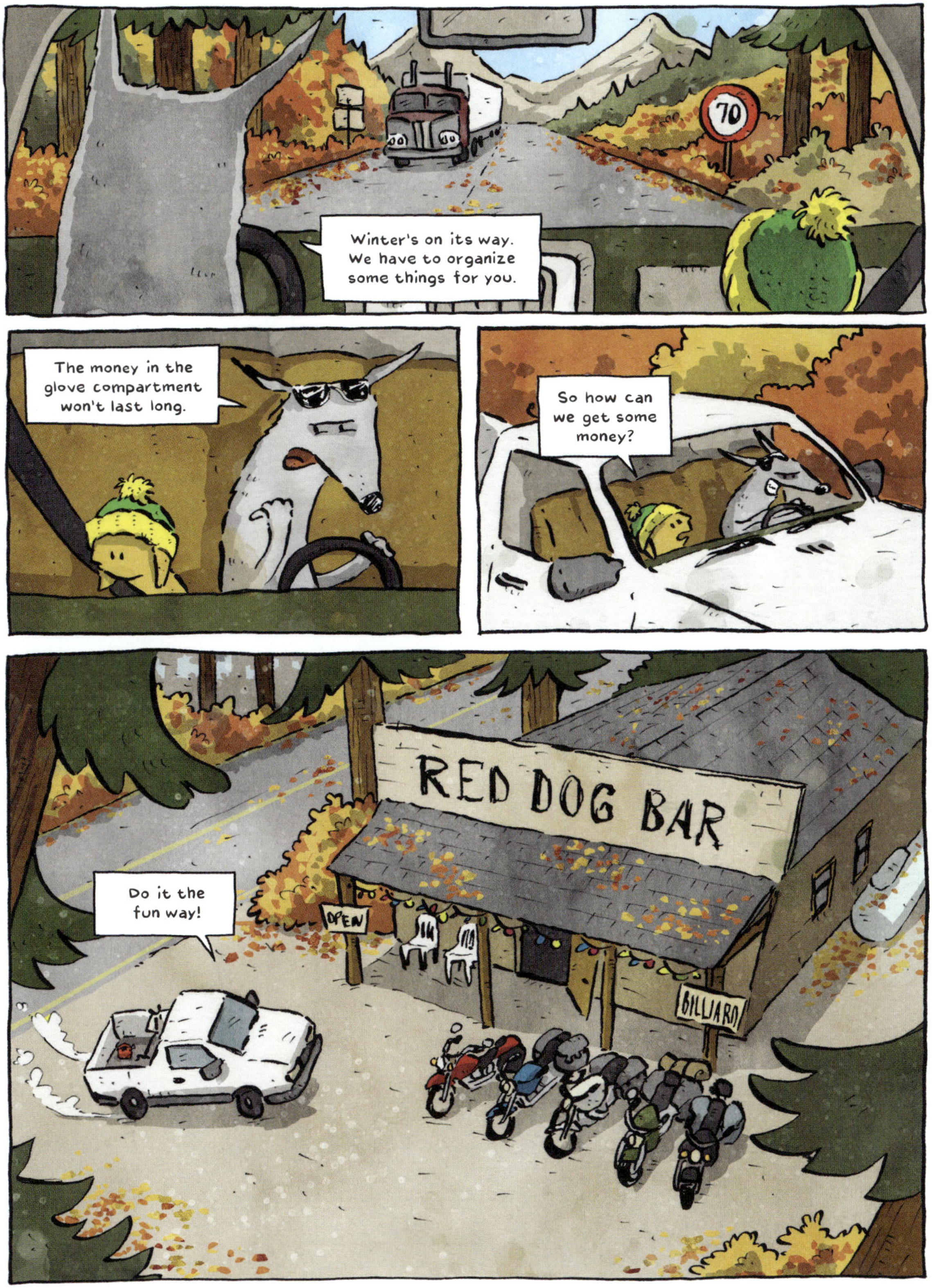
70
Winter's on its way. We have to organize some things for you.
The money in the glove compartment won't last long.
So how can we get some money?
RED DOG BAR
OPEN
BILLJARD
Do it the fun way!

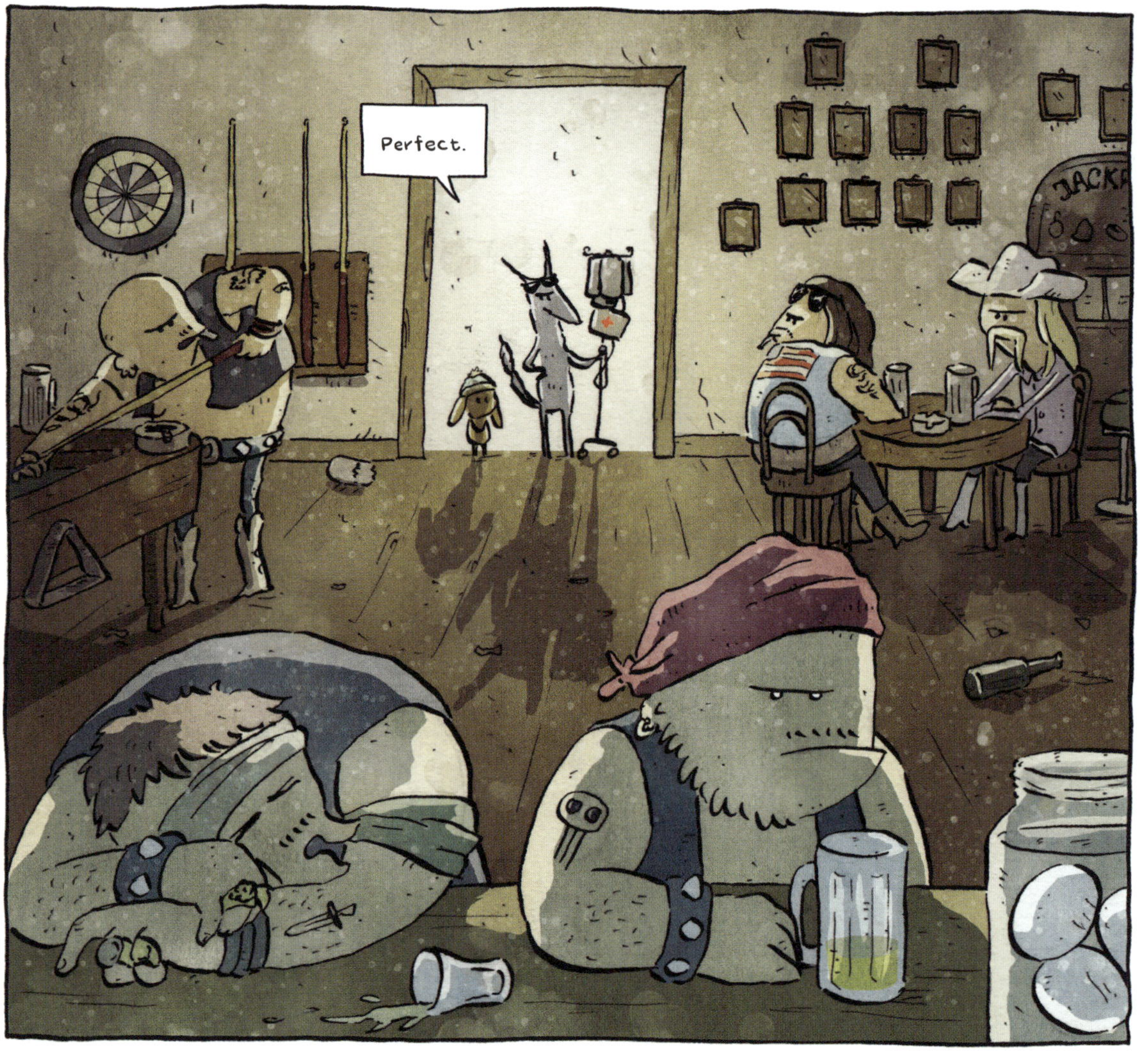
Perfect.

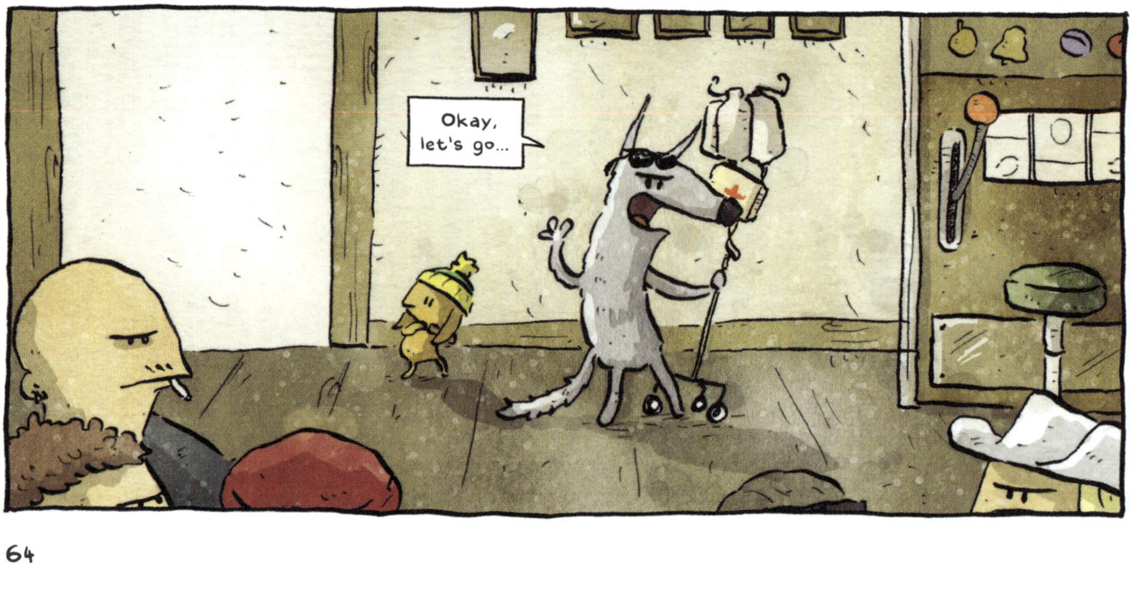
Okay,
let's go...

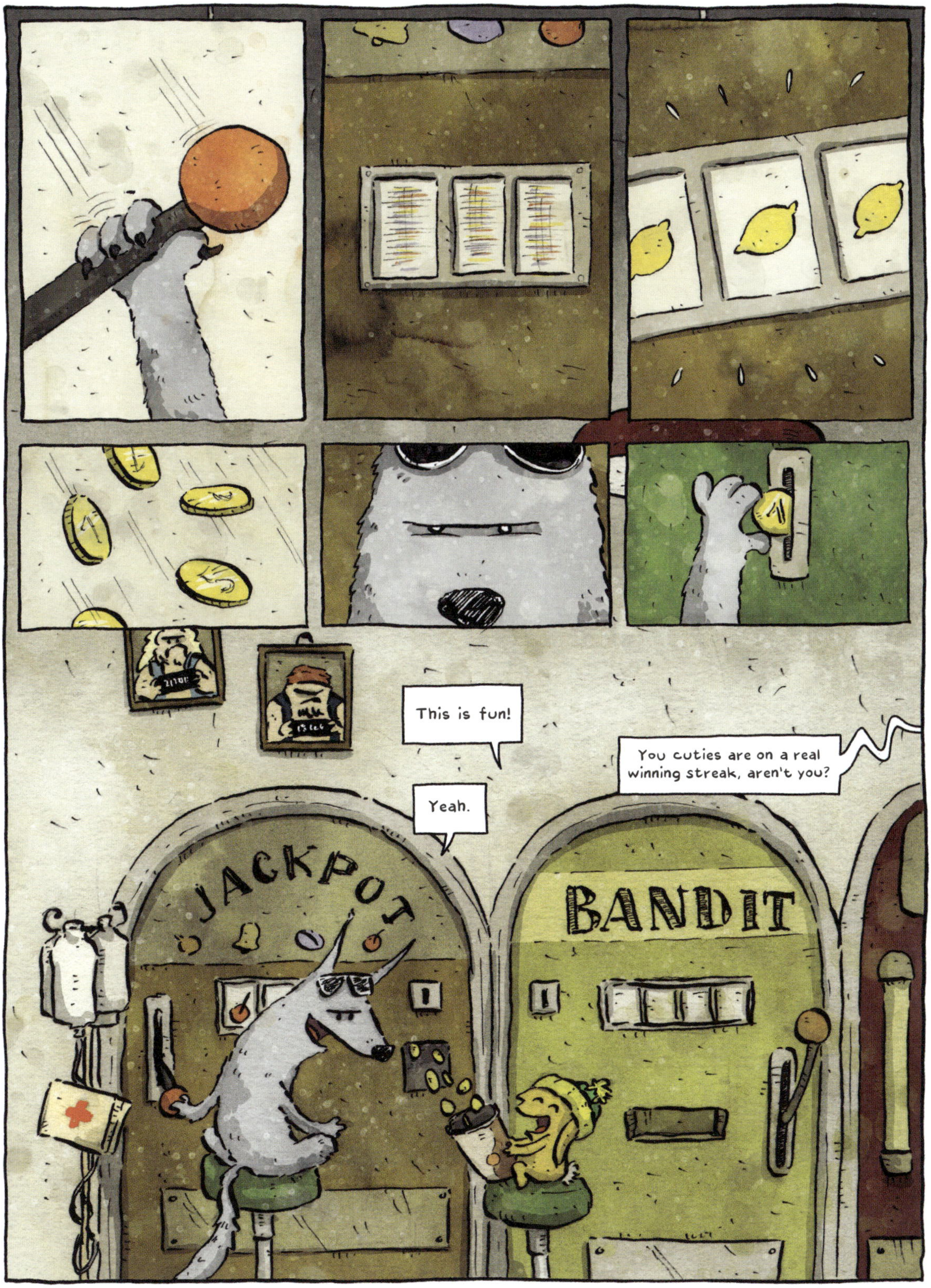

This is fun!
Yeah.
You cuties are on a real winning streak, aren't you?
JACKPOT
BANDIT

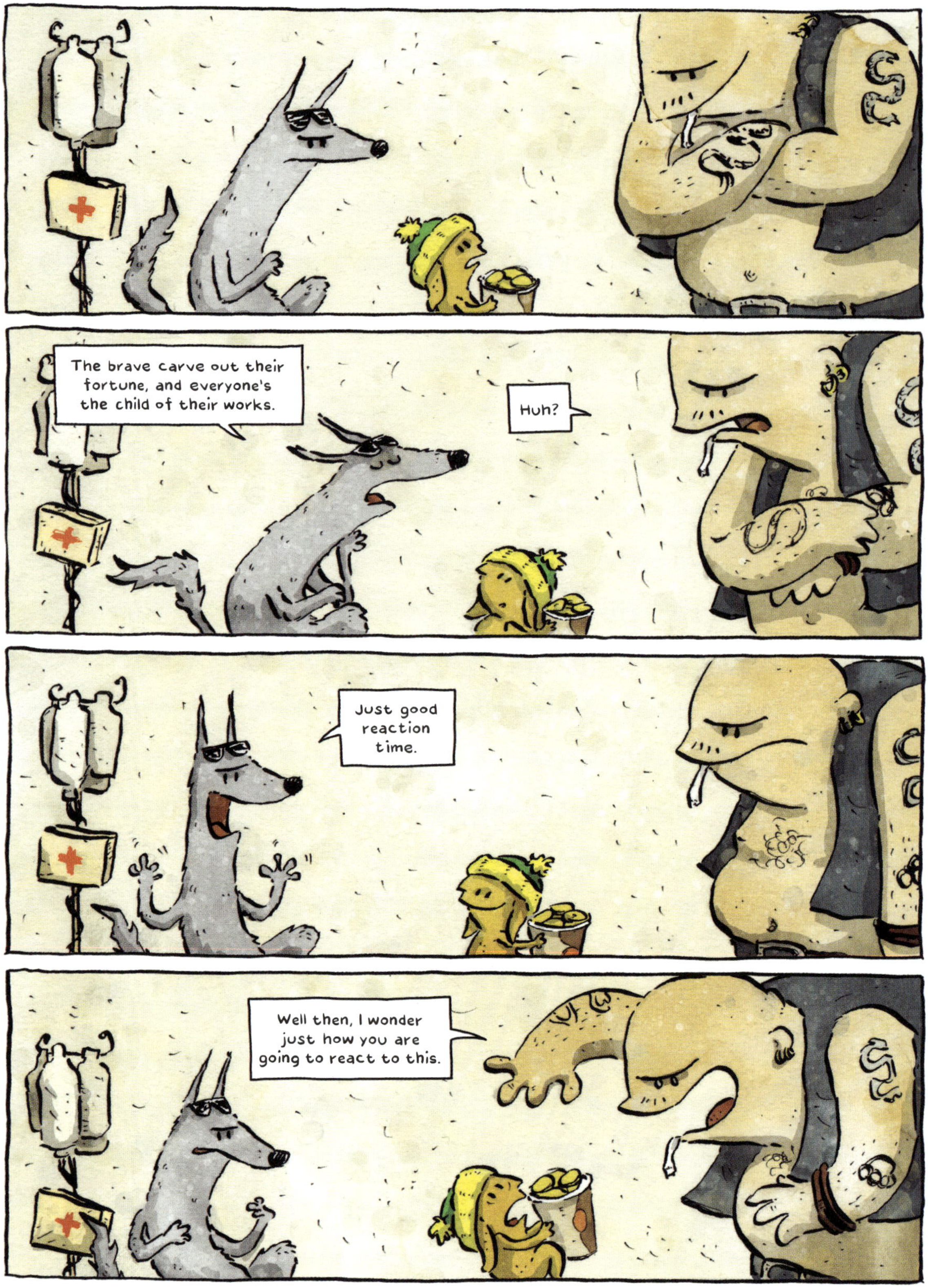
The brave carve out their fortune, and everyone's the child of their works.
Huh?
Just good reaction time.
Well then, I wonder just how you are going to react to this.

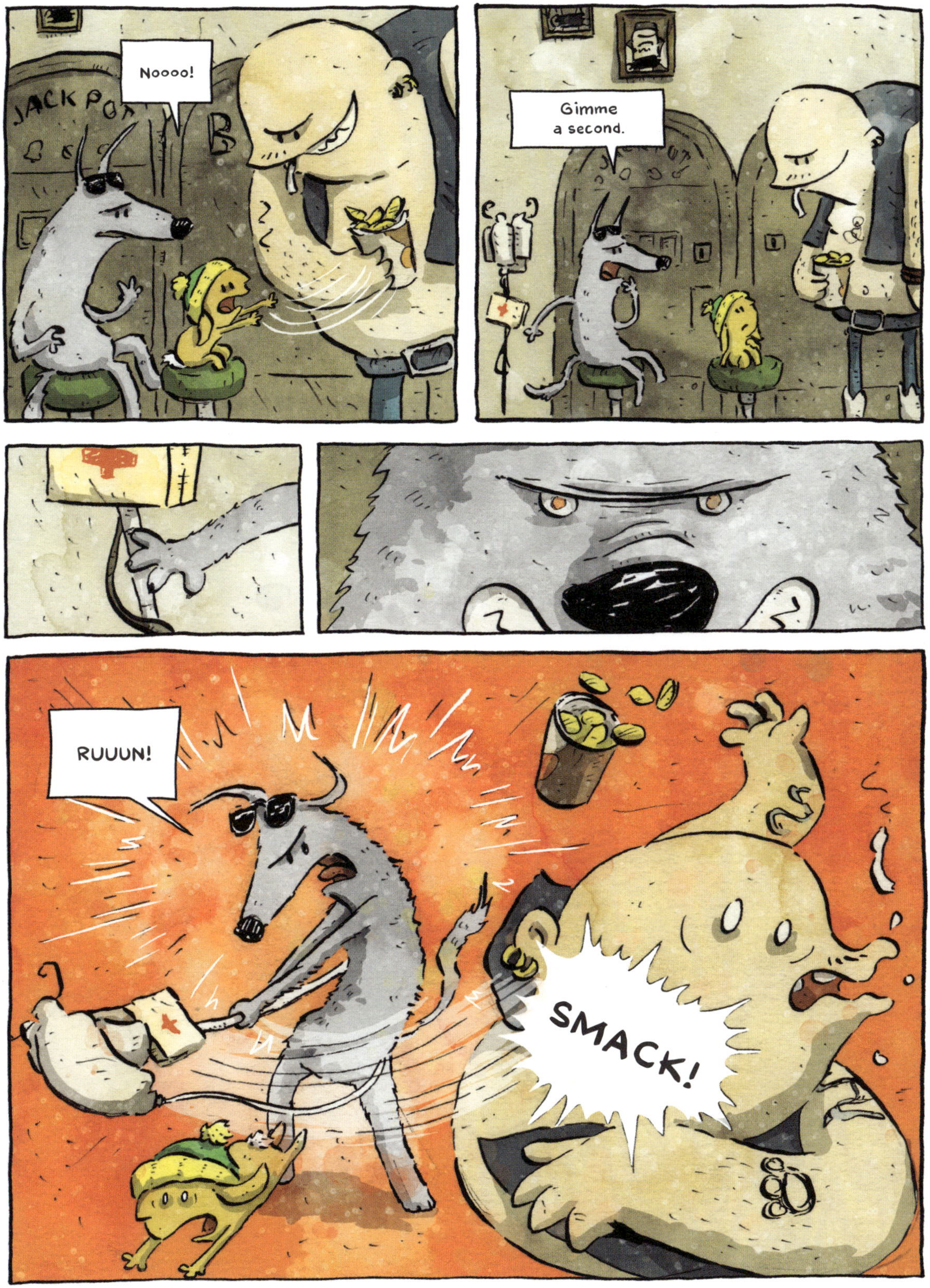
Noooo!
JACKPOT
Gimme a second.
RUUUN!
SMACK!

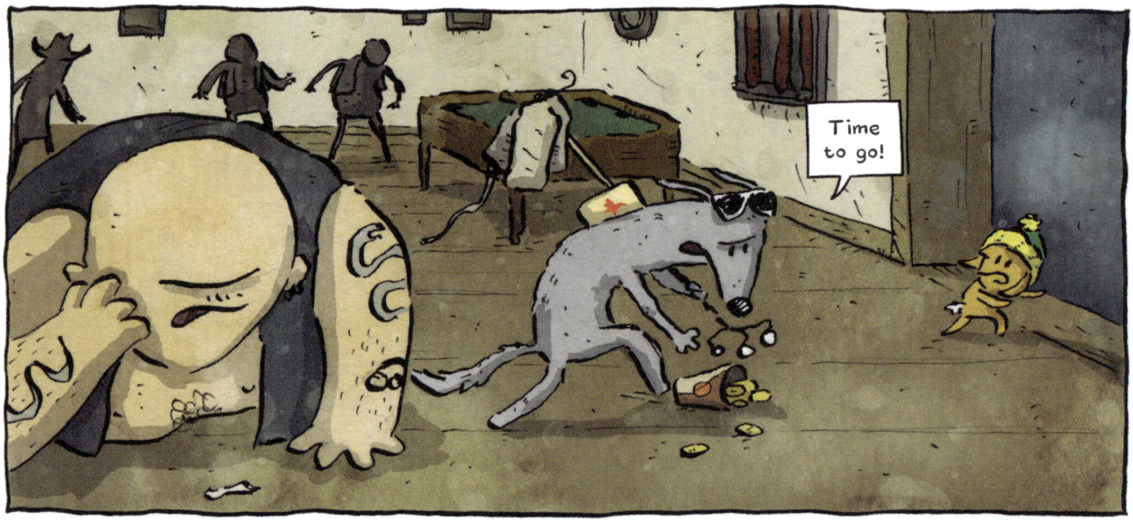
Time to go!

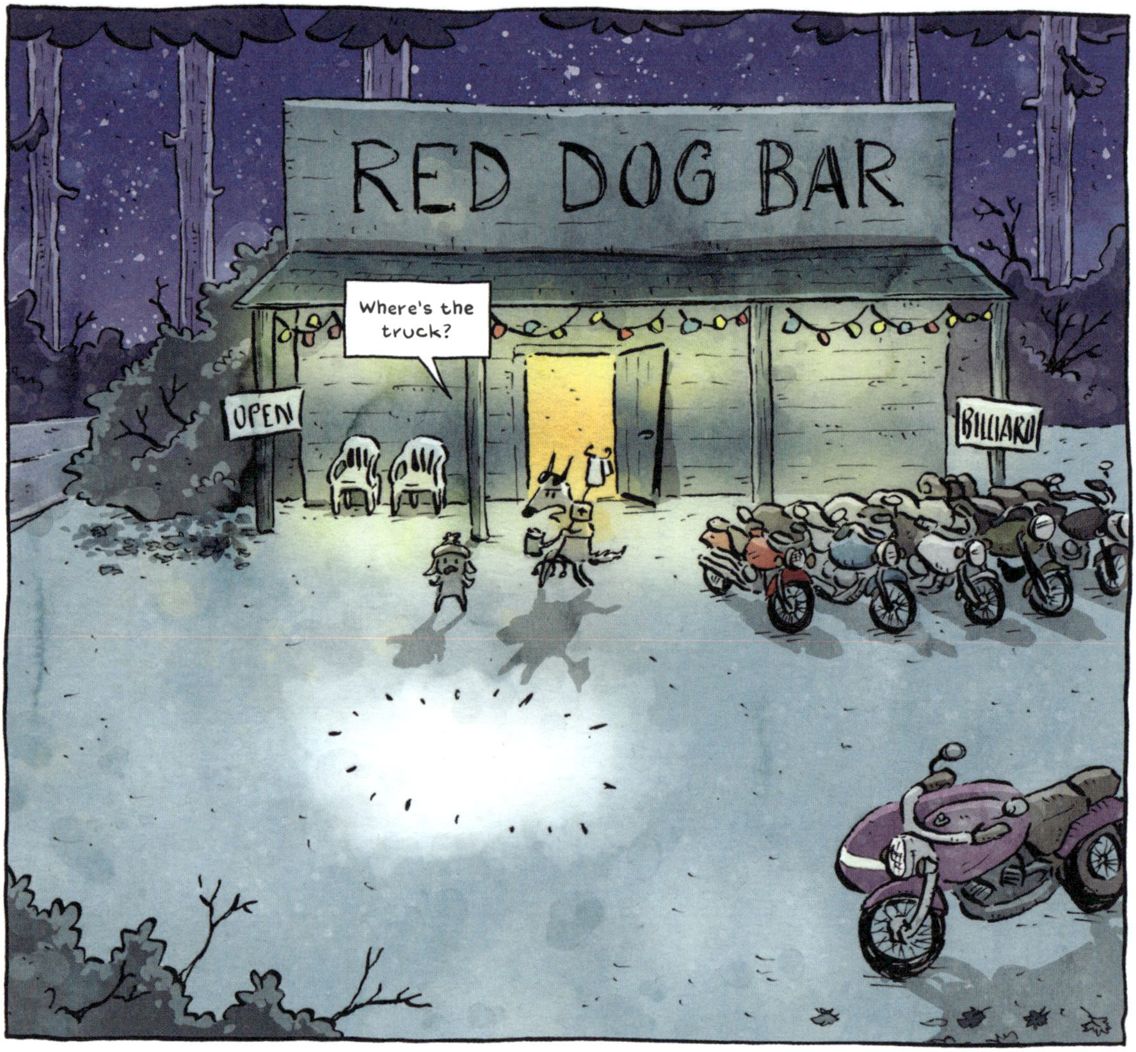
RED DOG BAR
Where's the truck?
OPEN
BILLIARD

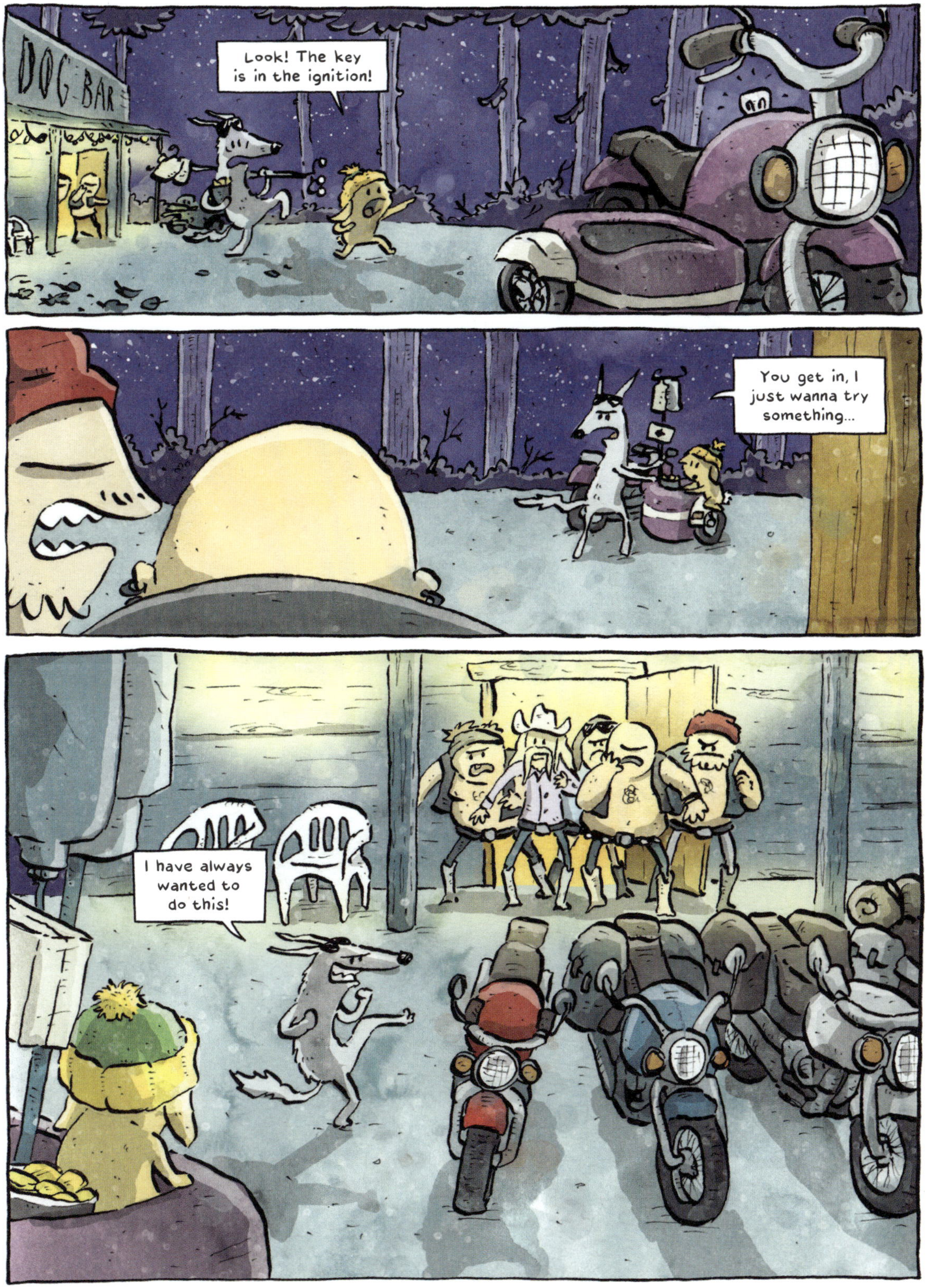
DOG BAR
Look! The key is in the ignition!
You get in, I just wanna try something...
I have always wanted to do this!

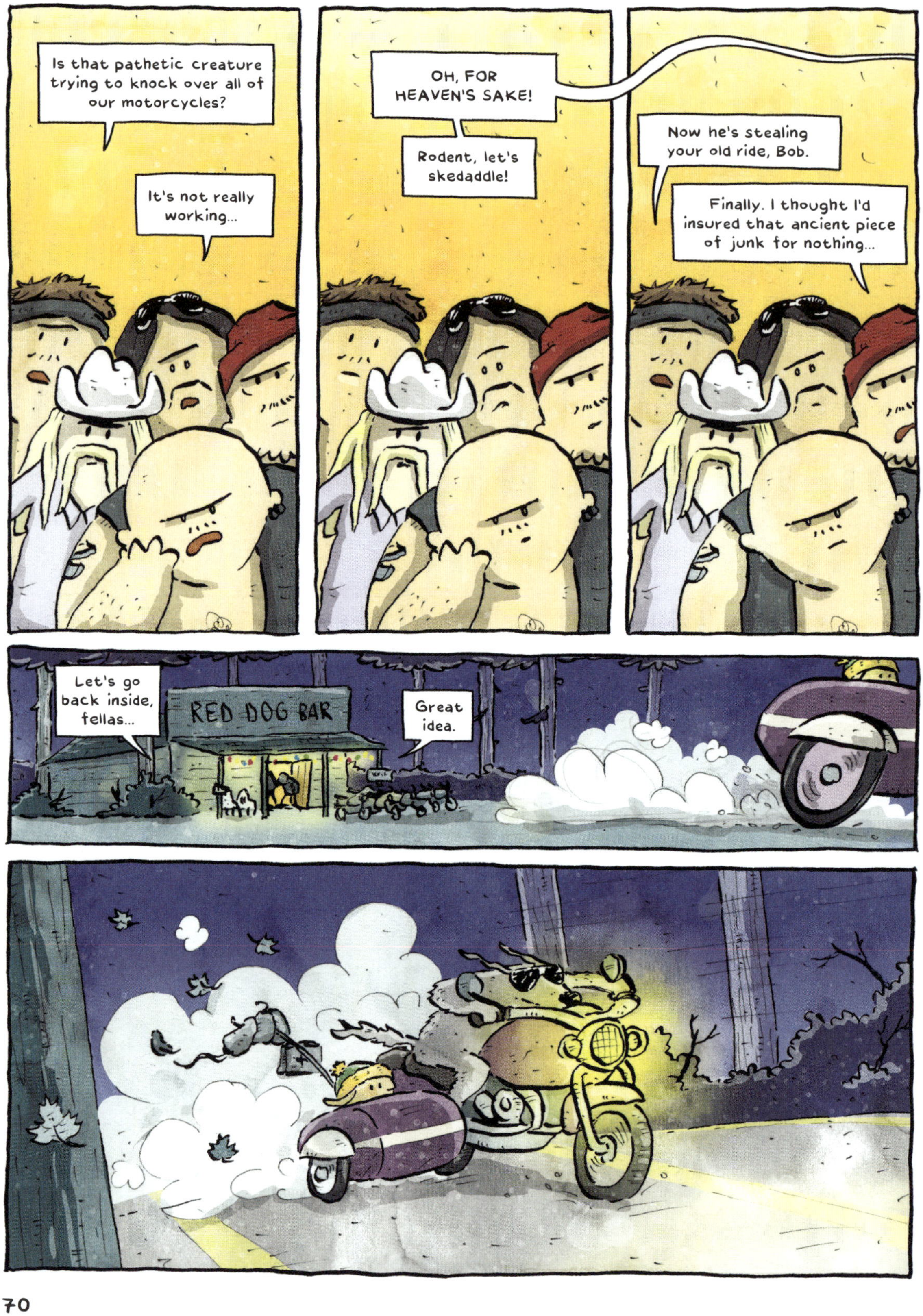

Is that pathetic creature trying to knock over all of our motorcycles?
It's not really working...
OH, FOR HEAVEN'S SAKE!
Rodent, let's skedaddle!
Now he's stealing your old ride, Bob.
Finally. I thought I'd insured that ancient piece of junk for nothing...
Let's go back inside, fellas...
RED DOG BAR
Great idea.

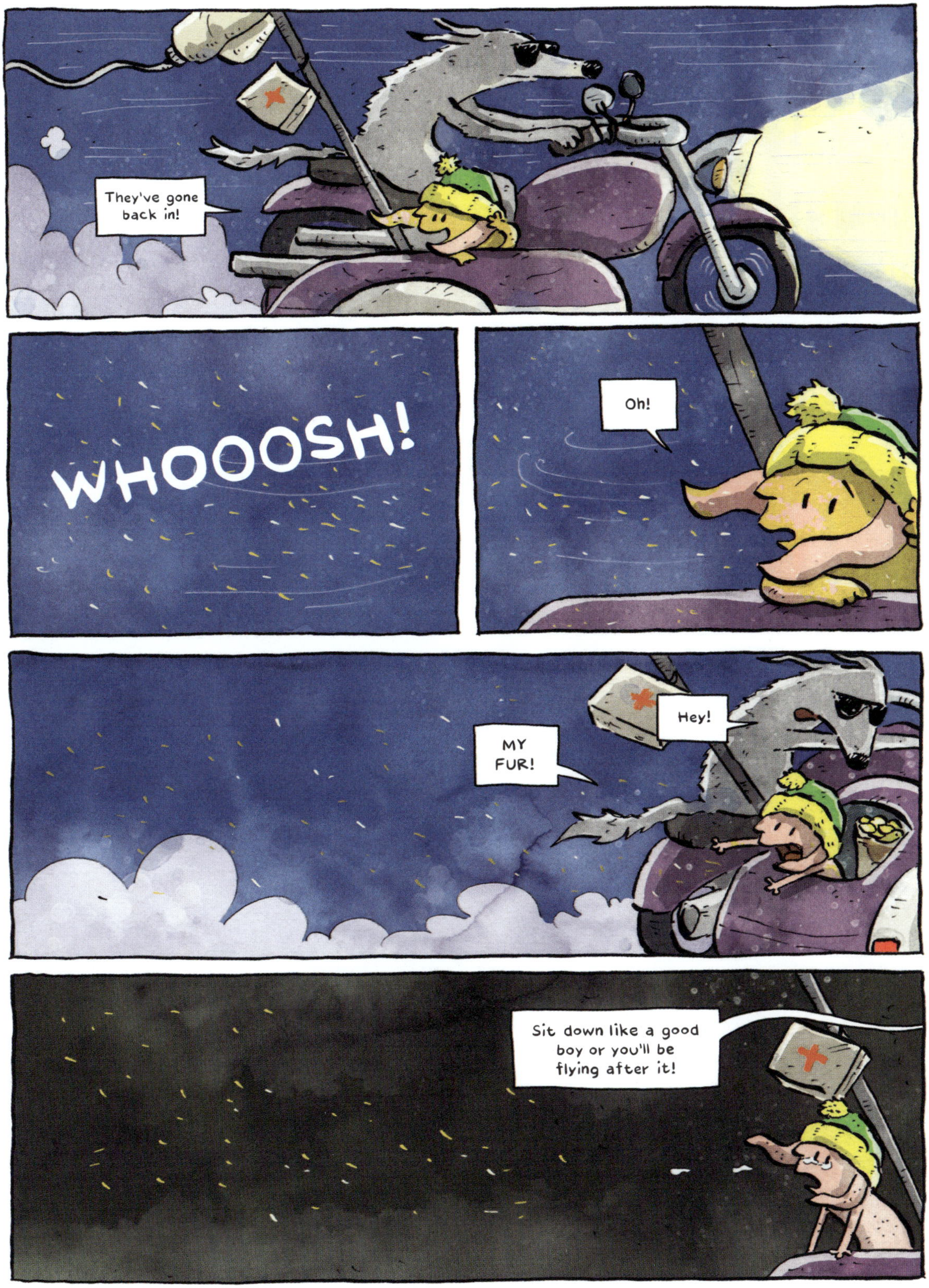
They've gone back in!
WHOOOSH!
Oh!
Hey!
MY FUR!
Sit down like a good boy or you'll be flying after it!

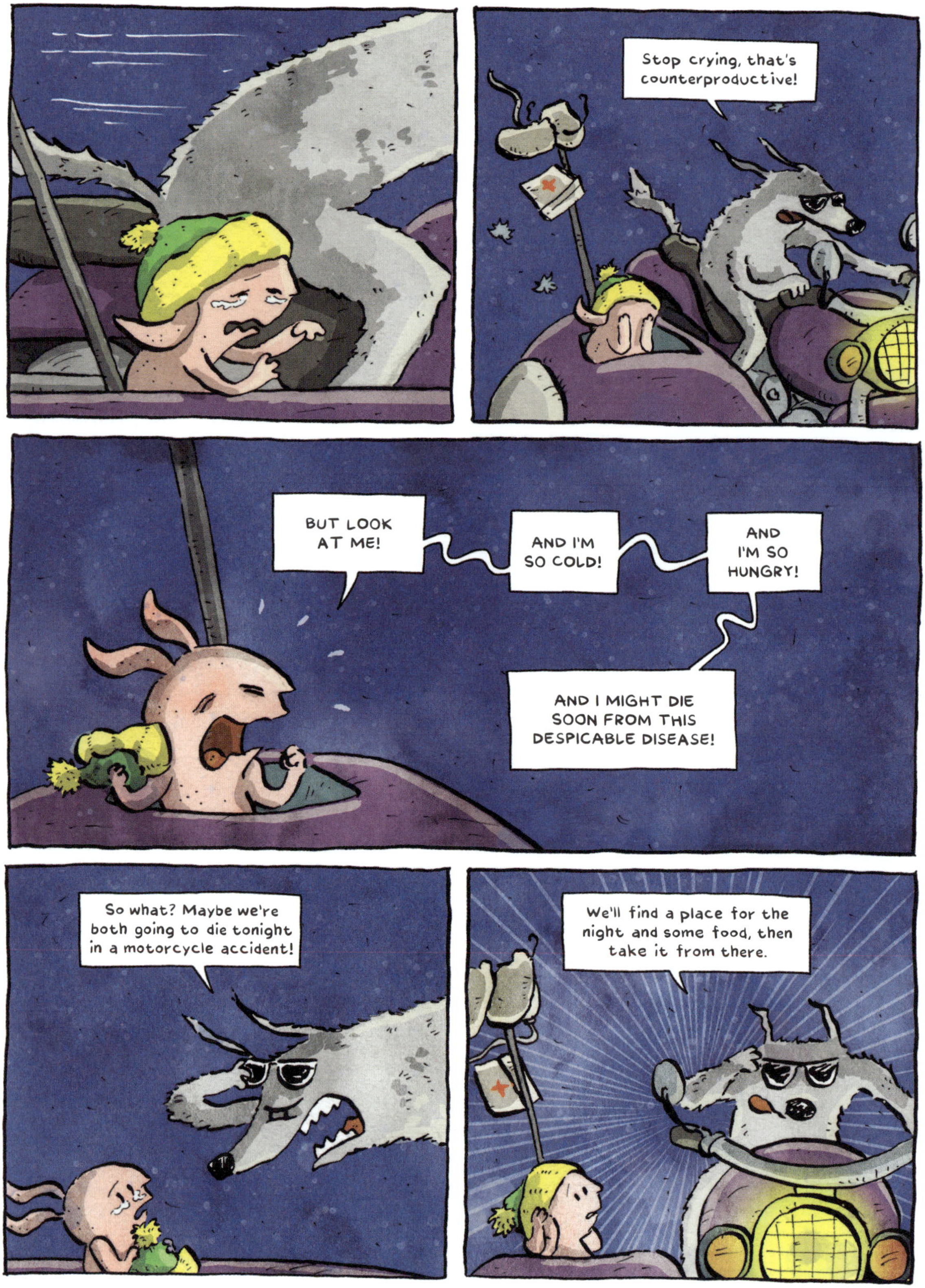
Stop crying, that's counterproductive!
BUT LOOK AT ME!
AND I'M SO COLD!
AND I'M SO HUNGRY!
AND I MIGHT DIE SOON FROM THIS DESPICABLE DISEASE!
So what? Maybe we're both going to die tonight in a motorcycle accident!
We'll find a place for the night and some food, then take it from there.

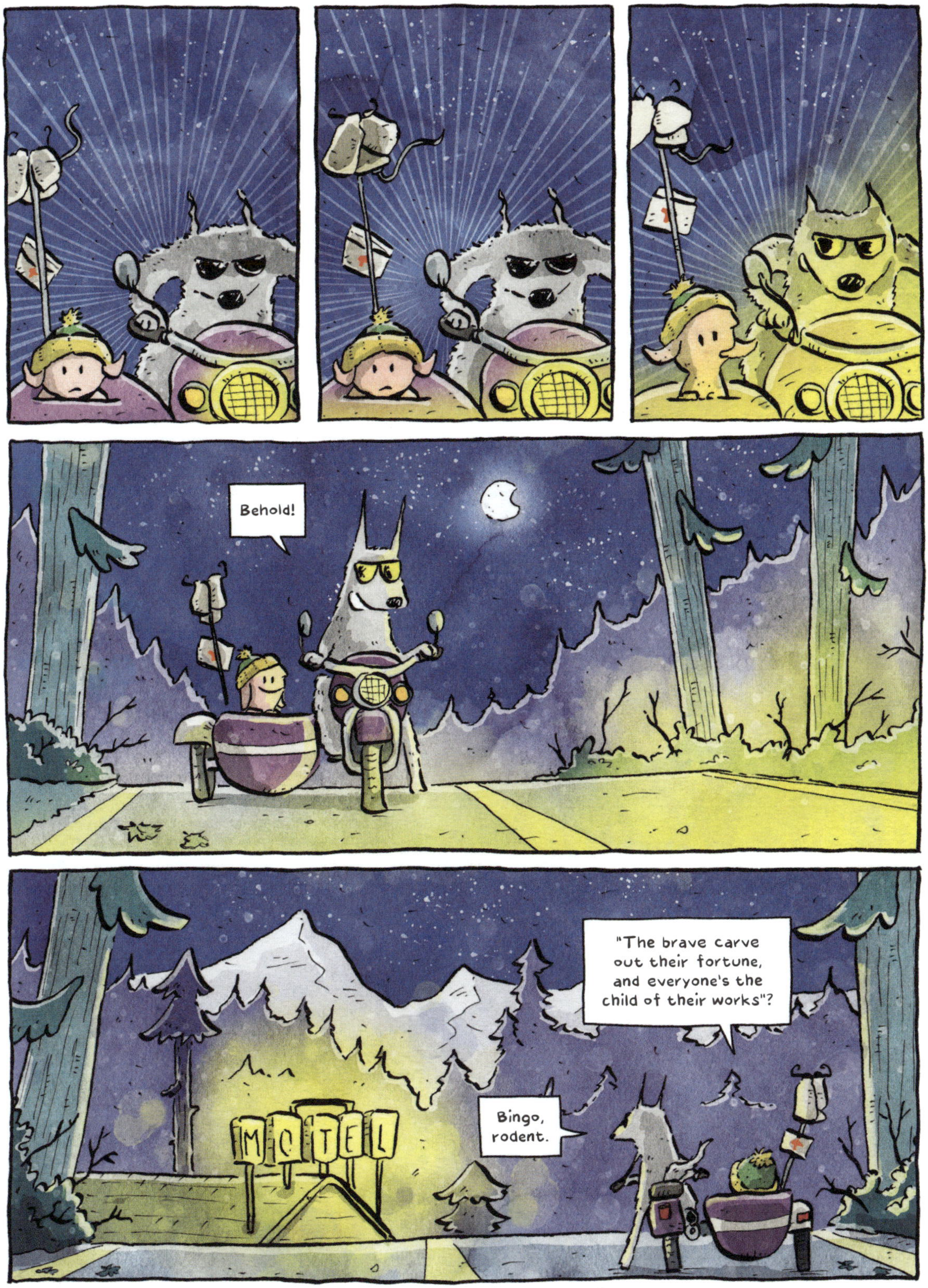
Behold!
"The brave carve out their fortune, and everyone's the child of their works"?
Bingo, rodent.
MOTEL

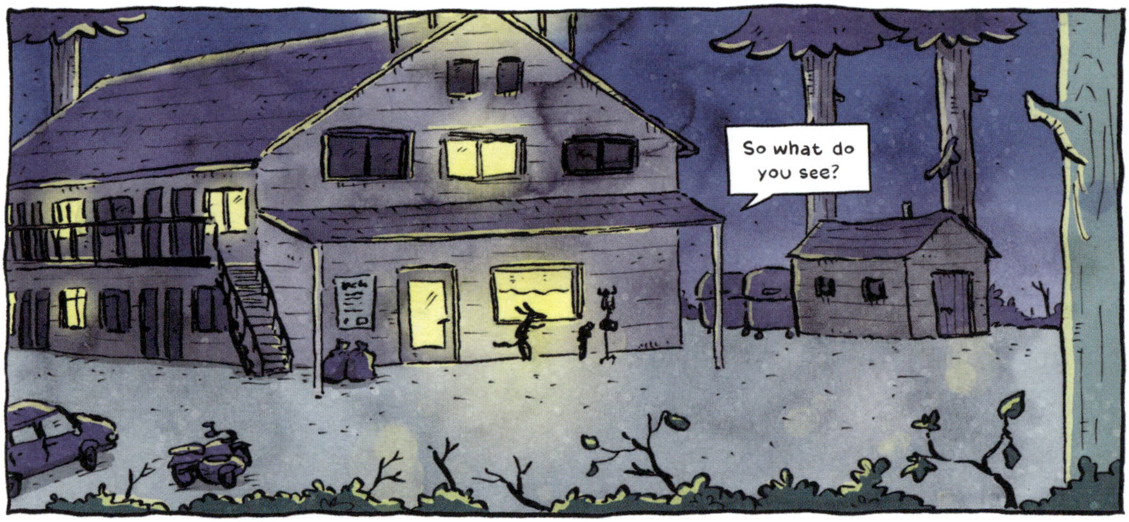
So what do you see?

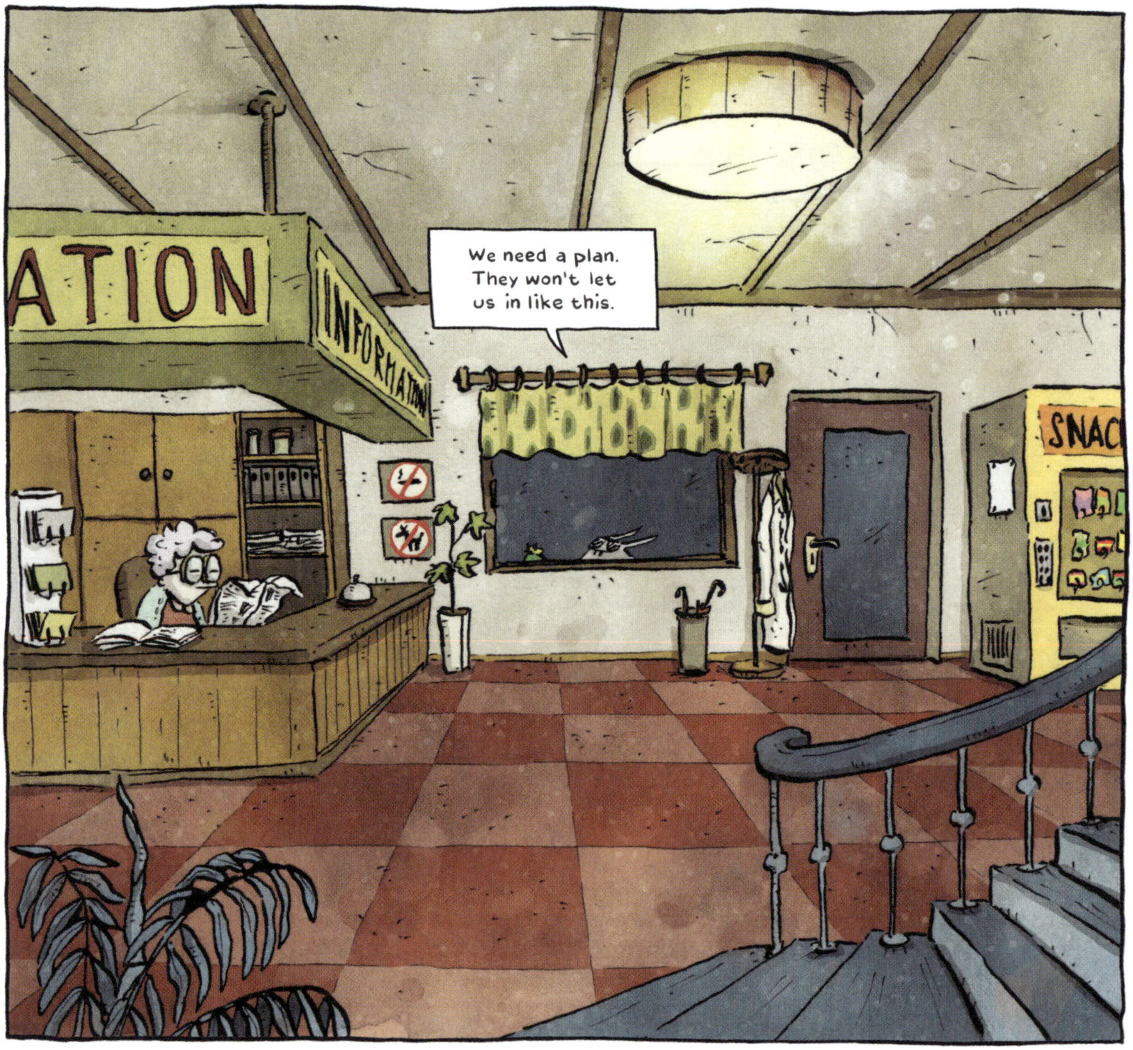
ATION
INFORMATION
We need a plan. They won't let us in like this.
SNAC

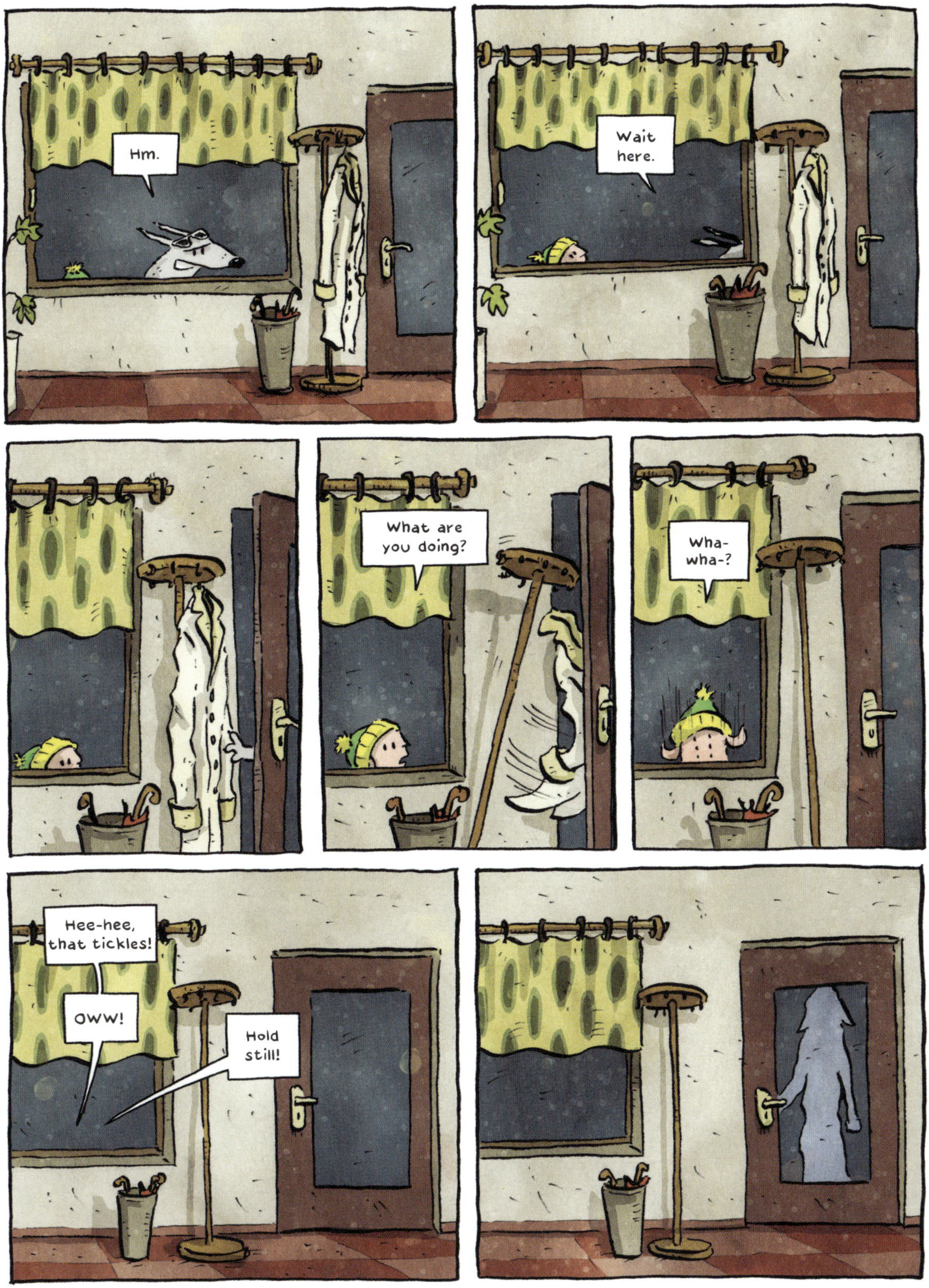
Hm.
Wait here.
What are you doing?
Wha-wha-?
Hee-hee, that tickles!
OWW!
Hold still!

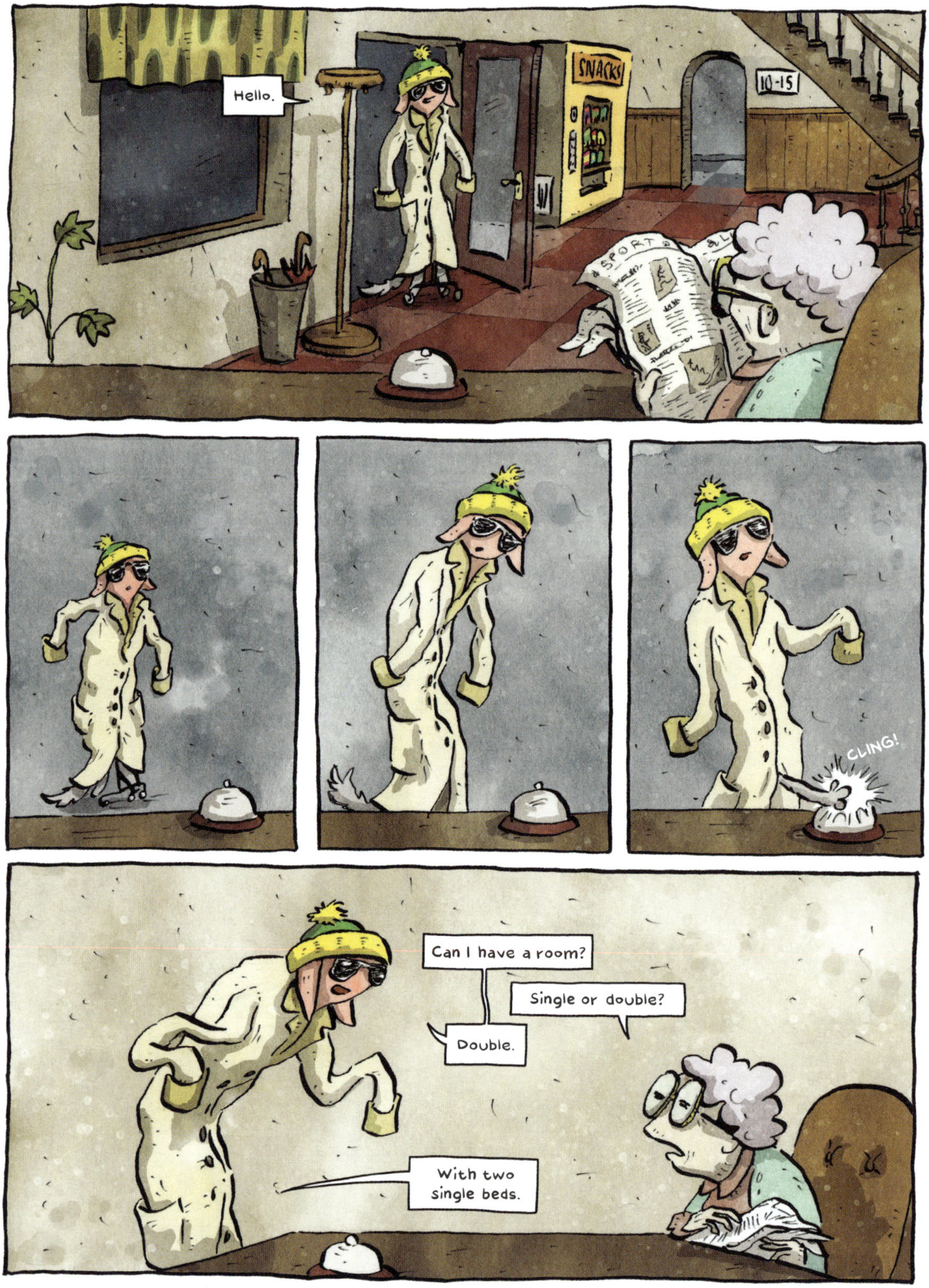
SNACKS
10-15
Hello.
SPORT
CLING!
Can I have a room?
Single or double?
Double.
With two single beds.

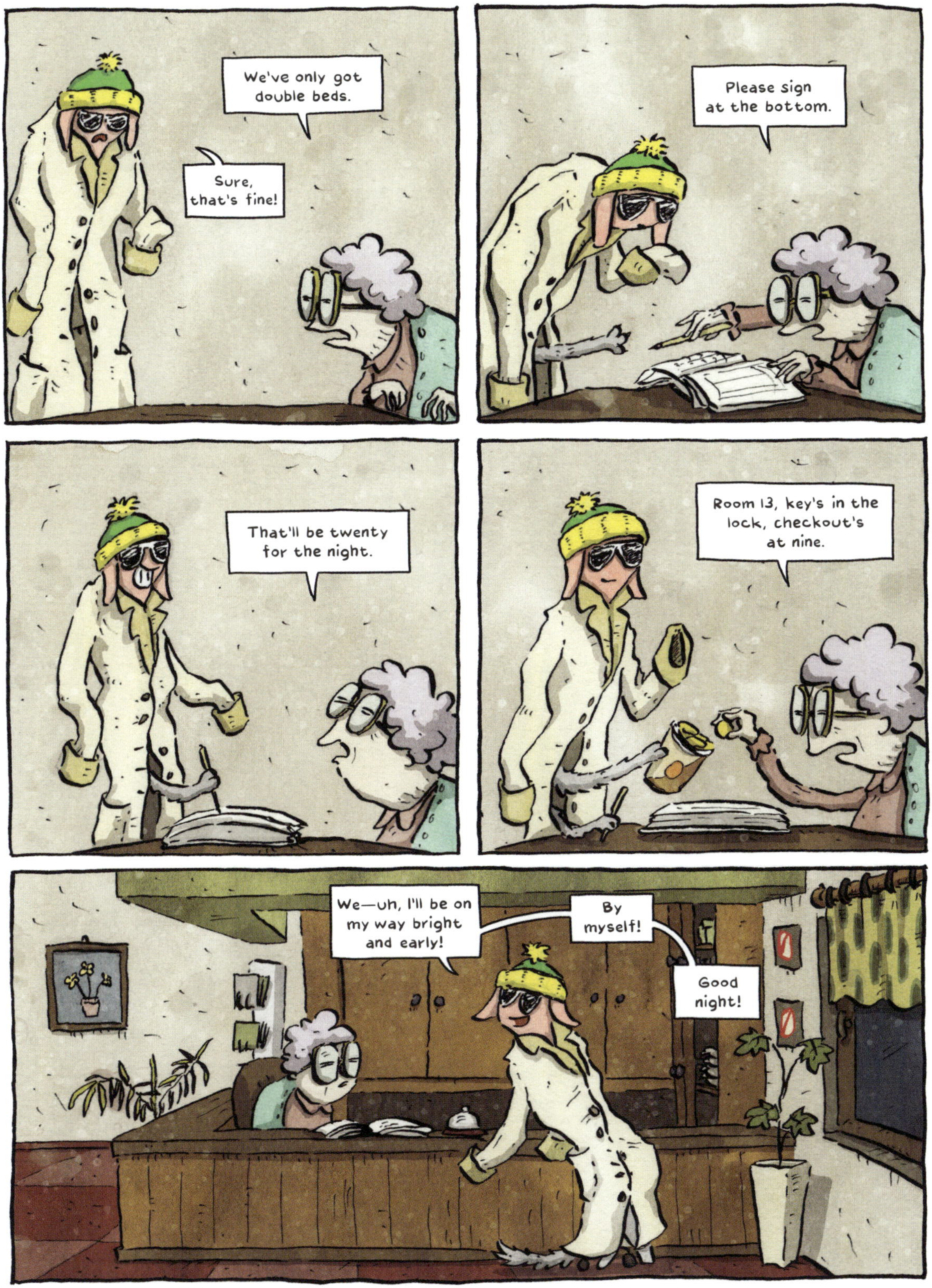
We've only got double beds.
Sure, that's fine!
Please sign at the bottom.
That'll be twenty for the night.
Room 13, key's in the lock, checkout's at nine.
We—uh, I'll be on my way bright and early!
By myself!
Good night!

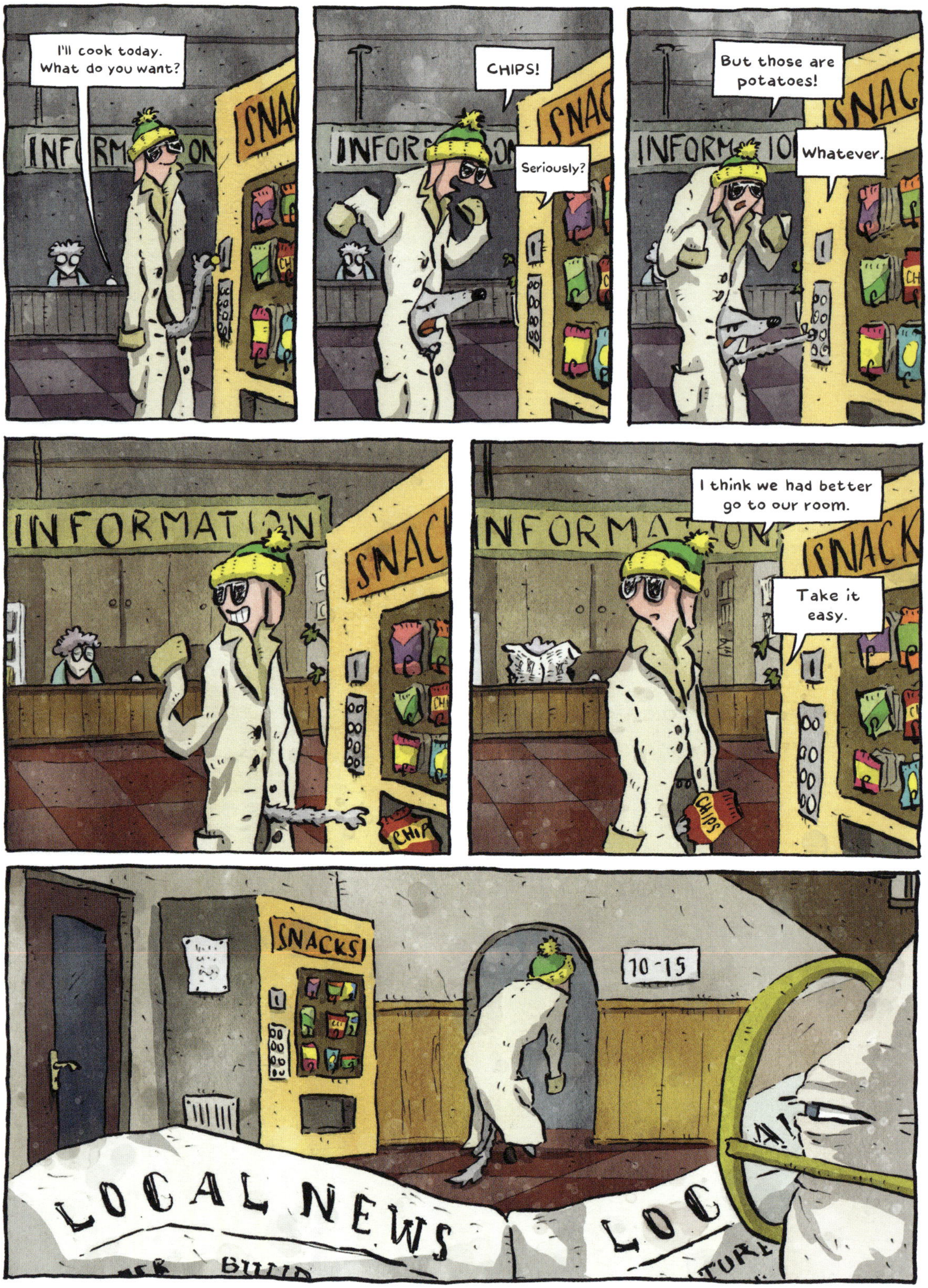
I'll cook today. What do you want?
SNAC
INFORM ON
CHIPS!
Seriously?
But those are potatoes!
Whatever.
INFORMATION
SNAC
CHIP
I think we had better go to our room.
Take it easy.
SNACK
CHIPS
SNACKS
10-15
LOCAL NEWS
LOC

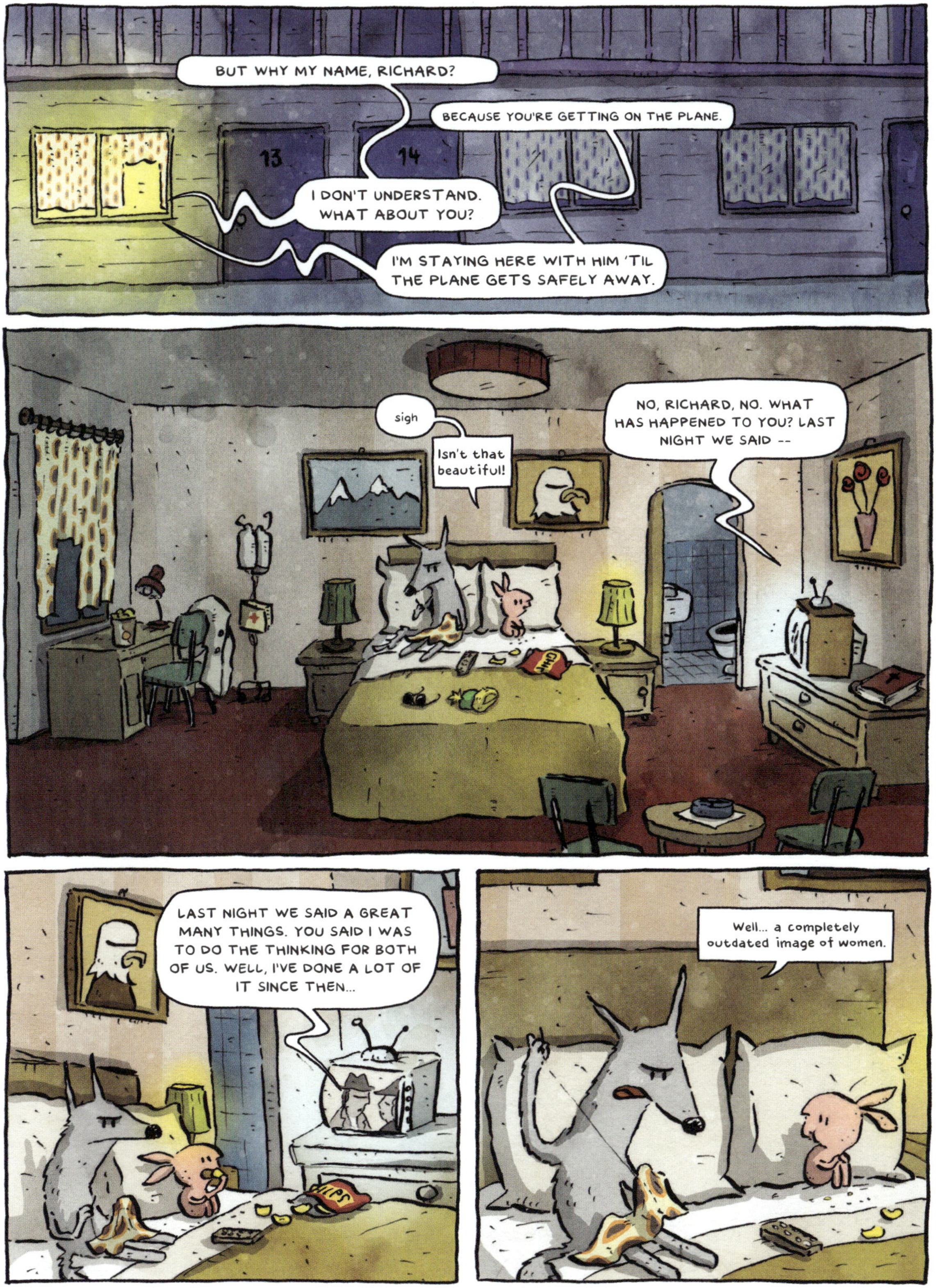
BUT WHY MY NAME, RICHARD?
BECAUSE YOU'RE GETTING ON THE PLANE.
I DON'T UNDERSTAND. WHAT ABOUT YOU?
I'M STAYING HERE WITH HIM 'TIL THE PLANE GETS SAFELY AWAY.
sigh
Isn't that beautiful!
NO, RICHARD, NO. WHAT HAS HAPPENED TO YOU? LAST NIGHT WE SAID --
LAST NIGHT WE SAID A GREAT MANY THINGS. YOU SAID I WAS TO DO THE THINKING FOR BOTH OF US. WELL, I'VE DONE A LOT OF IT SINCE THEN...
Well... a completely outdated image of women.

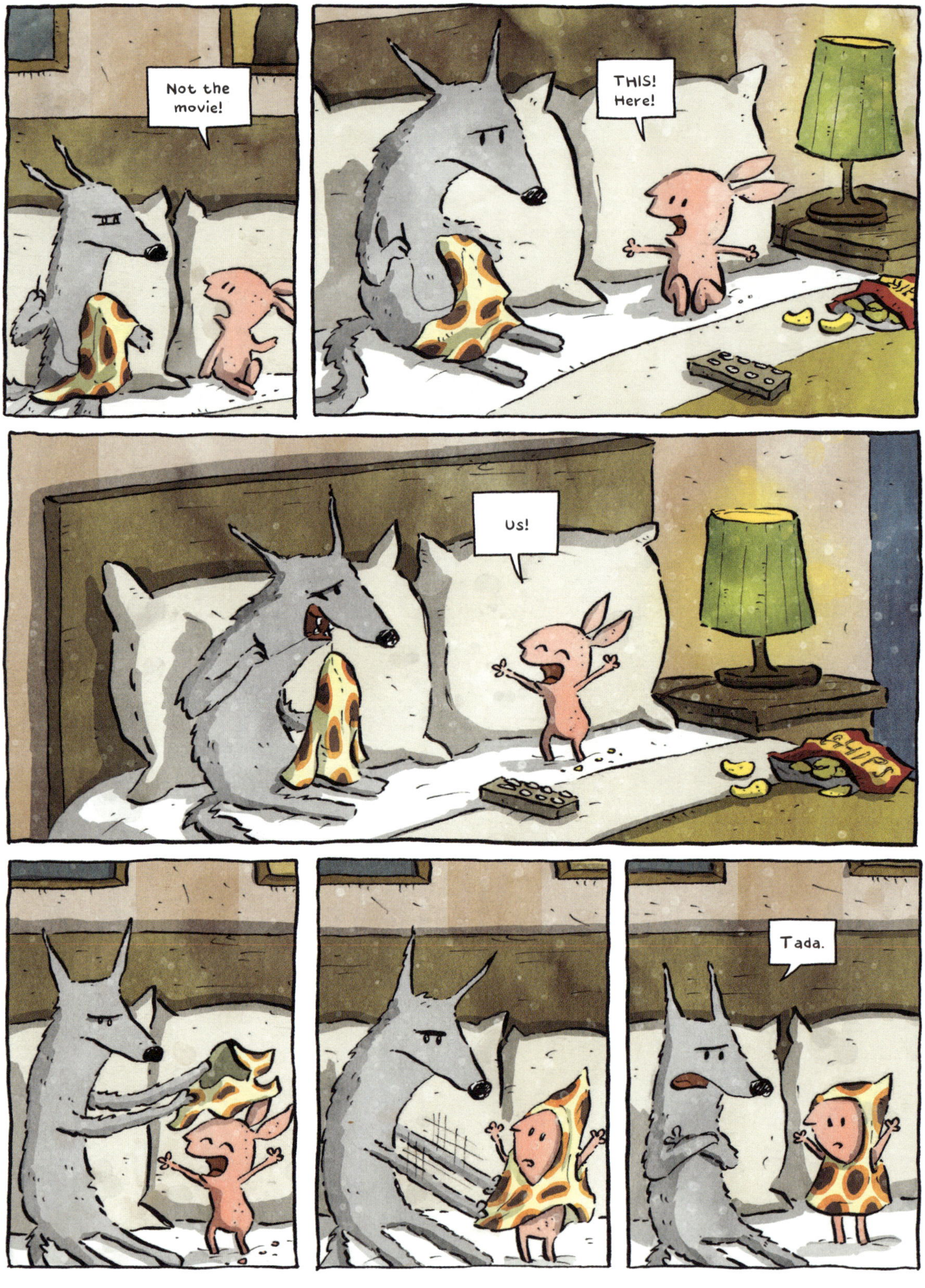
Not the movie!
THIS! Here!
Us!
Tada.

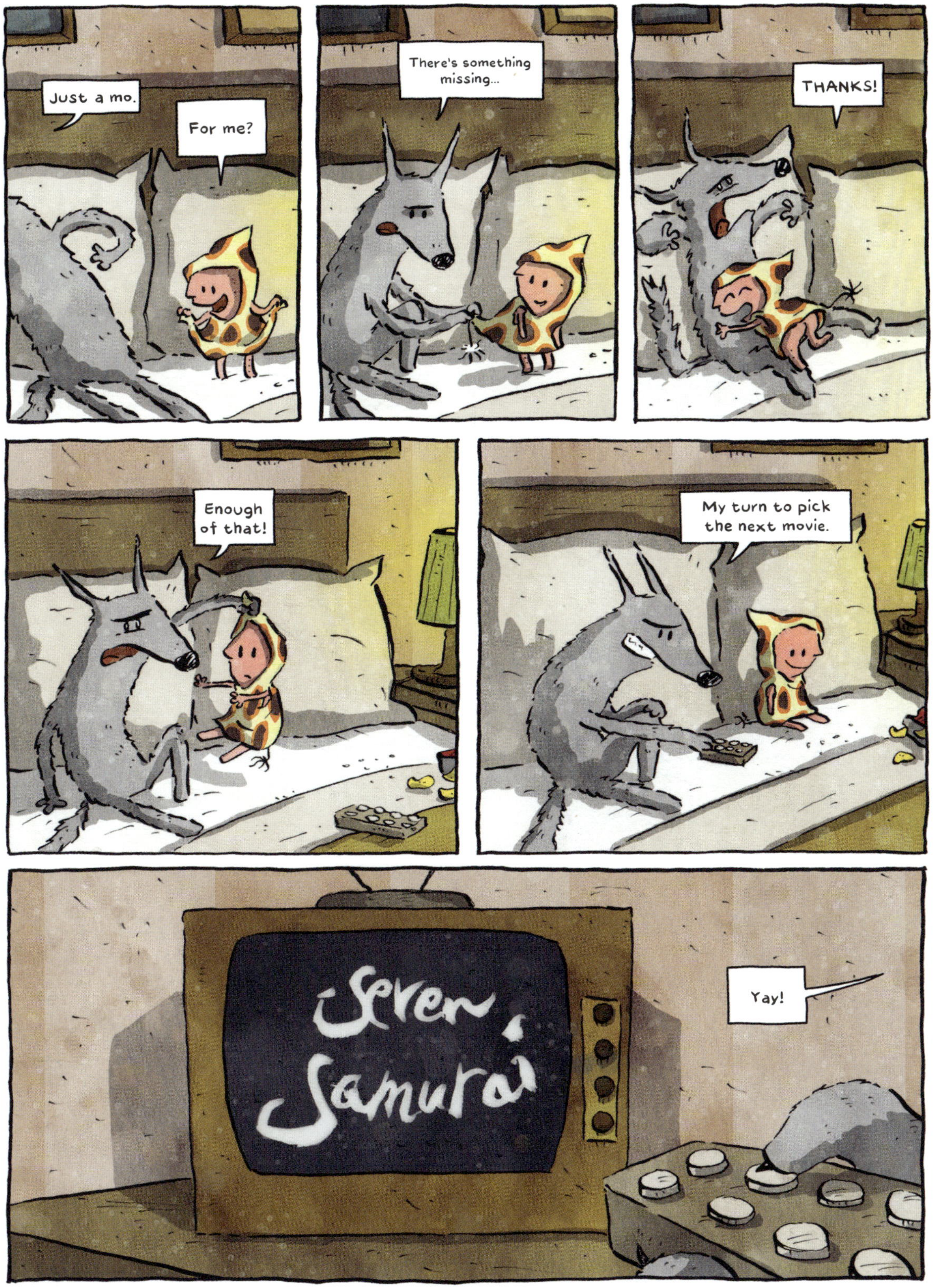
Just a mo.
For me?
There's something missing...
THANKS!
Enough of that!
My turn to pick the next movie.
Seven Samurai
Yay!

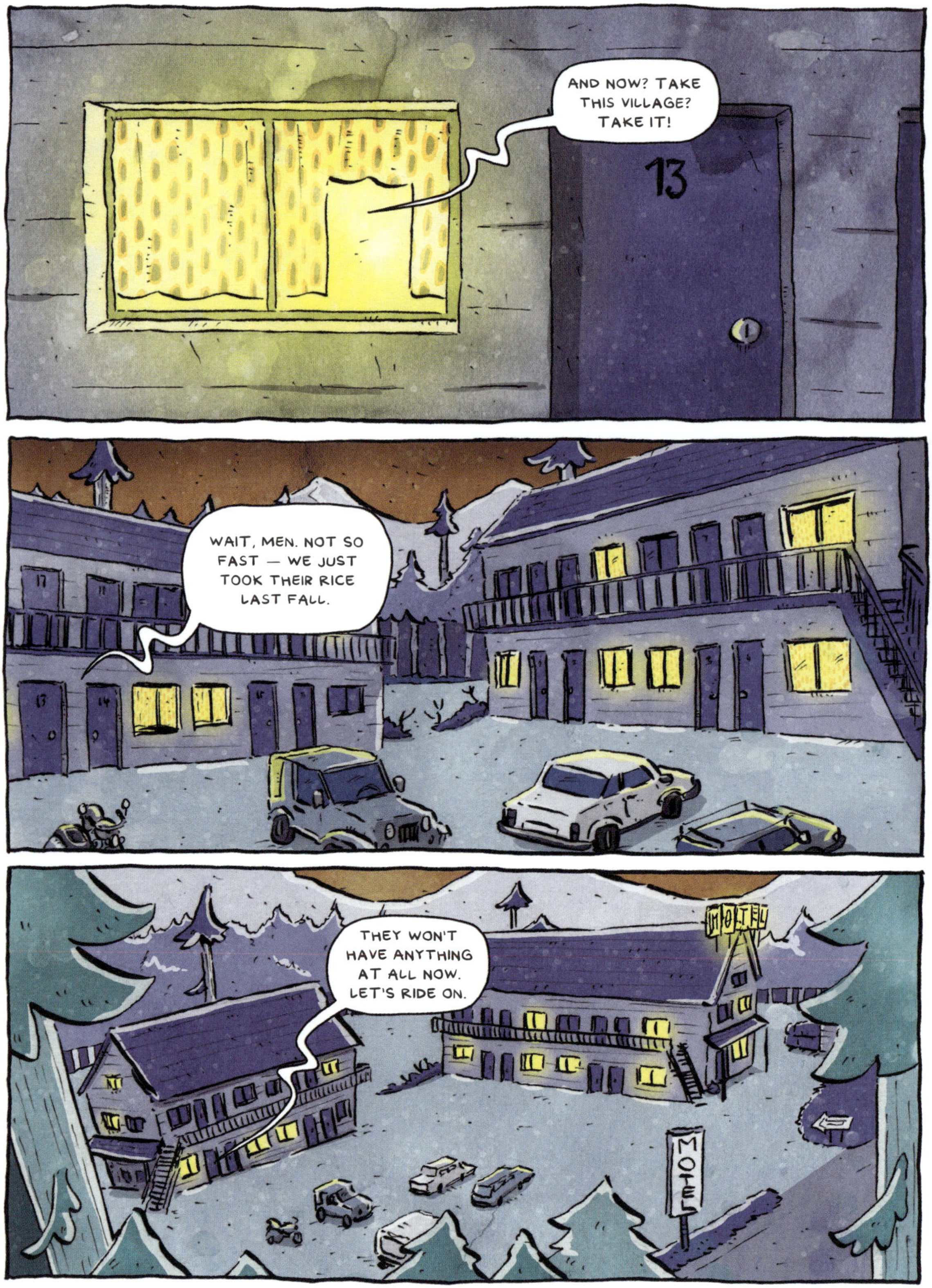
AND NOW? TAKE THIS VILLAGE? TAKE IT!
WAIT, MEN. NOT SO FAST — WE JUST TOOK THEIR RICE LAST FALL.
THEY WON'T HAVE ANYTHING AT ALL NOW. LET'S RIDE ON.
MOTEL

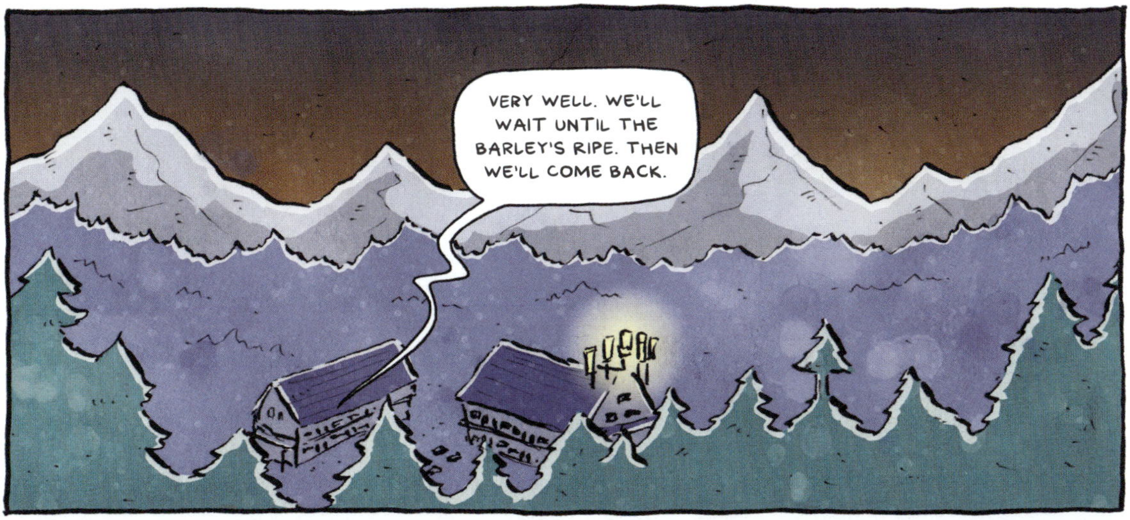
VERY WELL. WE'LL WAIT UNTIL THE BARLEY'S RIPE. THEN WE'LL COME BACK.

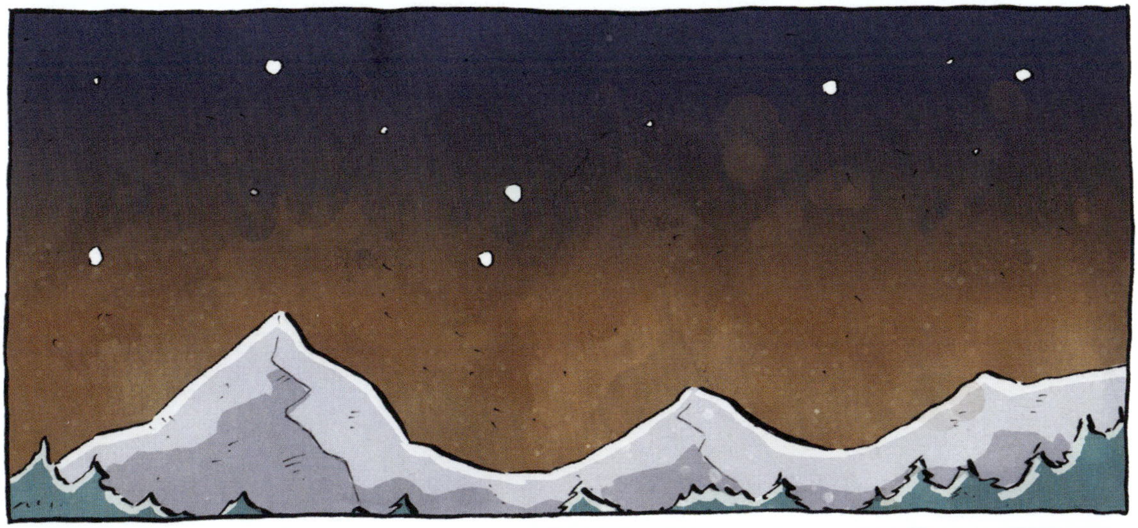

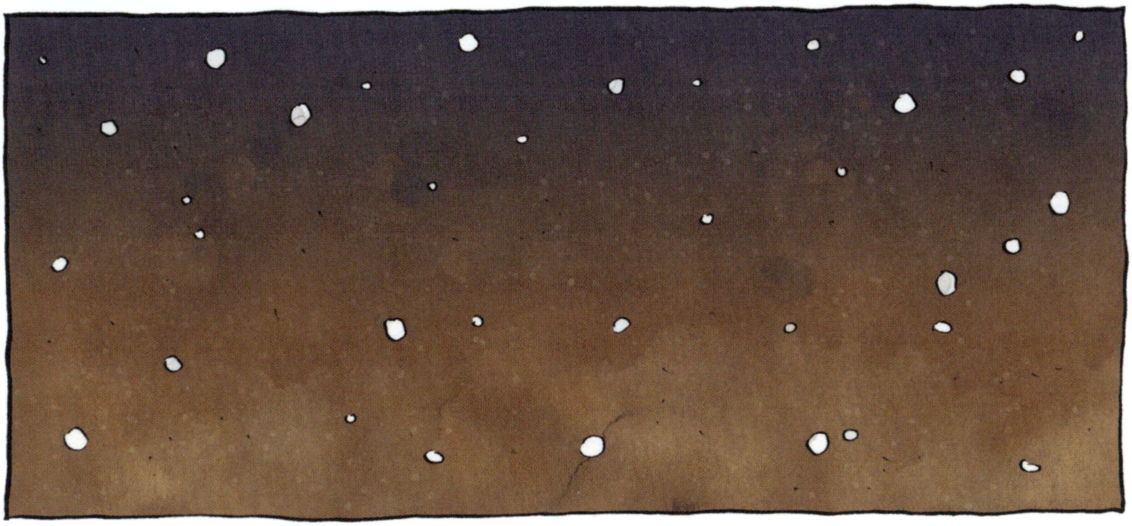

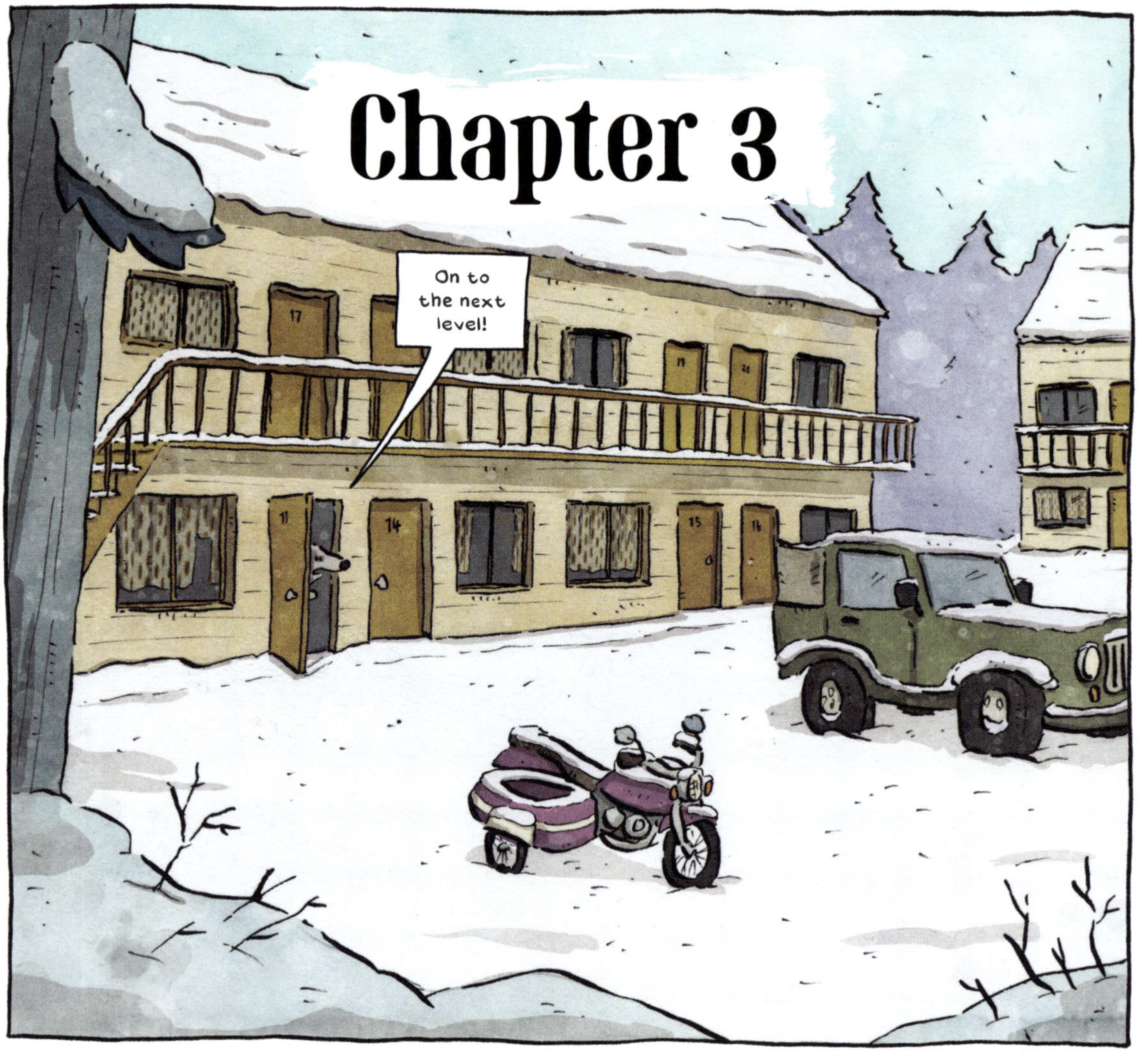
Chapter 3
On to the next level!

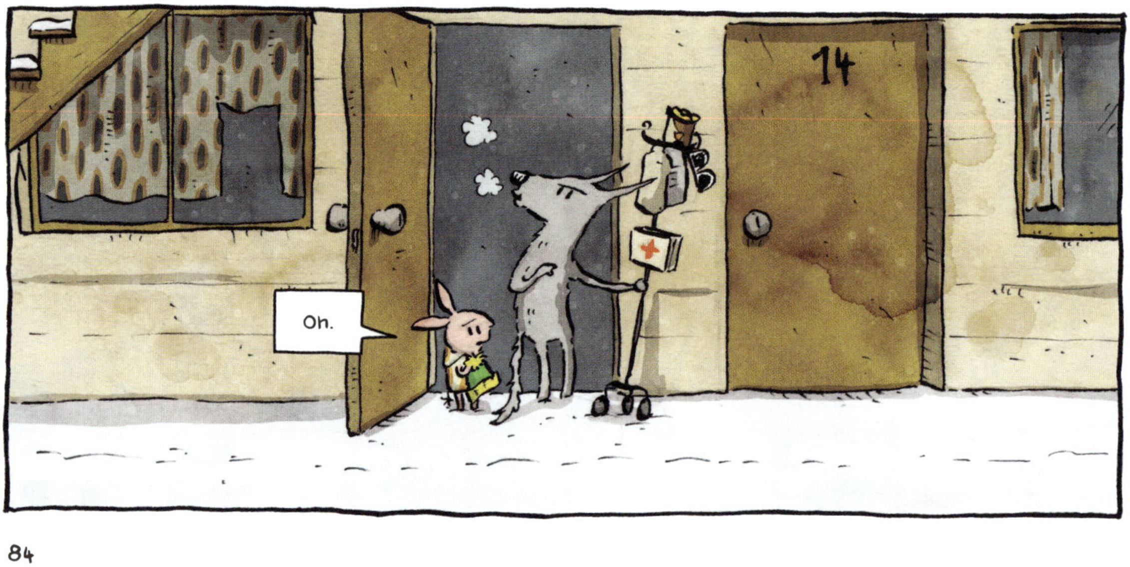
Oh.

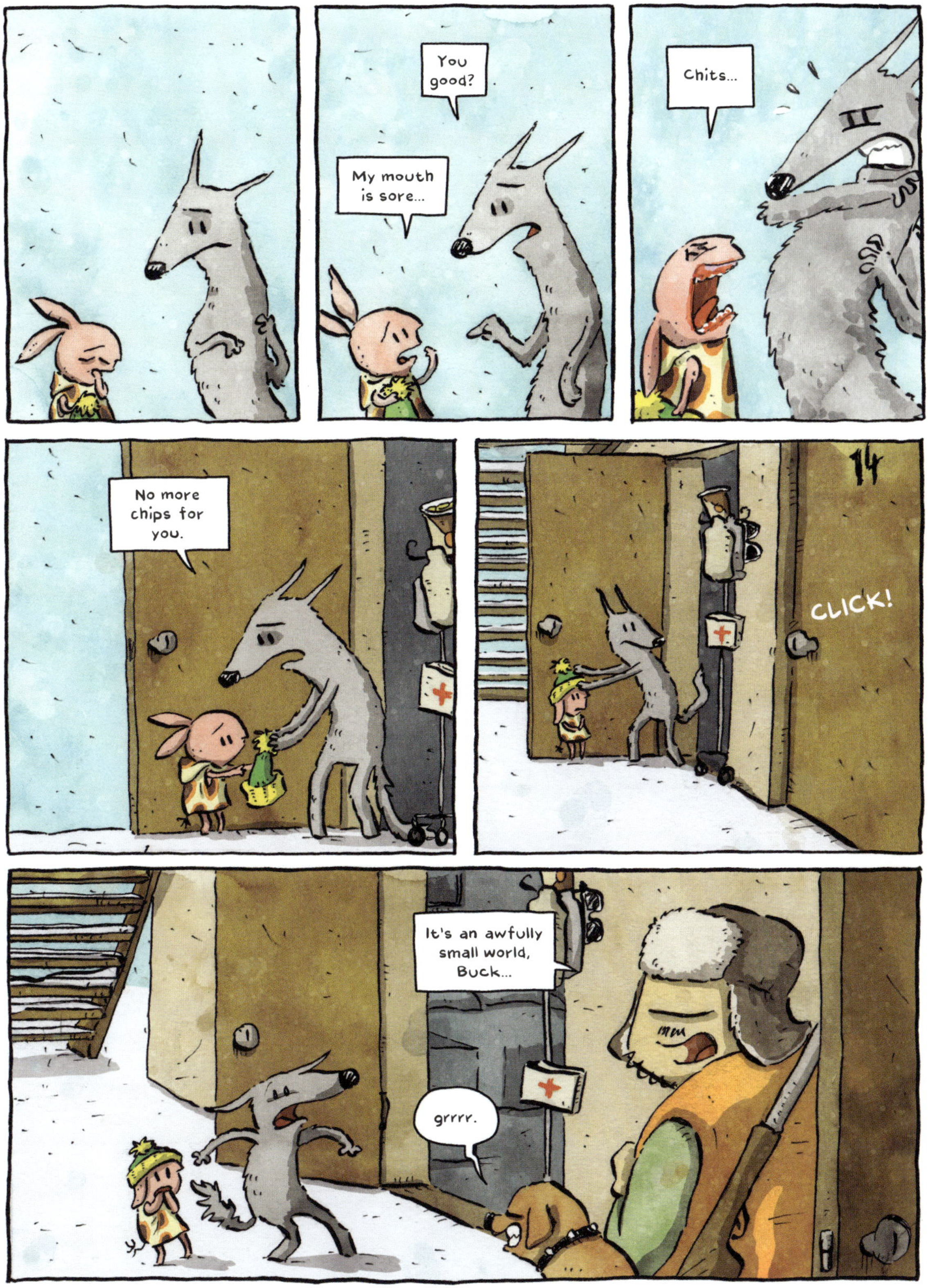
You good?
My mouth is sore...
Chits...
No more chips for you.
14
CLICK!
It's an awfully small world, Buck...
grrrr.

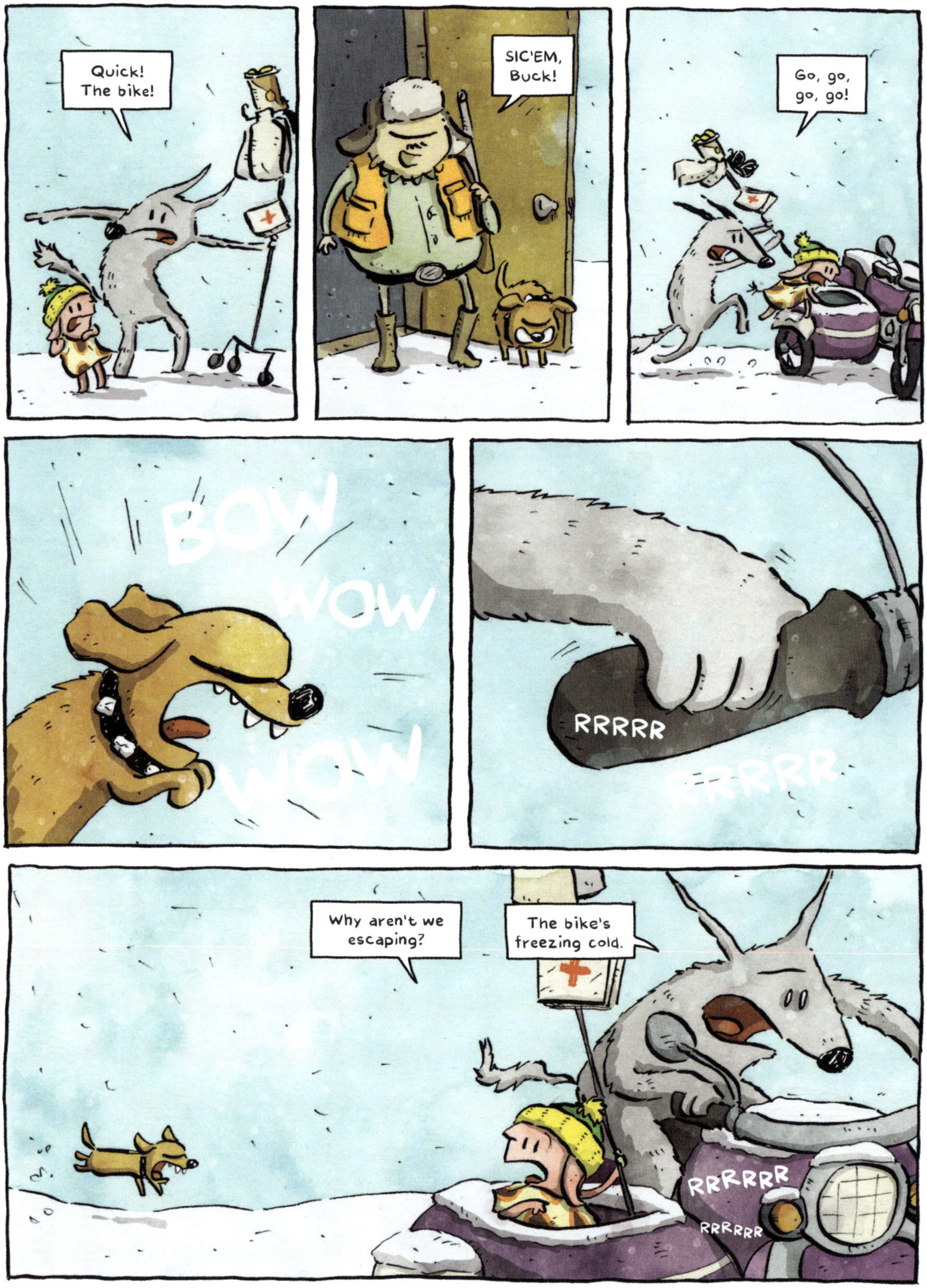
Quick! The bike!
SIC'EM, Buck!
Go, go, go, go!
BOW
WOW
WOW
RRRRR
RRRRR
Why aren't we escaping?
The bike's freezing cold.
RRRRRR
RRRRRR

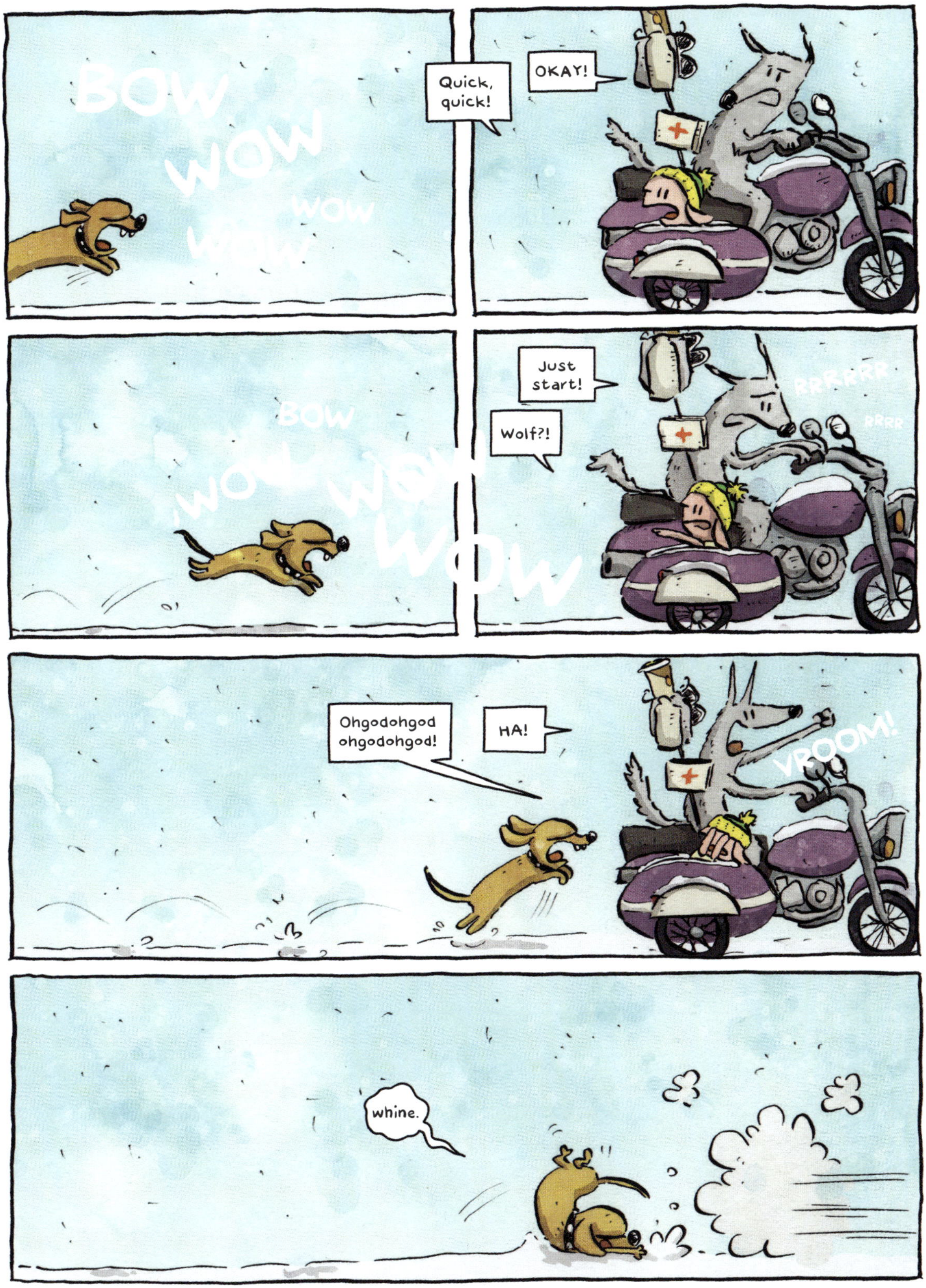
BOW
WOW
WOW
WOW
Quick, quick!
OKAY!
Just start!
Wolf?!
RRRRRR
RRRR
BOW
WOW
WOW
WOW
Ohgodohgod ohgodohgod!
HA!
VROOM!
whine.

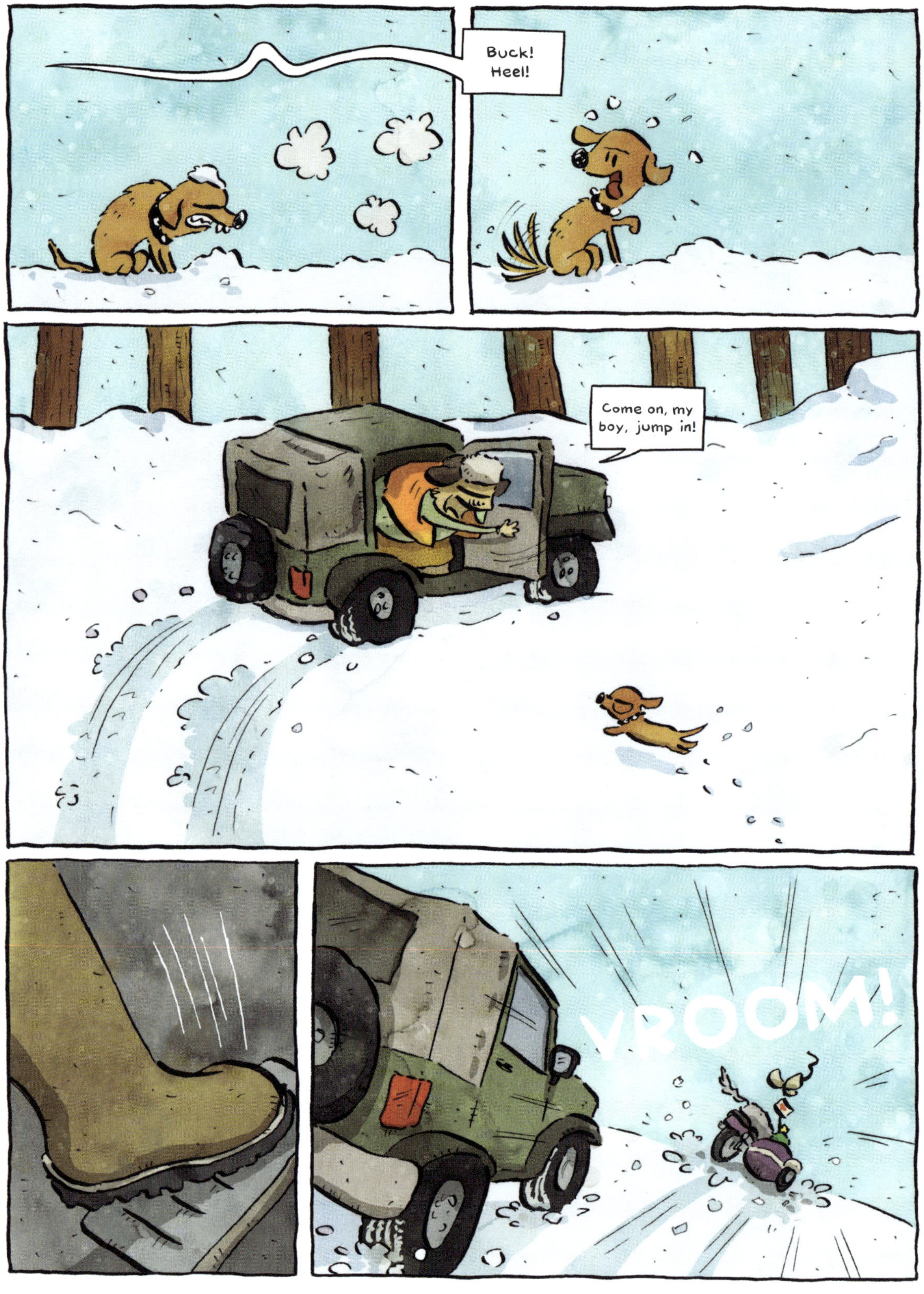
Buck!
Heel!
Come on, my boy, jump in!
VROOM!

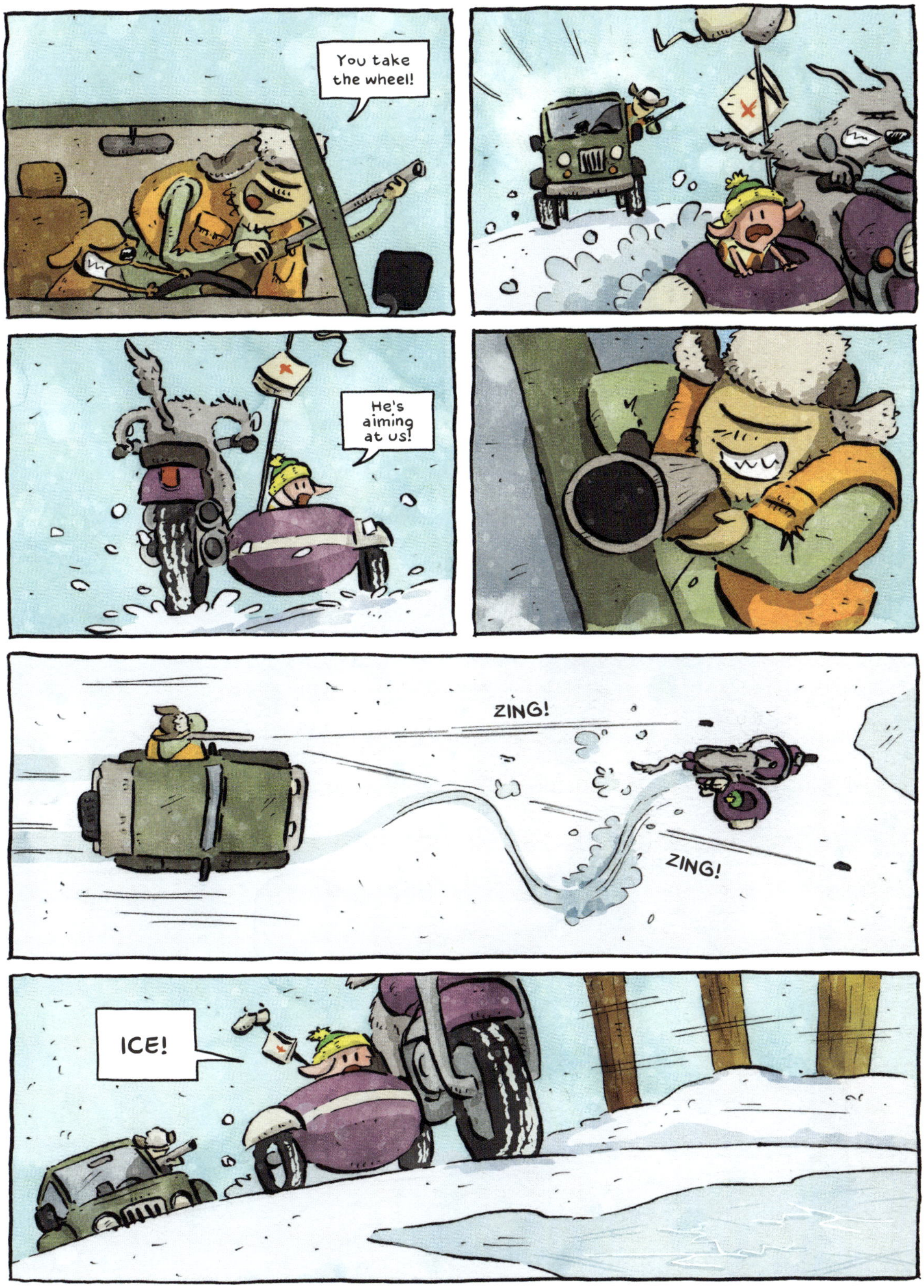
You take the wheel!
He's aiming at us!
ZING!
ZING!
ICE!

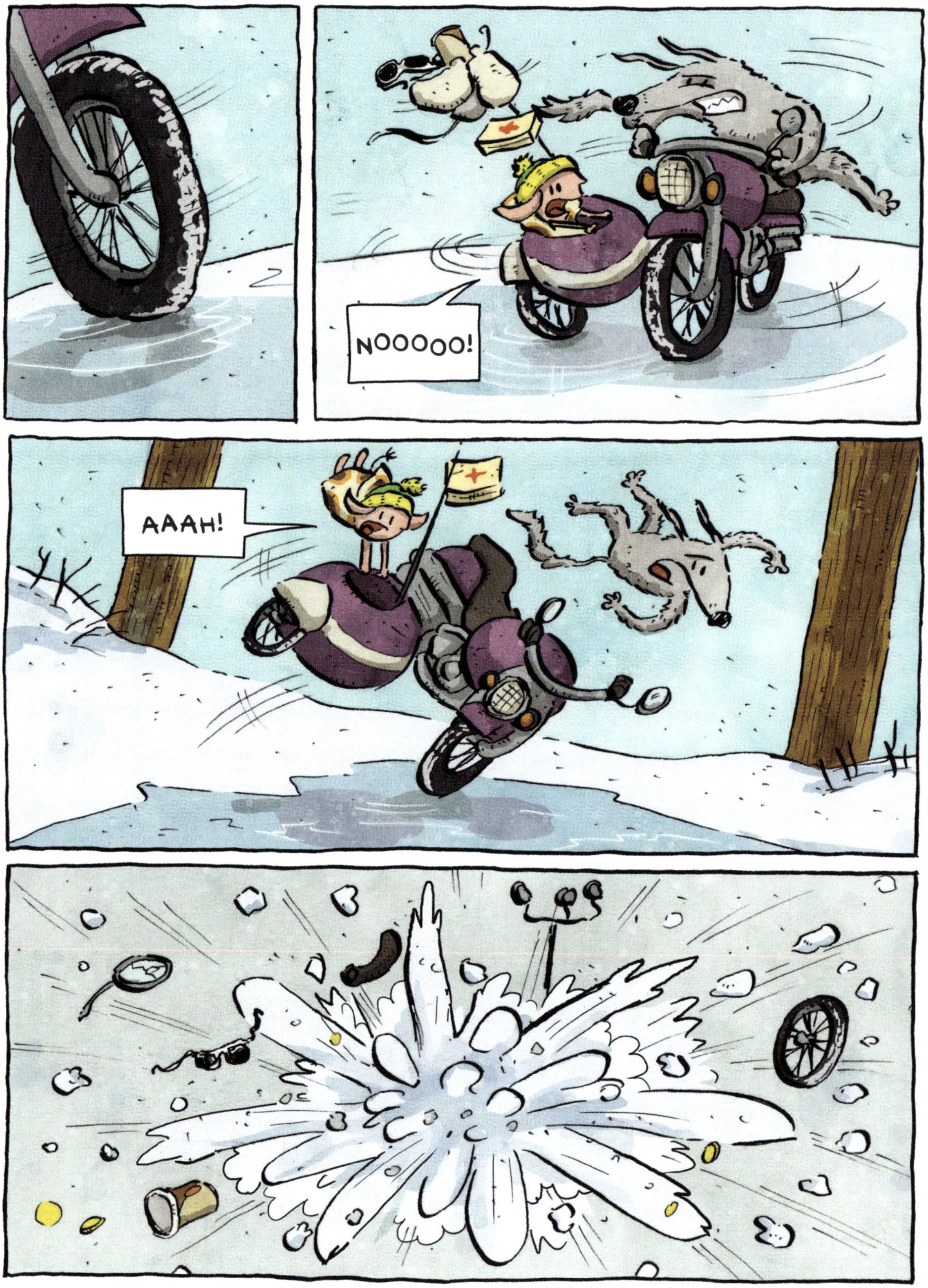
NOOOOO!
AAAH!

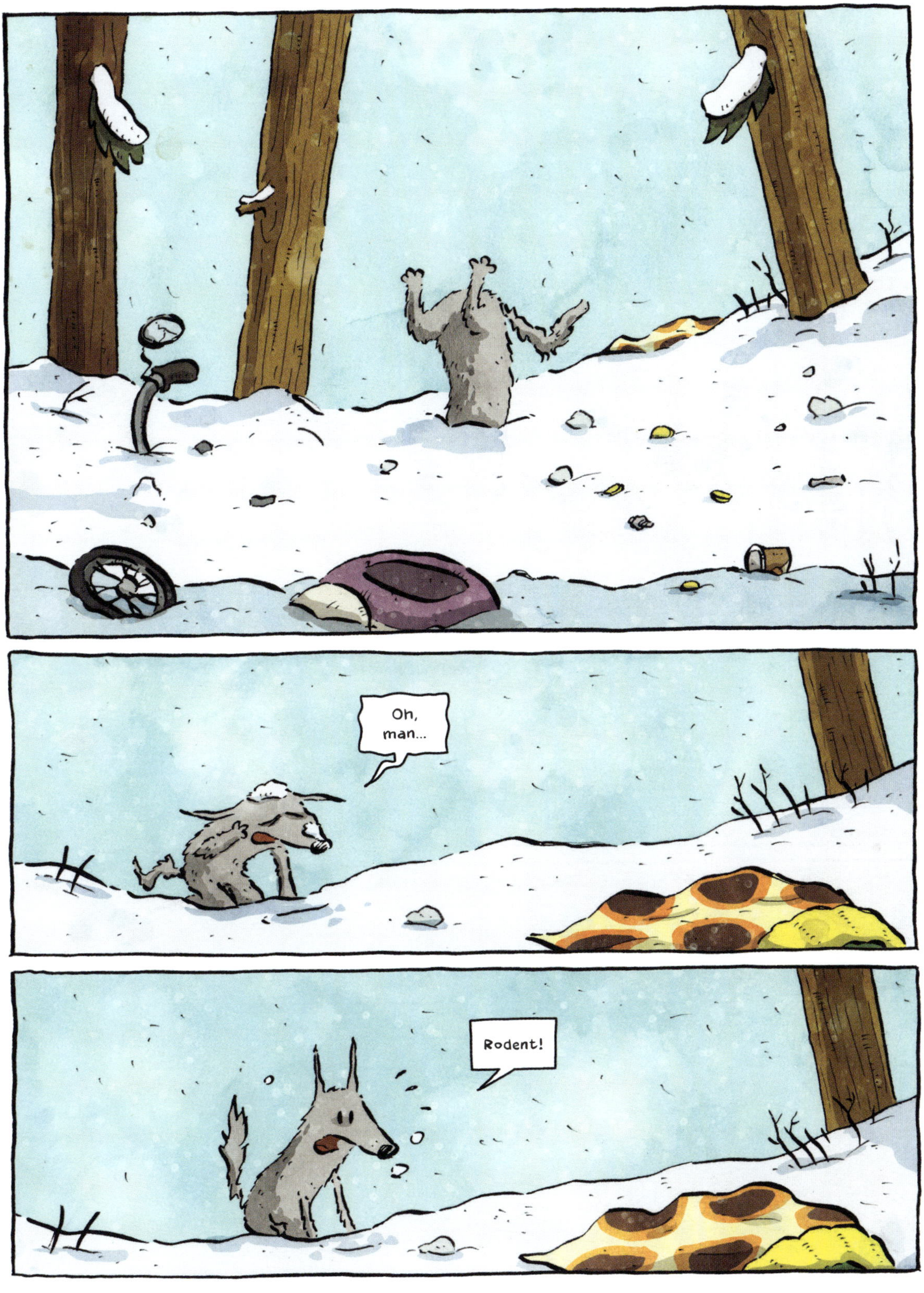
Oh, man...
Rodent!

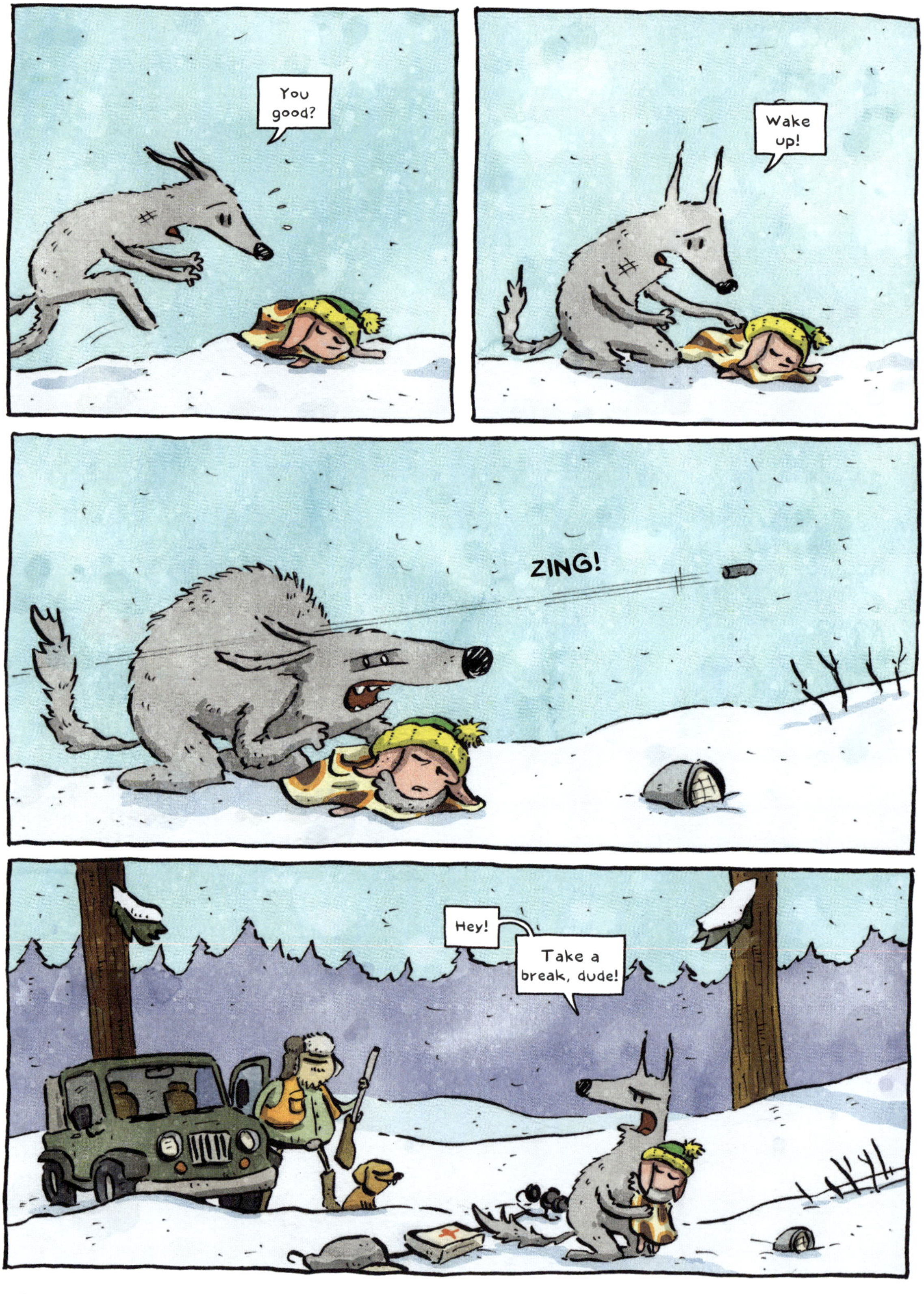

You good?
Wake up!
ZING!
Hey!
Take a break, dude!

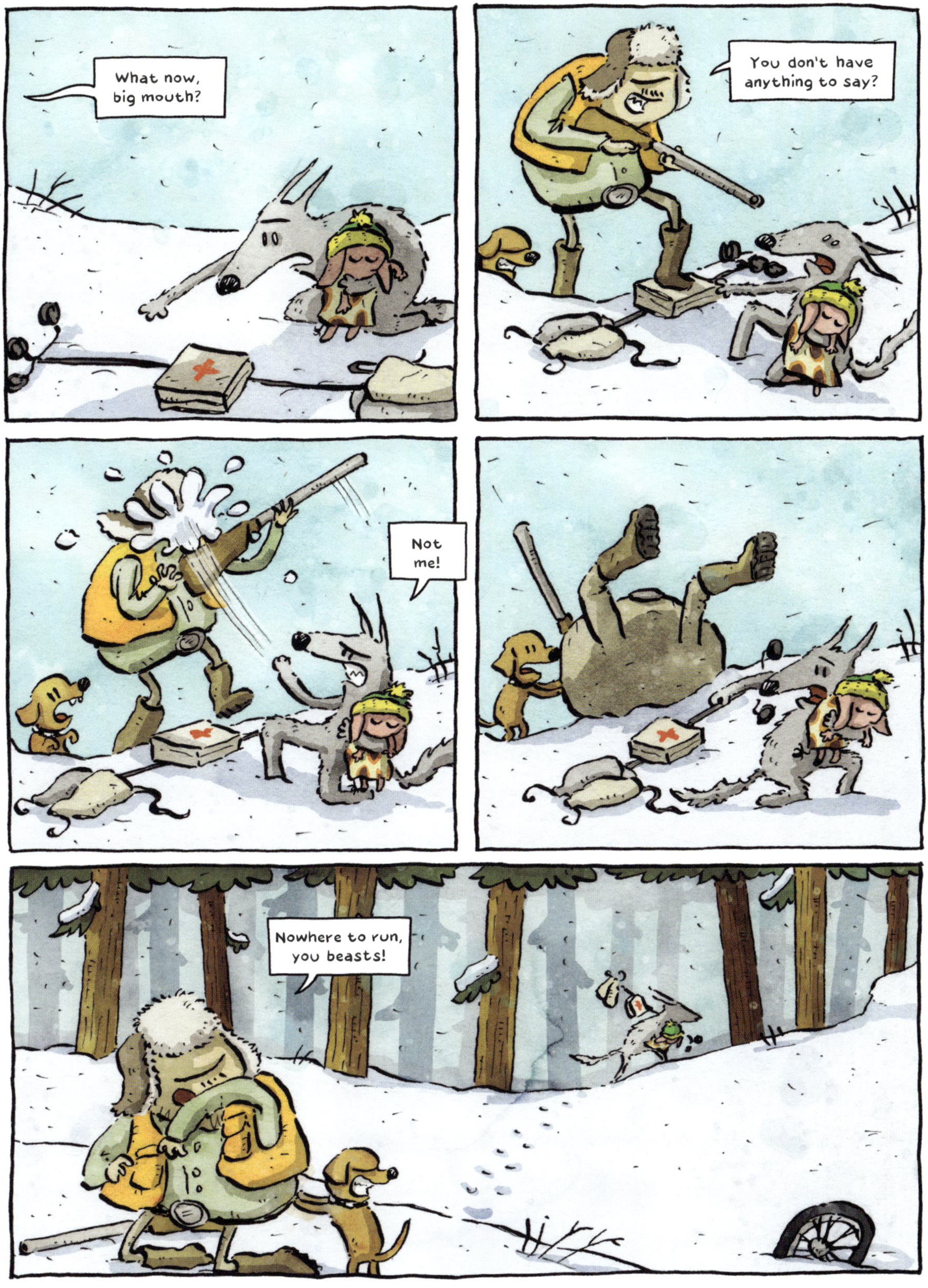
What now, big mouth?
You don't have anything to say?
Not me!
Nowhere to run, you beasts!

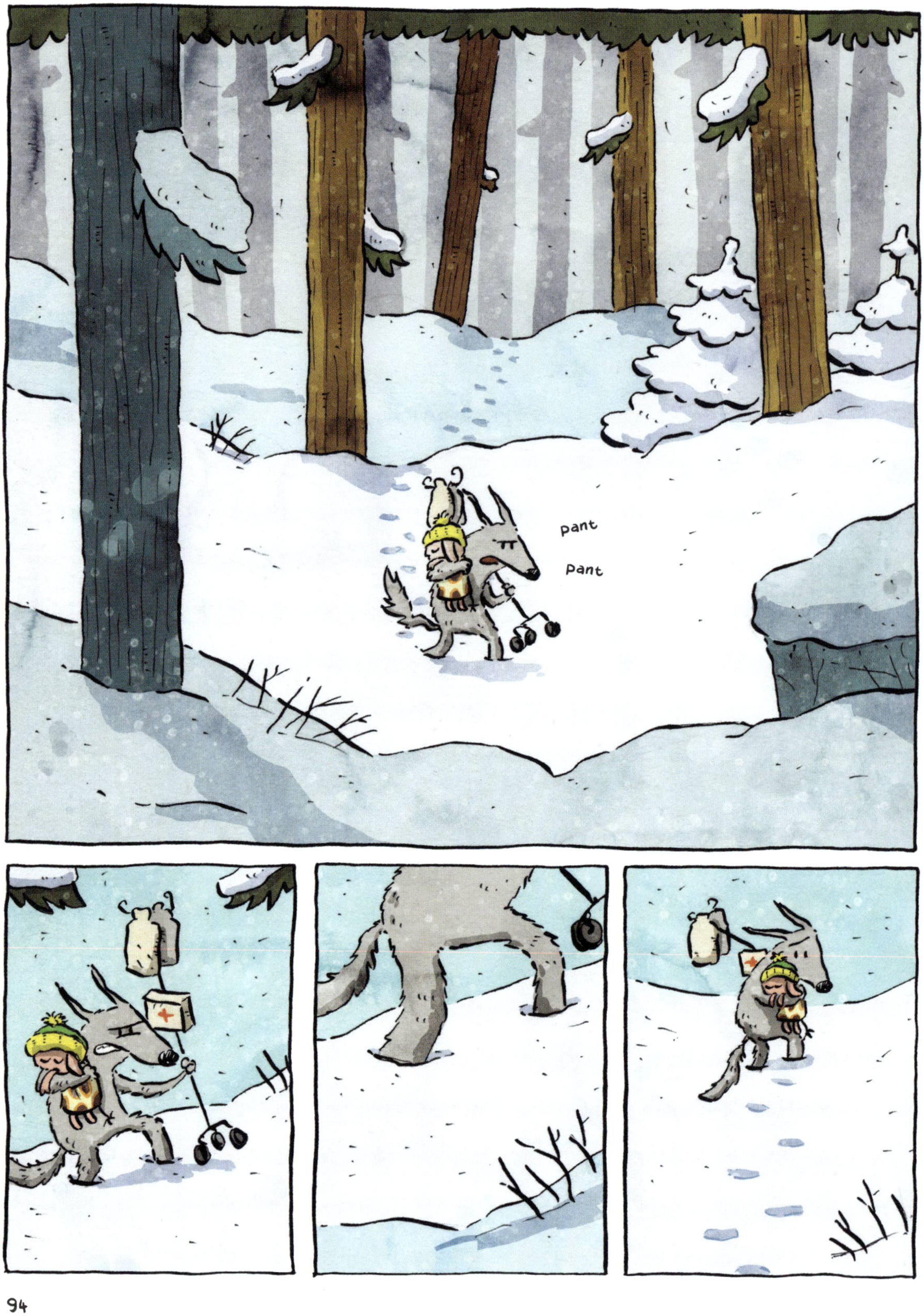
pant
pant

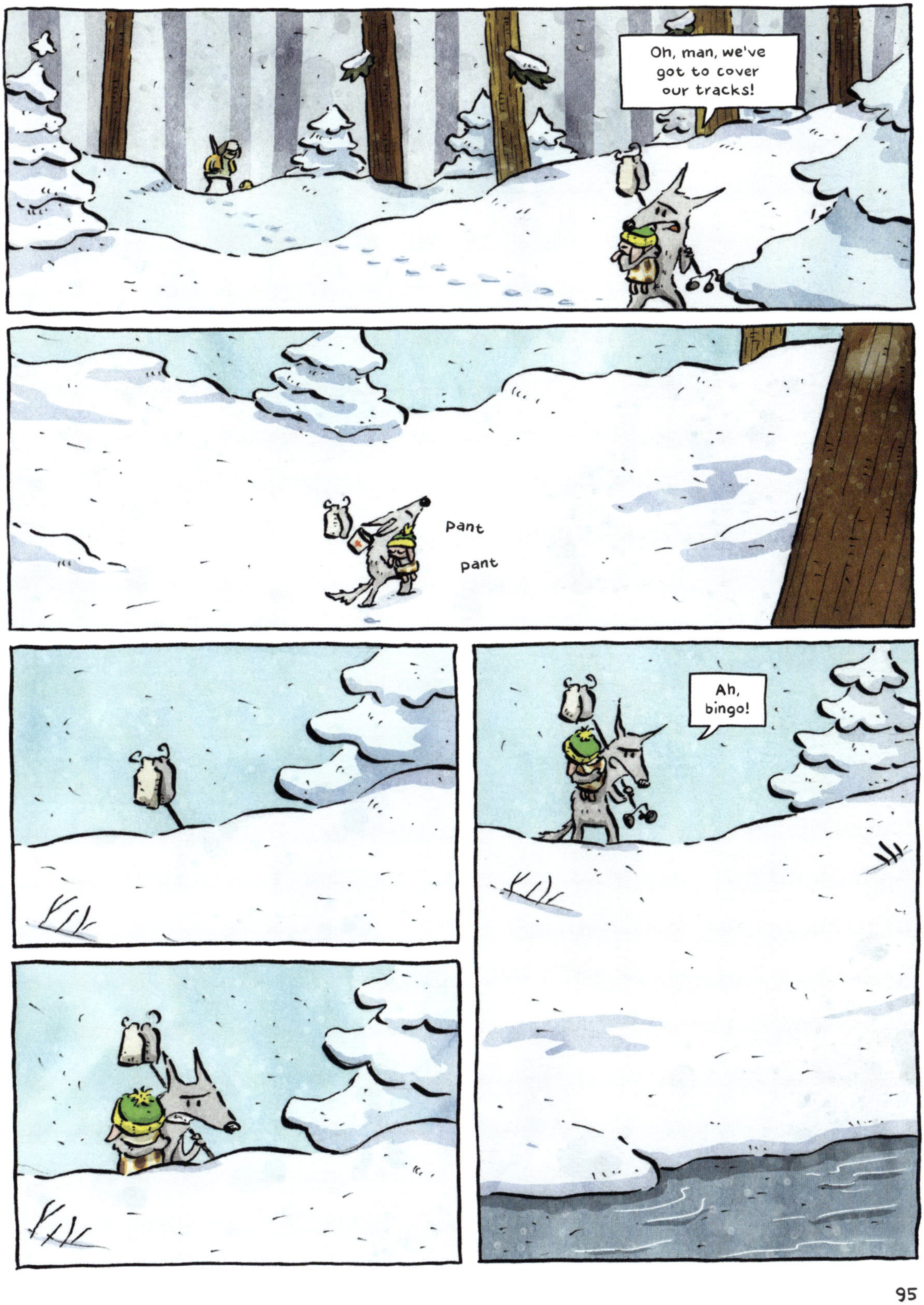
Oh, man, we've got to cover our tracks!
pant
pant
Ah, bingo!

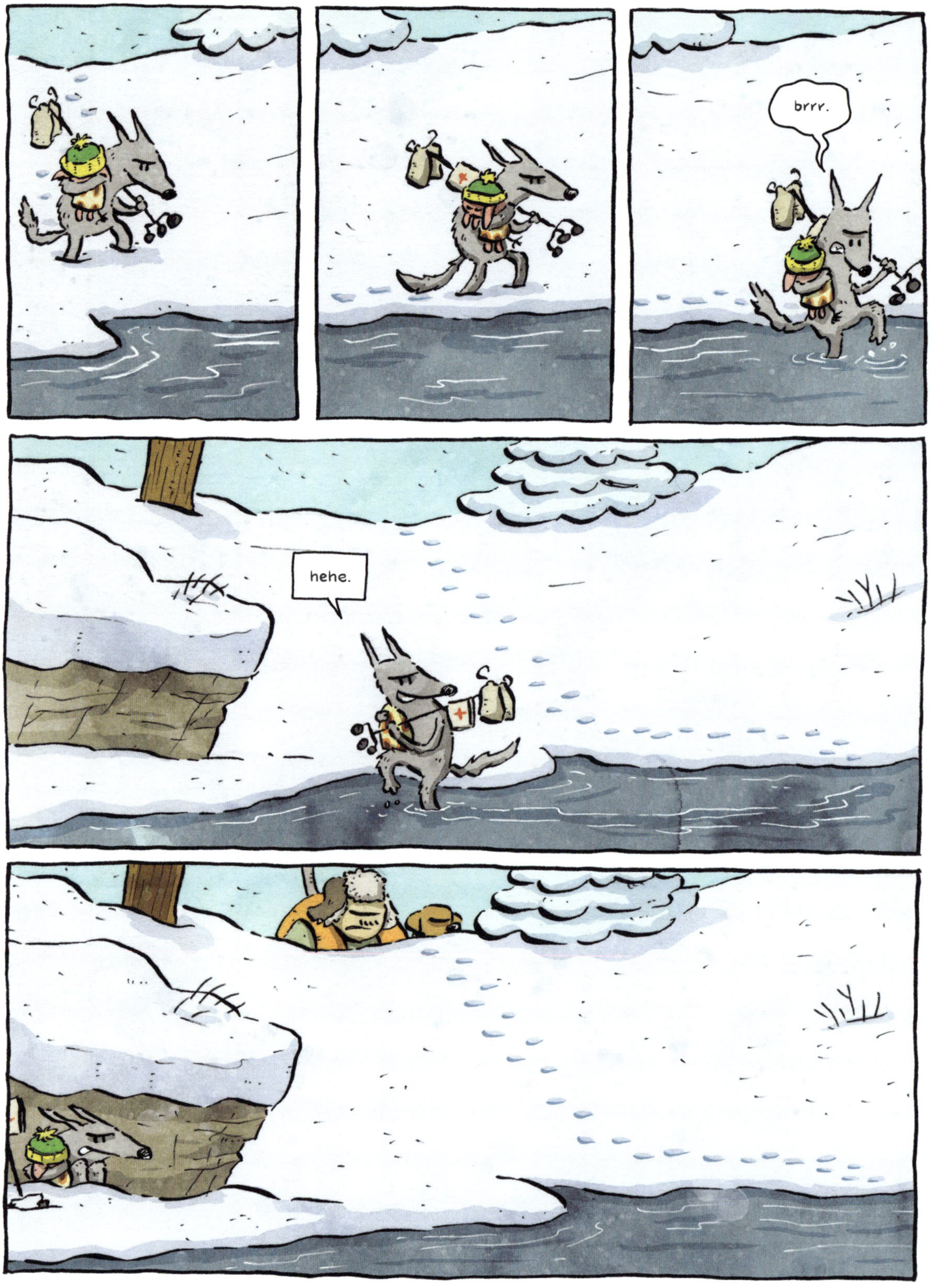
brrr.
hehe.

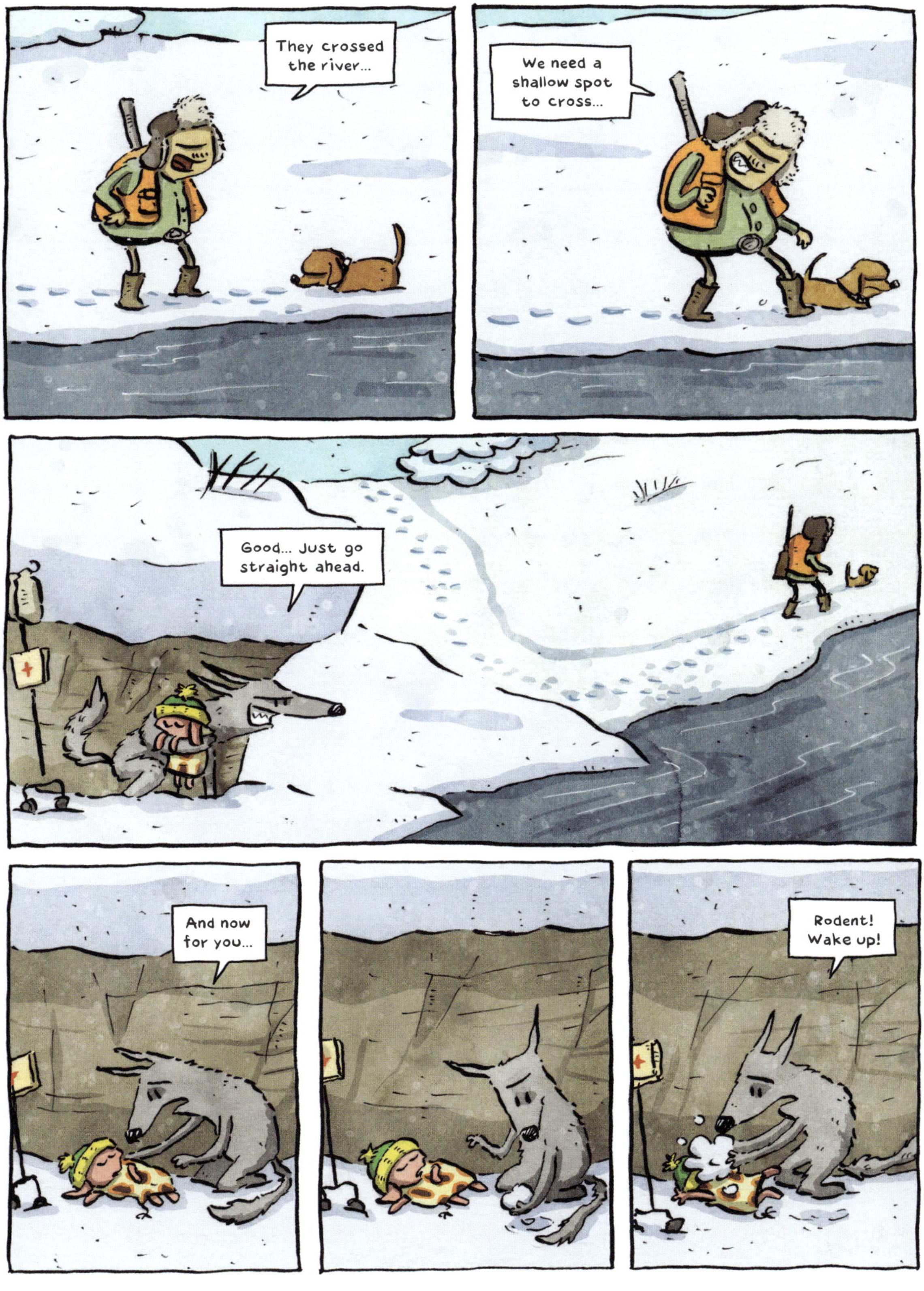
They crossed the river...
We need a shallow spot to cross...
Good... Just go straight ahead.
And now for you...
Rodent! Wake up!

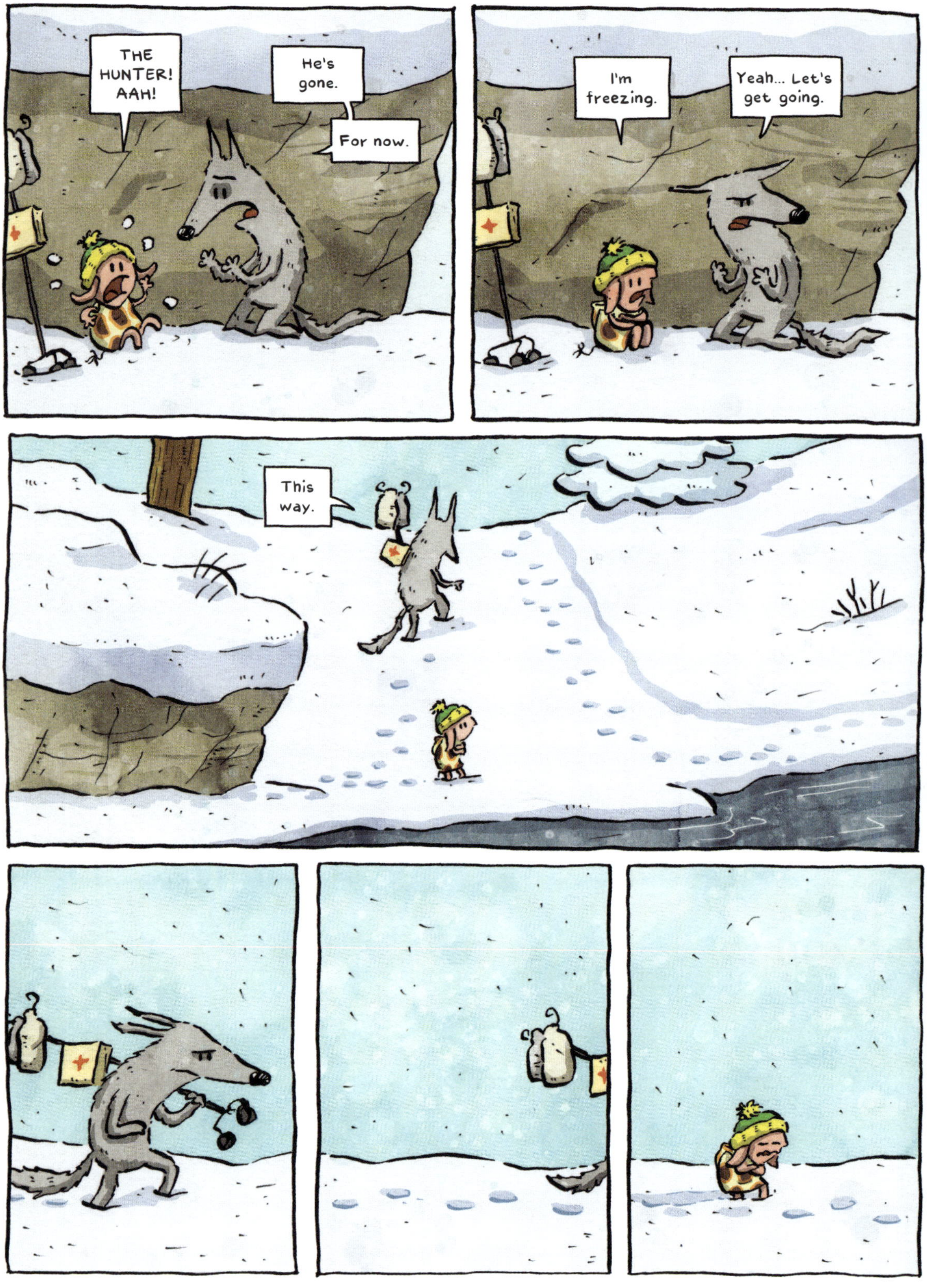
THE HUNTER! AAH!
He's gone.
For now.
I'm freezing.
Yeah... Let's get going.
This way.

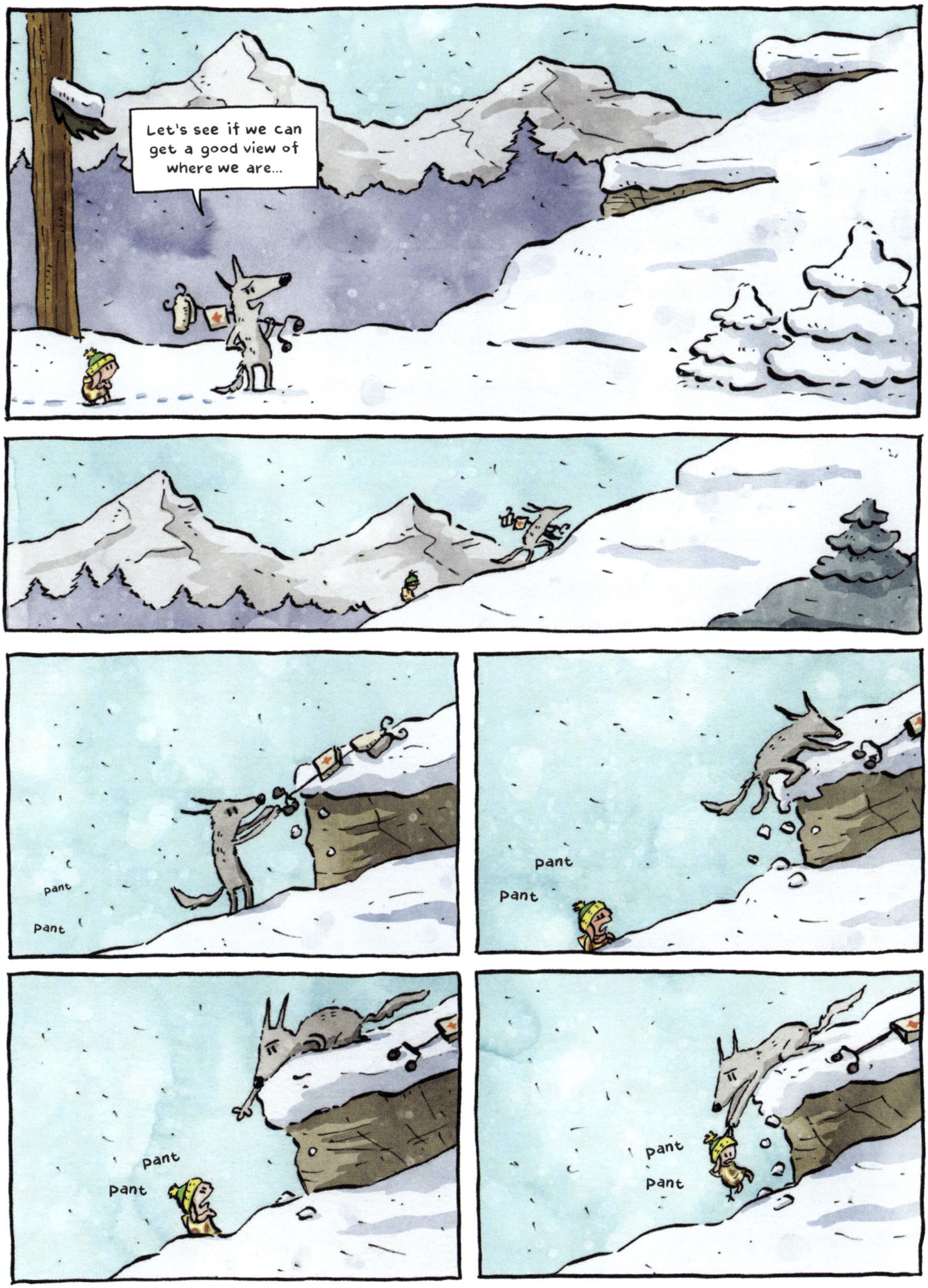

Let's see if we can get a good view of where we are...
pant
pant
pant
pant
pant
pant
pant
pant

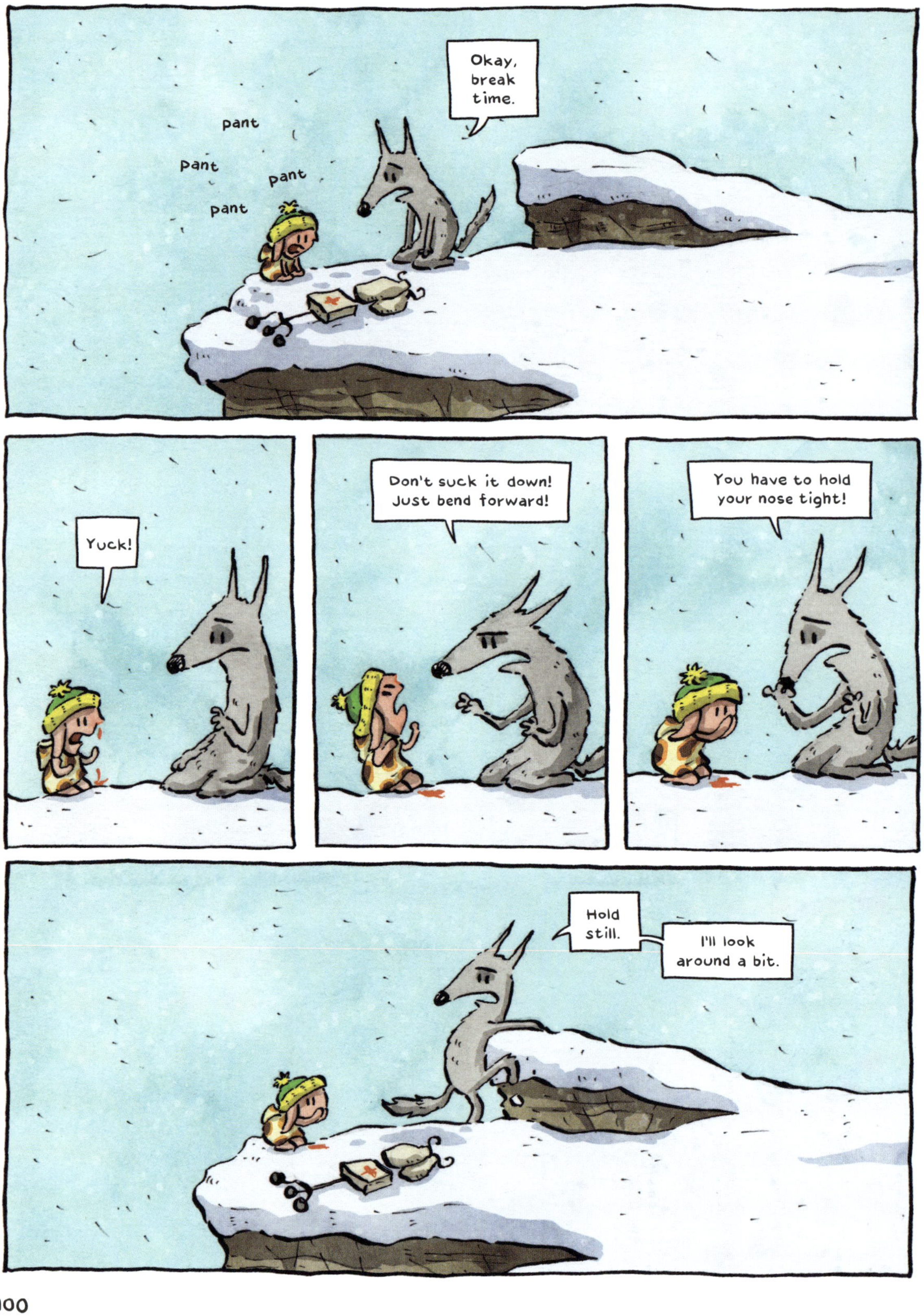
Okay, break time.
pant
pant
pant
pant
Yuck!
Don't suck it down! Just bend forward!
You have to hold your nose tight!
Hold still.
I'll look around a bit.

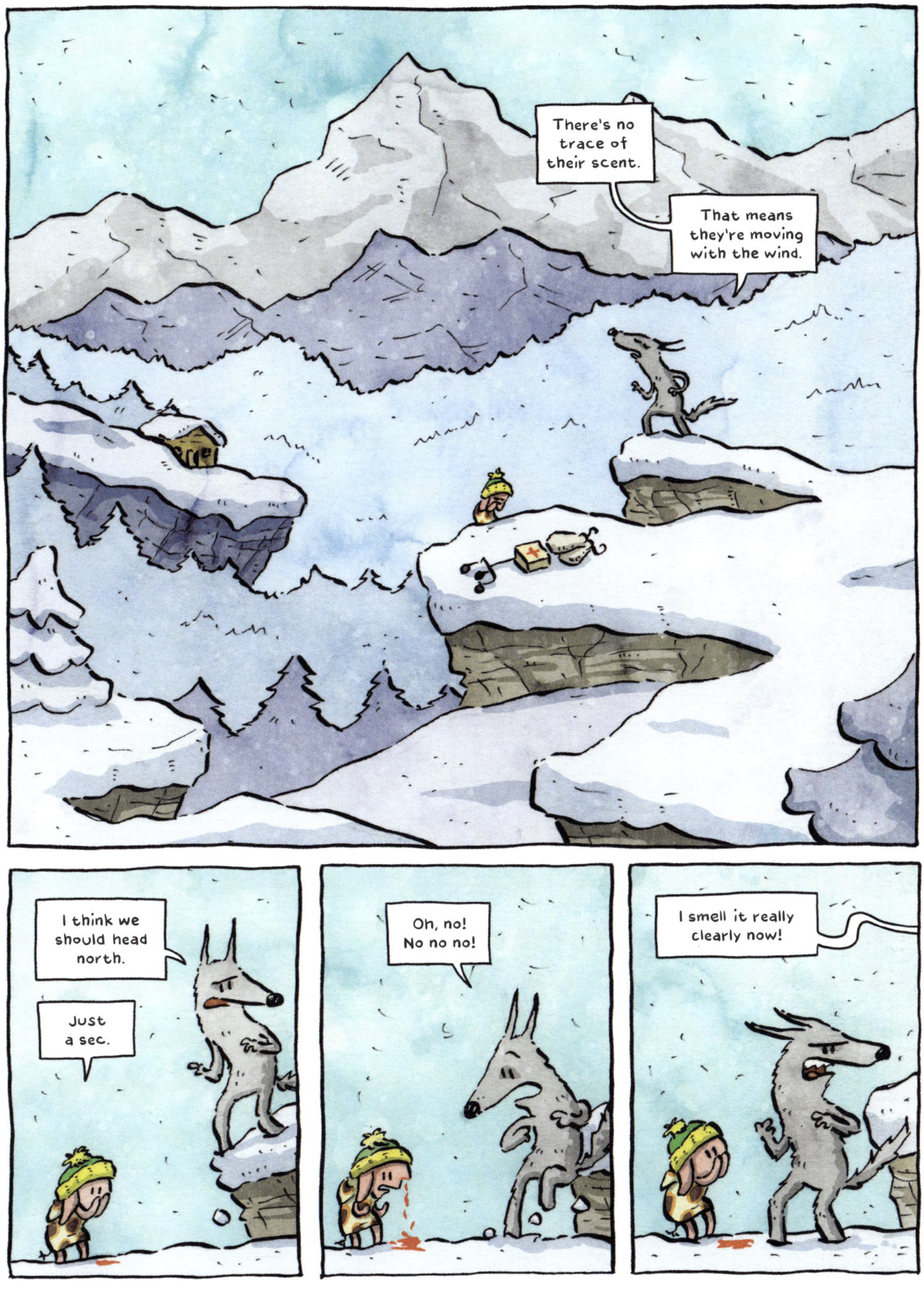
There's no trace of their scent.
That means they're moving with the wind.
I think we should head north.
Just a sec.
Oh, no! No no no!
I smell it really clearly now!

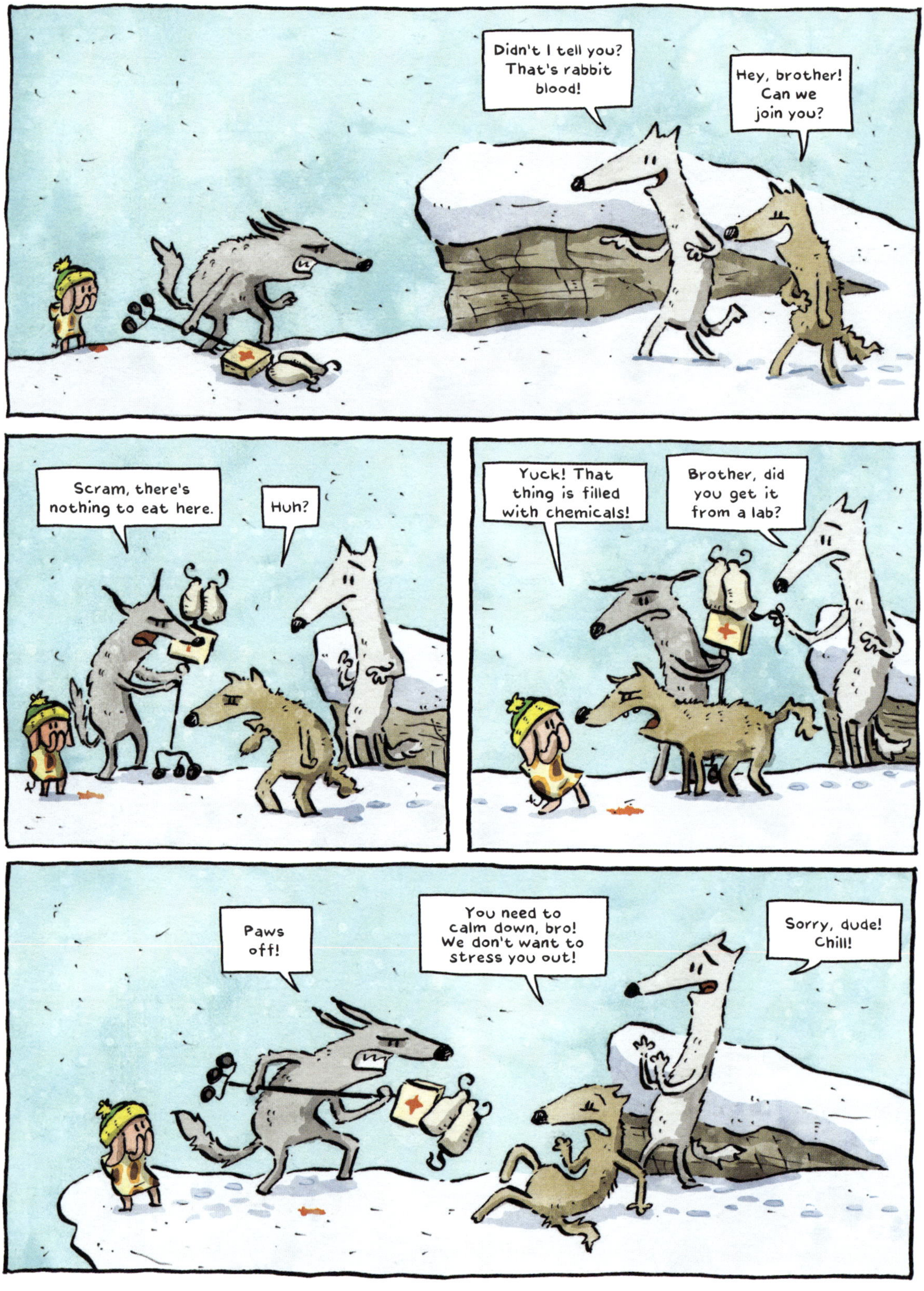
Didn't I tell you? That's rabbit blood!
Hey, brother! Can we join you?
Scram, there's nothing to eat here.
Huh?
Yuck! That thing is filled with chemicals!
Brother, did you get it from a lab?
Paws off!
You need to calm down, bro! We don't want to stress you out!
Sorry, dude! Chill!

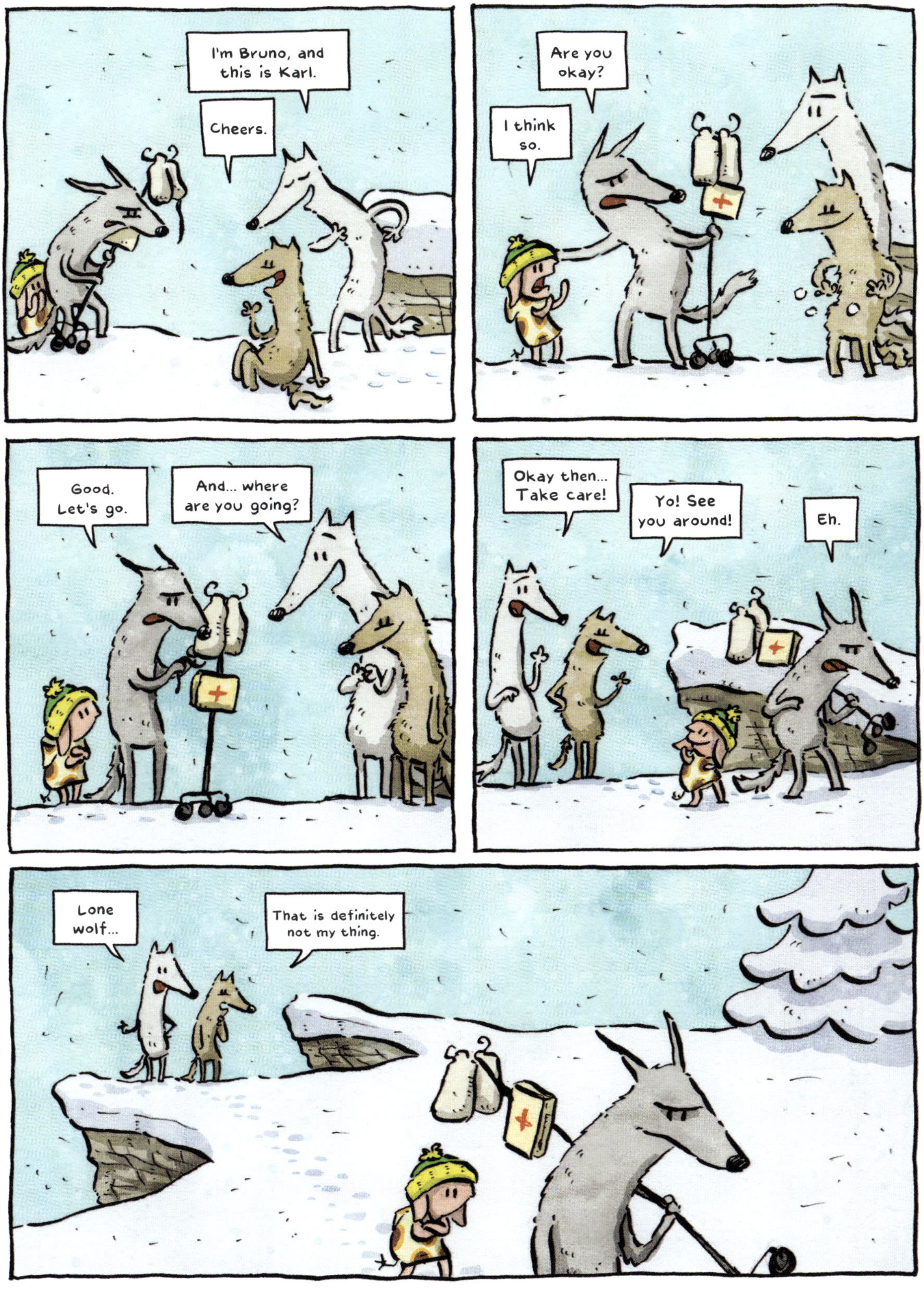
I'm Bruno, and this is Karl.
Cheers.
Are you okay?
I think so.
Good. Let's go.
And... where are you going?
Okay then... Take care!
Yo! See you around!
Eh.
Lone wolf...
That is definitely not my thing.

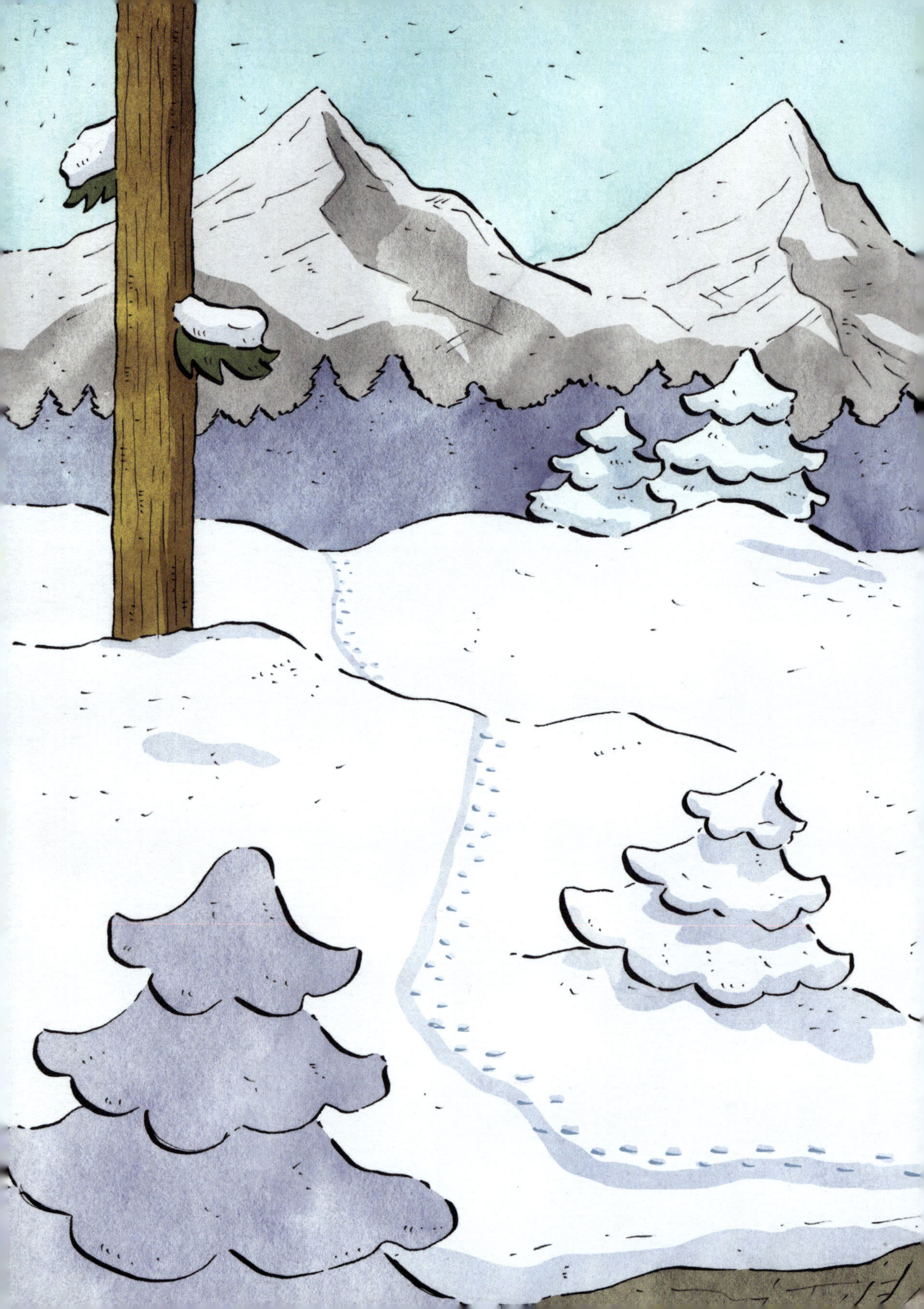

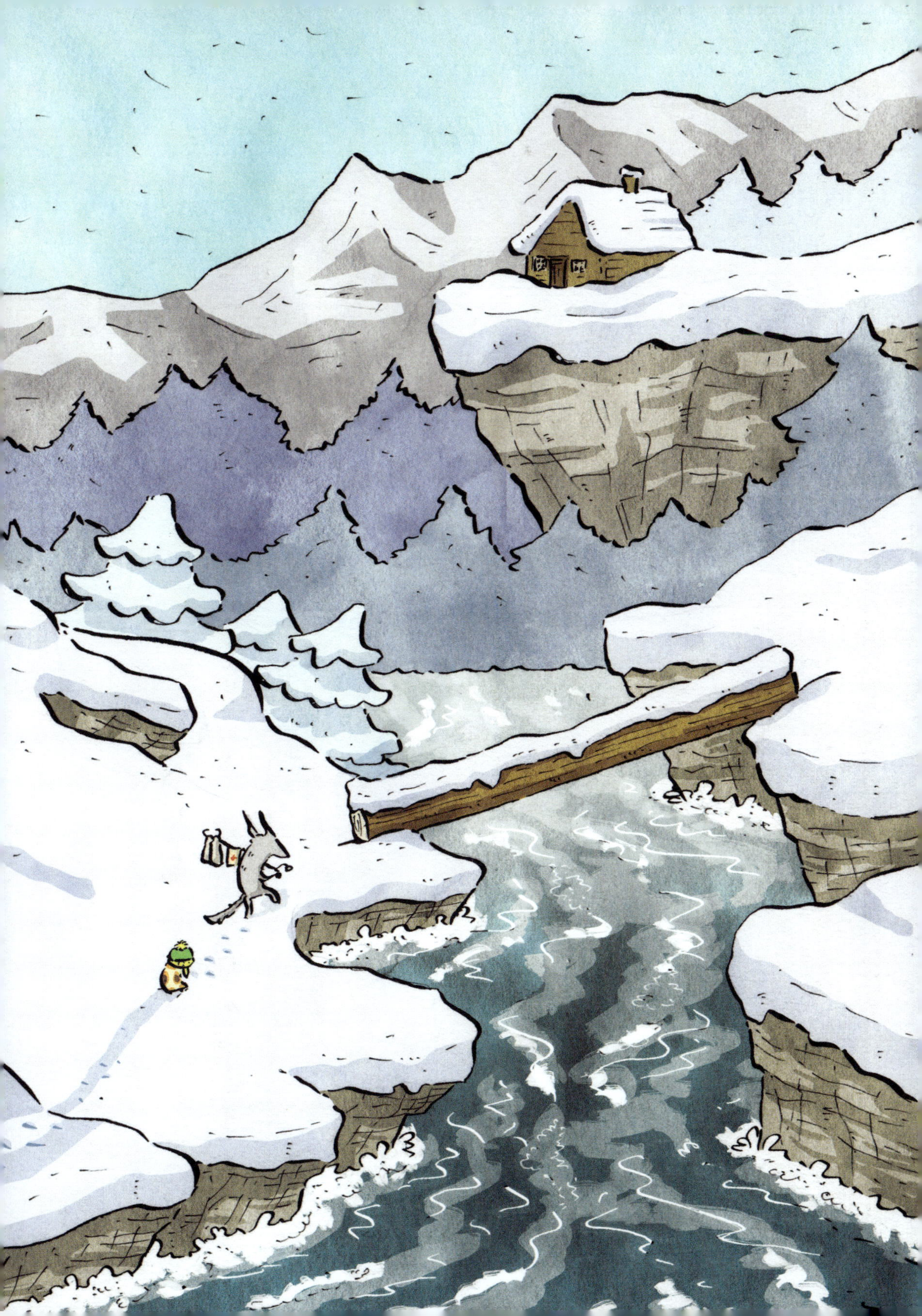

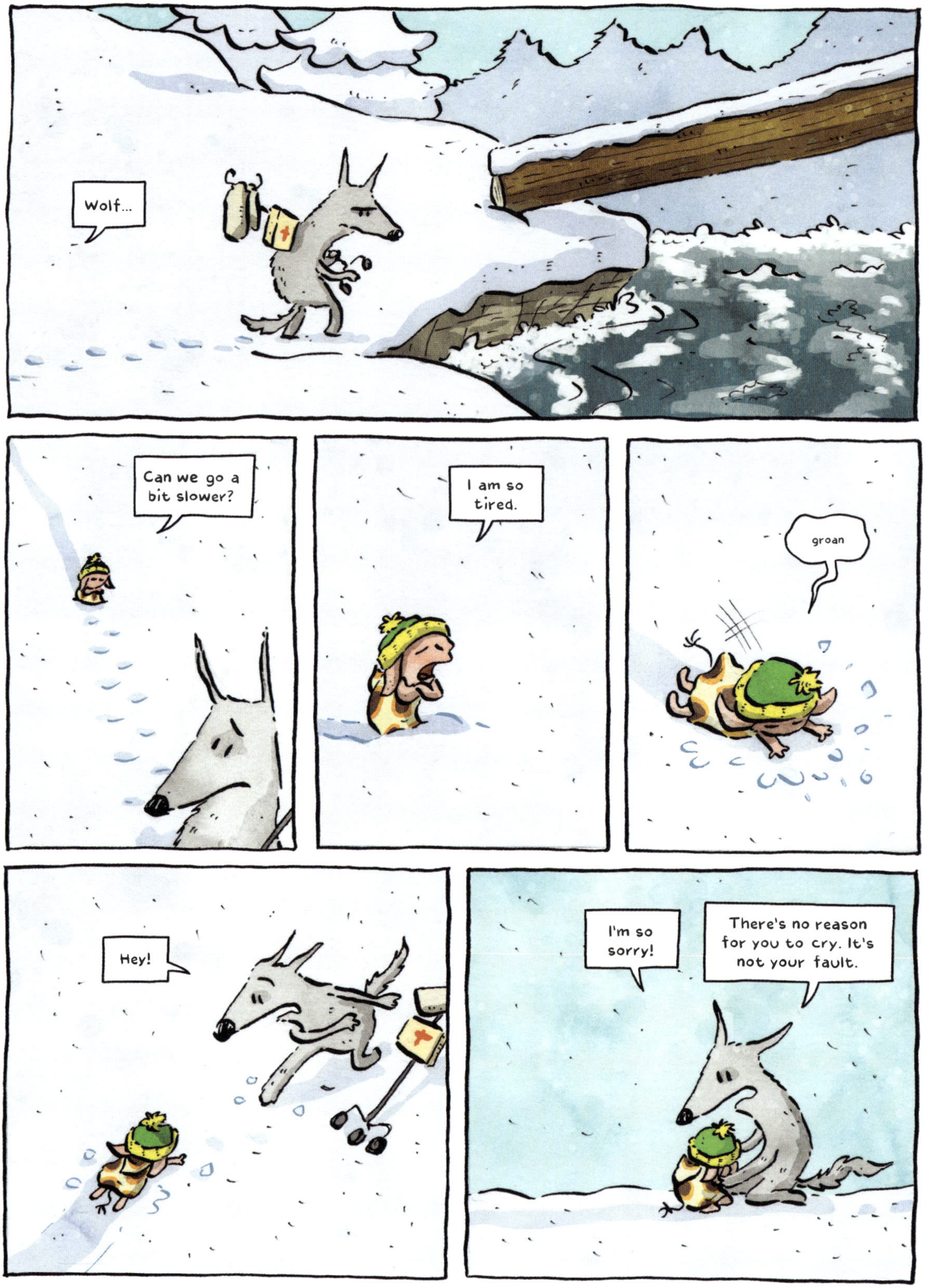

Wolf...
Can we go a bit slower?
I am so tired.
groan
Hey!
I'm so sorry!
There's no reason for you to cry. It's not your fault.

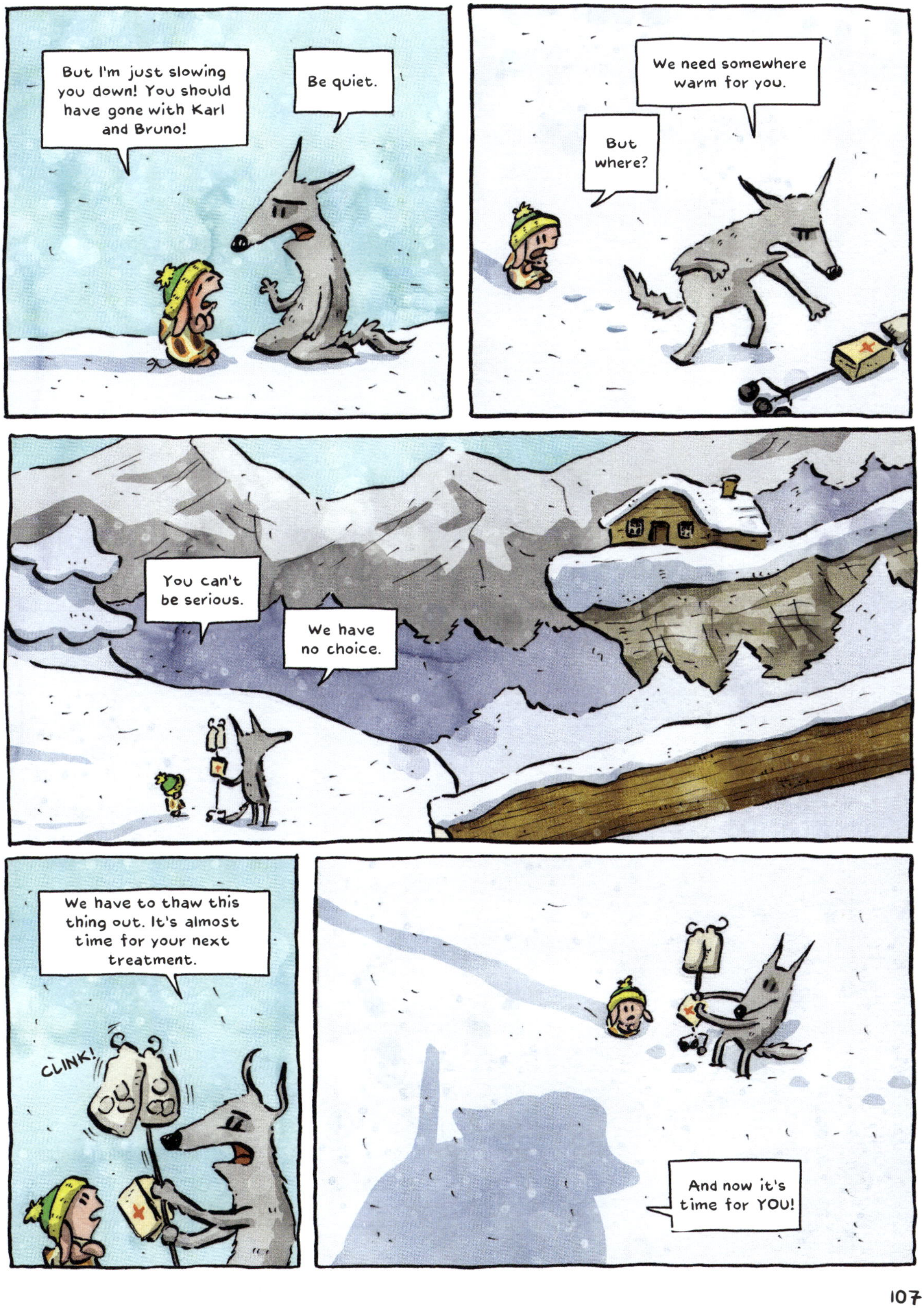

But I'm just slowing you down! You should have gone with Karl and Bruno!
Be quiet.
We need somewhere warm for you.
But where?
You can't be serious.
We have no choice.
We have to thaw this thing out. It's almost time for your next treatment.
CLINK!
And now it's time for YOU!

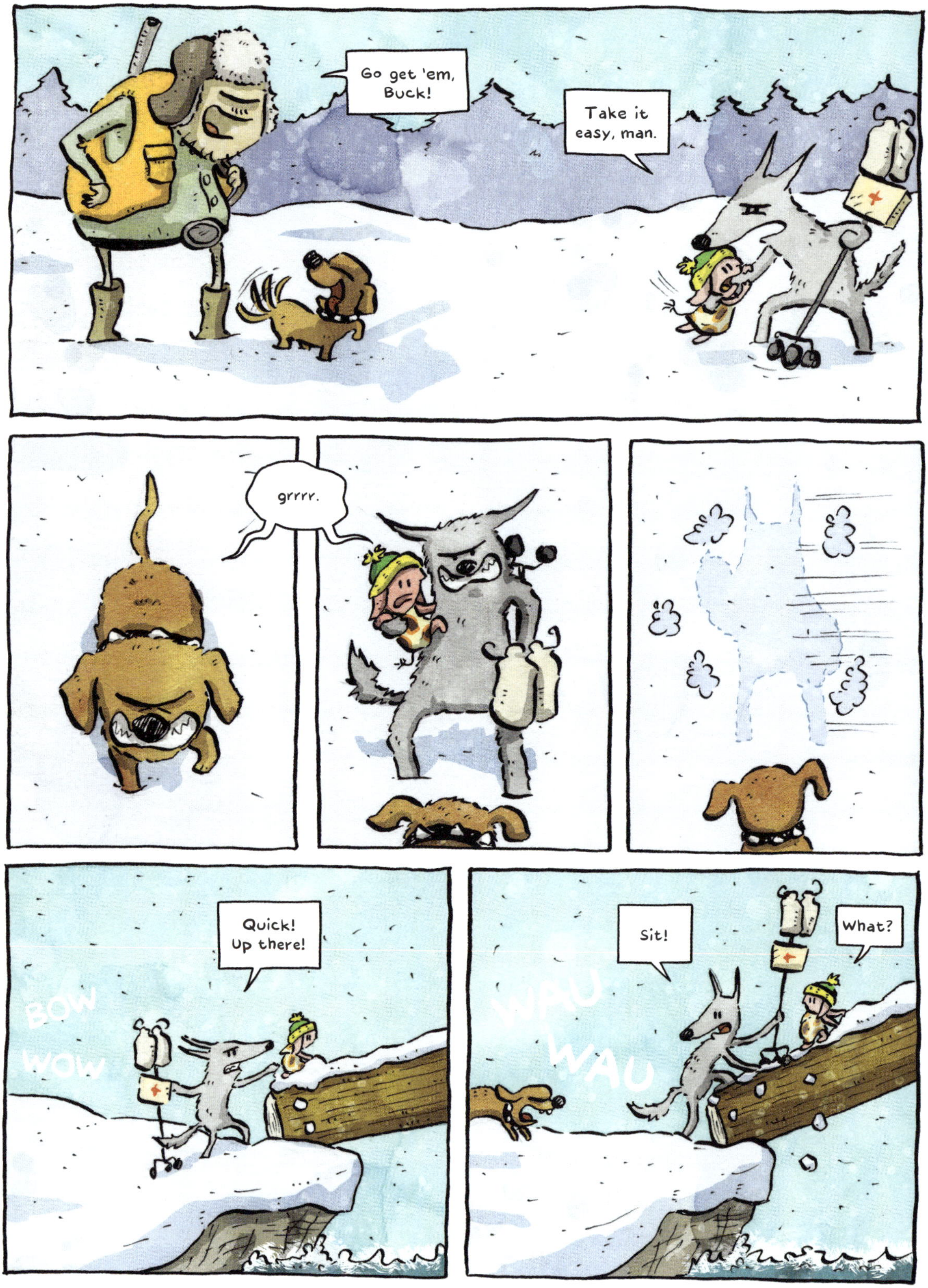
Go get 'em, Buck!
Take it easy, man.
grrrr.
BOW WOW
Quick! Up there!
WAU WAU
Sit!
What?

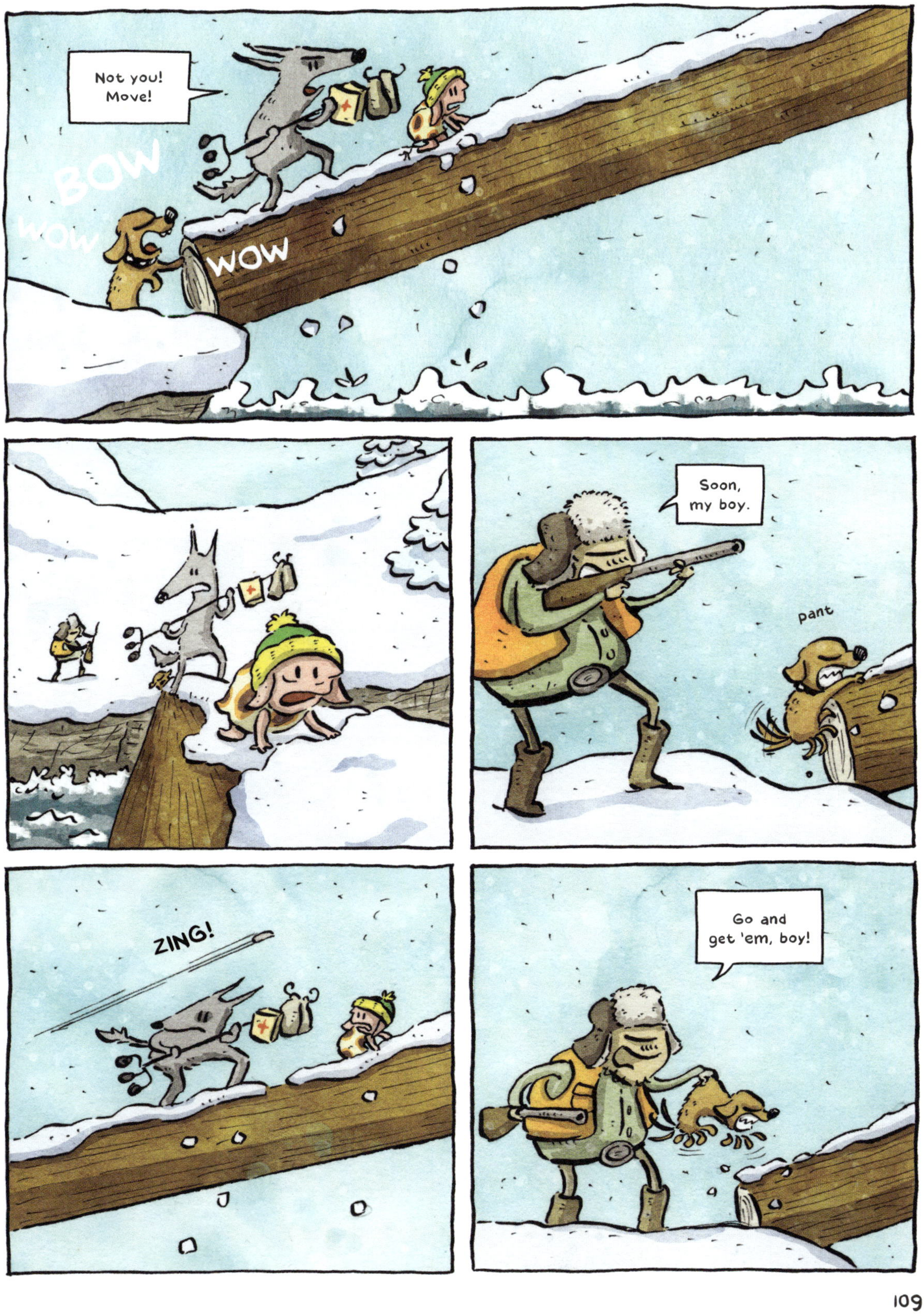
Not you! Move!
BOW WOW WOW
Soon, my boy.
pant
ZING!
Go and get 'em, boy!

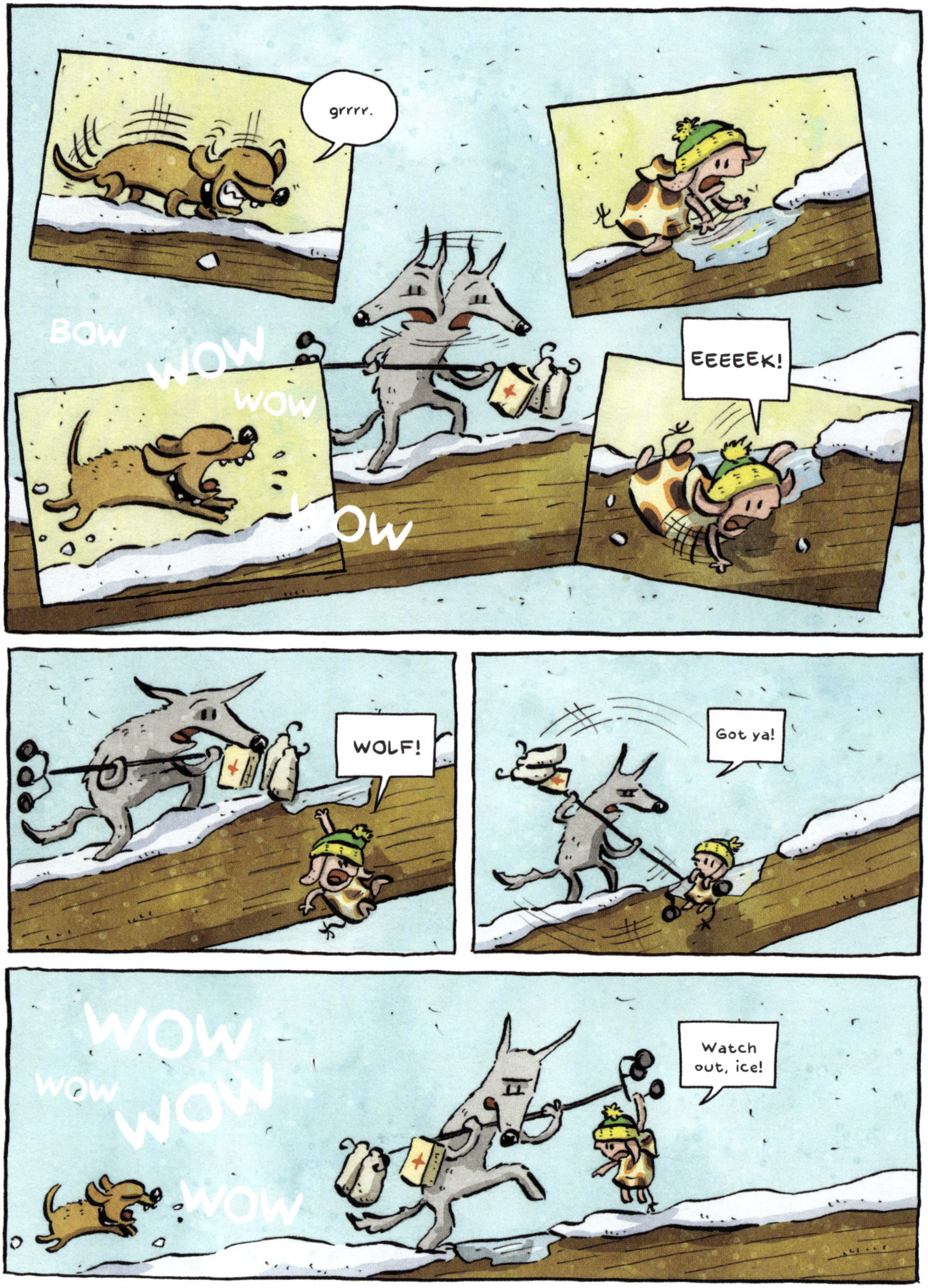
grrrr.
BOW
WOW
WOW
WOW
EEEEEK!
WOLF!
Got ya!
WOW
WOW
WOW
WOW
Watch out, ice!

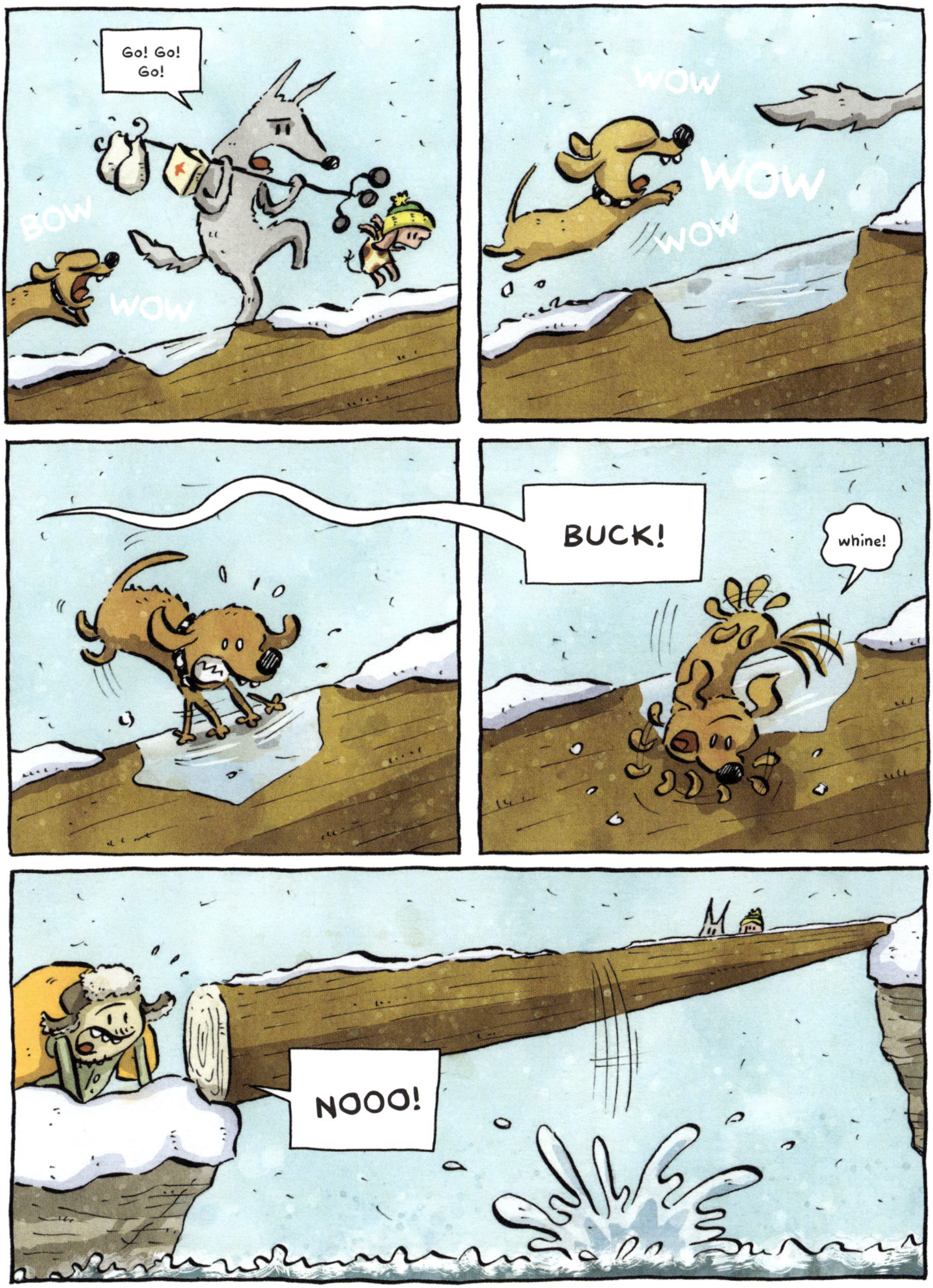
Go! Go! Go!
BOW
WOW
WOW
WOW
WOW
BUCK!
whine!
NOOO!

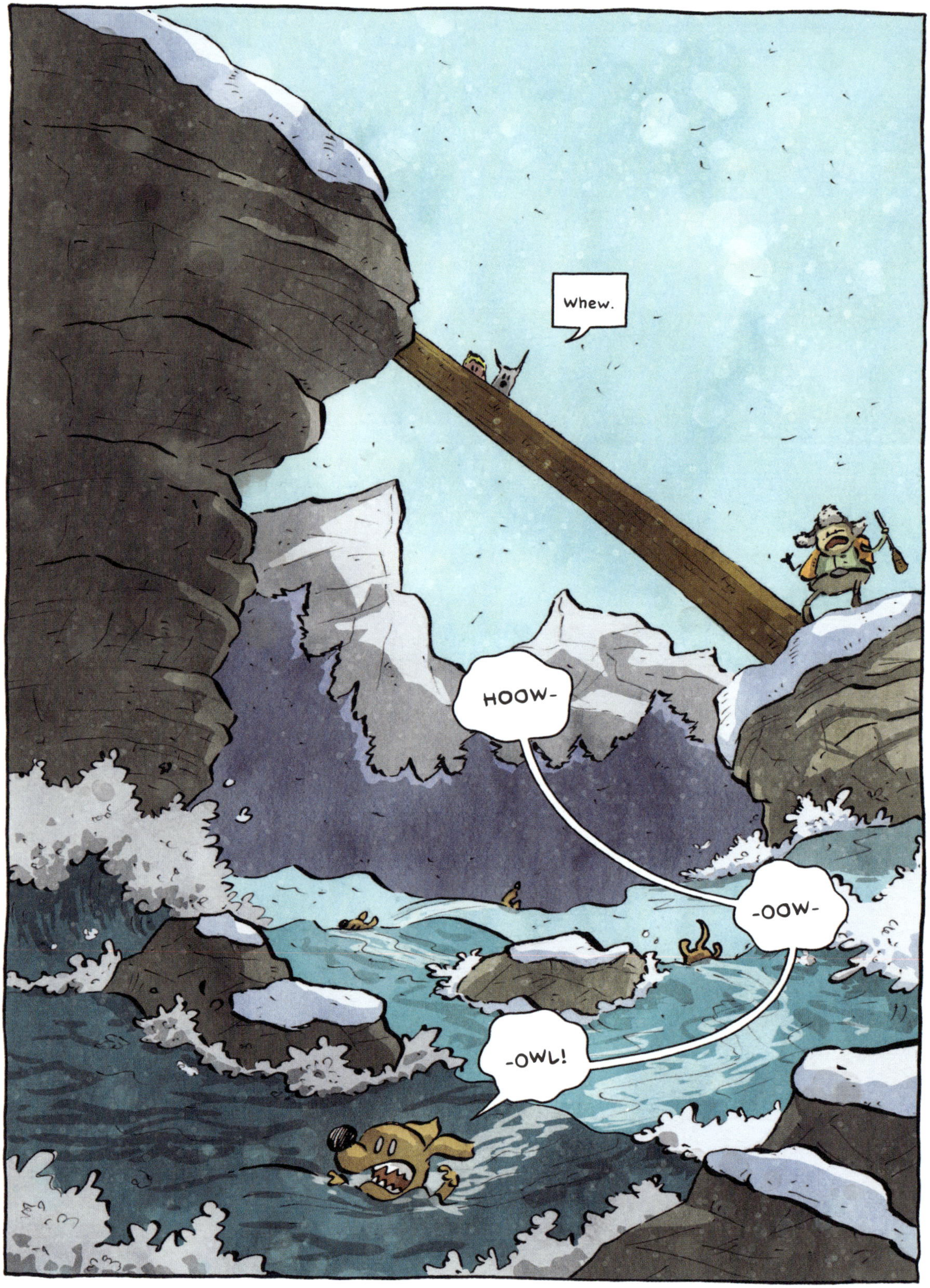
Whew.
HOOW-
-OOW-
-OWL!

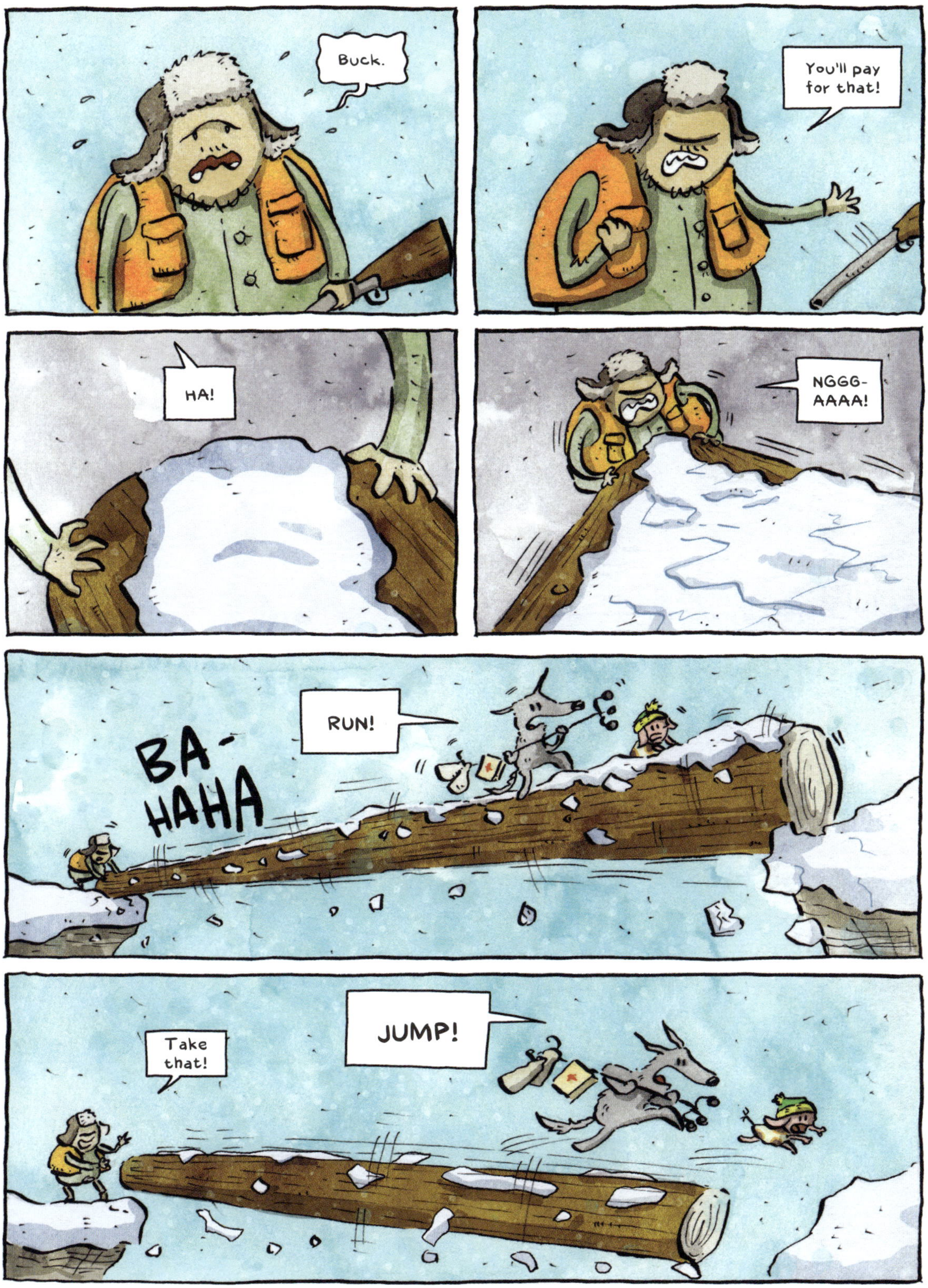
Buck.
You'll pay for that!
HA!
NGGG-AAAA!
BA-HAHA
RUN!
Take that!
JUMP!

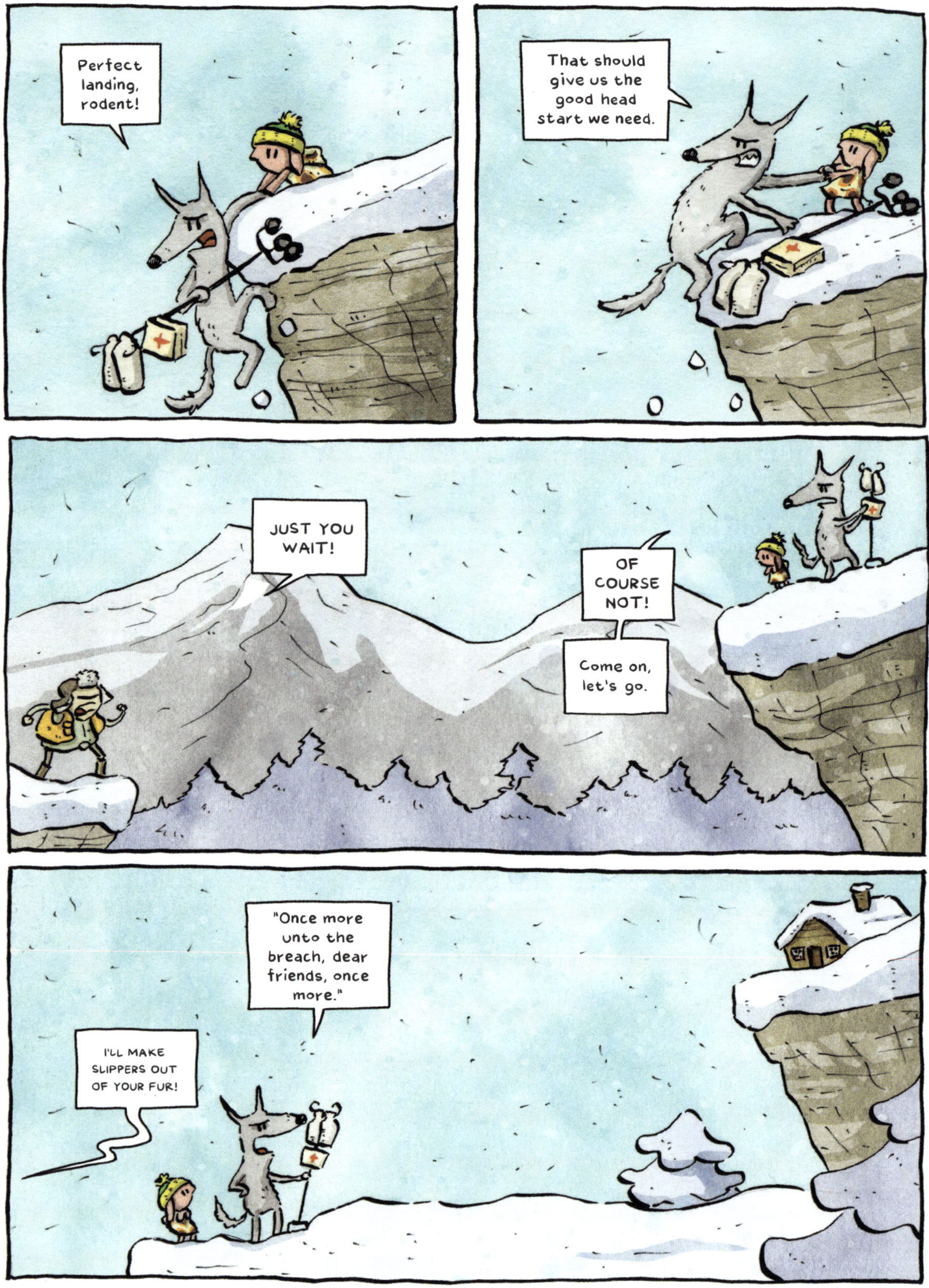
Perfect landing, rodent!
That should give us the good head start we need.
JUST YOU WAIT!
OF COURSE NOT!
Come on, let's go.
"Once more unto the breach, dear friends, once more."
I'LL MAKE SLIPPERS OUT OF YOUR FUR!

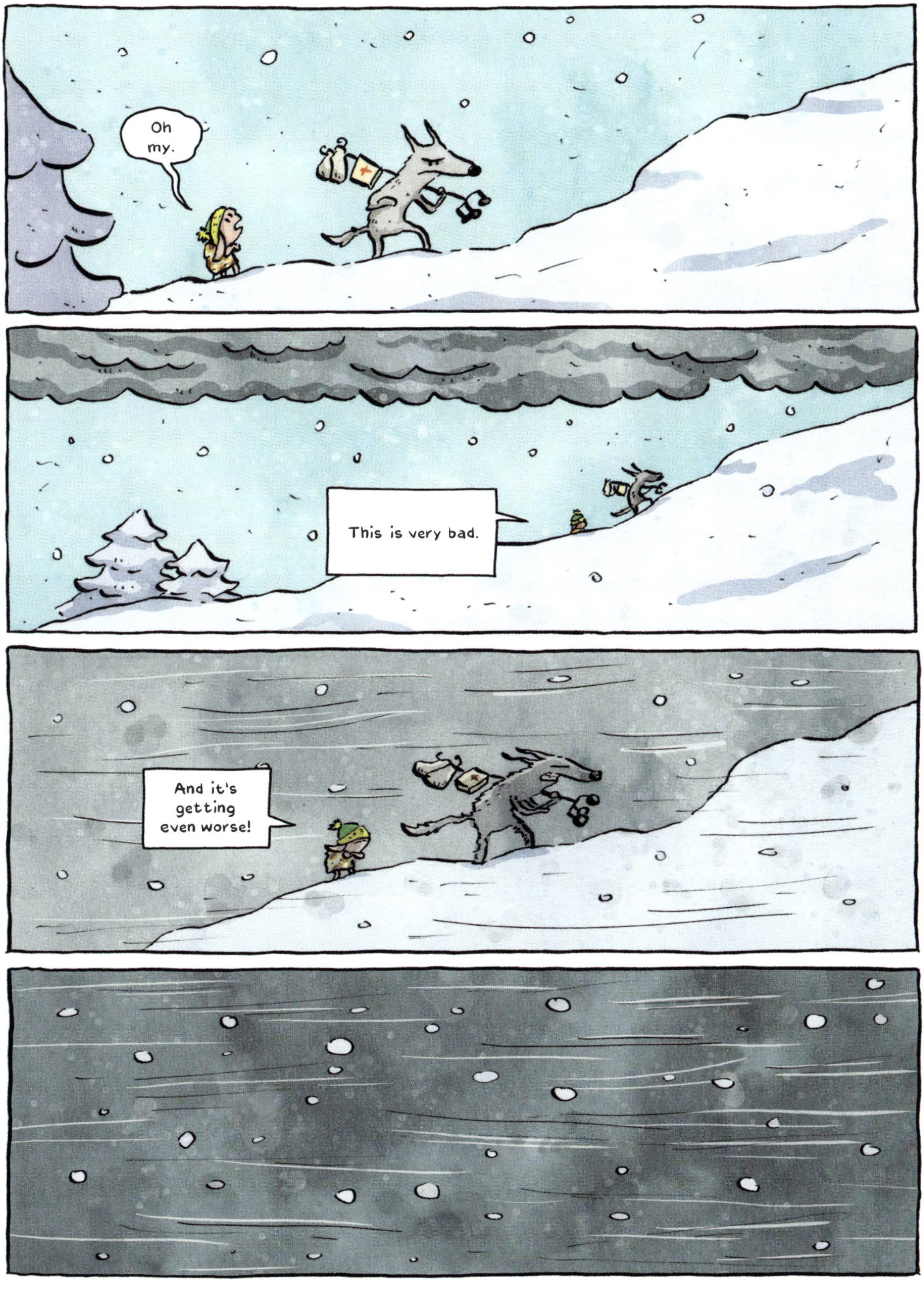
Oh my.
This is very bad.
And it's getting even worse!

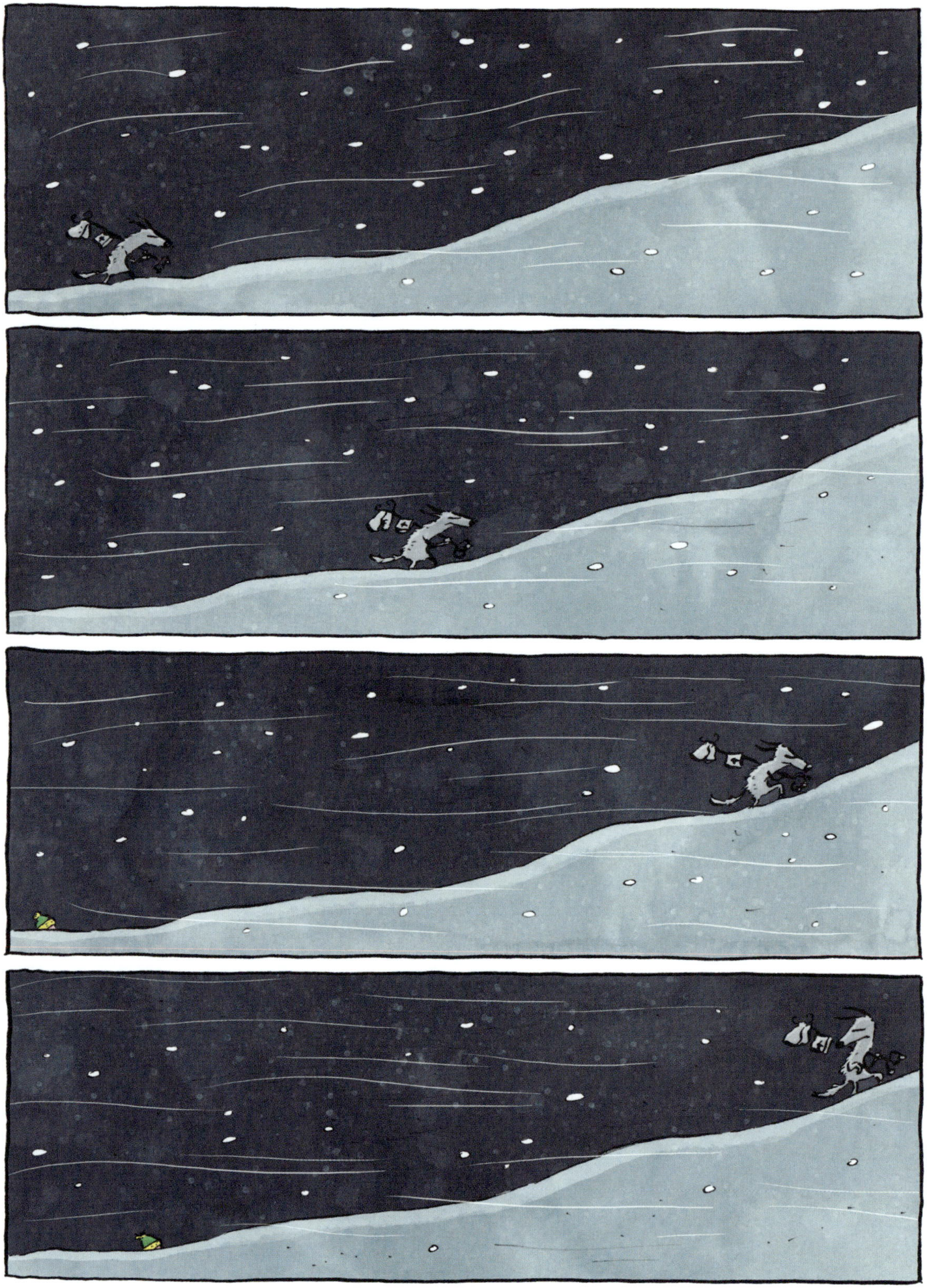

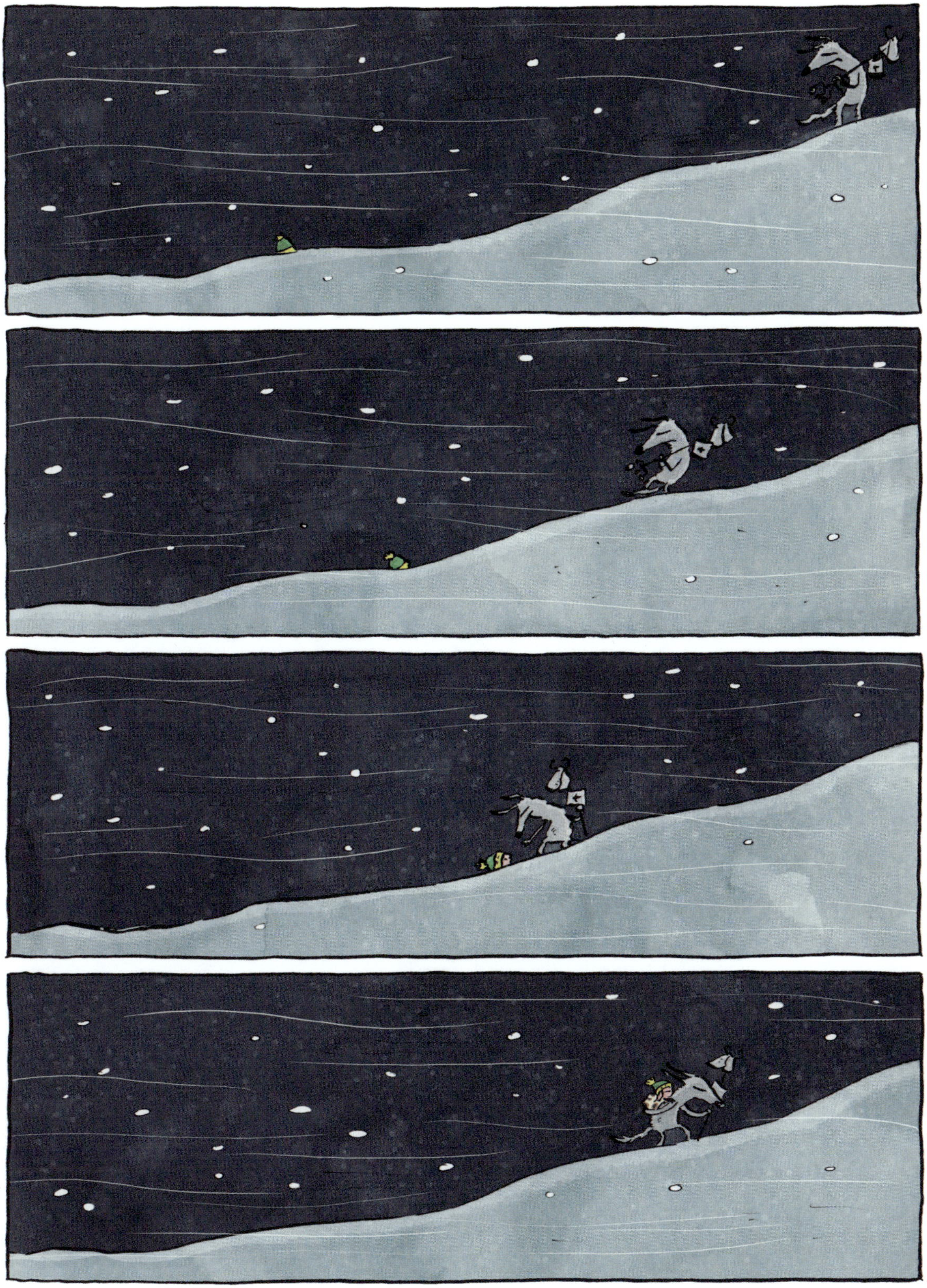

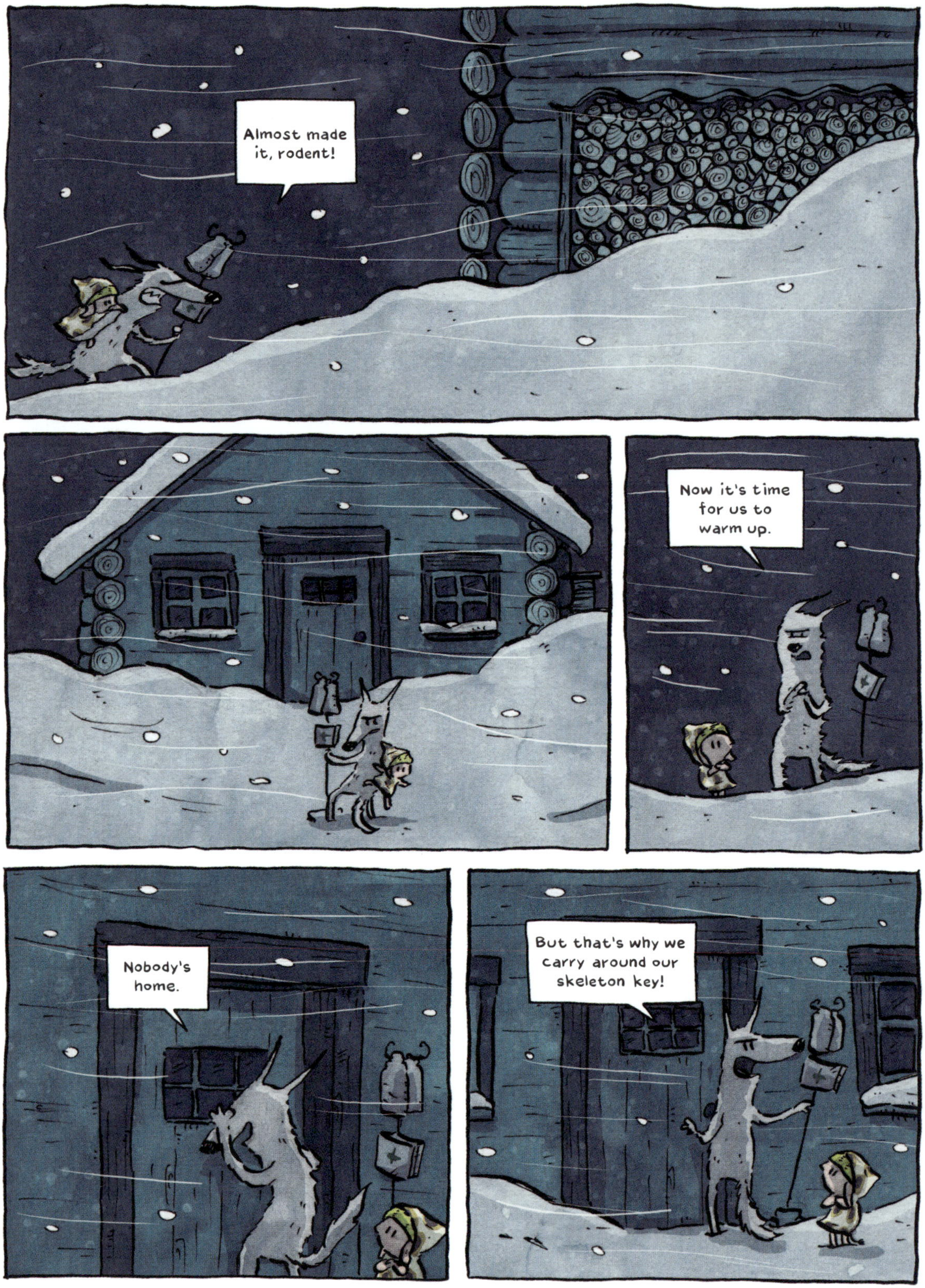

Almost made it, rodent!
Now it's time for us to warm up.
Nobody's home.
But that's why we carry around our skeleton key!

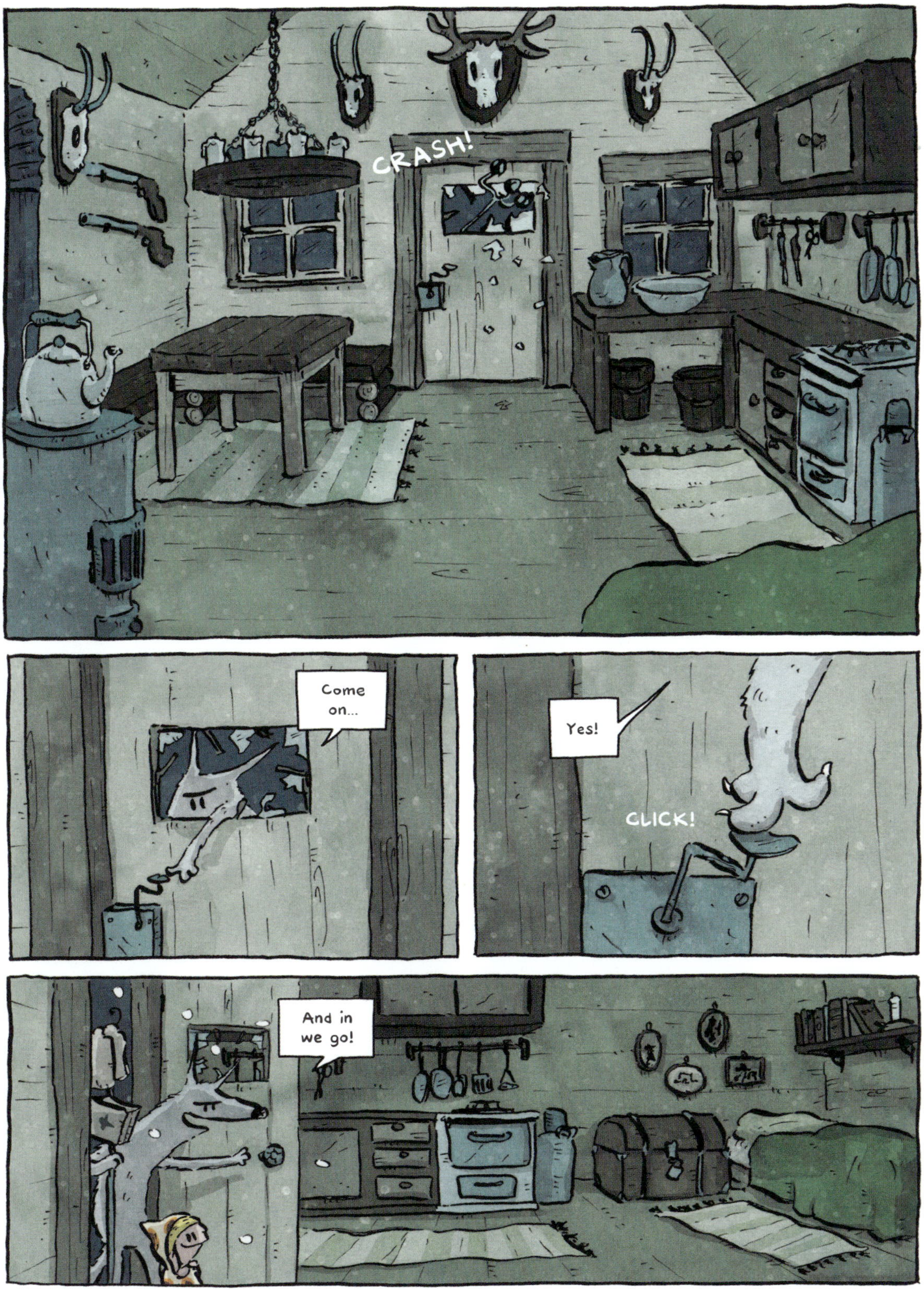
CRASH!
Come on...
Yes!
CLICK!
And in we go!

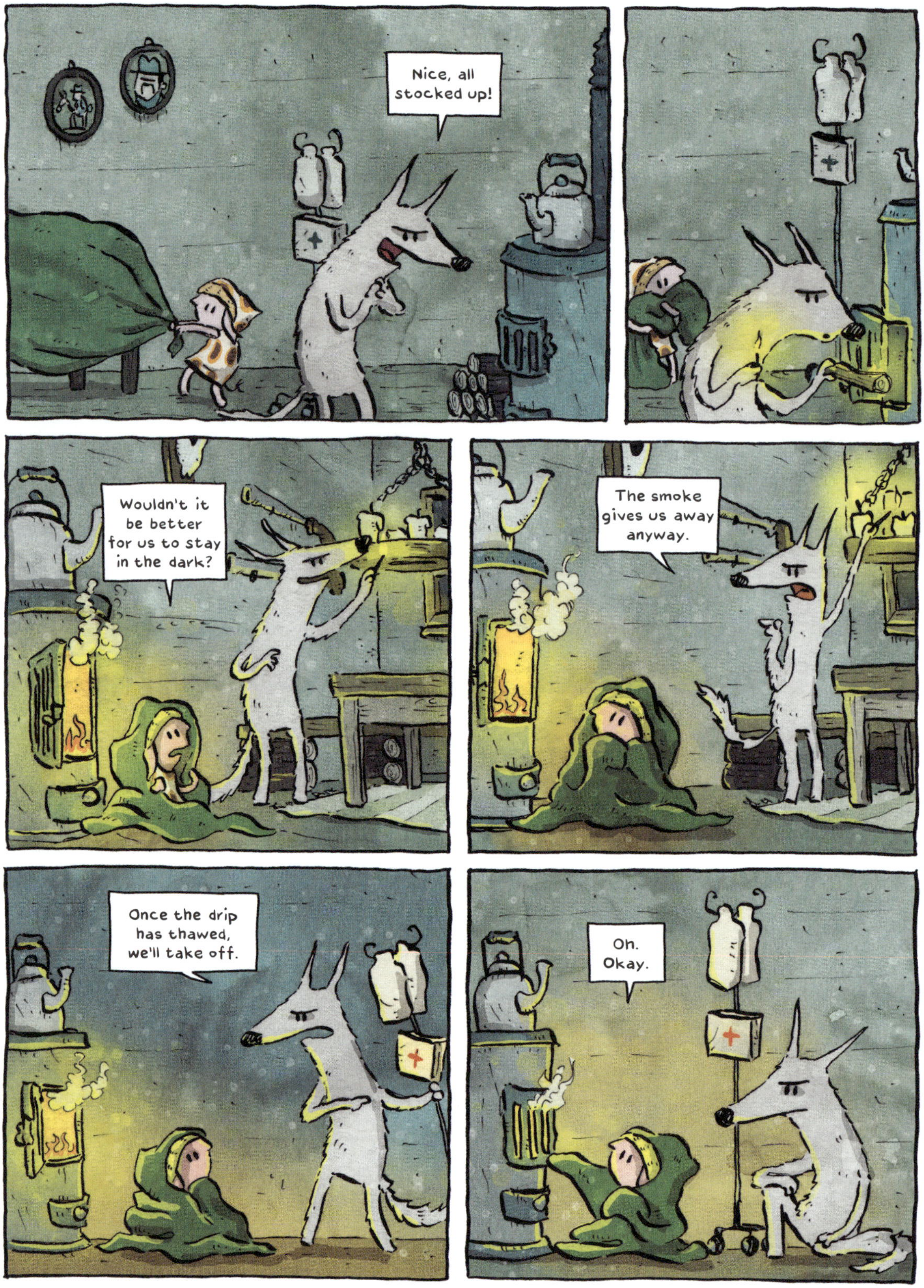
Nice, all stocked up!
Wouldn't it be better for us to stay in the dark?
The smoke gives us away anyway.
Once the drip has thawed, we'll take off.
Oh. Okay.

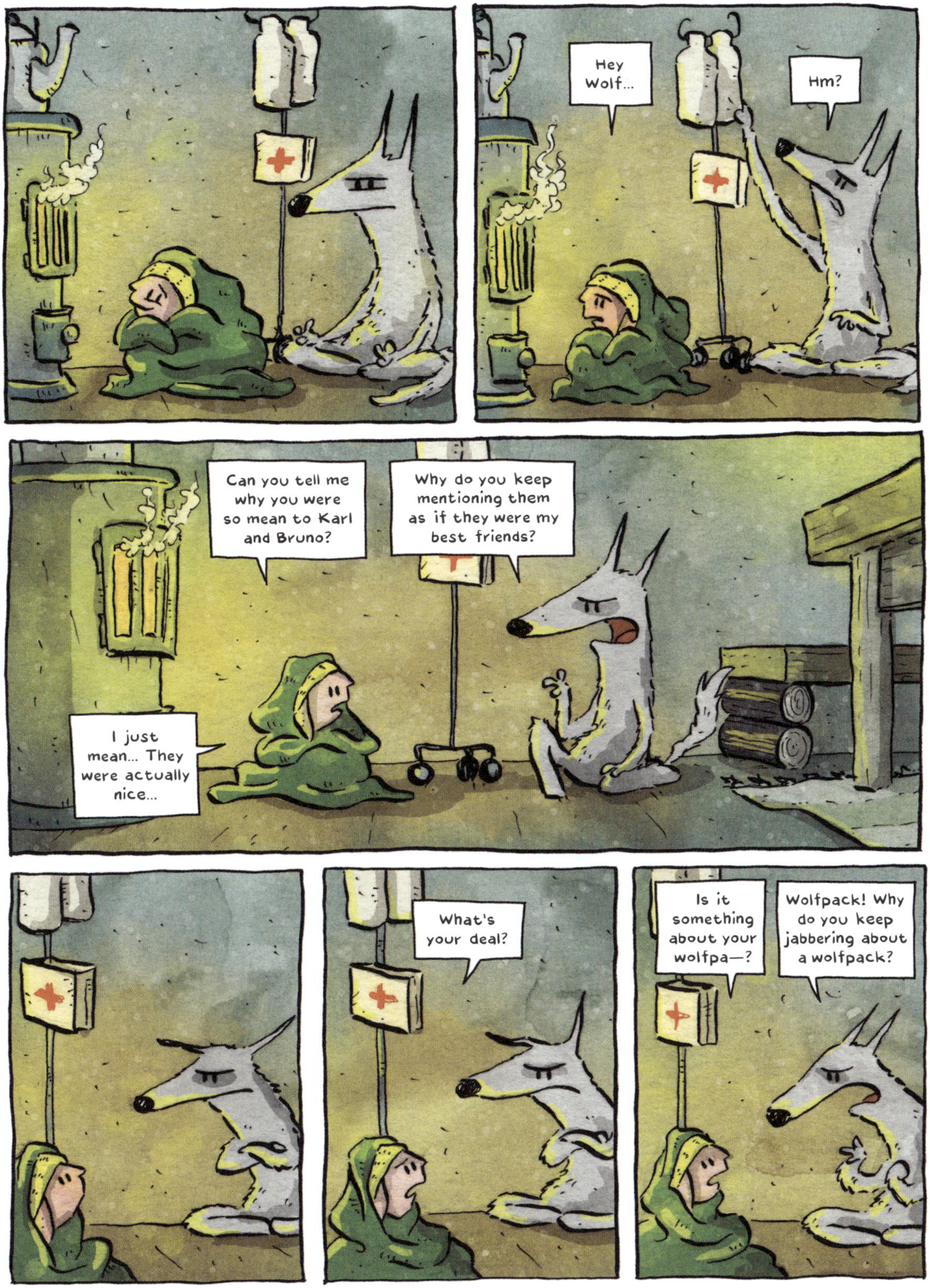
Hey Wolf...
Hm?
Can you tell me why you were so mean to Karl and Bruno?
Why do you keep mentioning them as if they were my best friends?
I just mean... They were actually nice...
What's your deal?
Is it something about your wolfpa—?
Wolfpack! Why do you keep jabbering about a wolfpack?

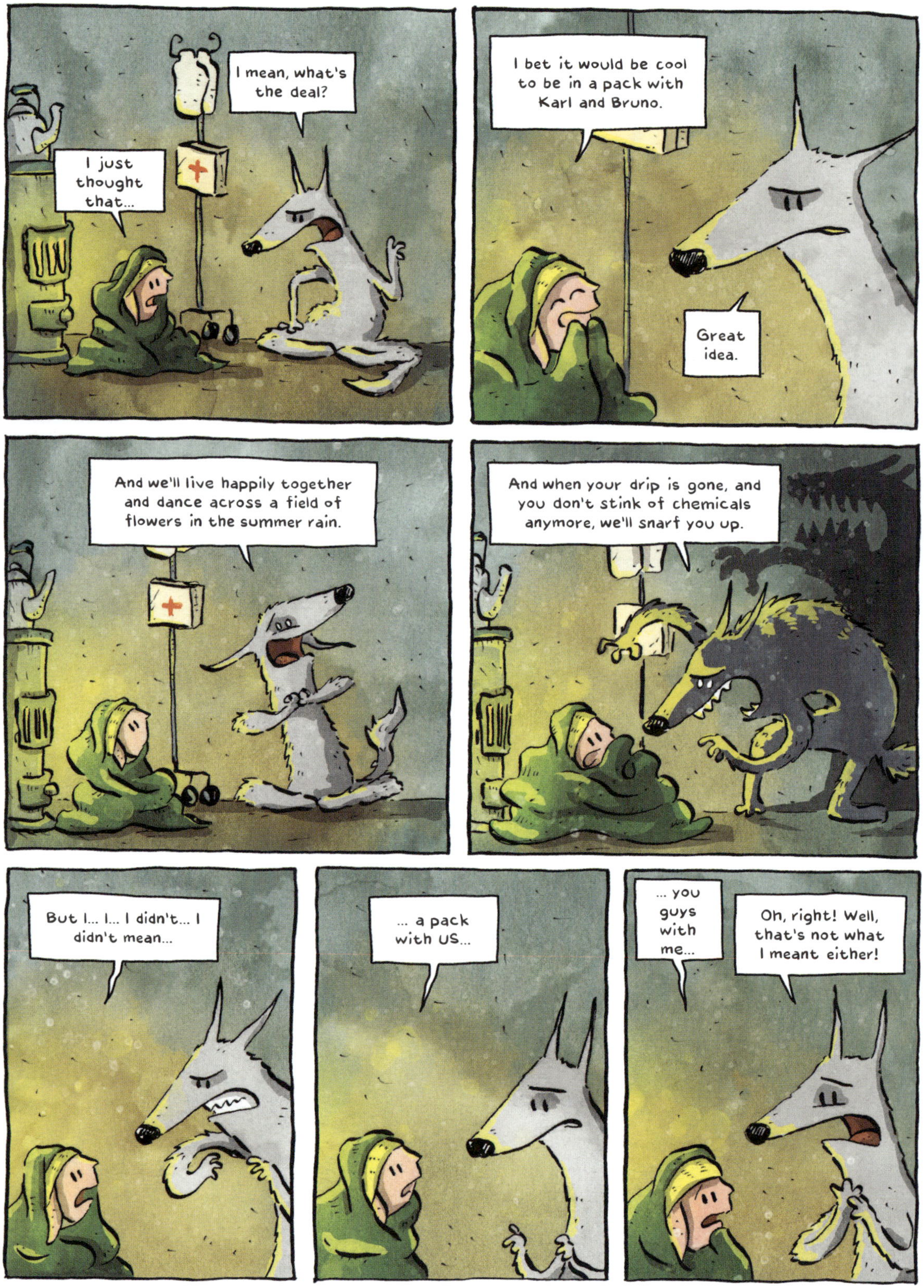
I mean, what's the deal?
I just thought that...
I bet it would be cool to be in a pack with Karl and Bruno.
Great idea.
And we'll live happily together and dance across a field of flowers in the summer rain.
And when your drip is gone, and you don't stink of chemicals anymore, we'll snarf you up.
But I... I... I didn't... I didn't mean...
... a pack with US...
... you guys with me...
Oh, right! Well, that's not what I meant either!

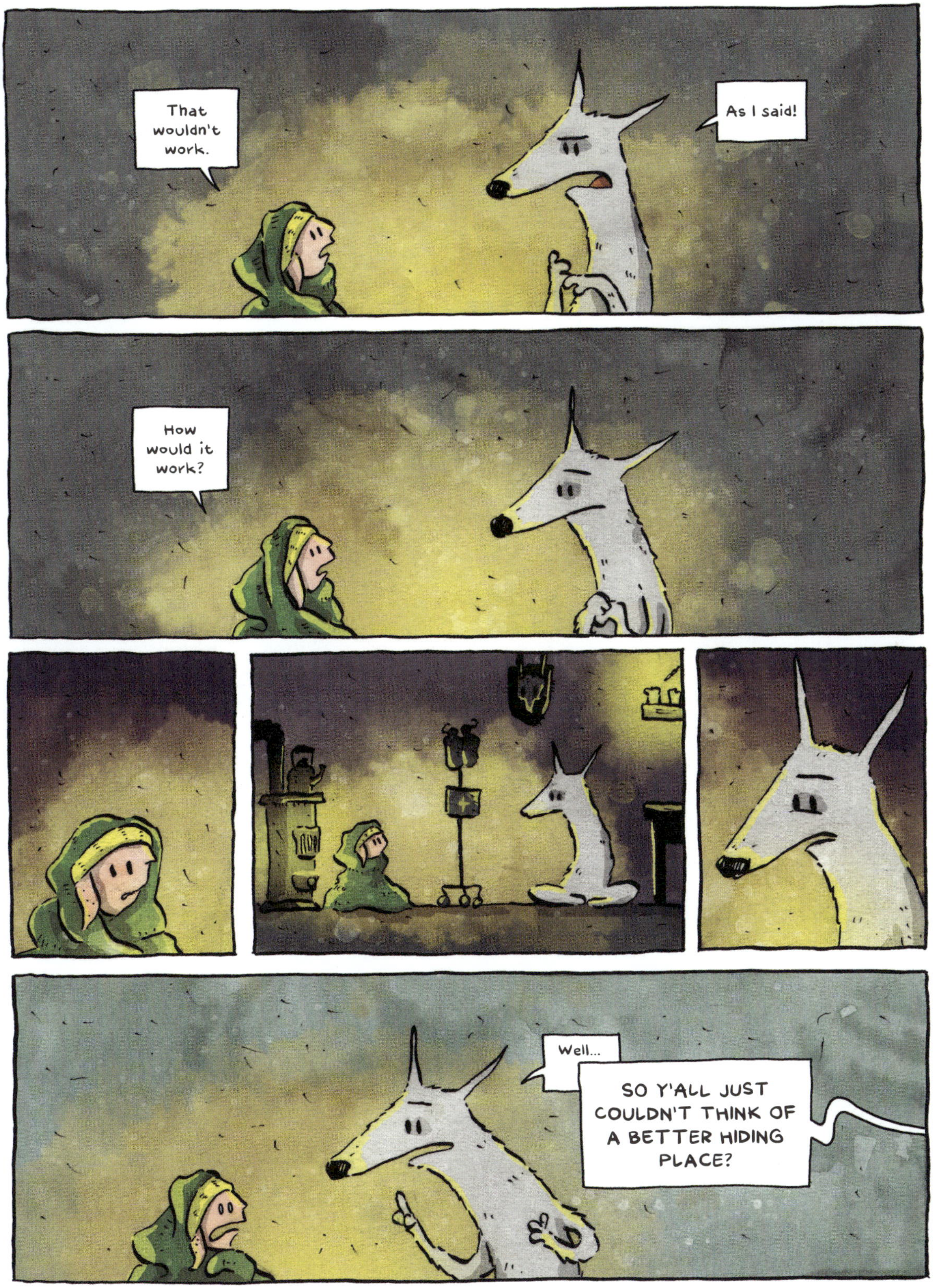
That wouldn't work.
As I said!
How would it work?
Well...
SO Y'ALL JUST COULDN'T THINK OF A BETTER HIDING PLACE?

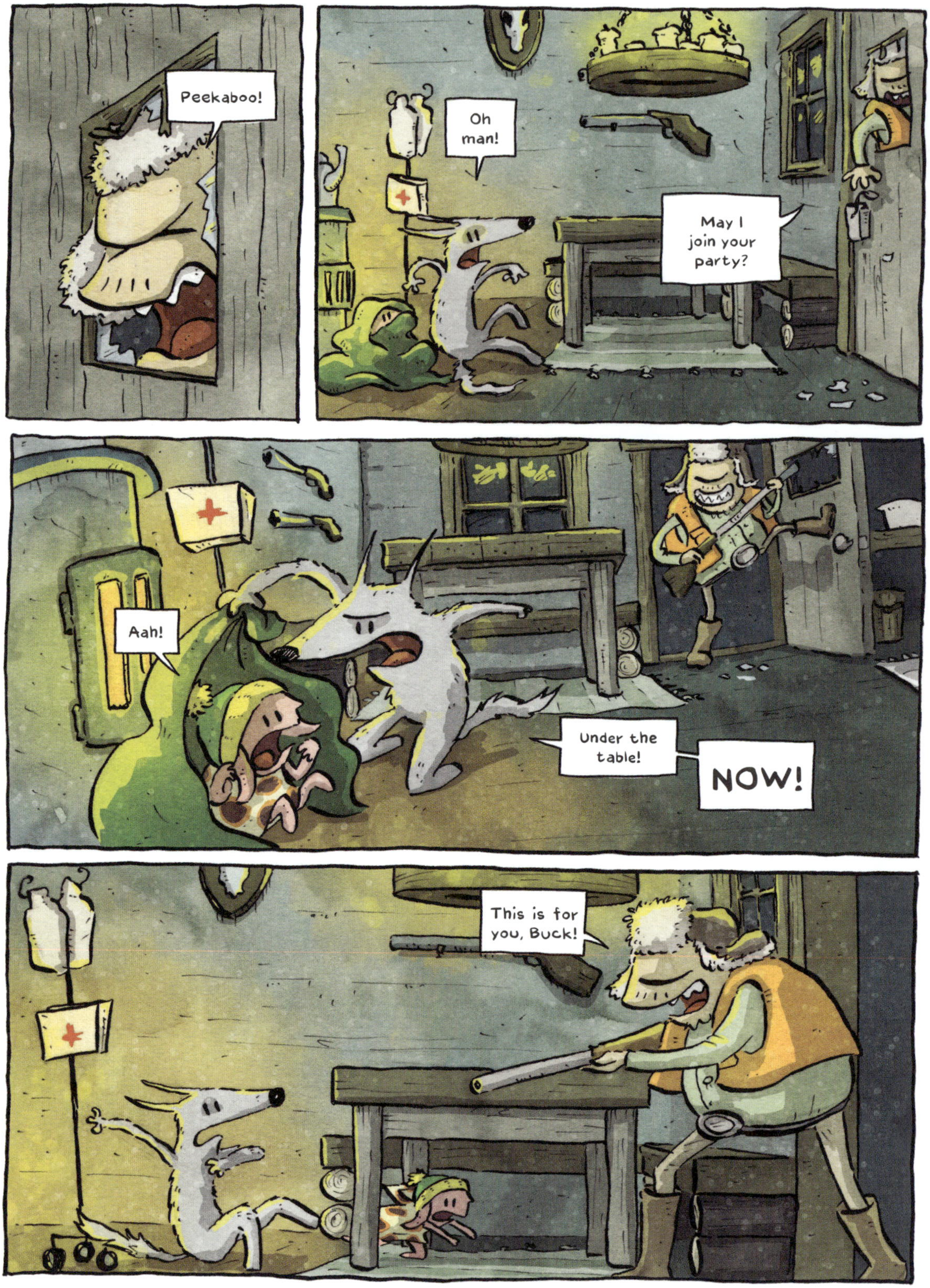
Peekaboo!
Oh man!
May I join your party?
Aah!
Under the table!
NOW!
This is for you, Buck!

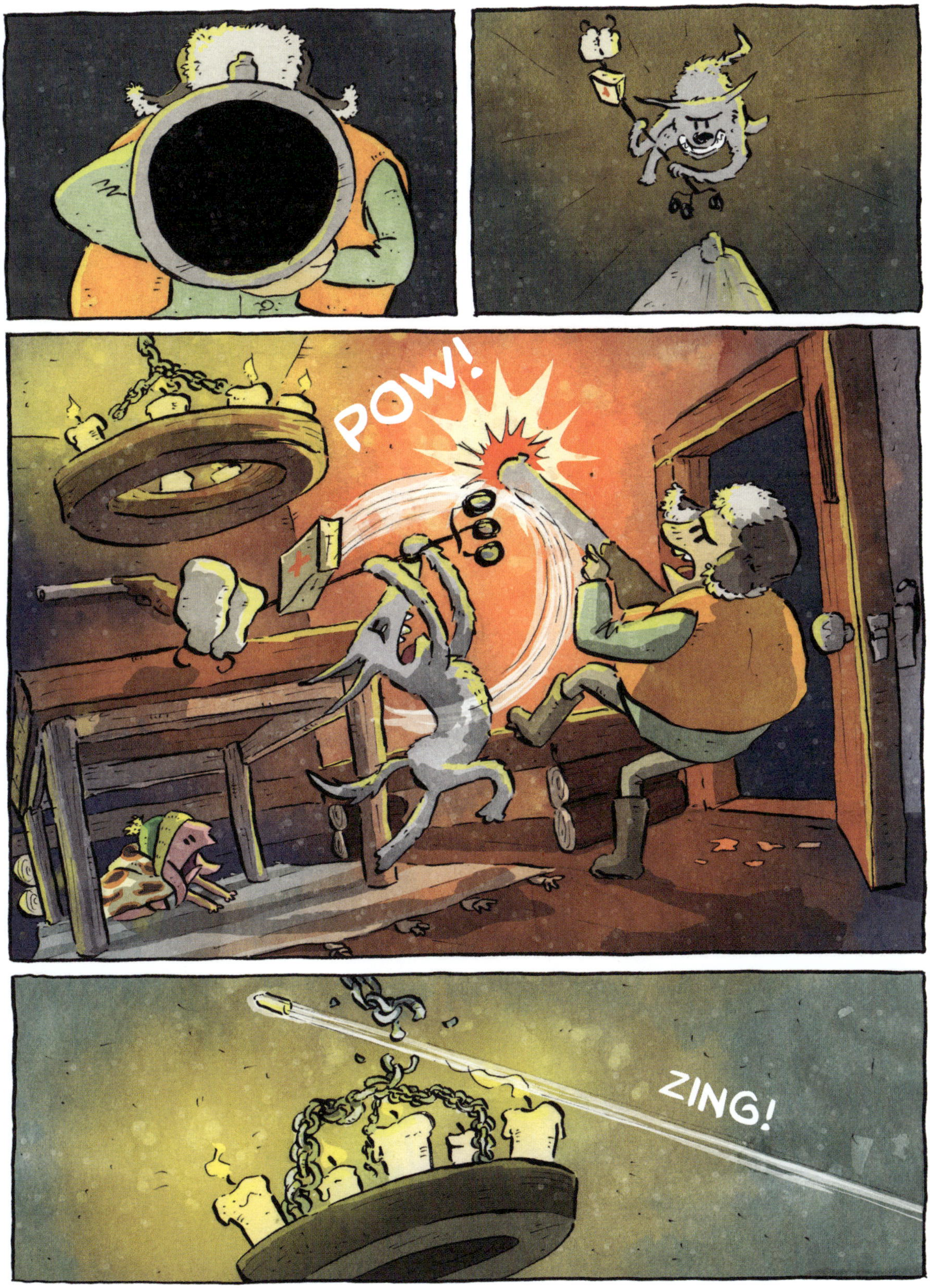
POW!
ZING!

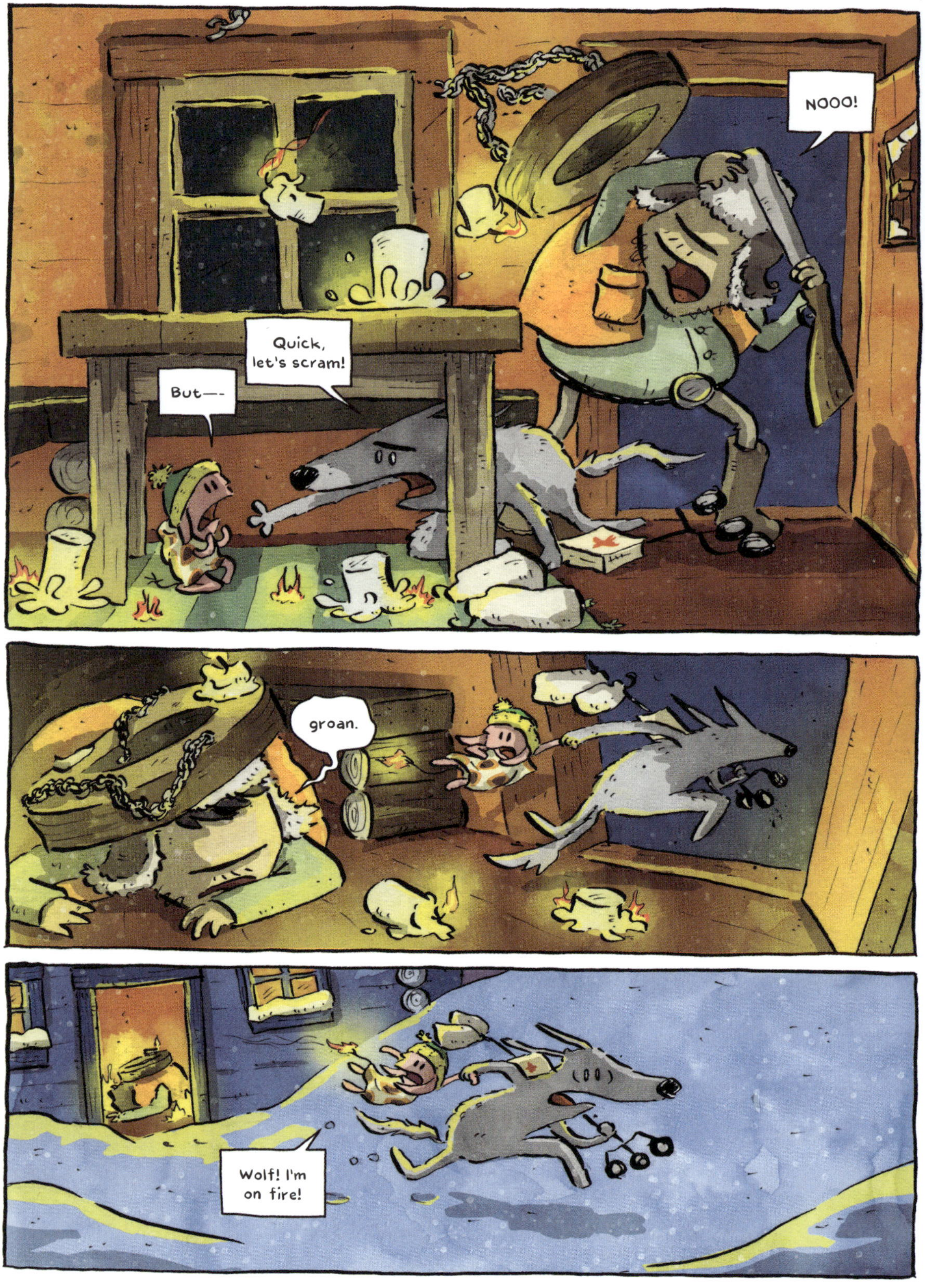
NOOO!
Quick, let's scram!
But—-
groan.
Wolf! I'm on fire!

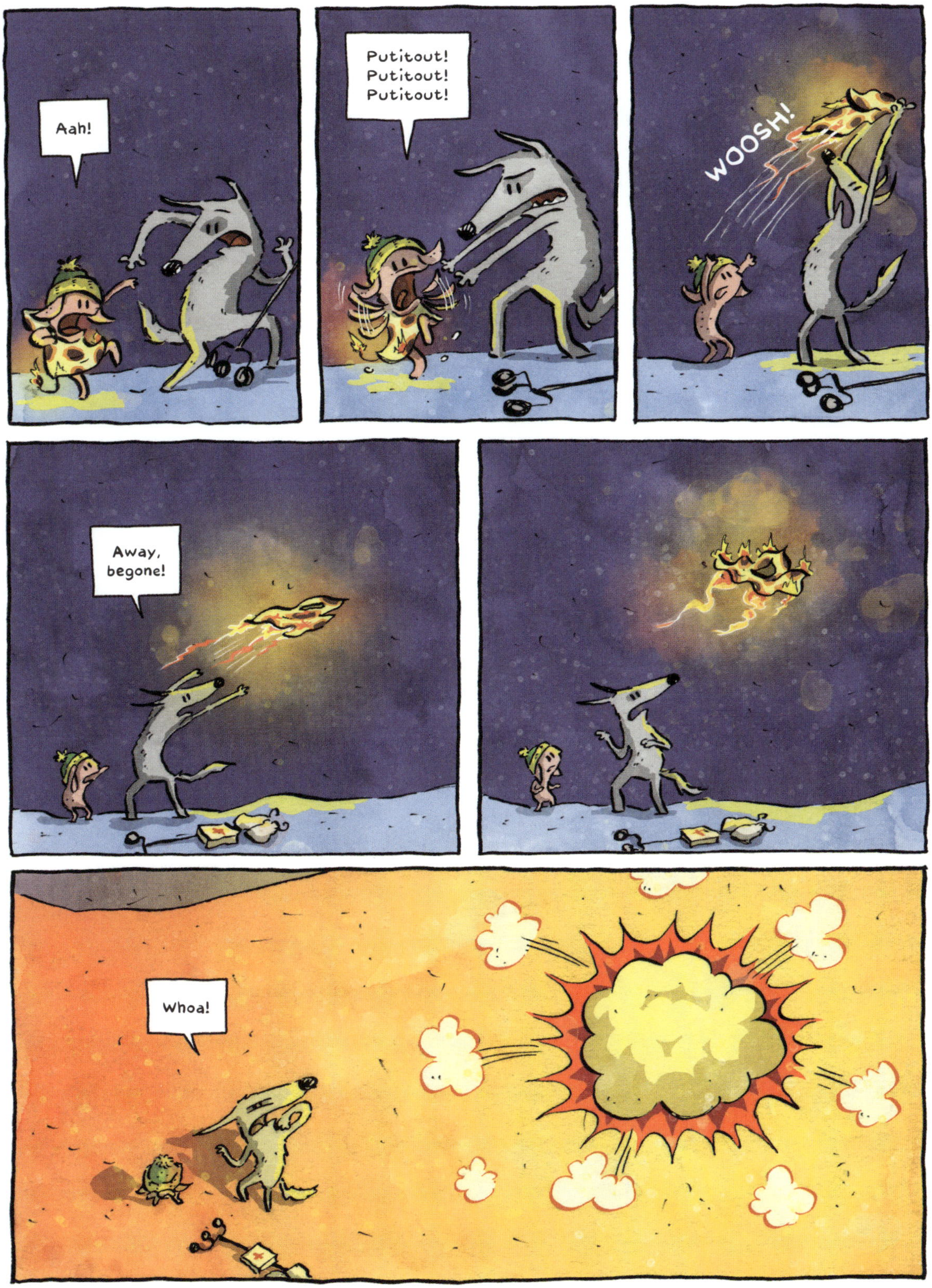
Aah!
Putitout!
Putitout!
Putitout!
WOOSH!
Away,
begone!
Whoa!

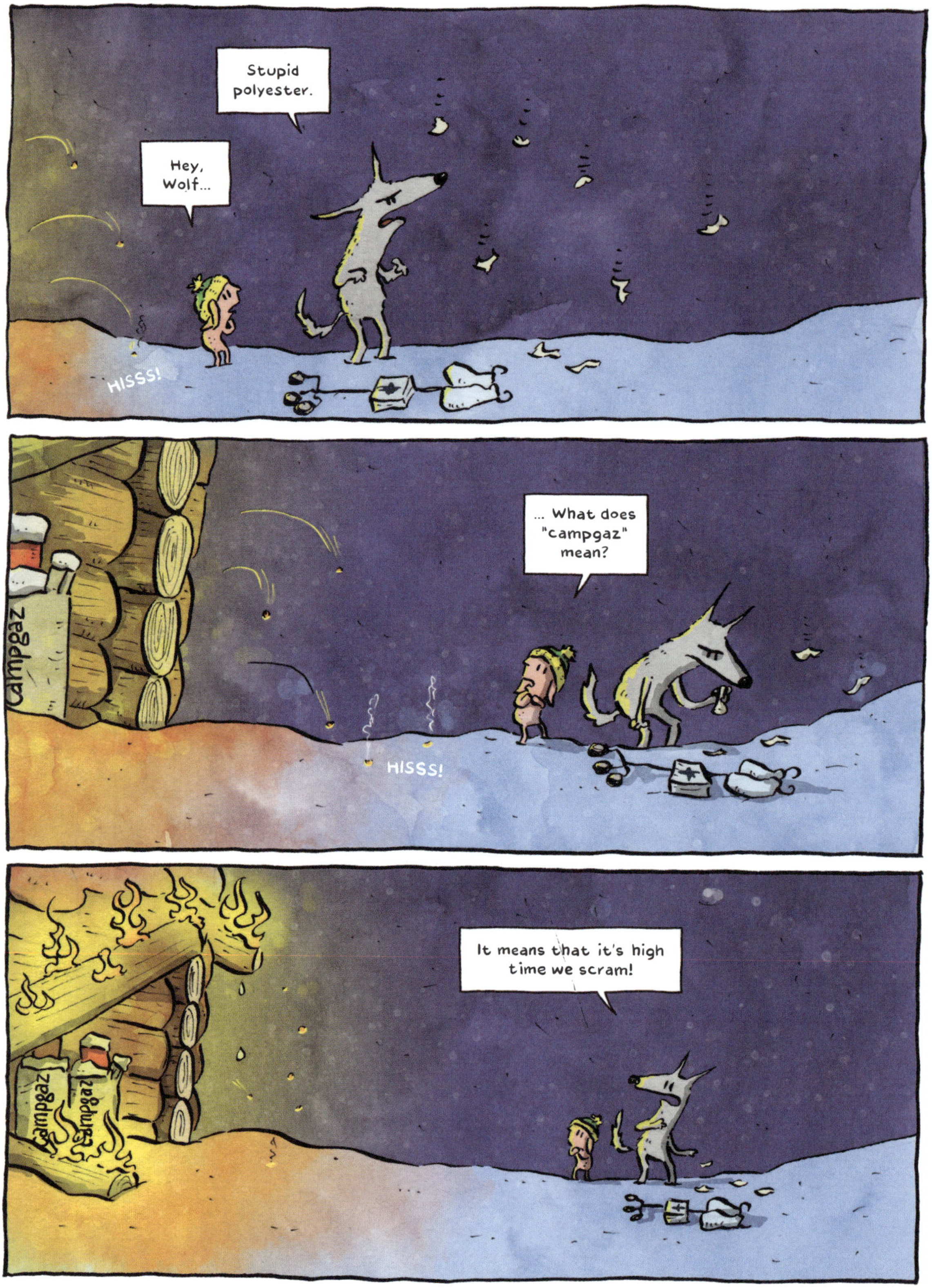
Stupid polyester.
Hey, Wolf...
HISSS!
Campgaz
... What does "campgaz" mean?
HISSS!
Campgaz
Campgaz
It means that it's high time we scram!

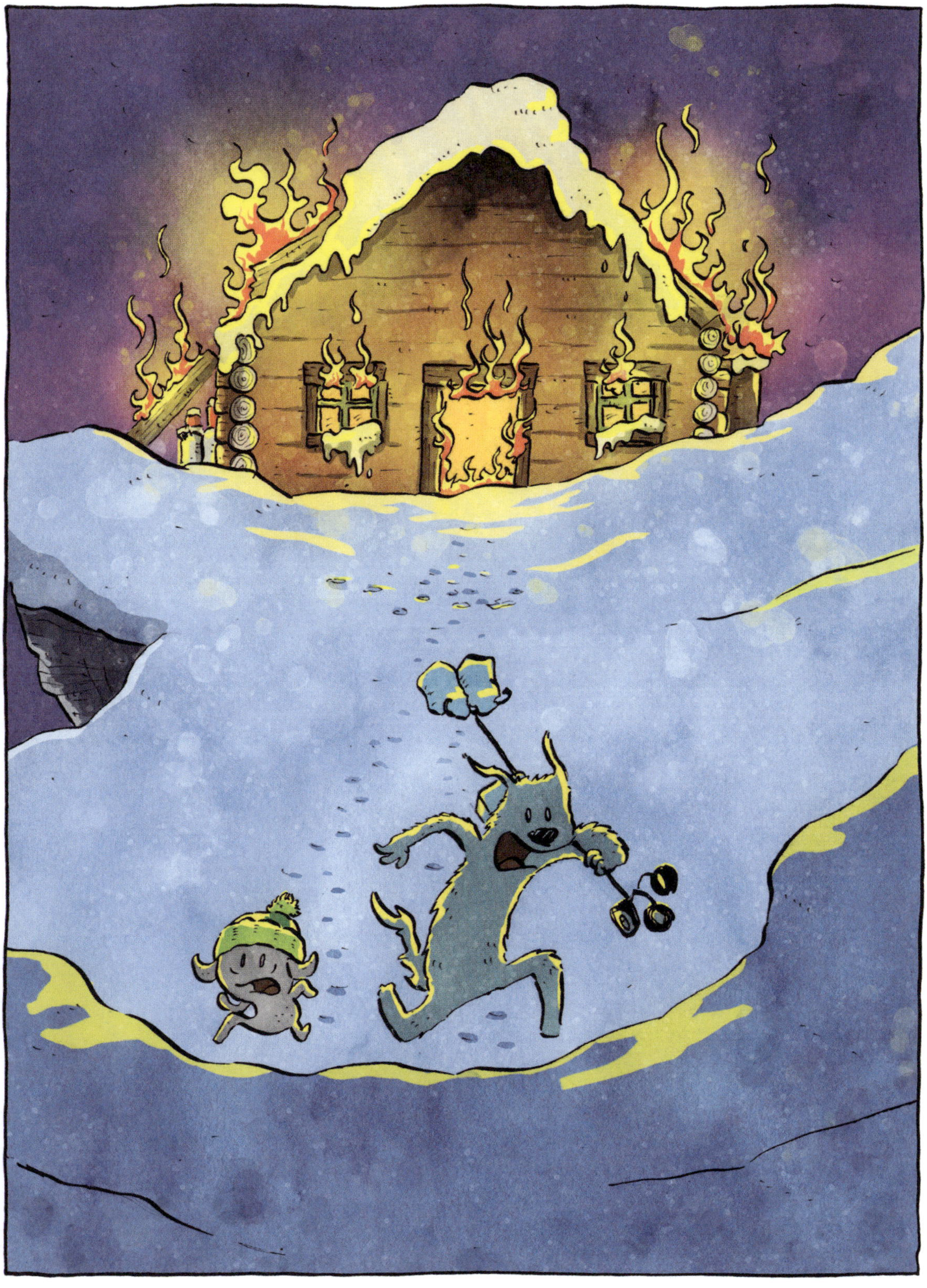

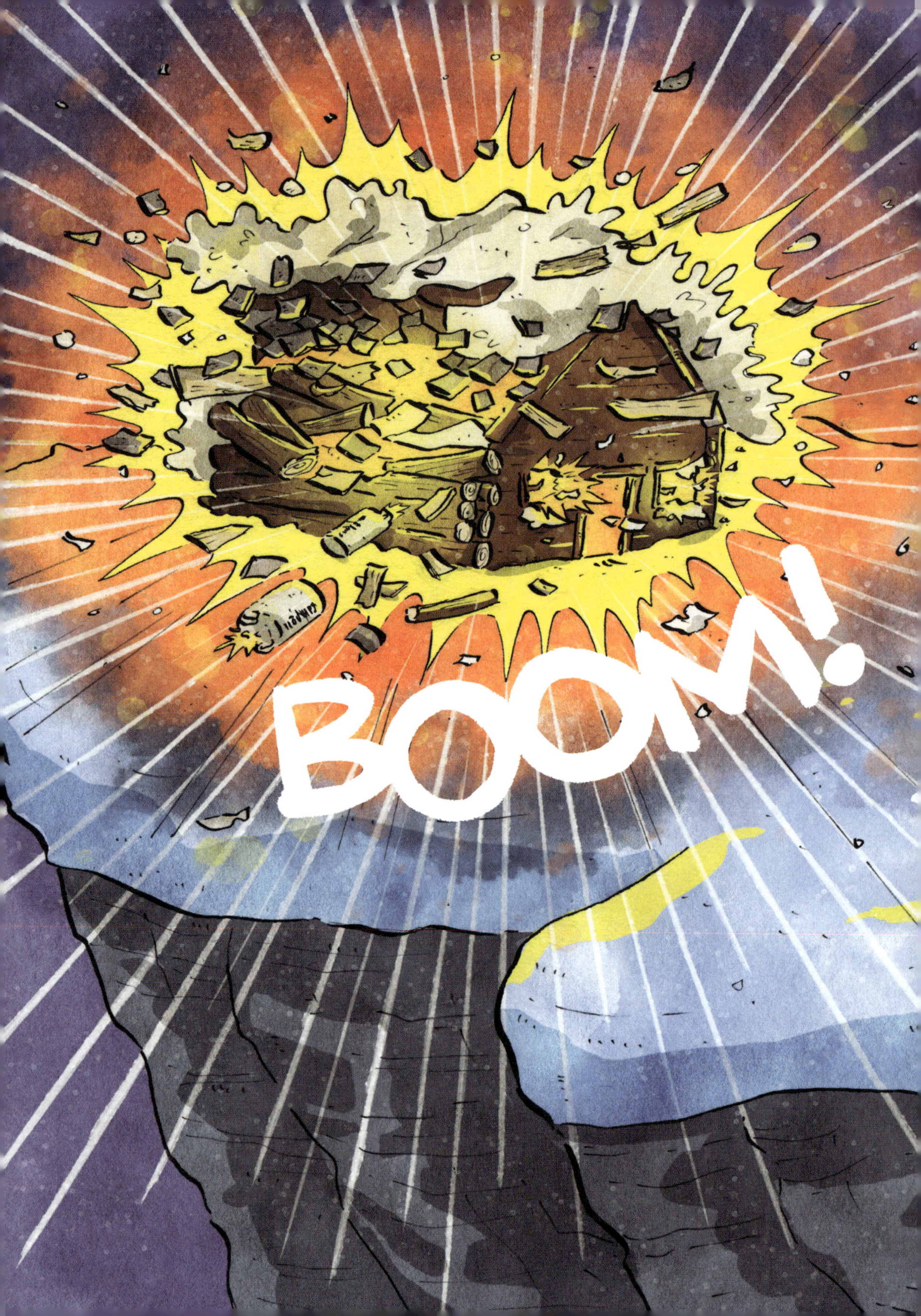
BOOM!

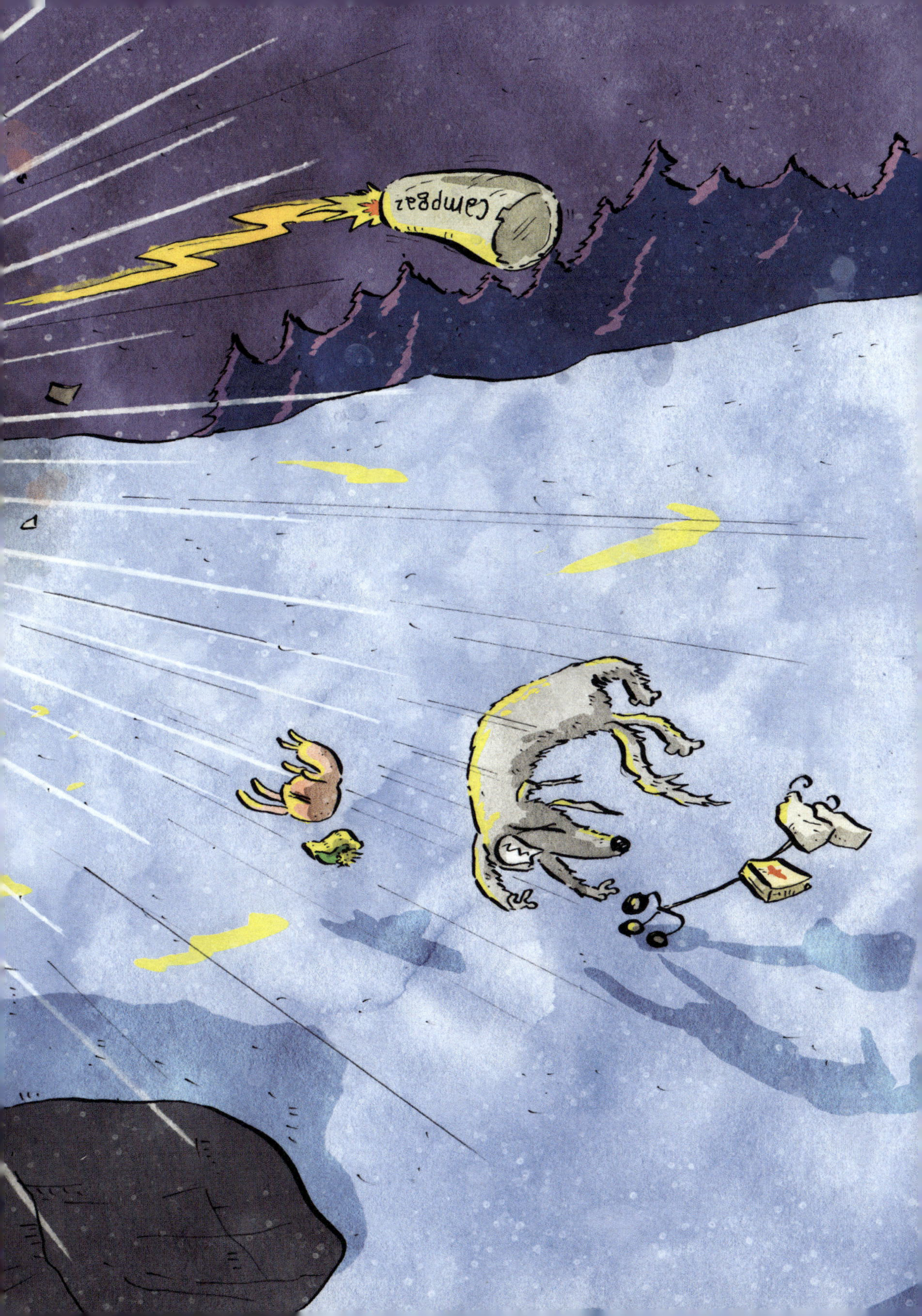
Campgaz

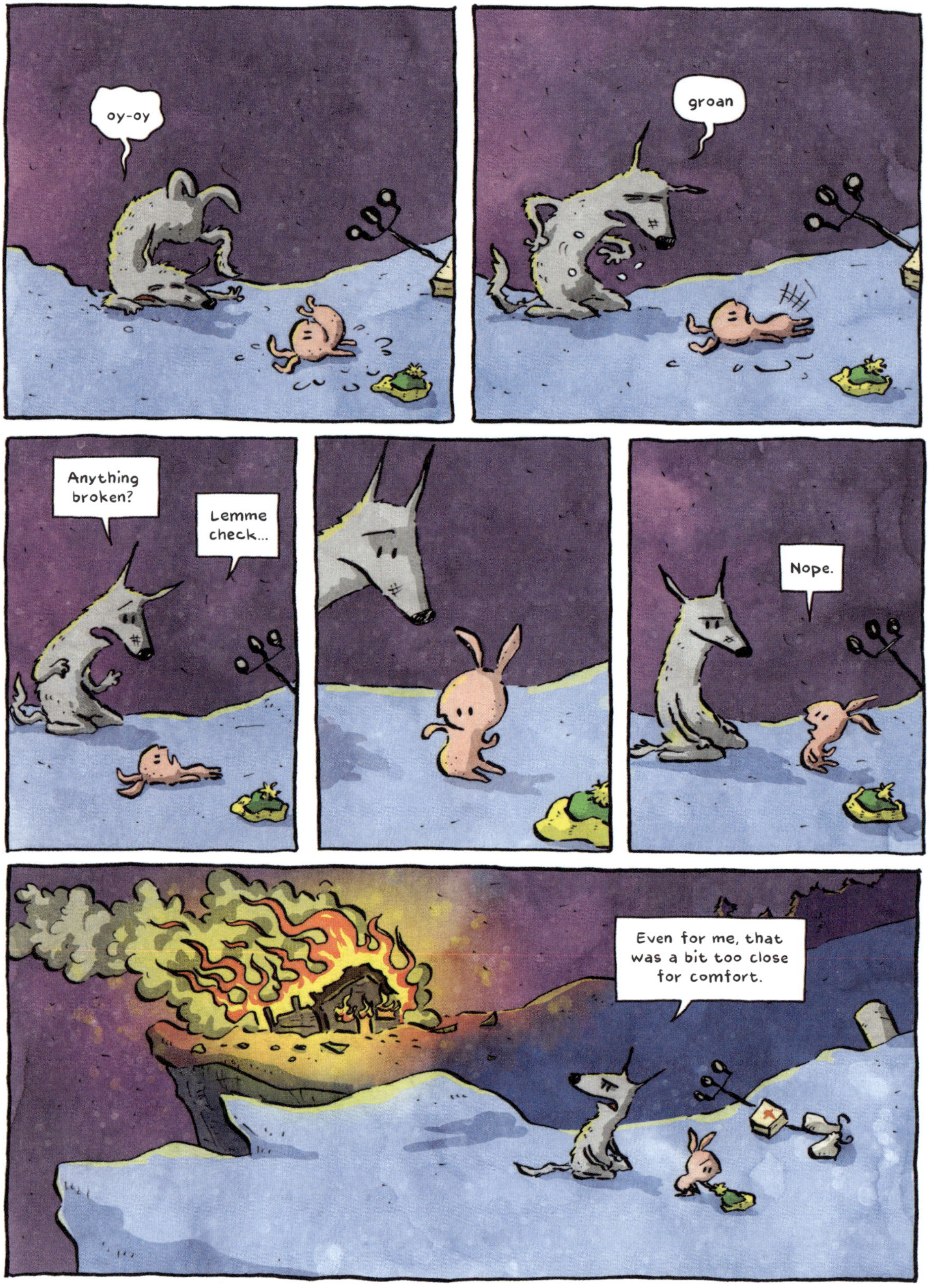
oy-oy
groan
Anything broken?
Lemme check...
Nope.
Even for me, that was a bit too close for comfort.

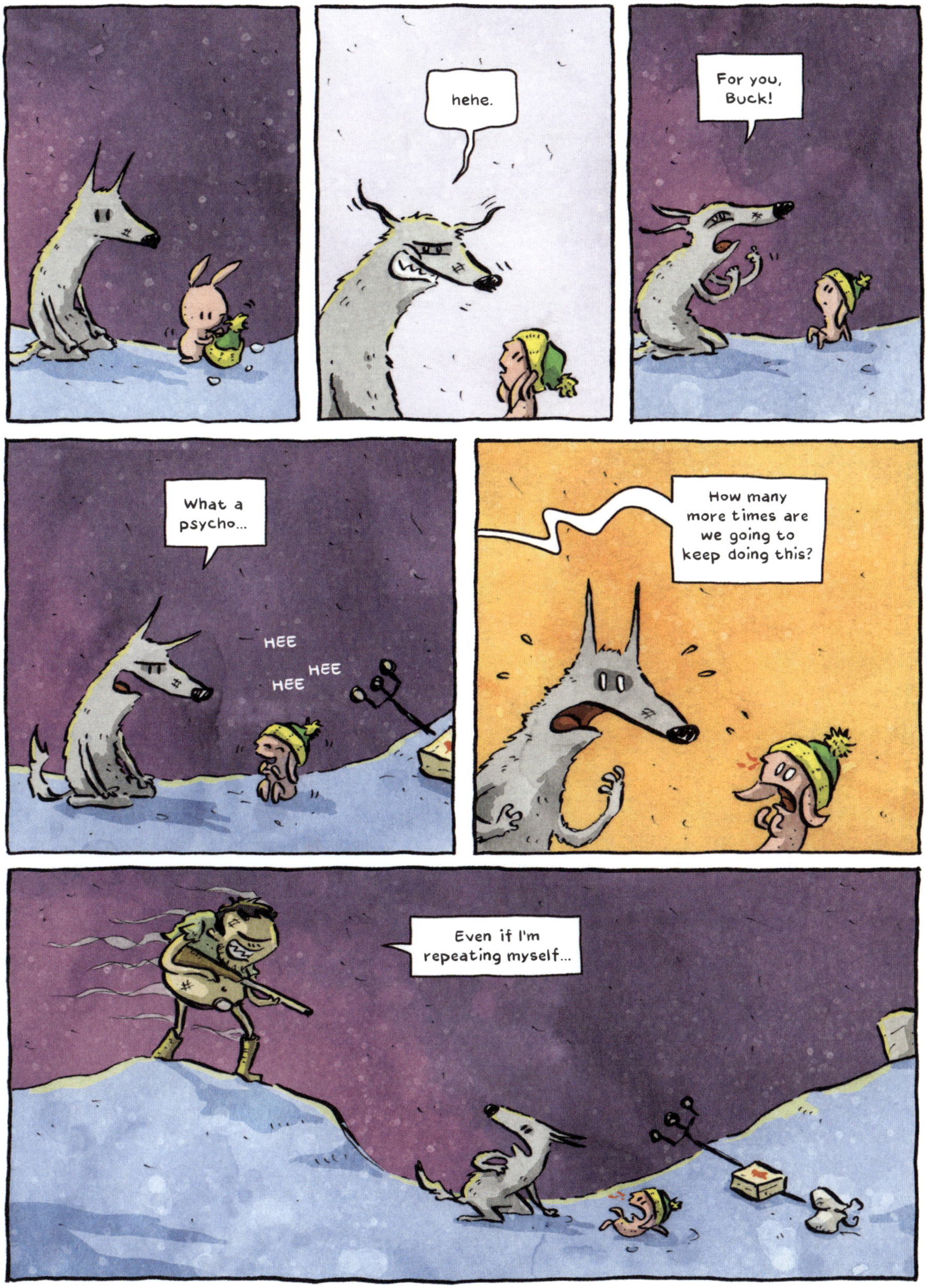
hehe.
For you, Buck!
What a psycho...
HEE
HEE HEE
How many more times are we going to keep doing this?
Even if I'm repeating myself...

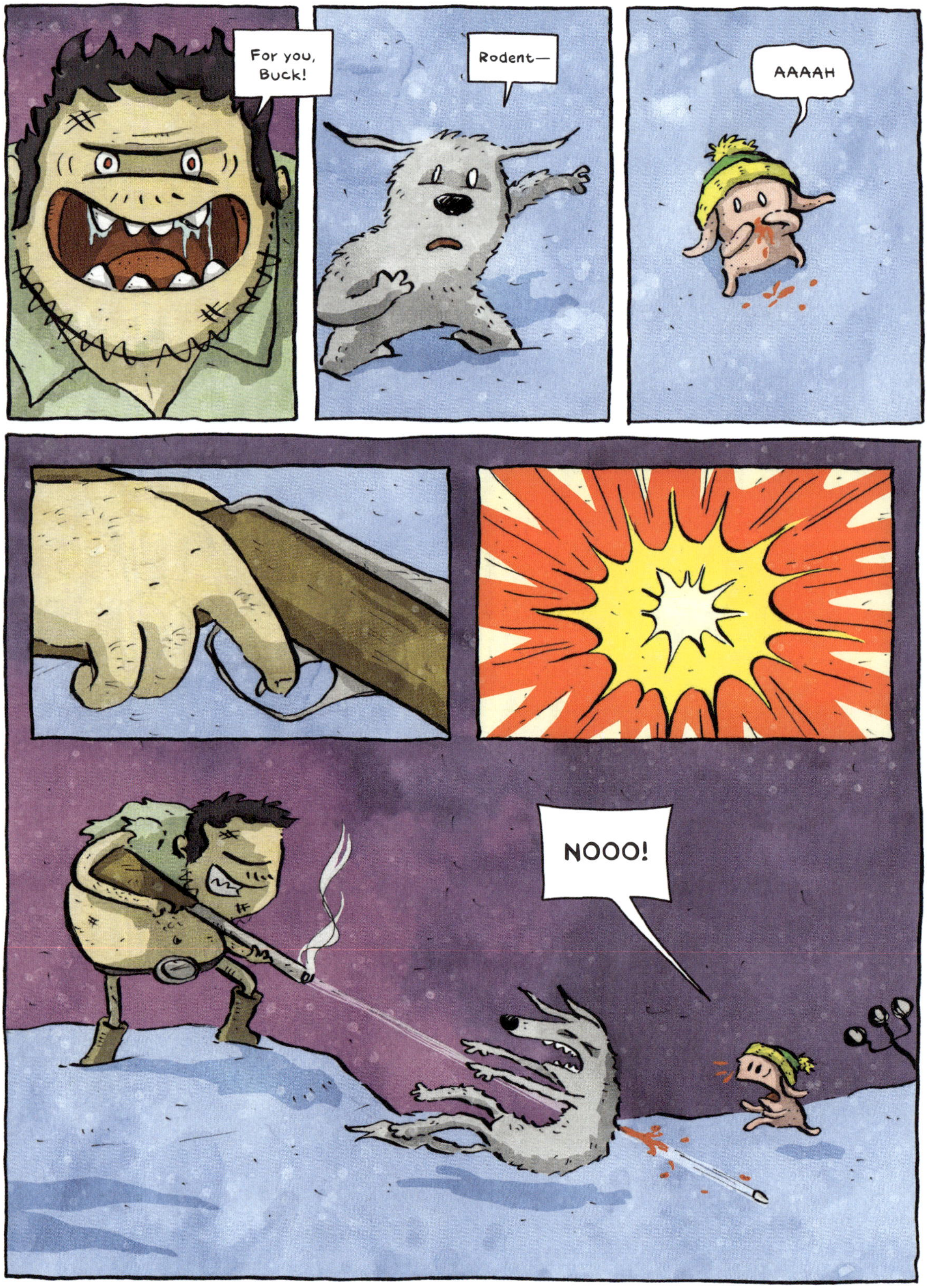

For you, Buck!
Rodent—
AAAAH
NOOO!

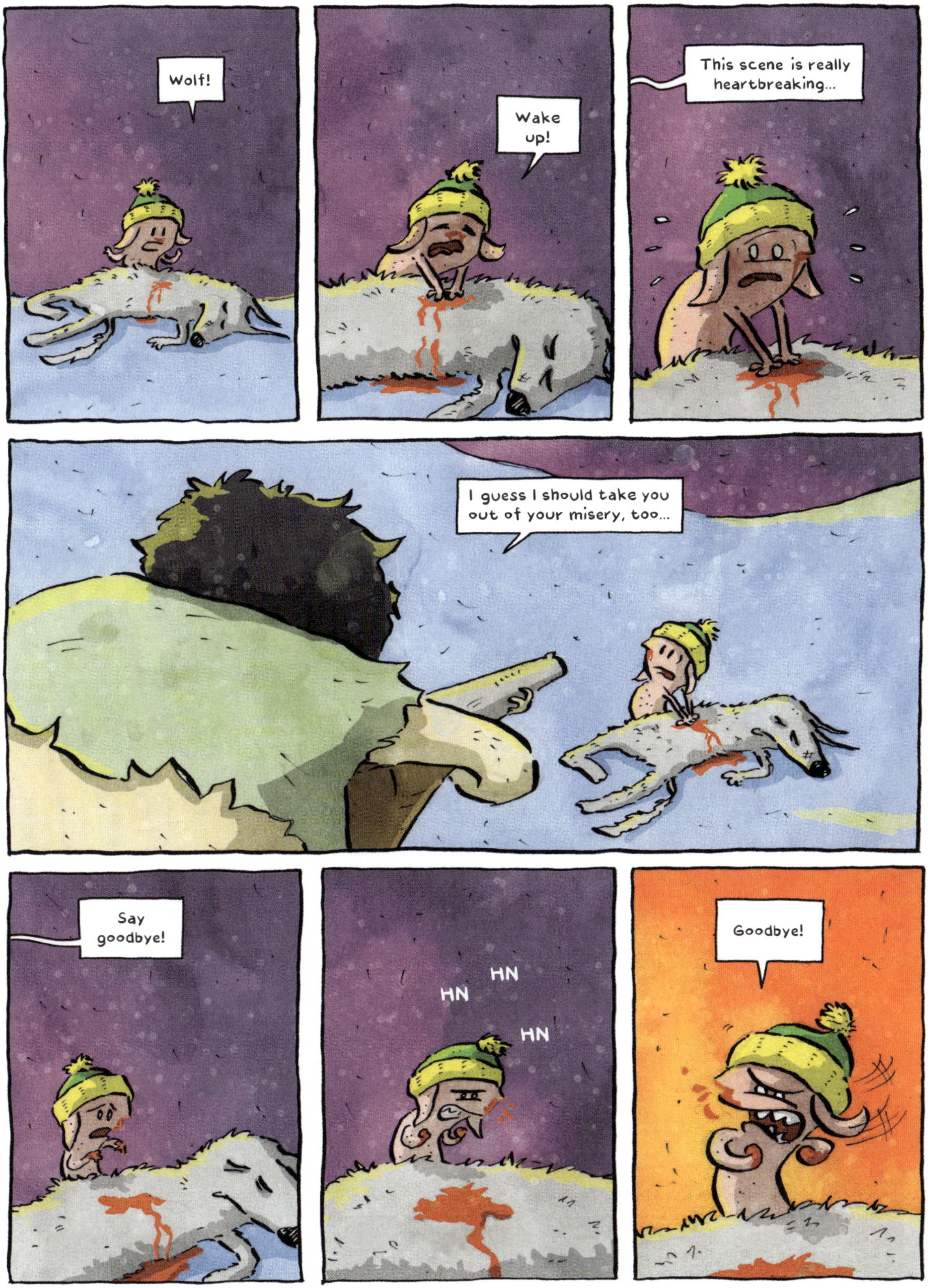
Wolf!
Wake up!
This scene is really heartbreaking...
I guess I should take you out of your misery, too...
Say goodbye!
HN
HN
HN
Goodbye!

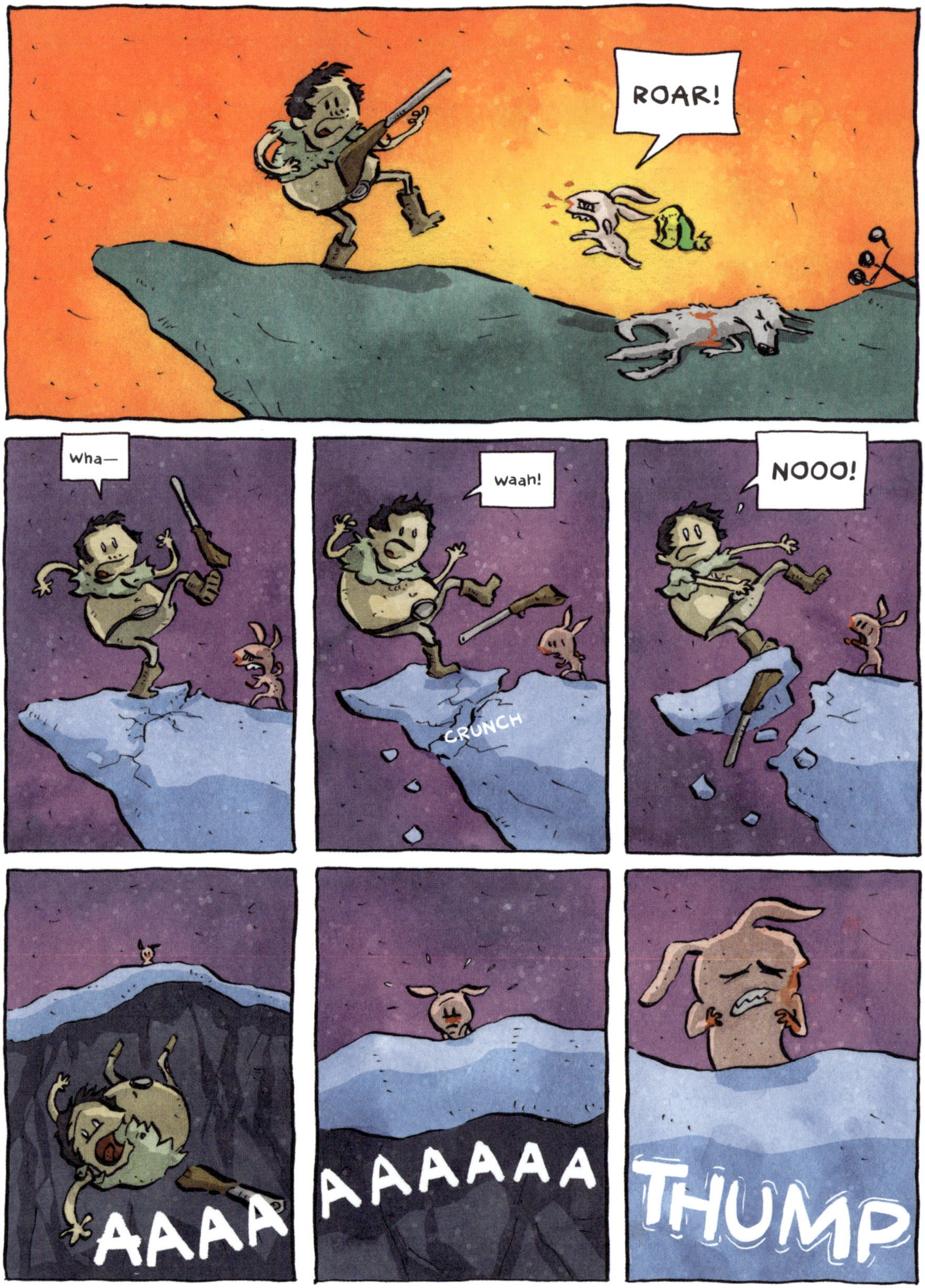
ROAR!
Wha—
Waah!
CRUNCH
NOOO!
AAAA
AAAAAA
THUMP

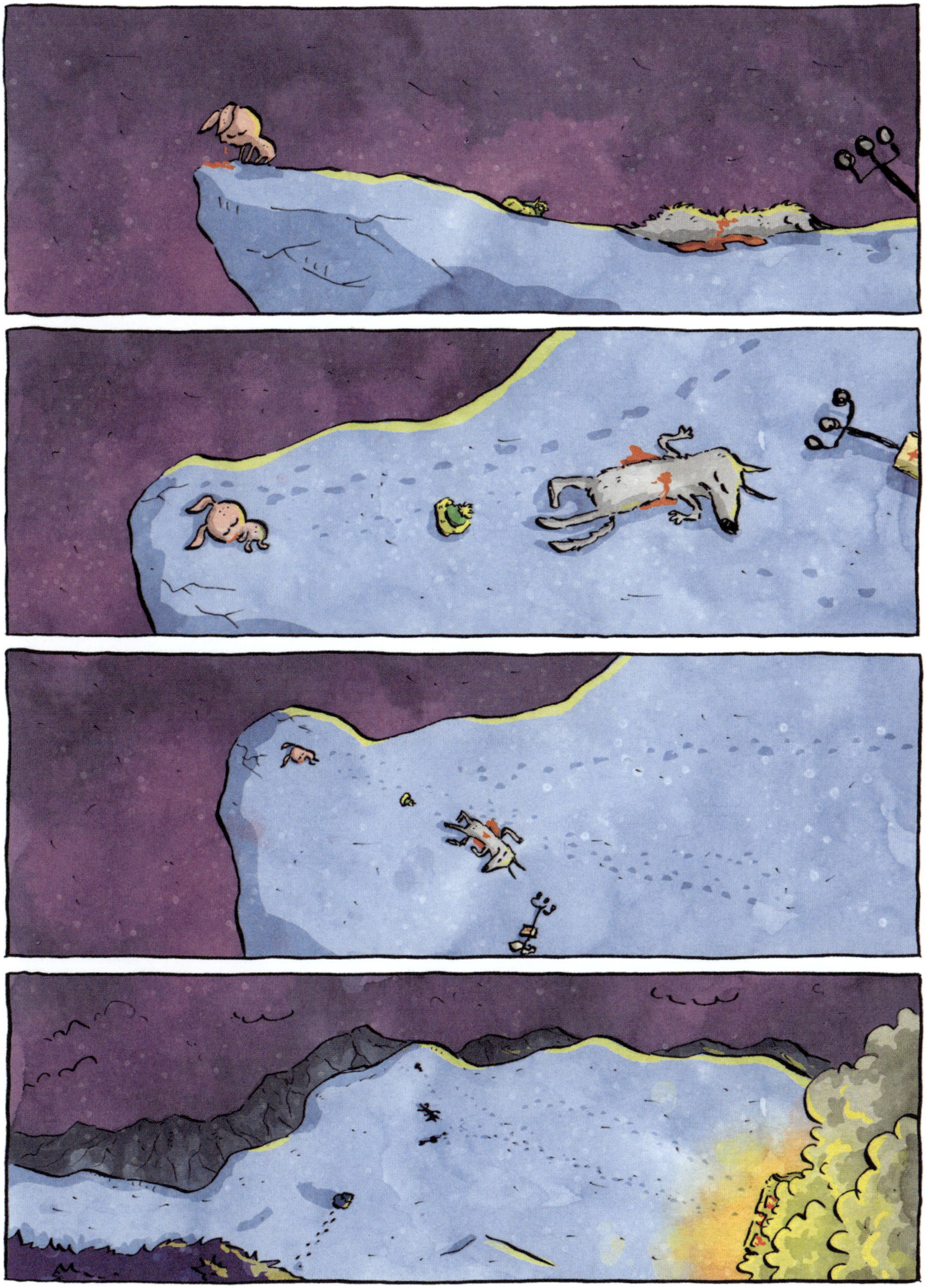

crunch
　　crunch
　　　　crunch

　　　　　　　crunch

　　　　　　　　　crunch

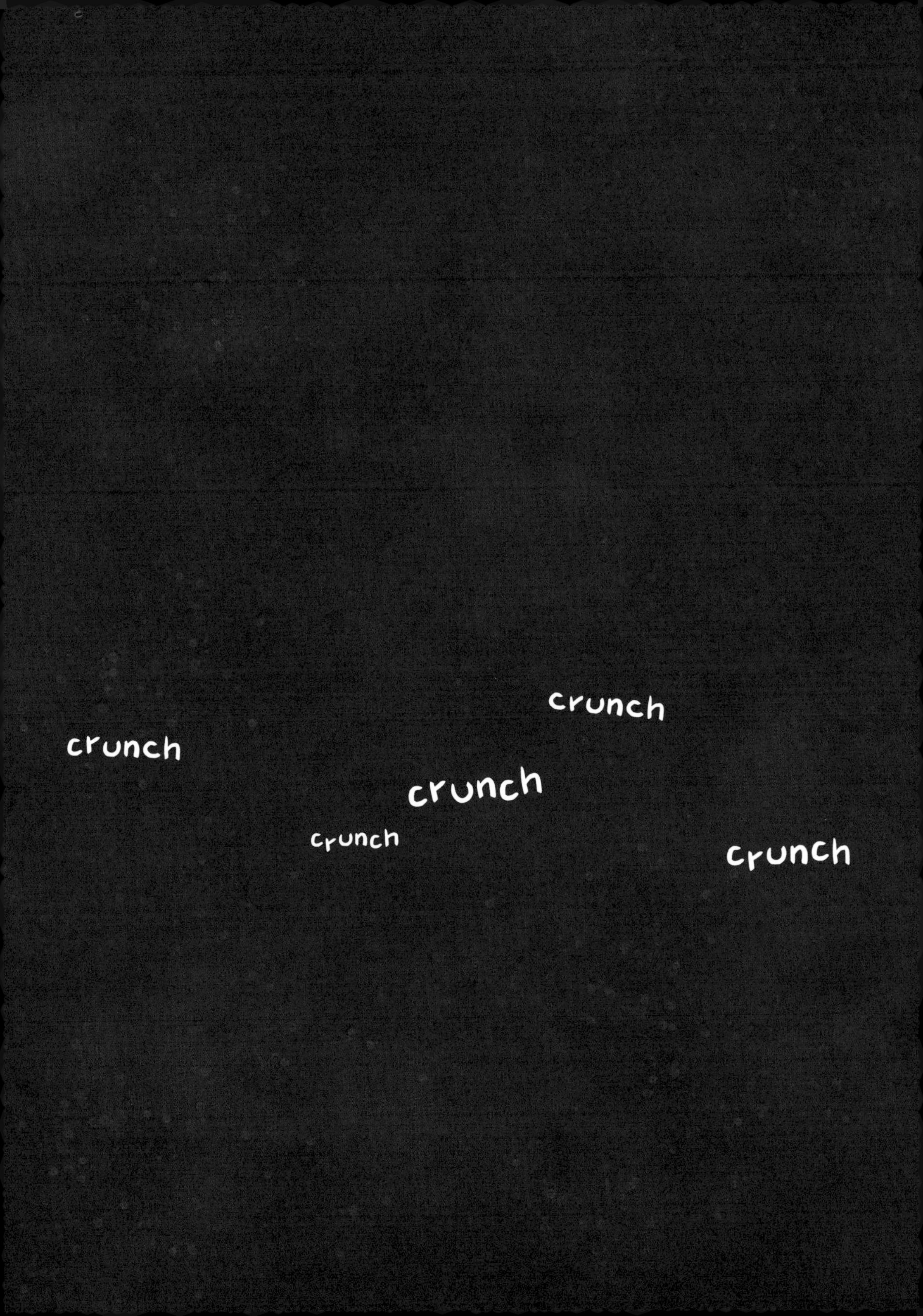
crunch
crunch
crunch
crunch
crunch

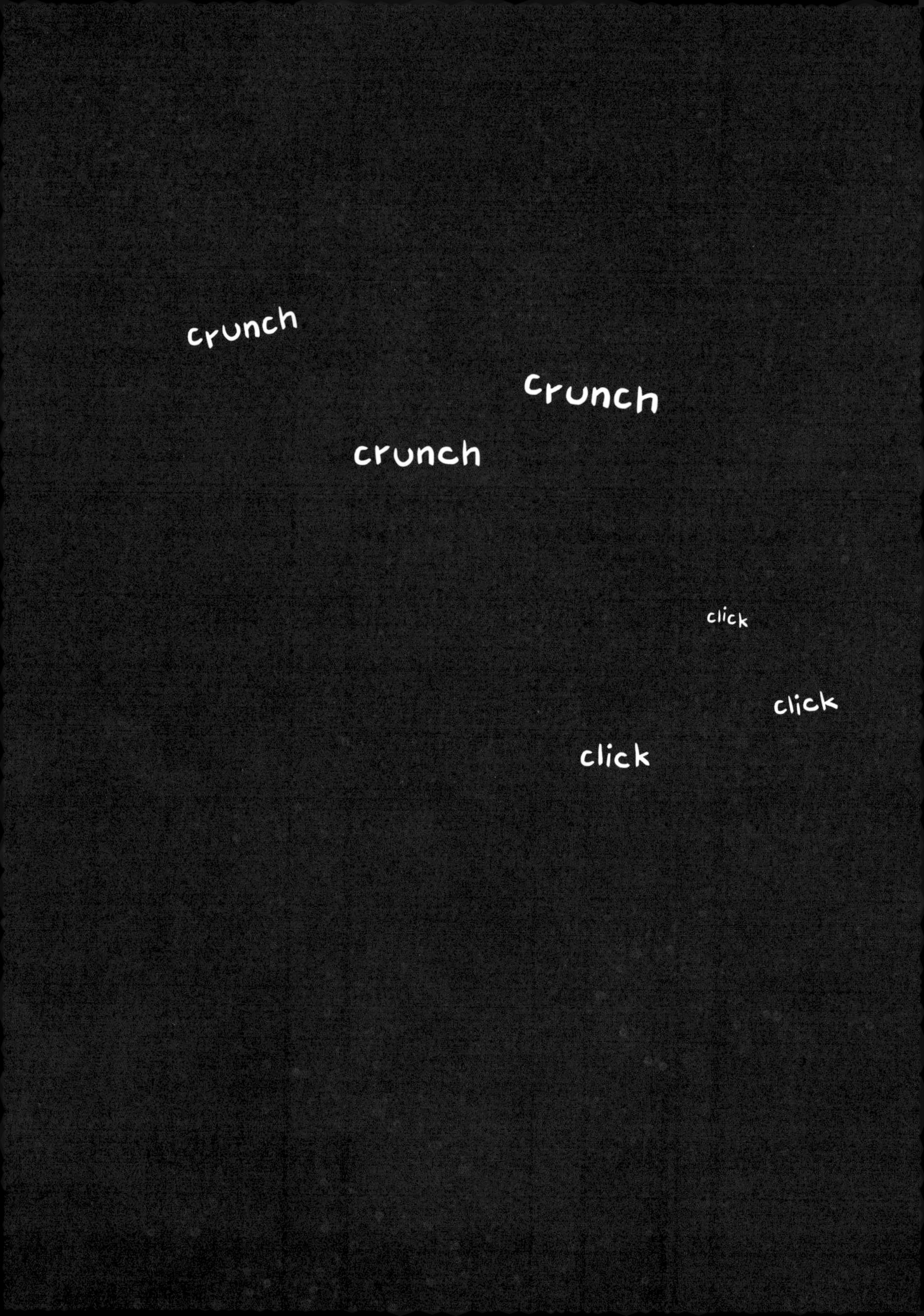
crunch
crunch
crunch
click
click
click

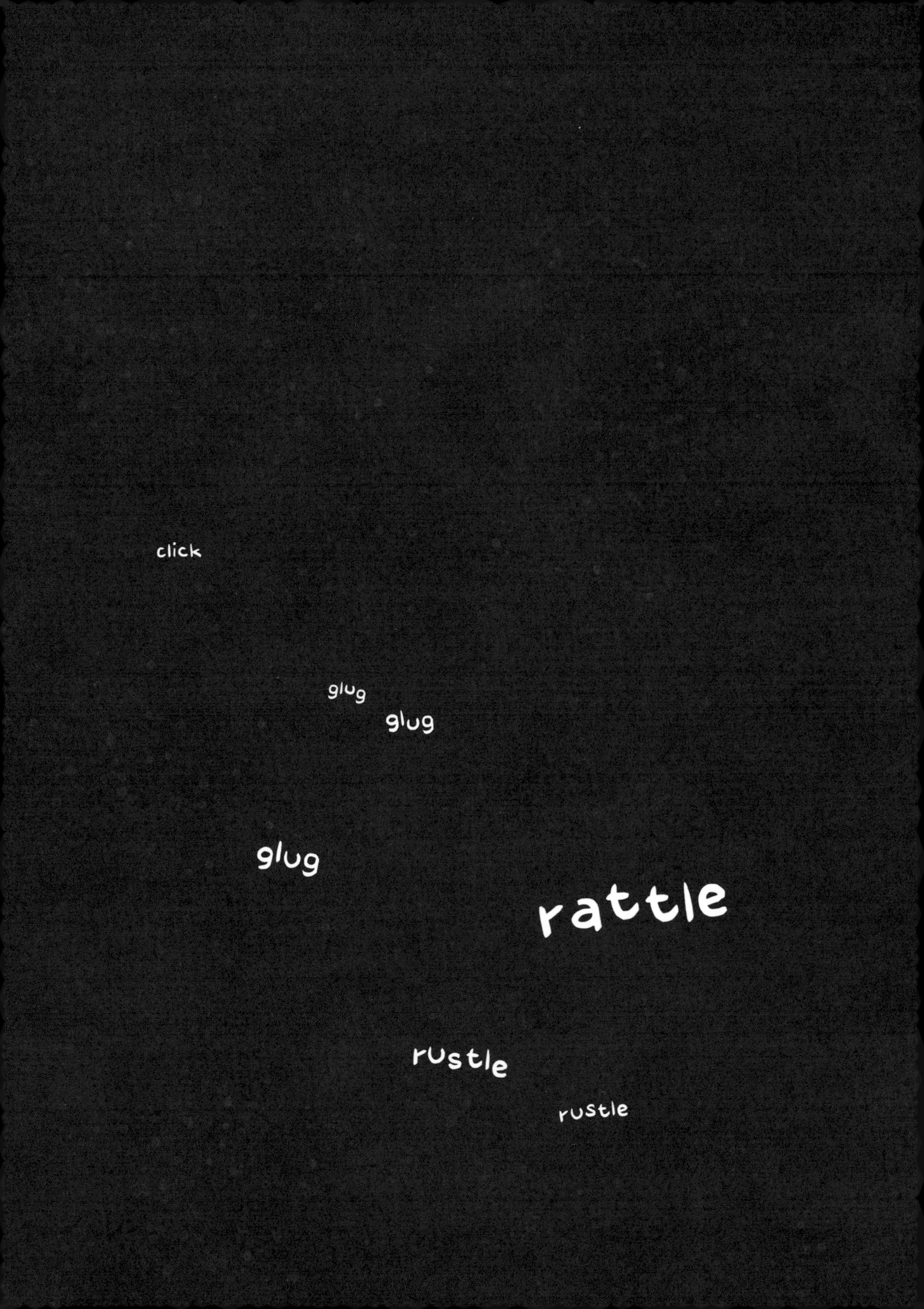
click
glug
glug
glug
rattle
rustle
rustle

Chapter 4

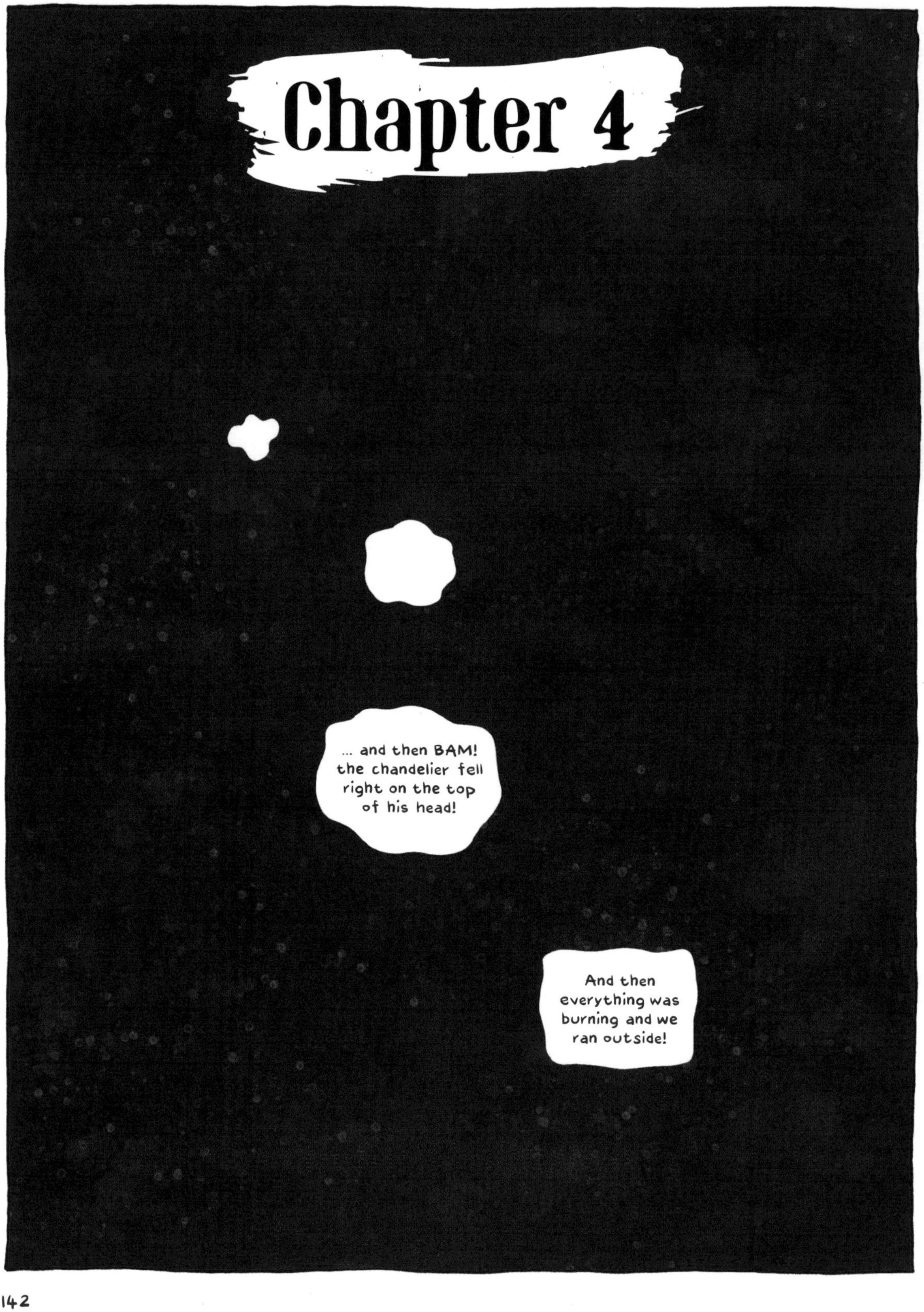
... and then BAM! the chandelier fell right on the top of his head!
And then everything was burning and we ran outside!

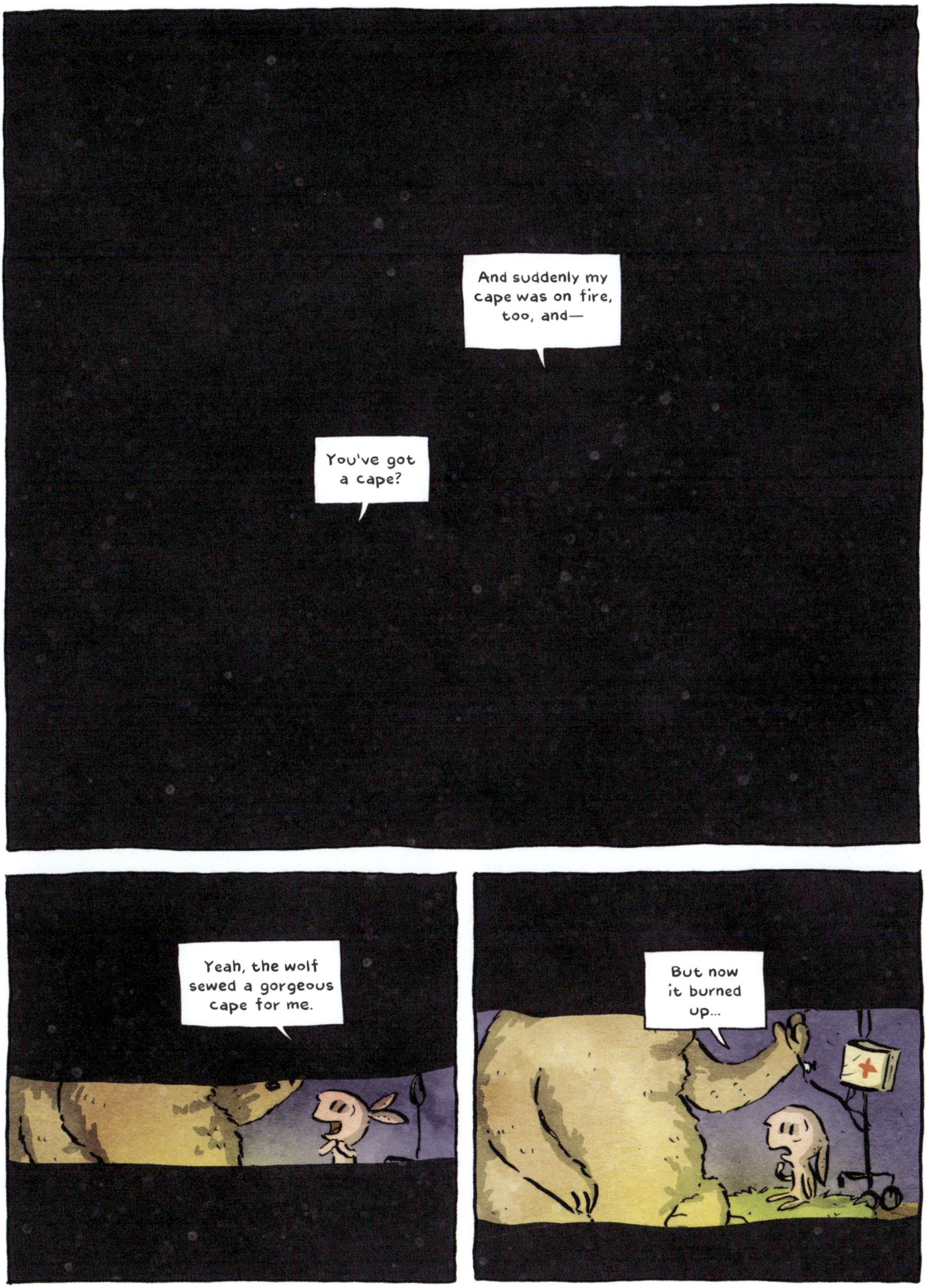
And suddenly my cape was on fire, too, and—
You've got a cape?
Yeah, the wolf sewed a gorgeous cape for me.
But now it burned up...

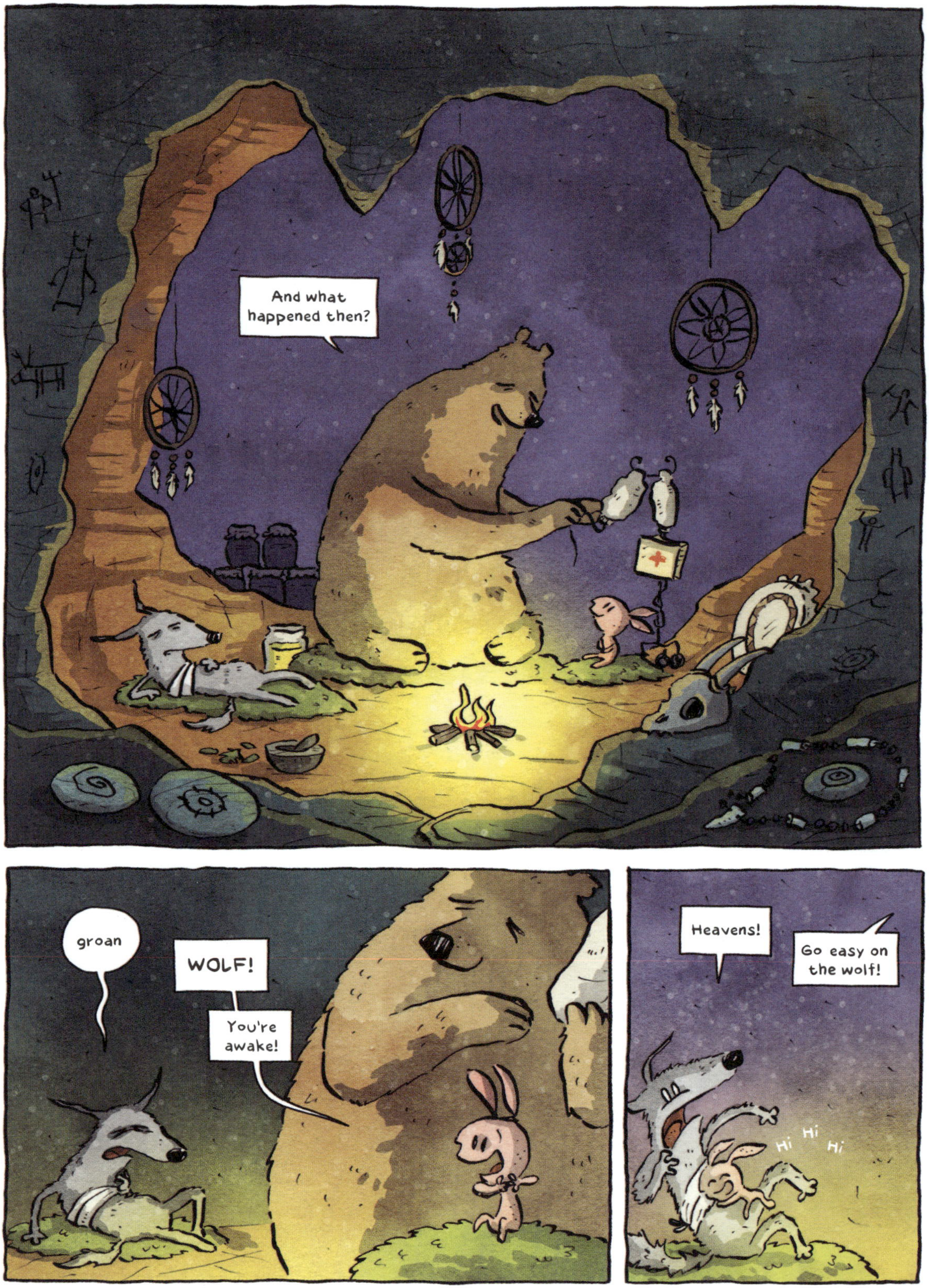
And what happened then?
groan
WOLF!
You're awake!
Heavens!
Go easy on the wolf!
Hi Hi Hi

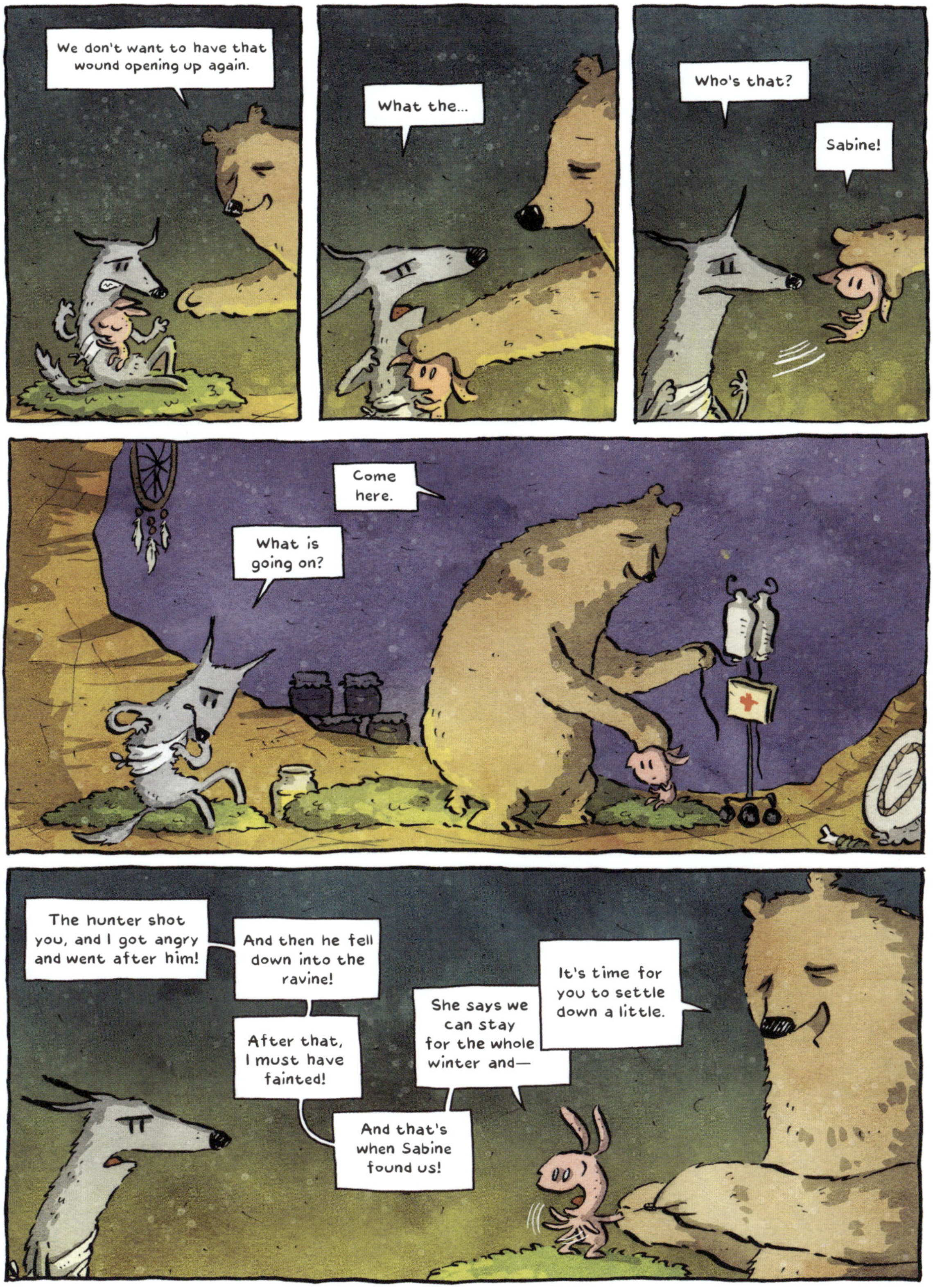
We don't want to have that wound opening up again.
What the...
Who's that?
Sabine!
What is going on?
Come here.
The hunter shot you, and I got angry and went after him!
And then he fell down into the ravine!
After that, I must have fainted!
And that's when Sabine found us!
She says we can stay for the whole winter and—
It's time for you to settle down a little.

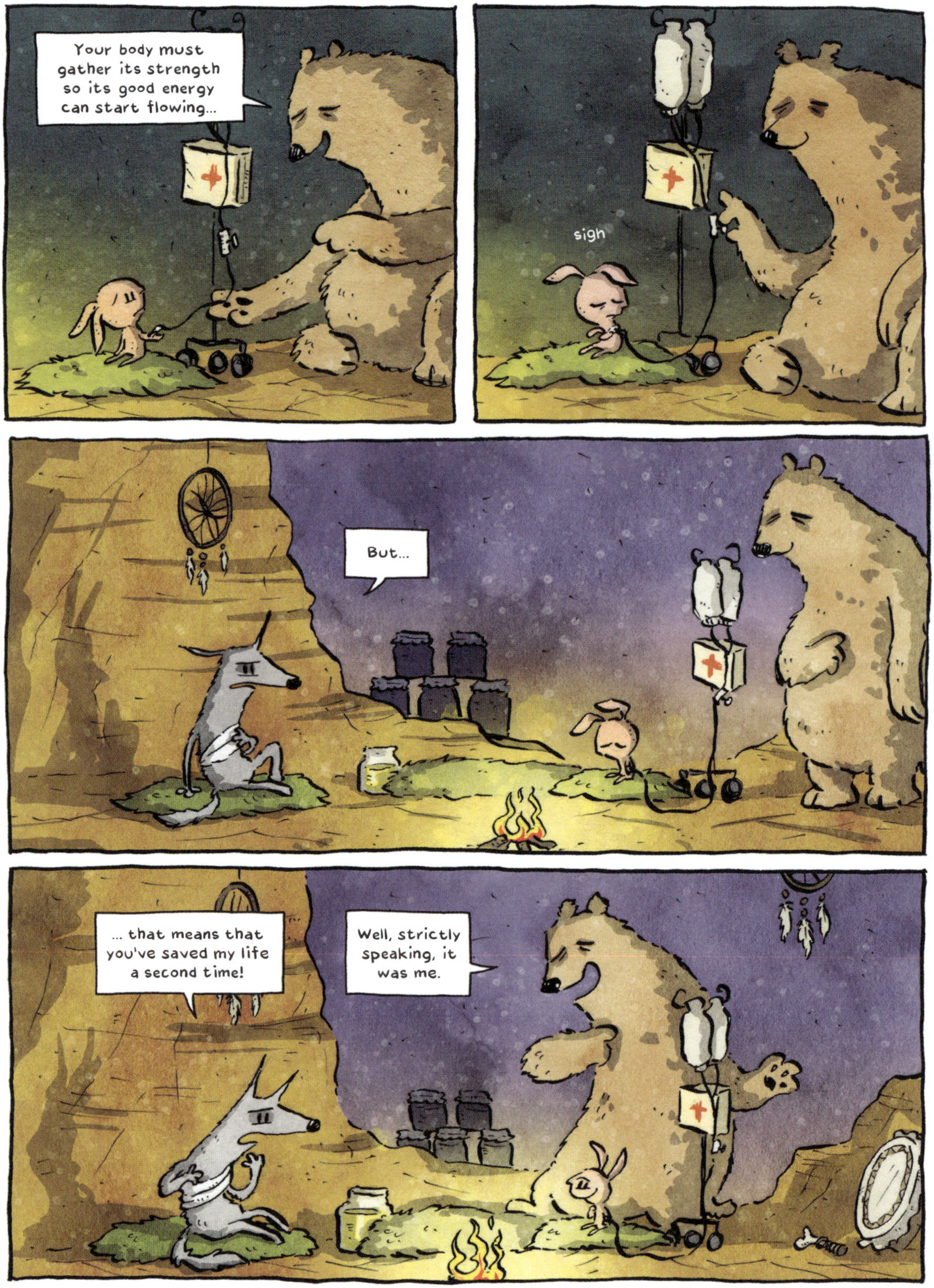
Your body must gather its strength so its good energy can start flowing...
sigh
But...
... that means that you've saved my life a second time!
Well, strictly speaking, it was me.

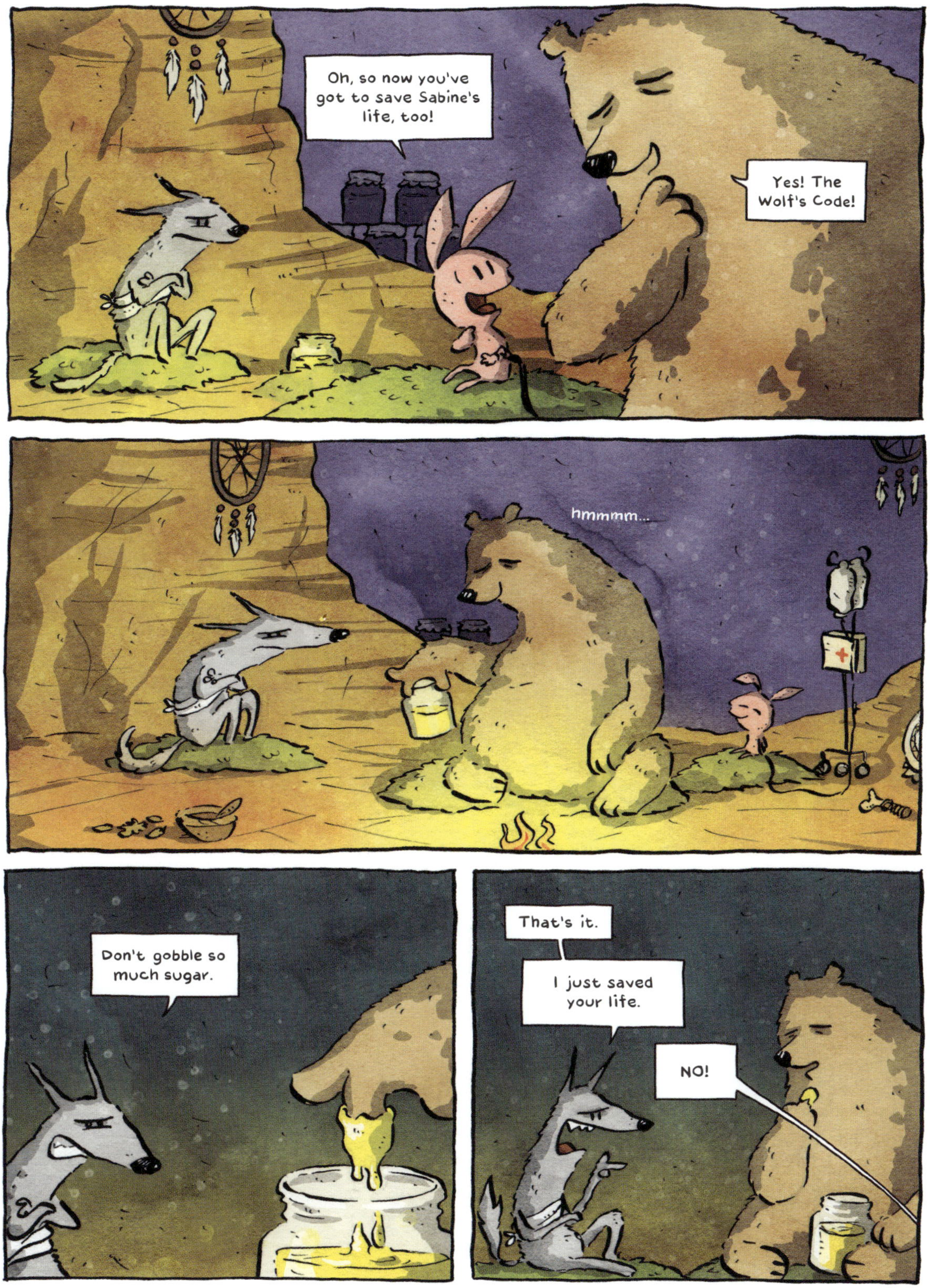
Oh, so now you've got to save Sabine's life, too!
Yes! The Wolf's Code!
hmmmm...
Don't gobble so much sugar.
That's it.
I just saved your life.
NO!

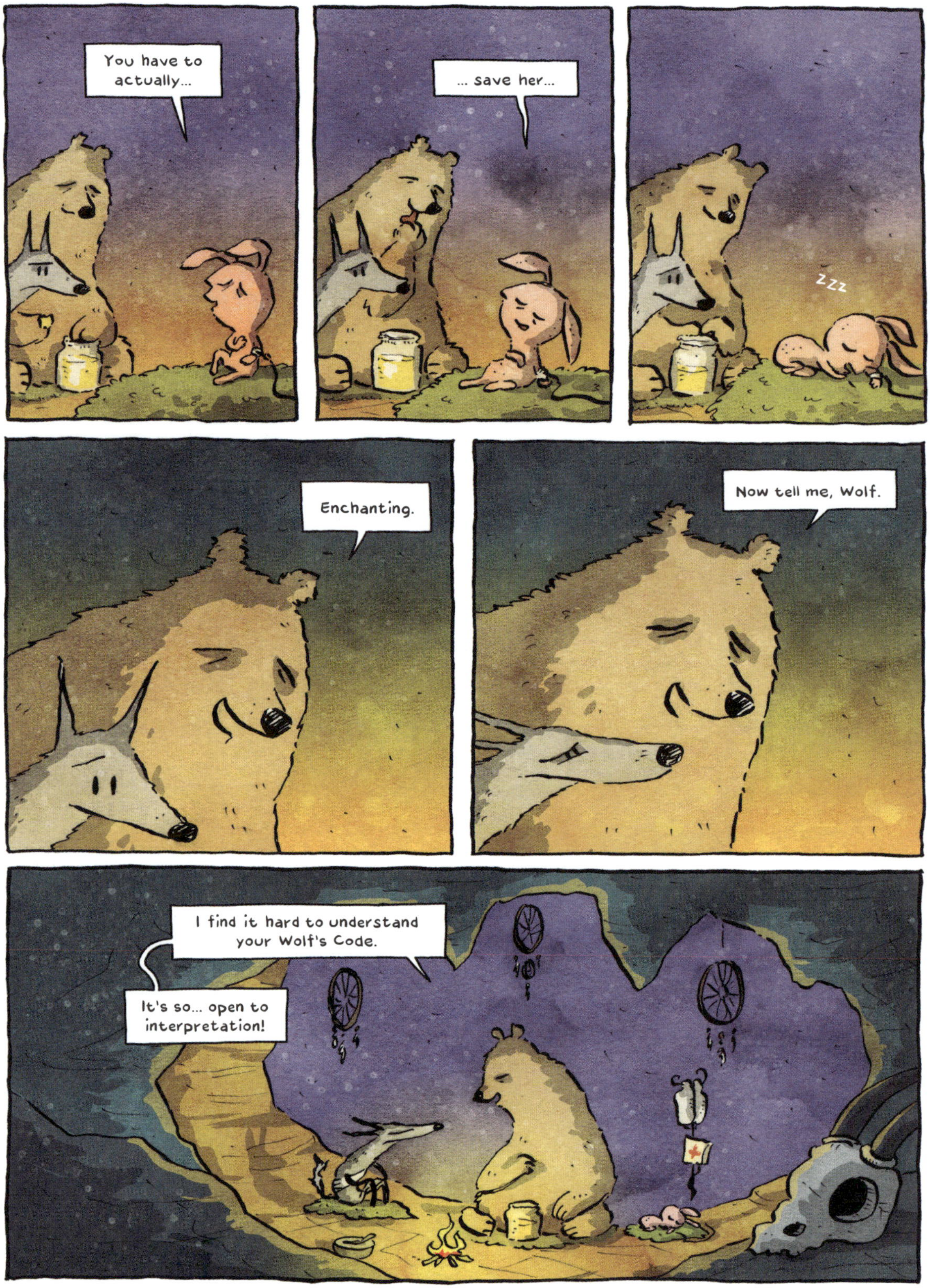
You have to actually...
... save her...
ZZZ
Enchanting.
Now tell me, Wolf.
I find it hard to understand your Wolf's Code.
It's so... open to interpretation!

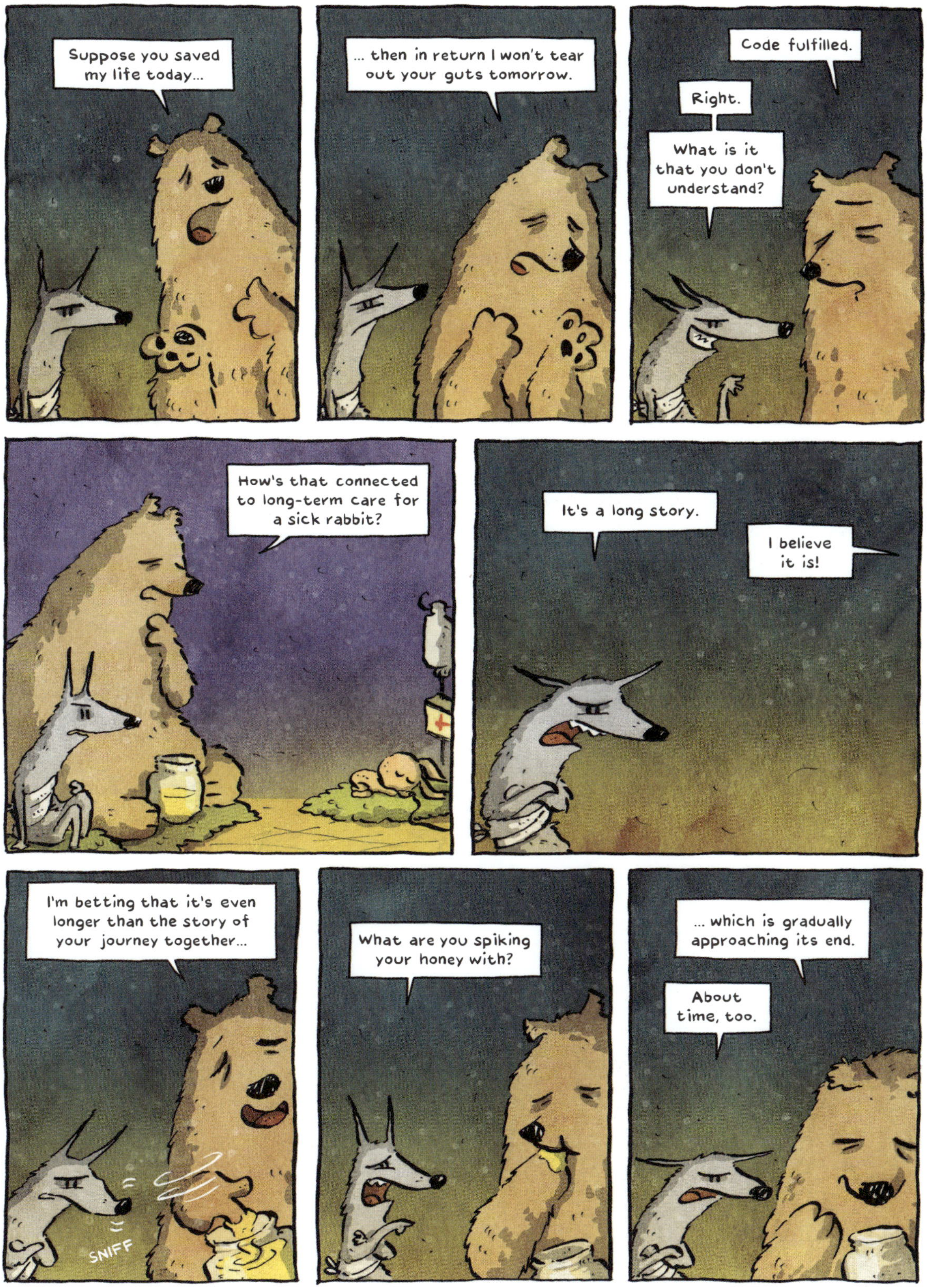
Suppose you saved my life today...
... then in return I won't tear out your guts tomorrow.
Code fulfilled.
Right.
What is it that you don't understand?
How's that connected to long-term care for a sick rabbit?
It's a long story.
I believe it is!
I'm betting that it's even longer than the story of your journey together...
SNIFF
What are you spiking your honey with?
... which is gradually approaching its end.
About time, too.

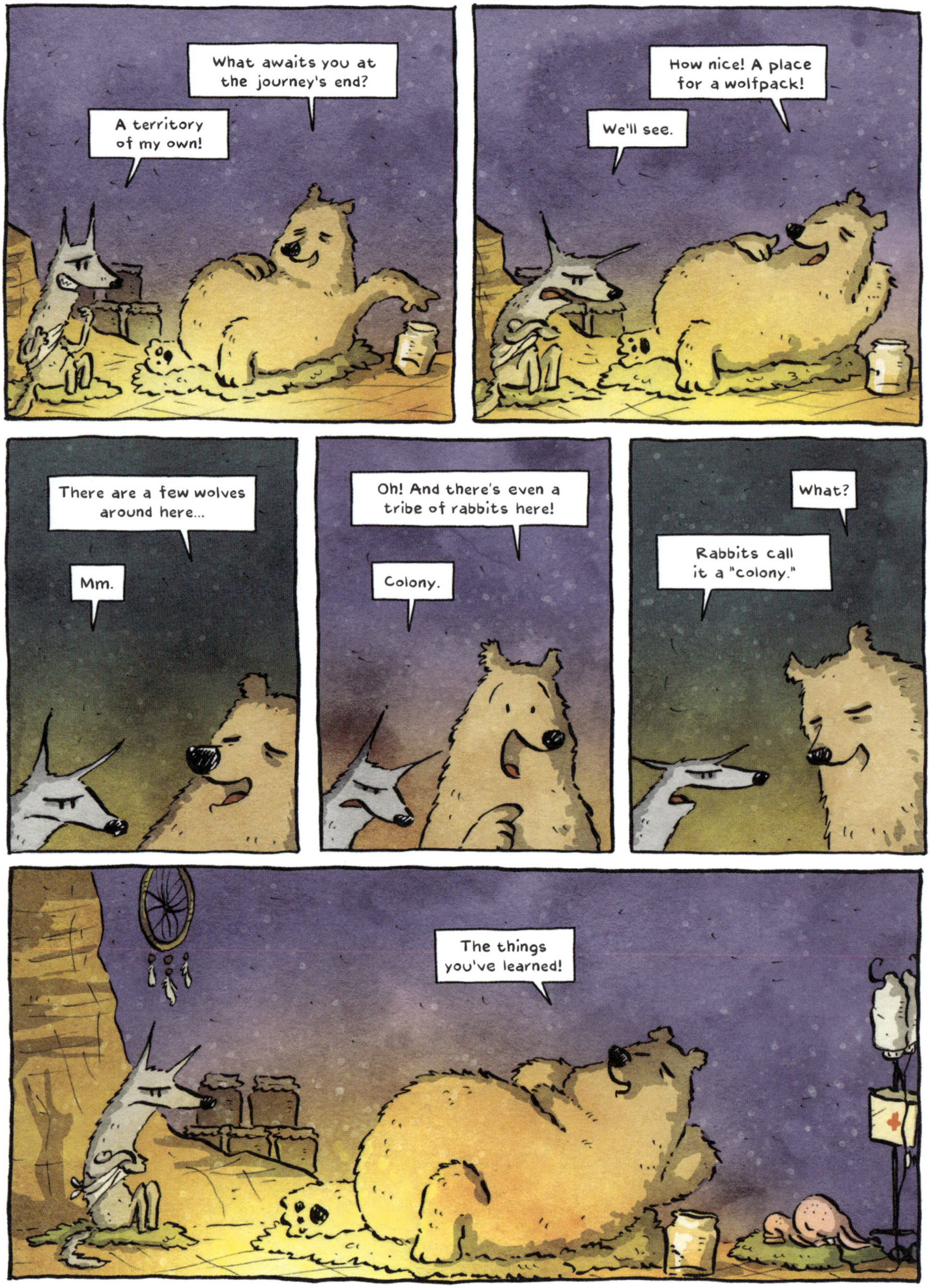
What awaits you at the journey's end?
A territory of my own!
How nice! A place for a wolfpack!
We'll see.
There are a few wolves around here...
Mm.
Oh! And there's even a tribe of rabbits here!
Colony.
What?
Rabbits call it a "colony."
The things you've learned!

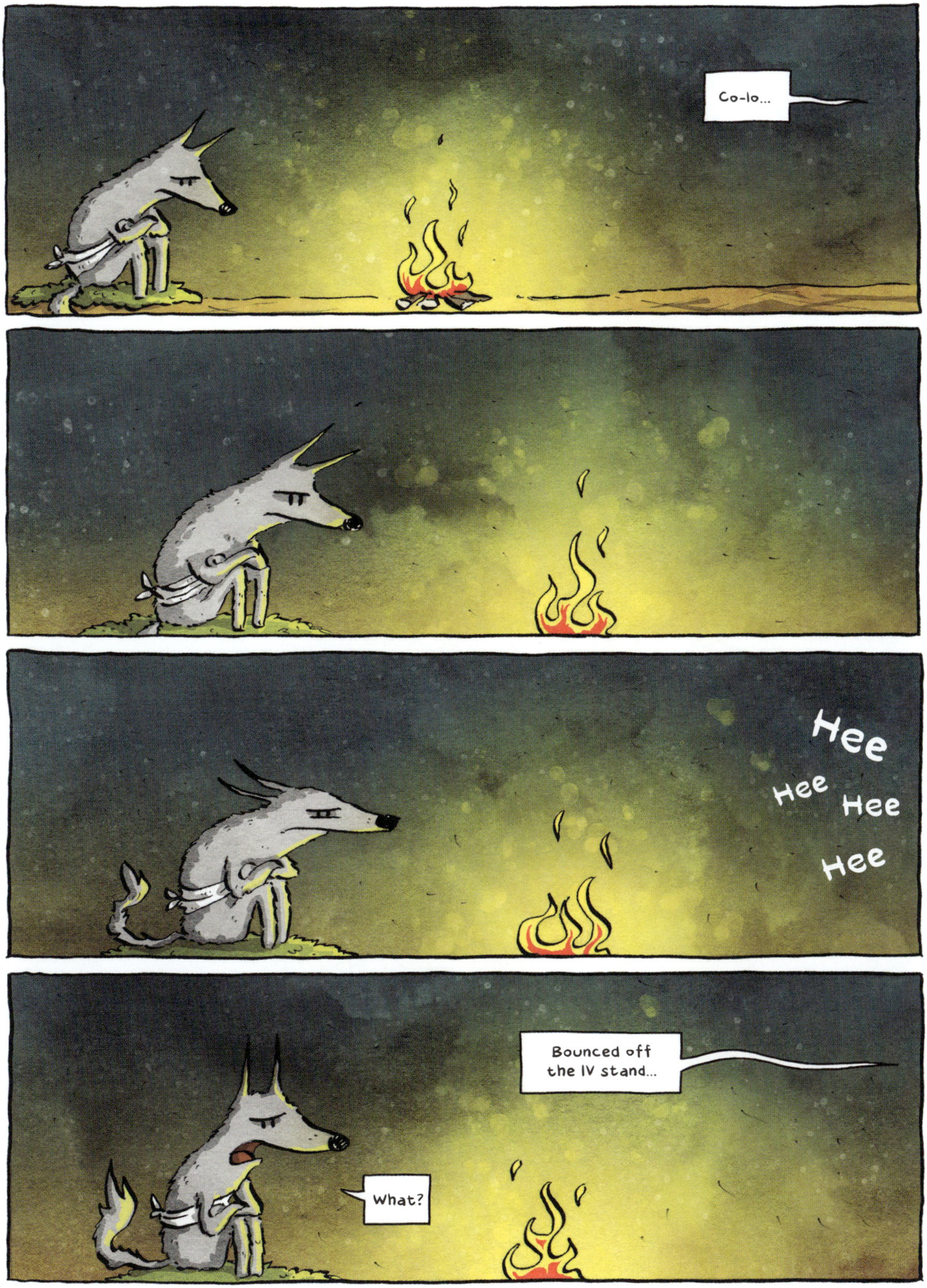
Co-lo...
Hee
Hee
Hee
Hee
Bounced off the IV stand...
What?

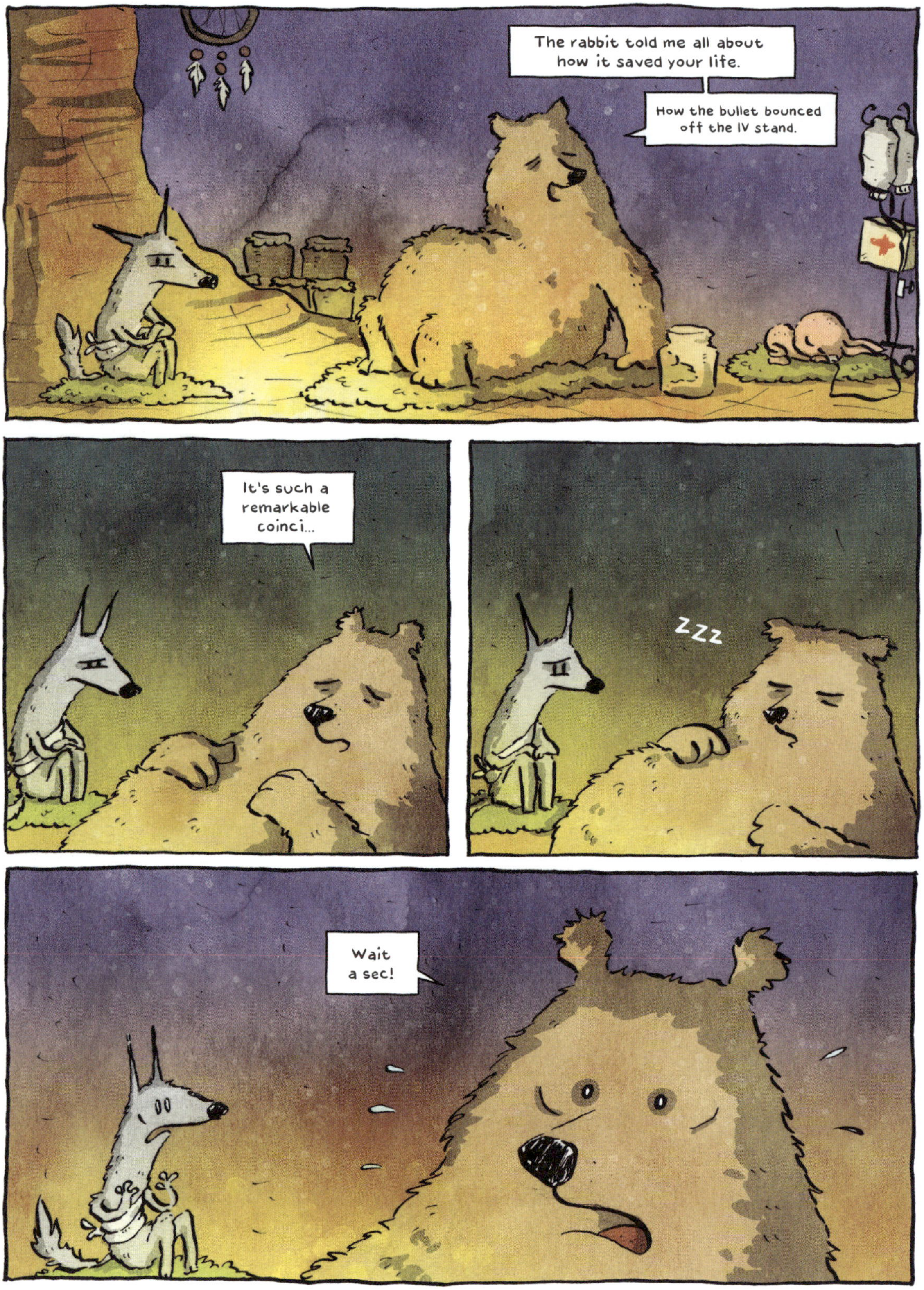
The rabbit told me all about how it saved your life.
How the bullet bounced off the IV stand.
It's such a remarkable coinci...
ZZZ
Wait a sec!

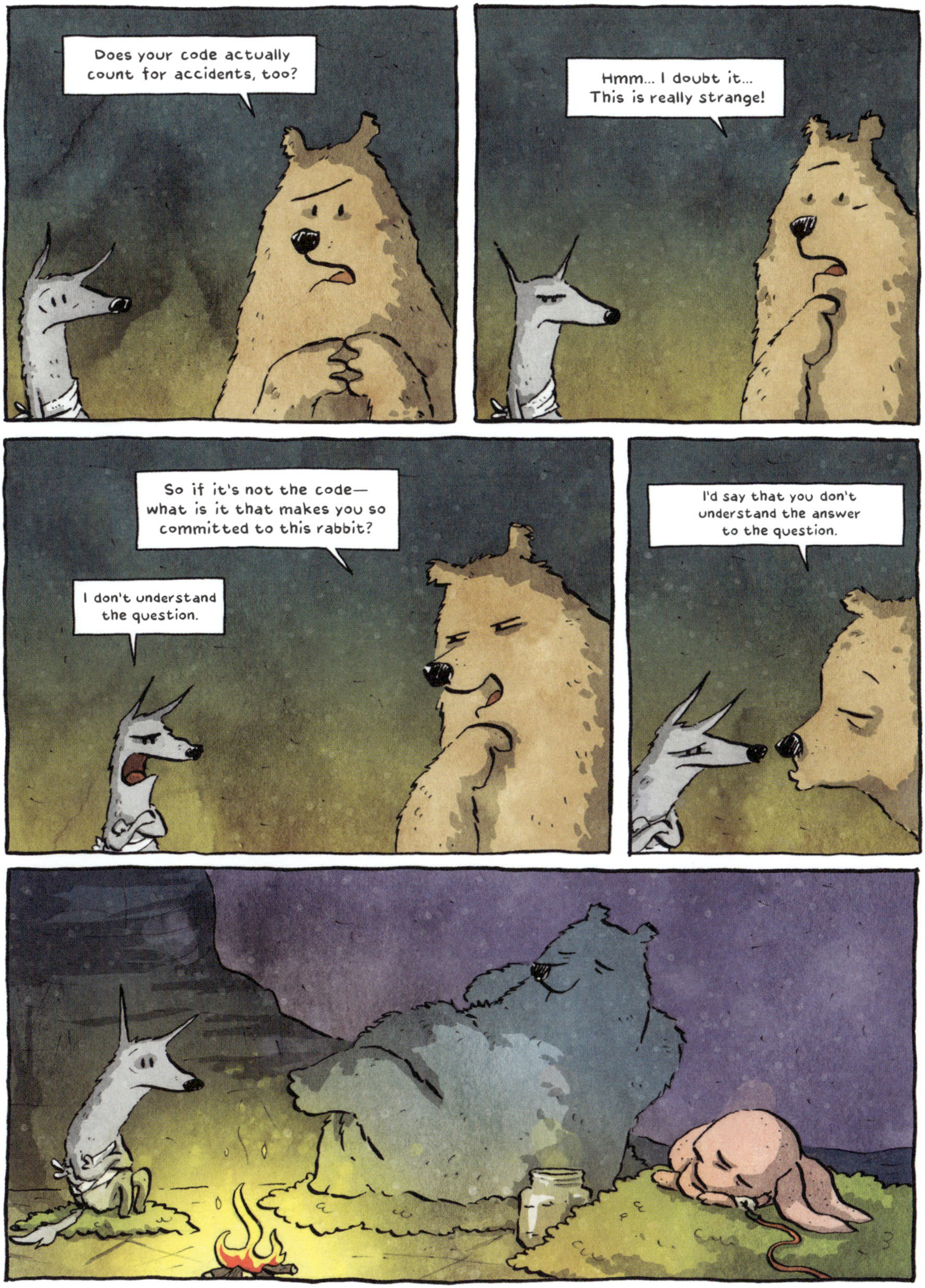
Does your code actually count for accidents, too?
Hmm... I doubt it... This is really strange!
So if it's not the code— what is it that makes you so committed to this rabbit?
I don't understand the question.
I'd say that you don't understand the answer to the question.

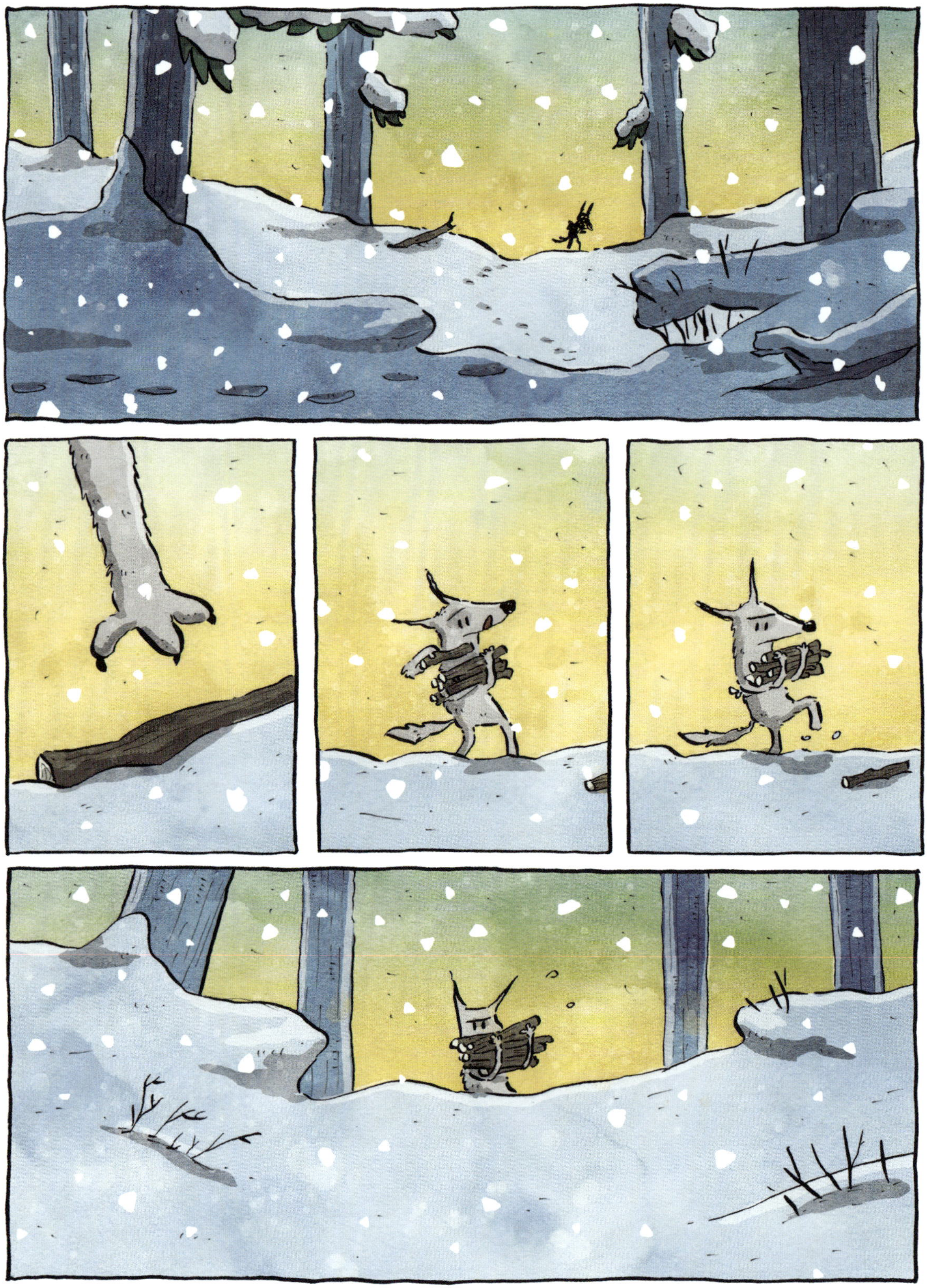

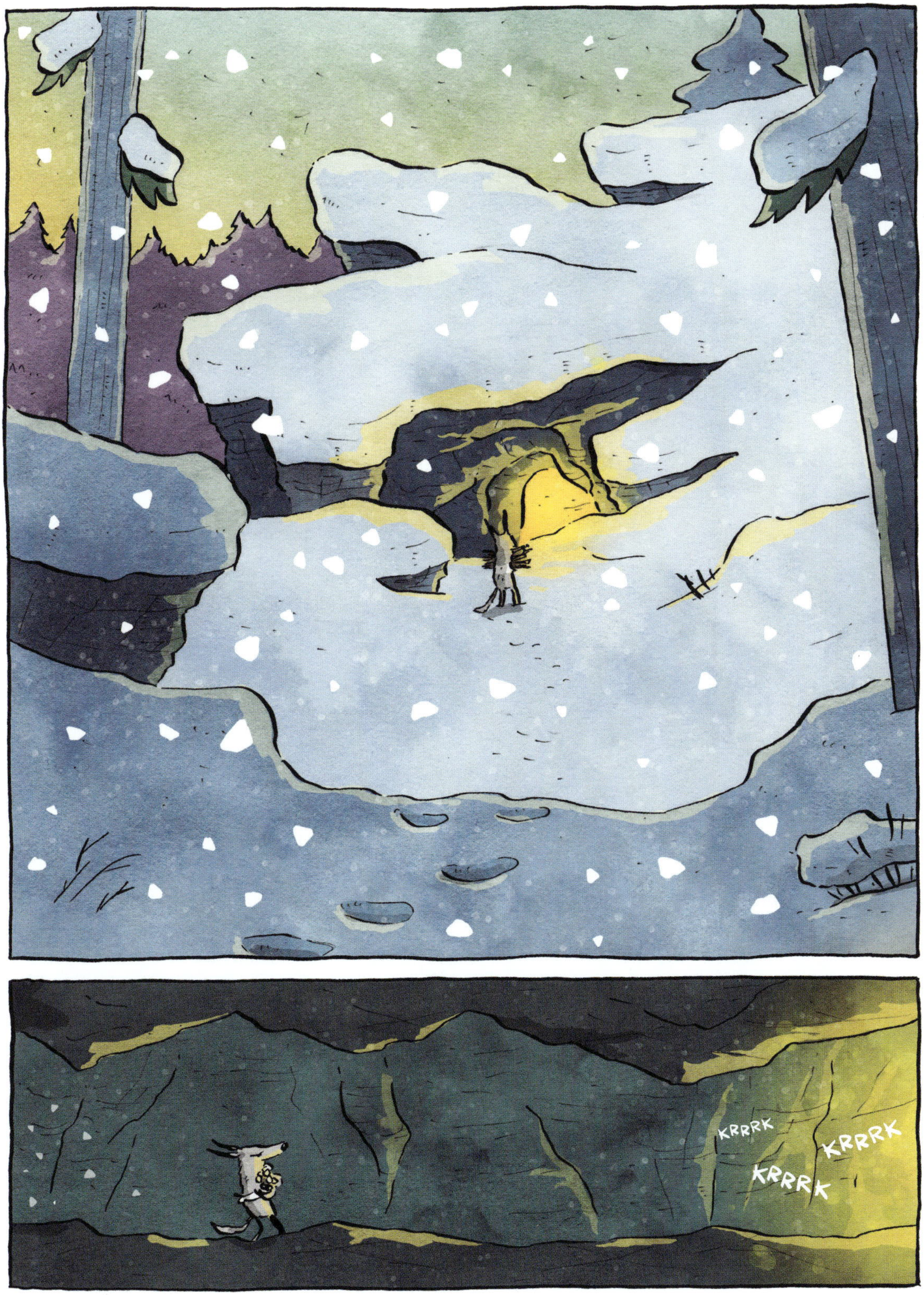
KRRRK
KRRRK
KRRRK

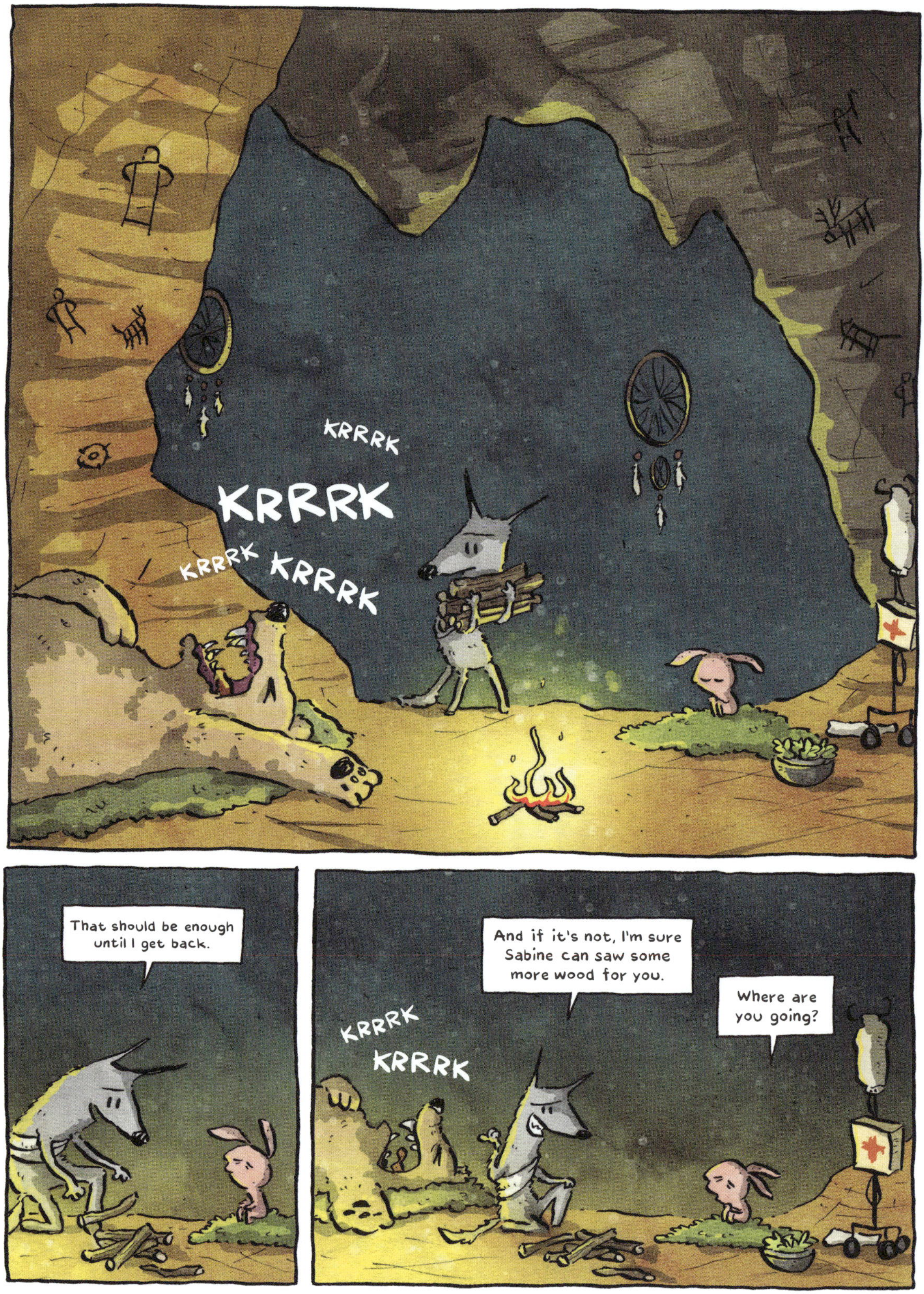
KRRRK
KRRRK
KRRRK
KRRRK
That should be enough until I get back.
KRRRK
KRRRK
And if it's not, I'm sure Sabine can saw some more wood for you.
Where are you going?

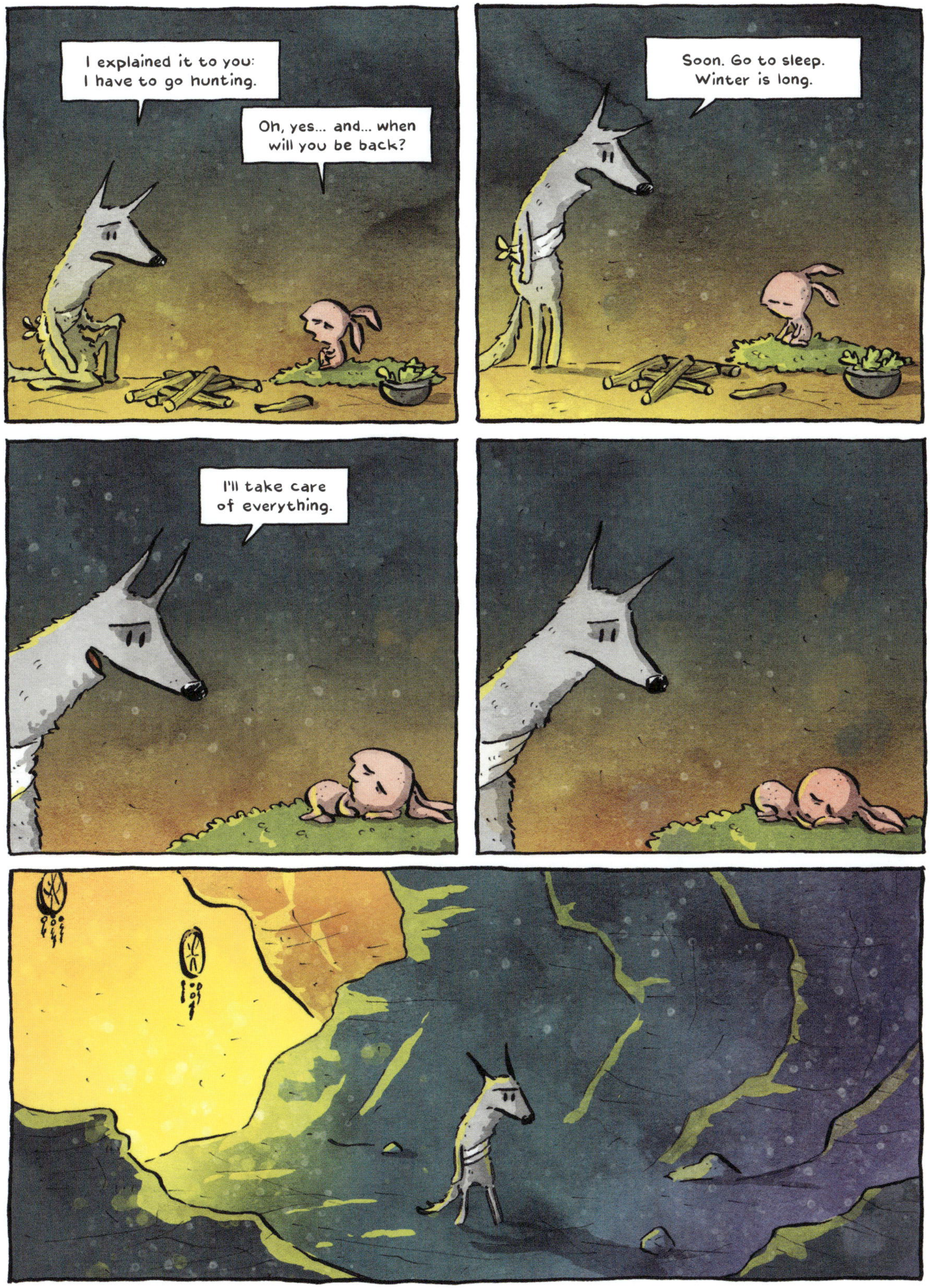
I explained it to you:
I have to go hunting.
Oh, yes... and... when will you be back?
Soon. Go to sleep.
Winter is long.
I'll take care of everything.

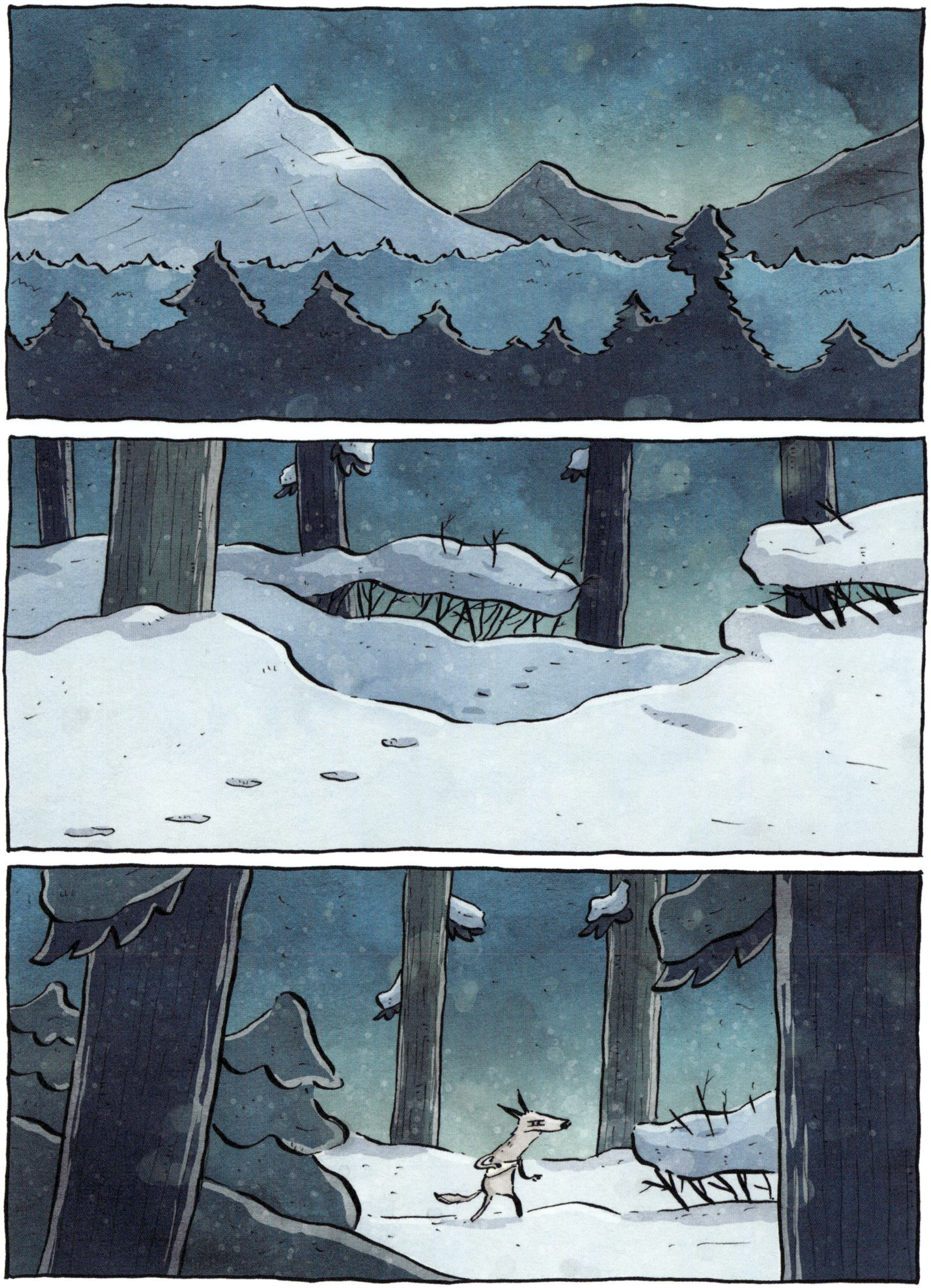

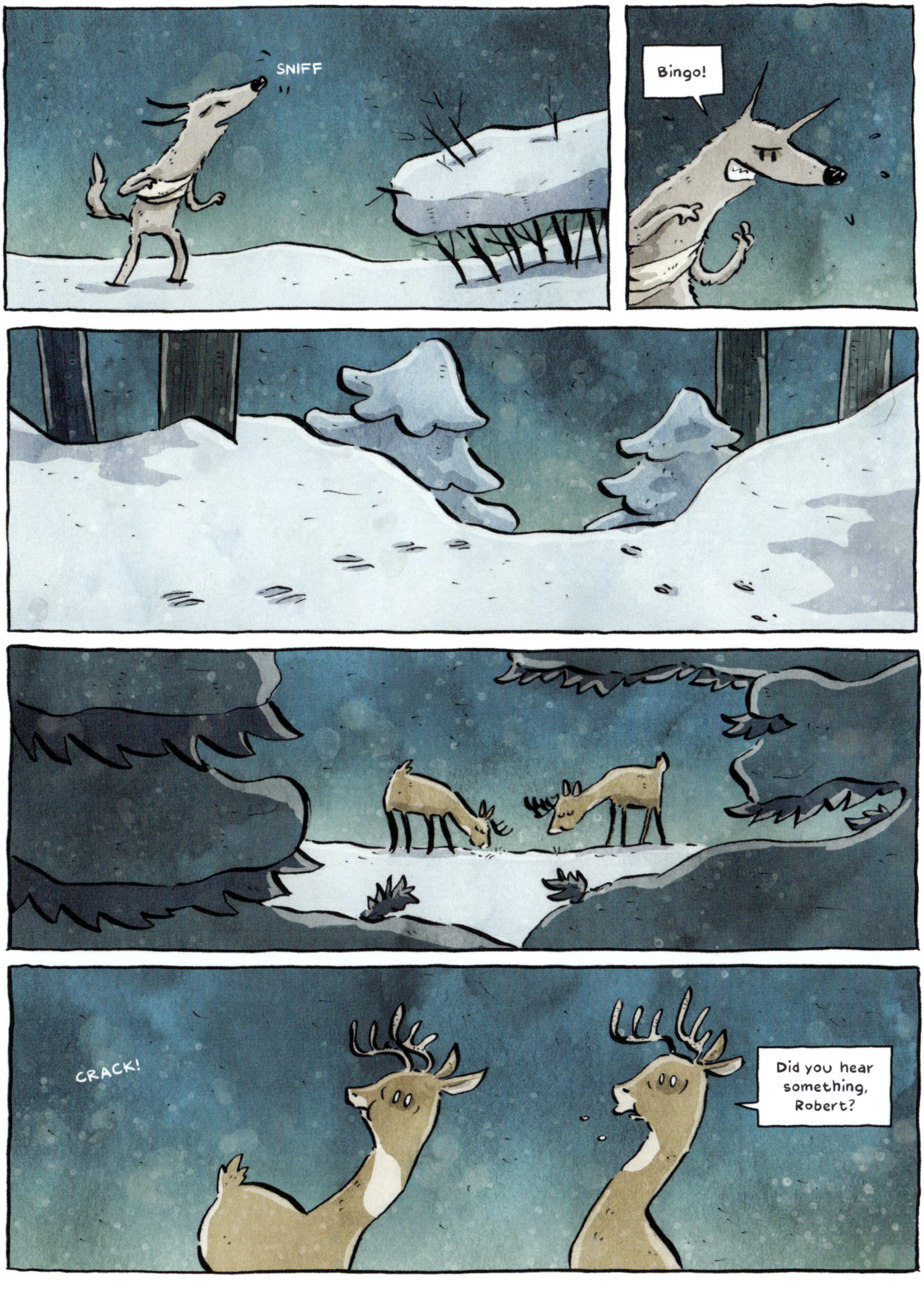
SNIFF
Bingo!
CRACK!
Did you hear something, Robert?

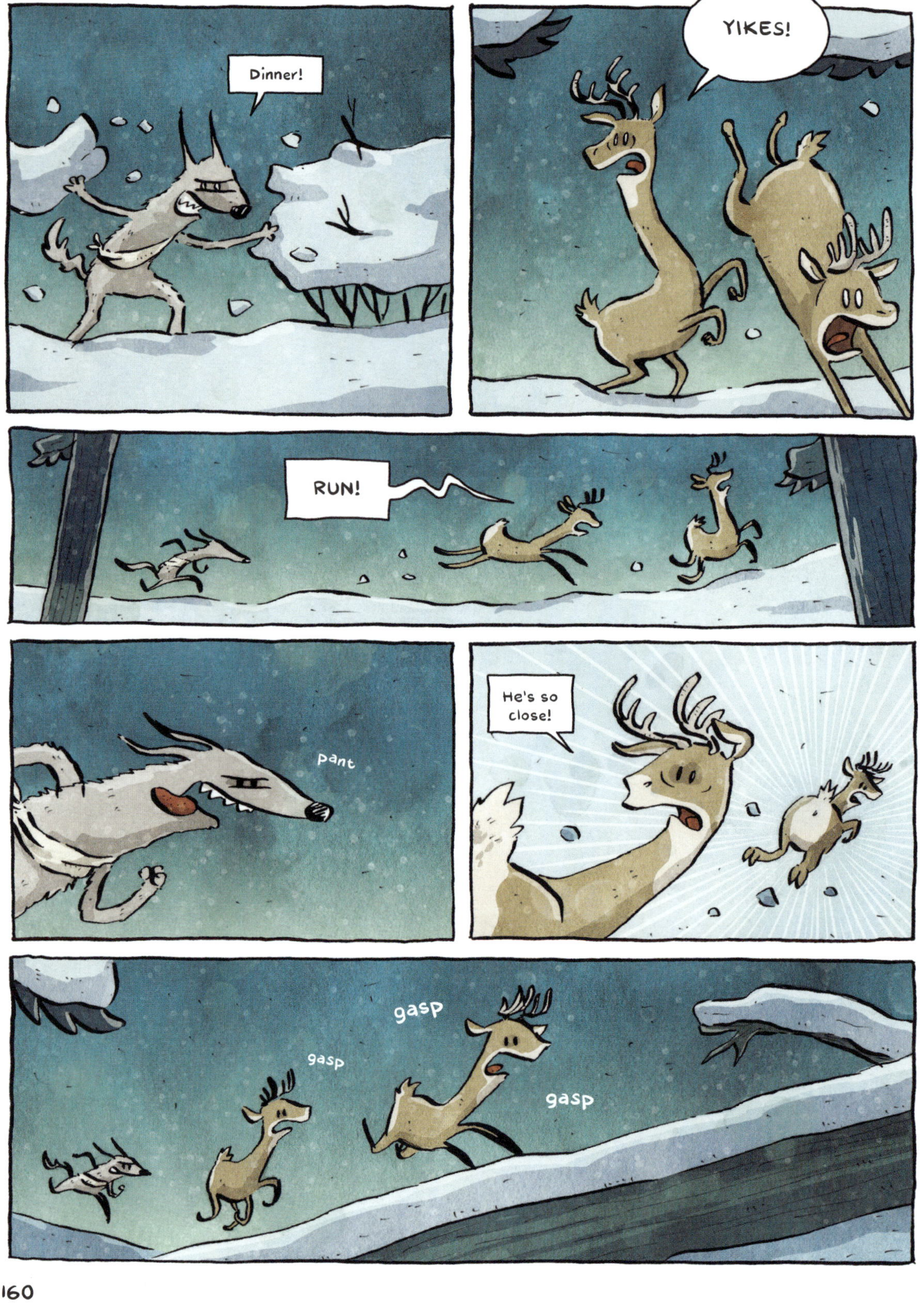
Dinner!
YIKES!
RUN!
pant
He's so close!
gasp
gasp
gasp

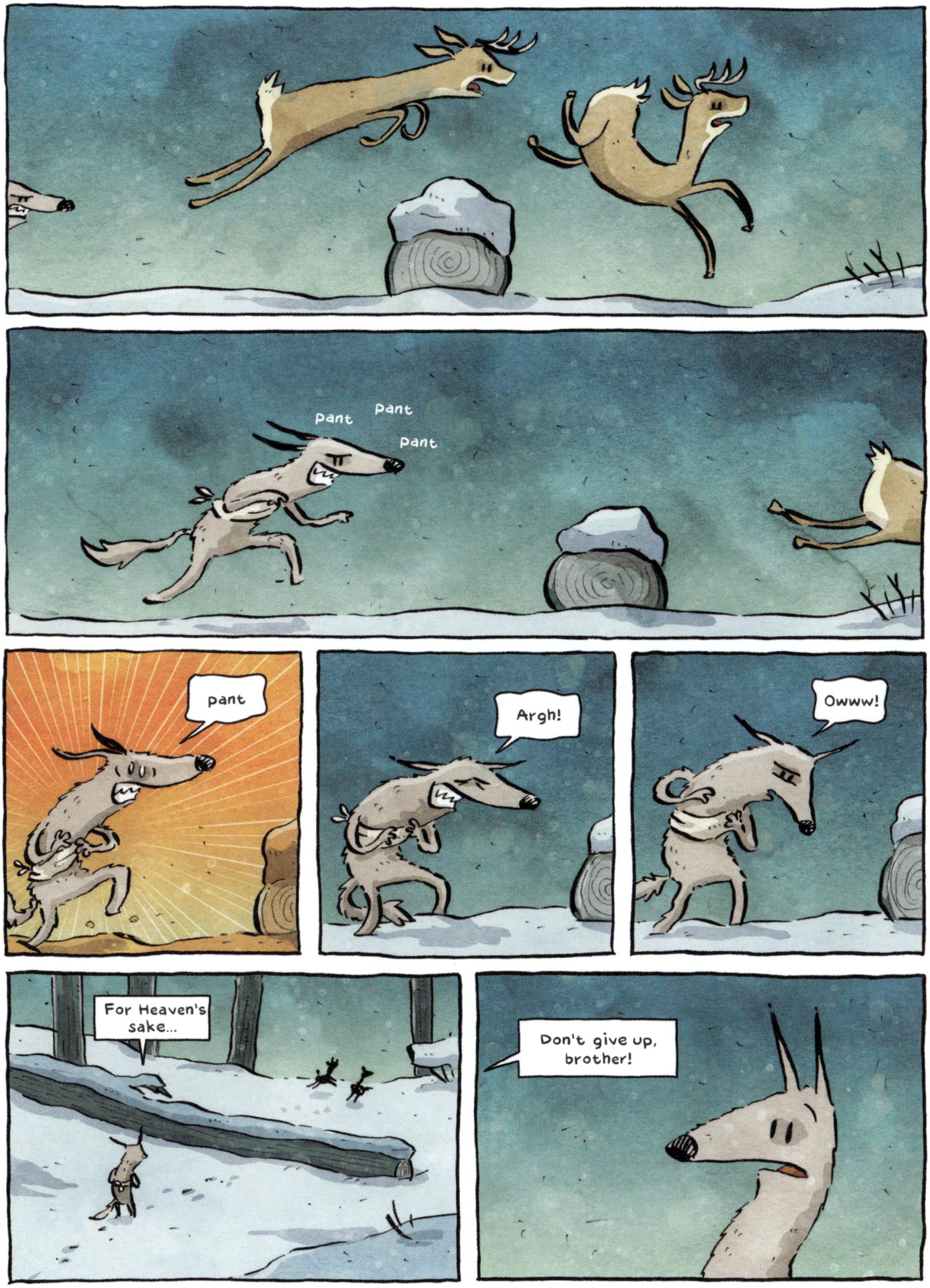
pant
pant
pant
pant
Argh!
Owww!
For Heaven's sake...
Don't give up, brother!

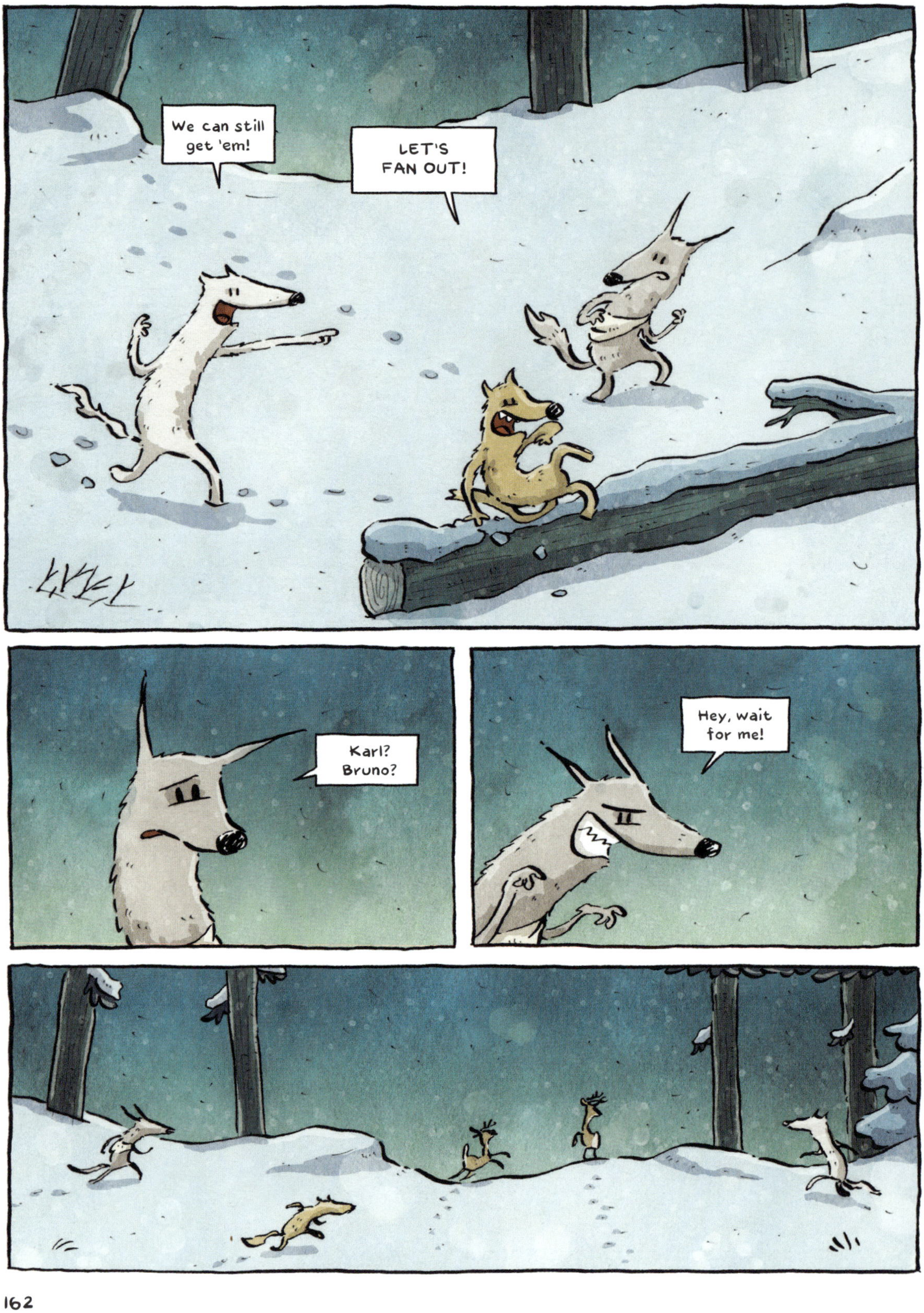
We can still get 'em!
LET'S FAN OUT!
Karl? Bruno?
Hey, wait for me!

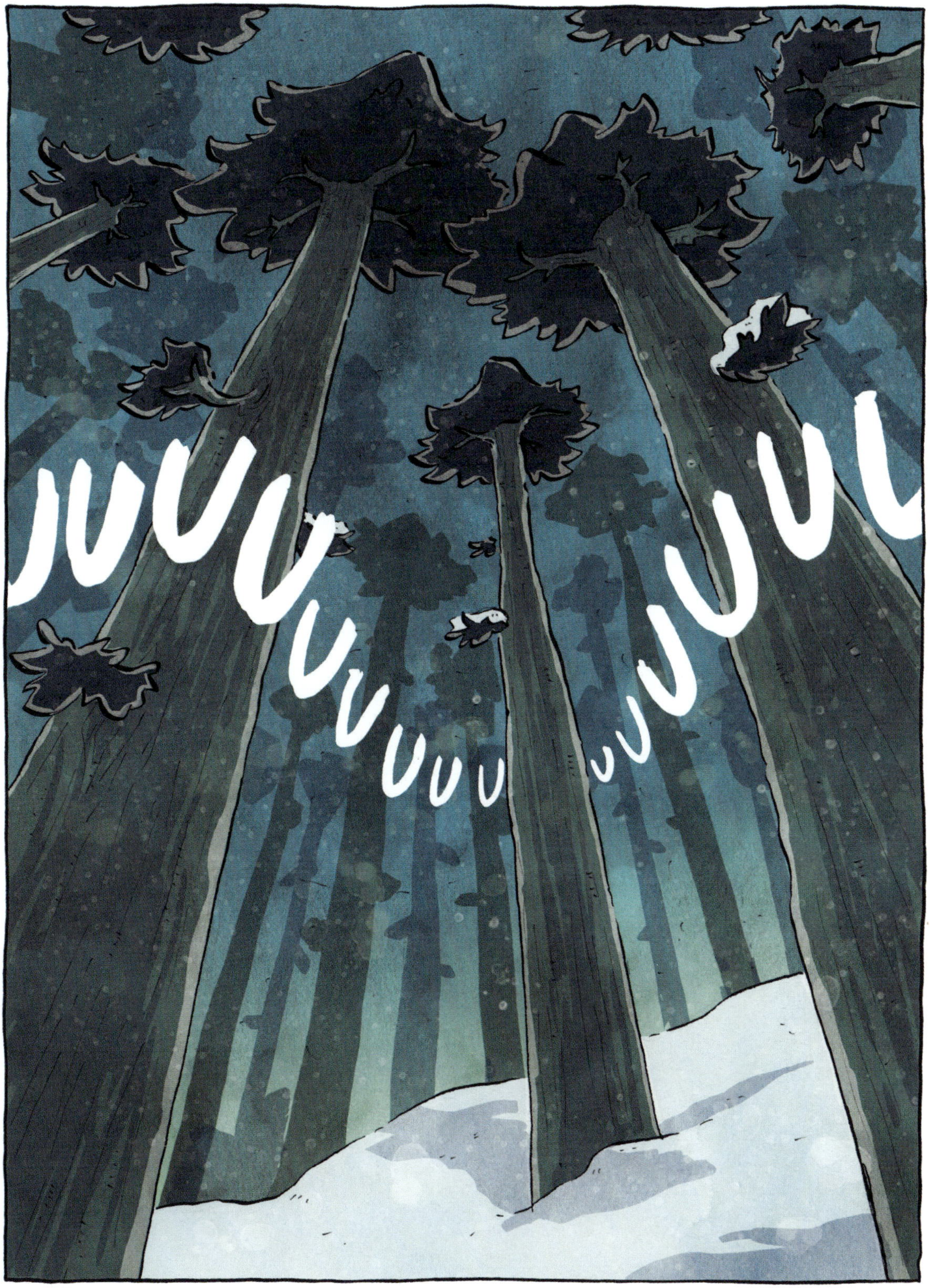
UUUUUUUUUUU UUUUUUUU

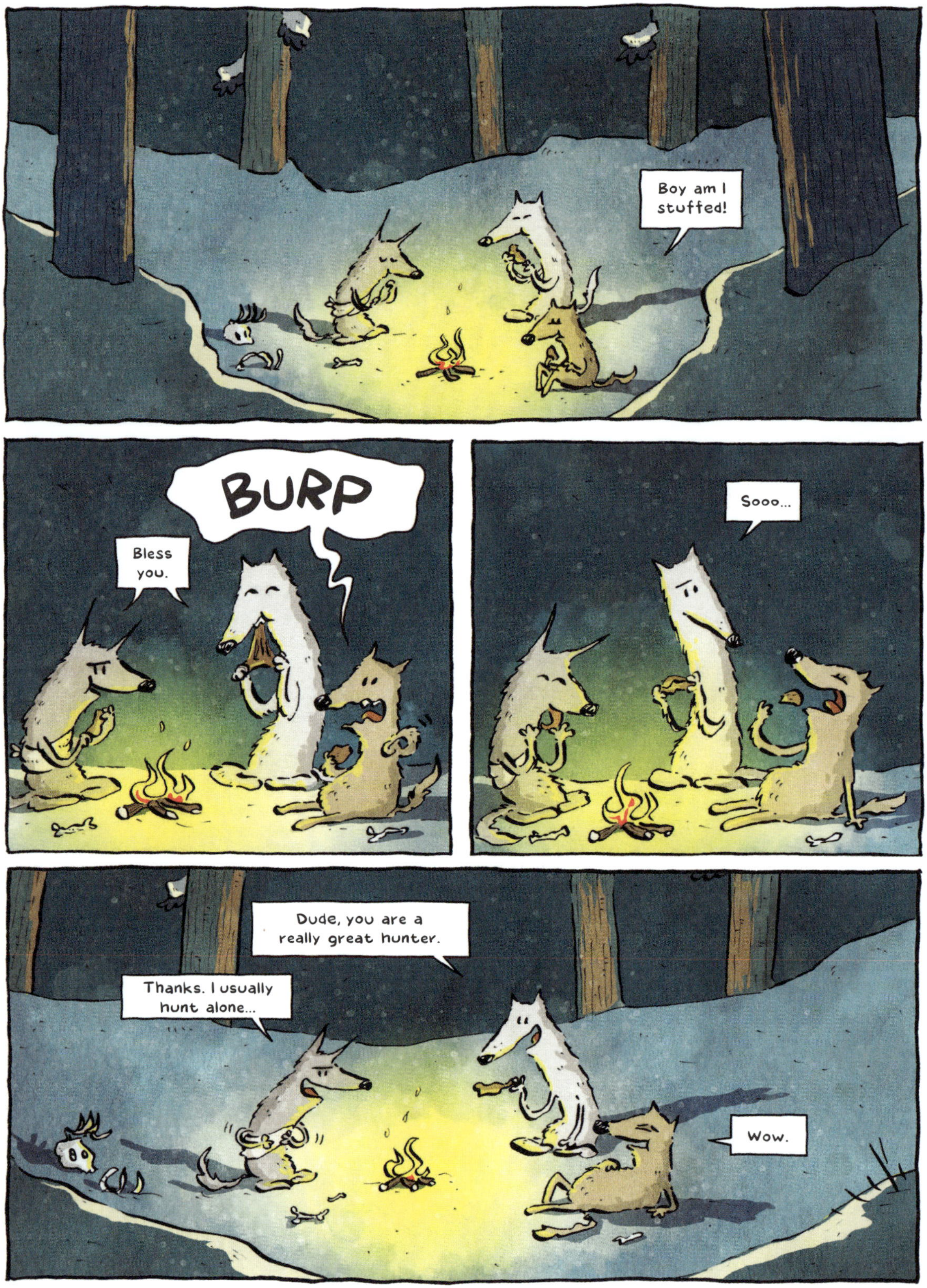
Boy am I stuffed!
BURP
Bless you.
Sooo...
Dude, you are a really great hunter.
Thanks. I usually hunt alone...
Wow.

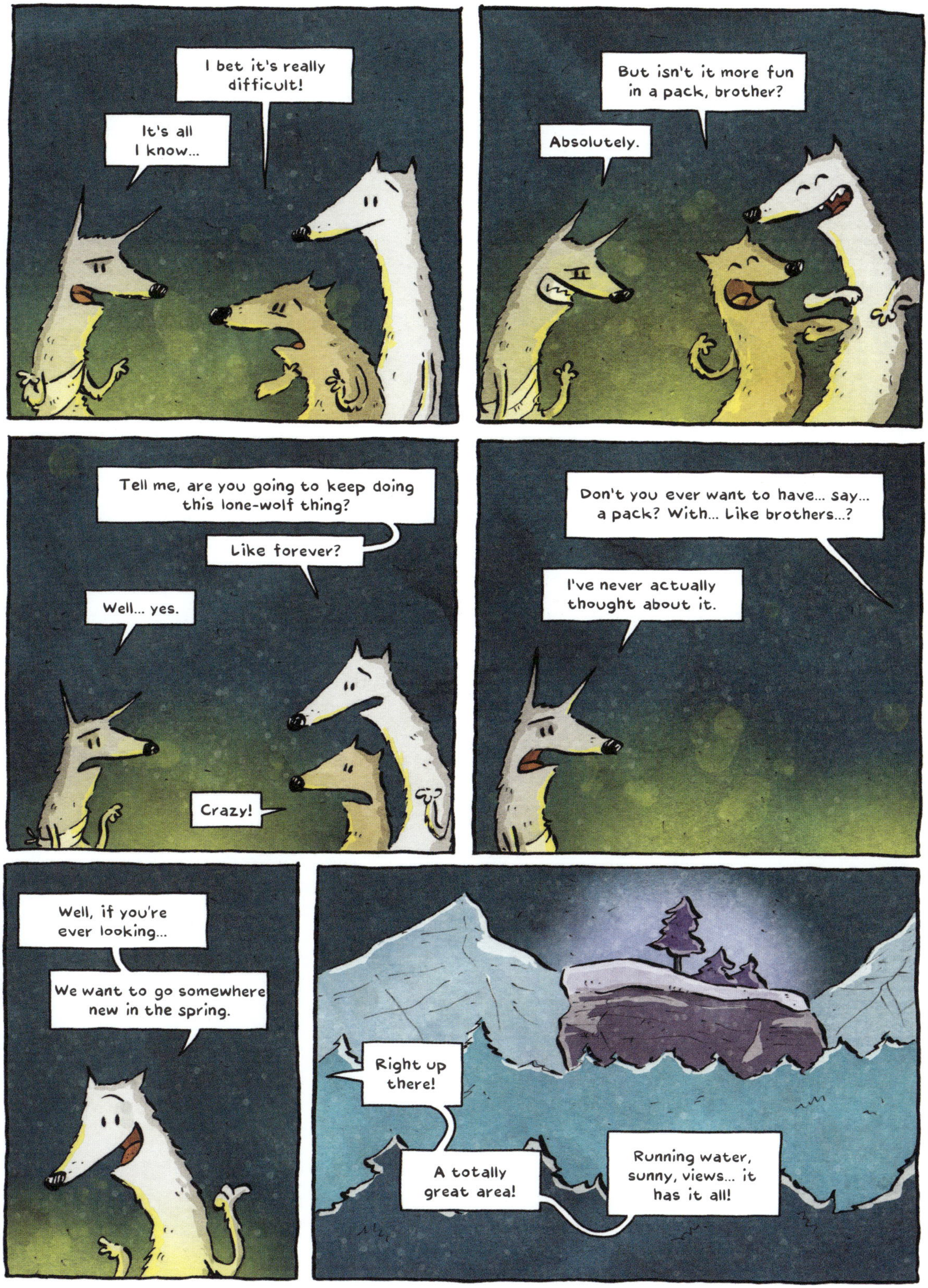
I bet it's really difficult!
It's all I know...
But isn't it more fun in a pack, brother?
Absolutely.
Tell me, are you going to keep doing this lone-wolf thing?
Like forever?
Well... yes.
Crazy!
Don't you ever want to have... say... a pack? With... Like brothers...?
I've never actually thought about it.
Well, if you're ever looking...
We want to go somewhere new in the spring.
Right up there!
A totally great area!
Running water, sunny, views... it has it all!

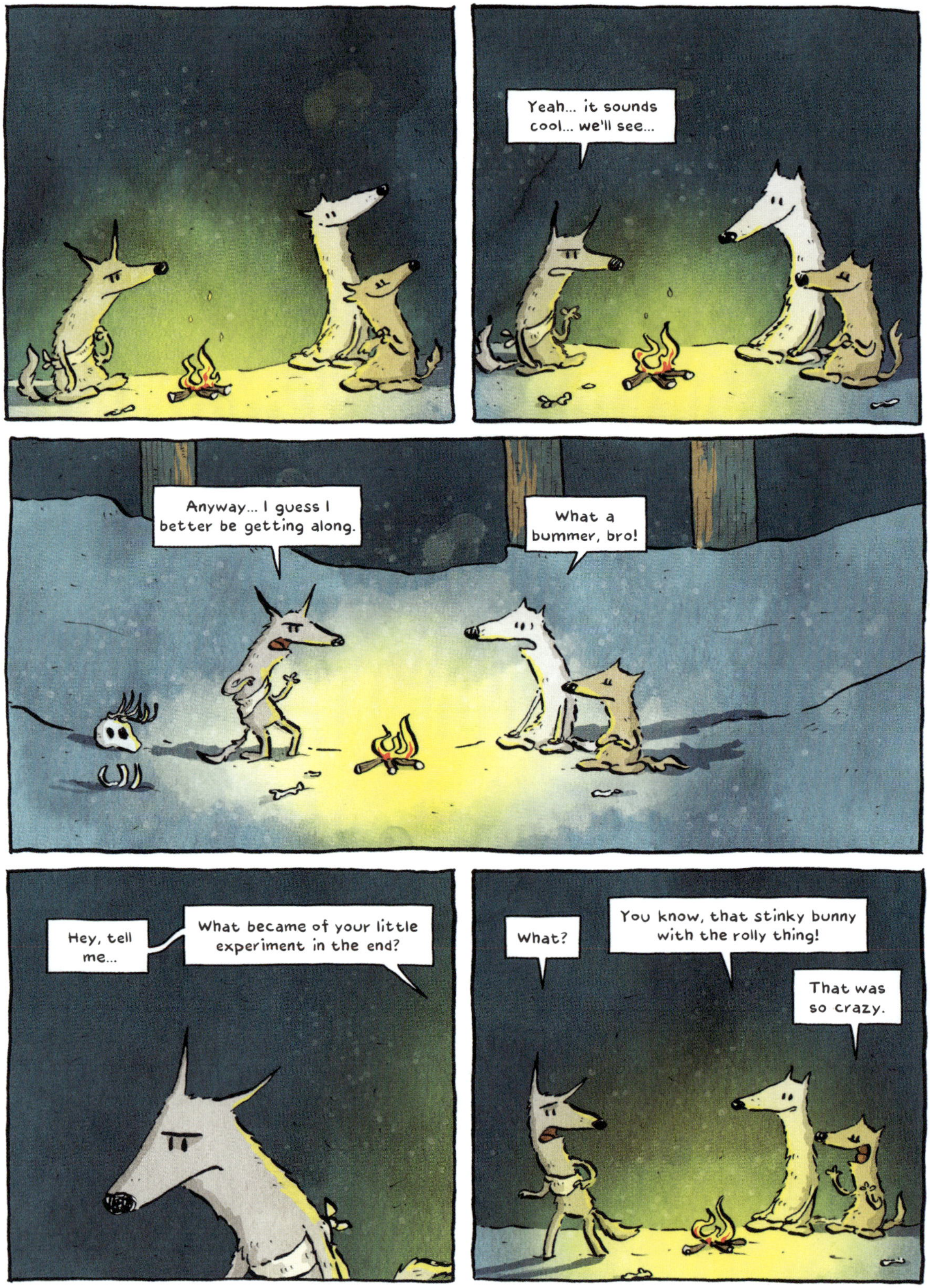
Yeah... it sounds cool... we'll see...
Anyway... I guess I better be getting along.
What a bummer, bro!
Hey, tell me...
What became of your little experiment in the end?
What?
You know, that stinky bunny with the rolly thing!
That was so crazy.

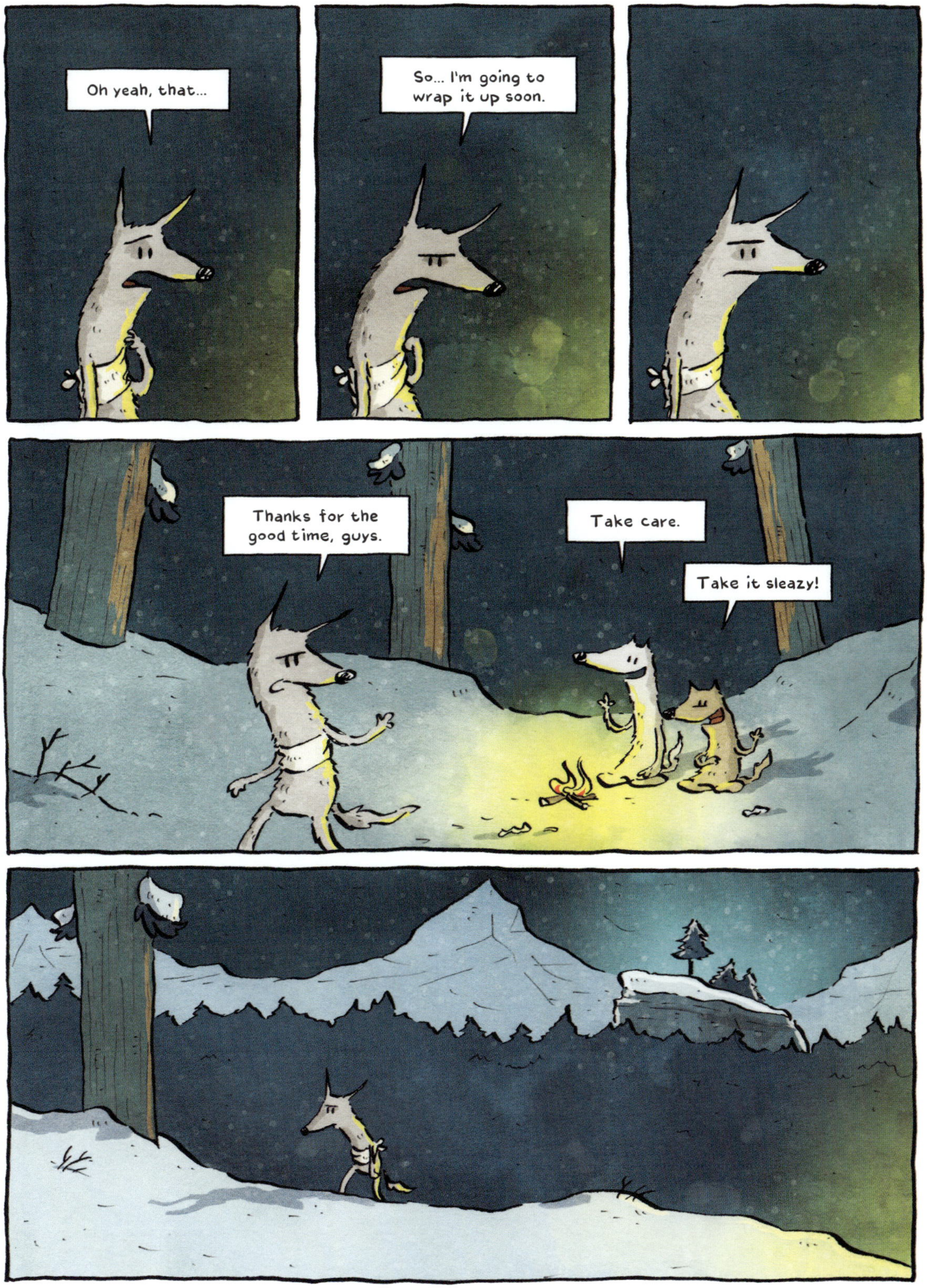
Oh yeah, that...
So... I'm going to wrap it up soon.
Thanks for the good time, guys.
Take care.
Take it sleazy!

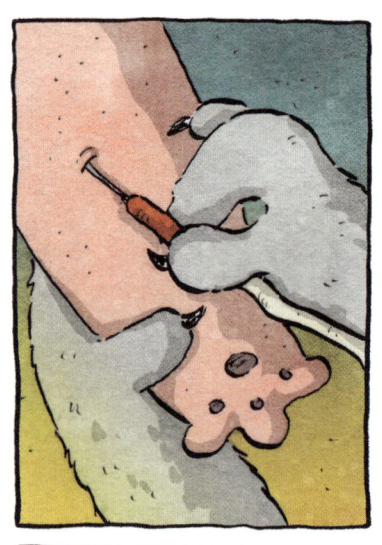

GURGLE

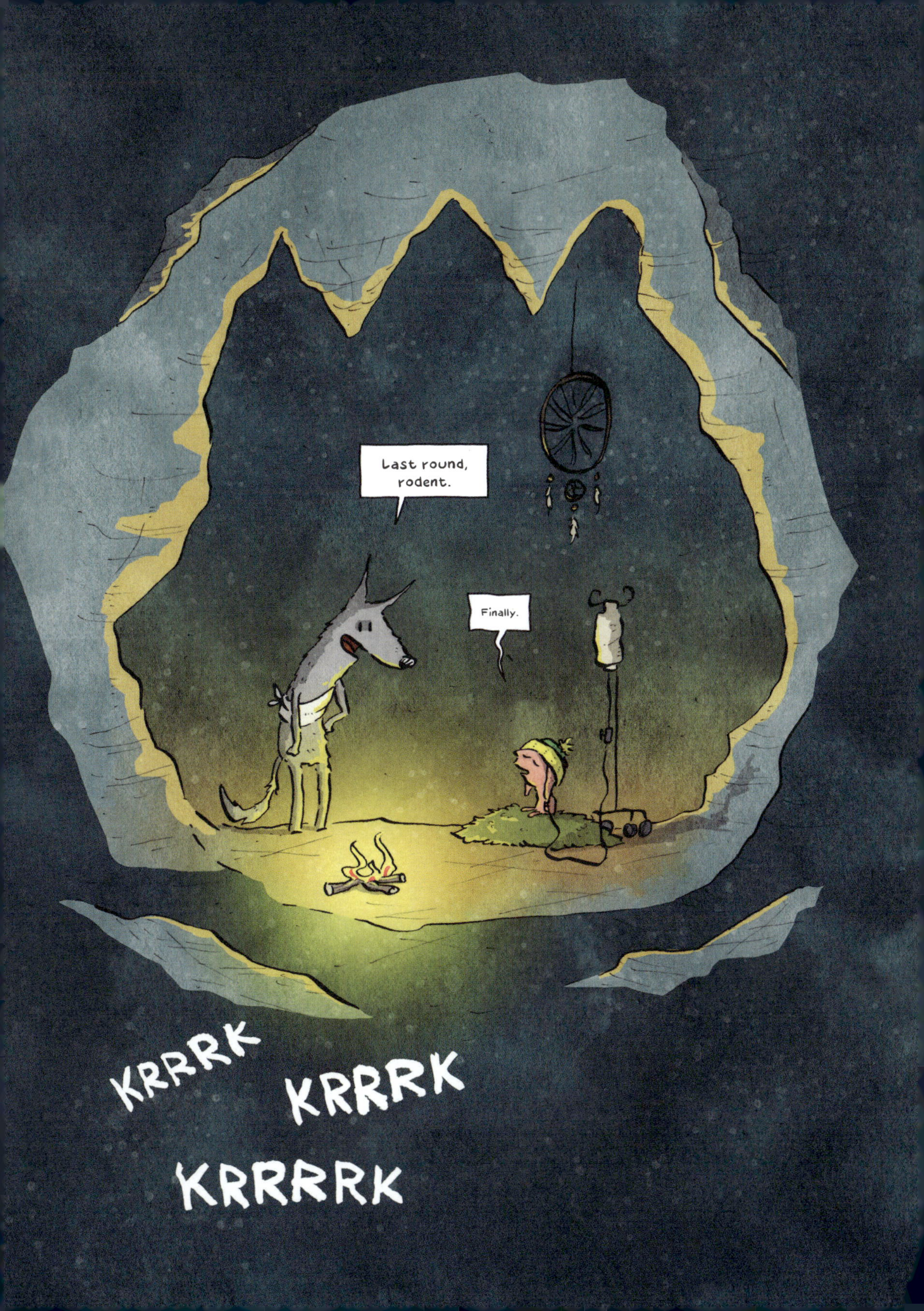
Last round, rodent.
Finally.
KRRRK
KRRRK
KRRRRK

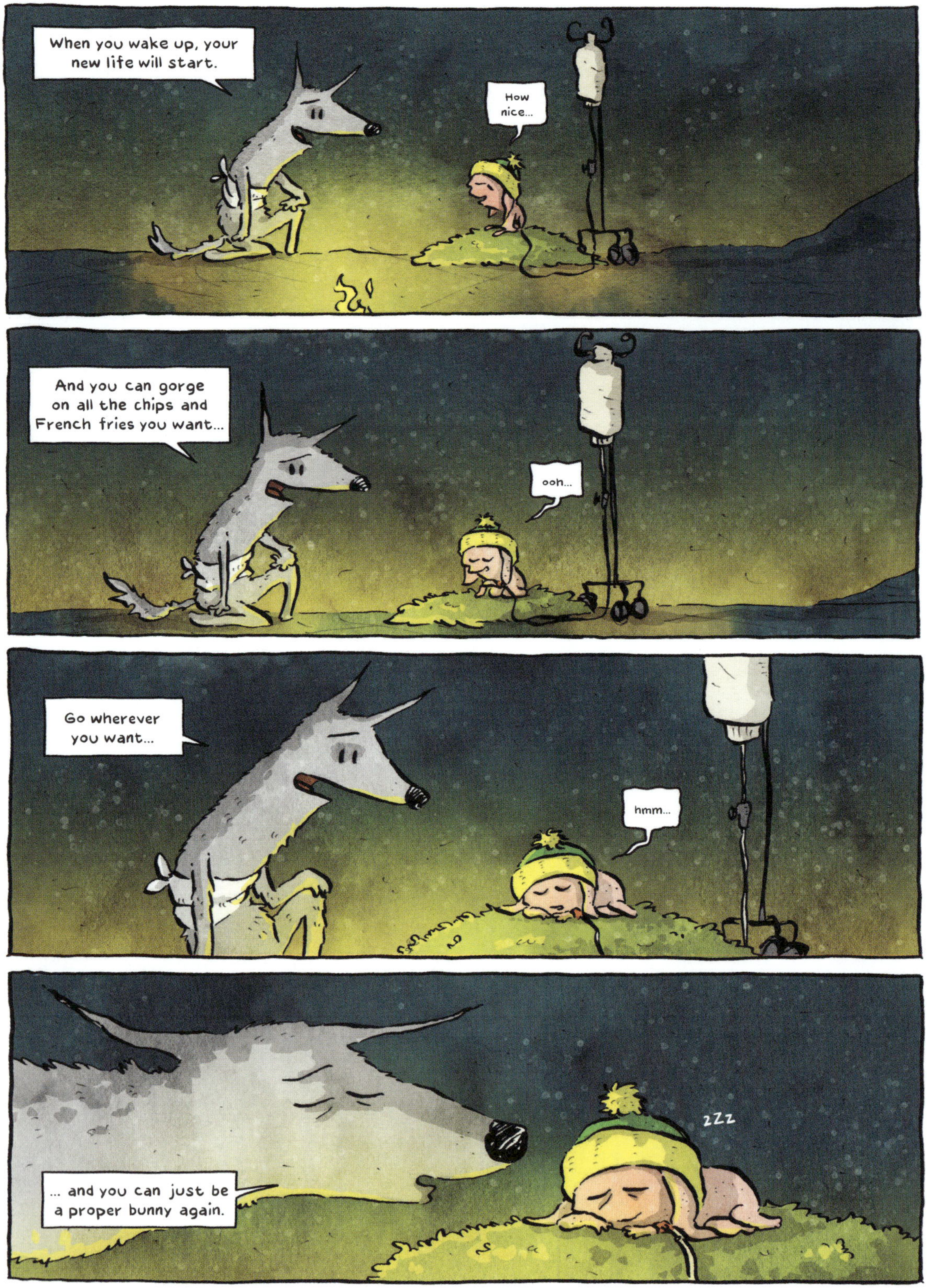
When you wake up, your new life will start.
How nice...
And you can gorge on all the chips and French fries you want...
ooh...
Go wherever you want...
hmm...
zzz
... and you can just be a proper bunny again.

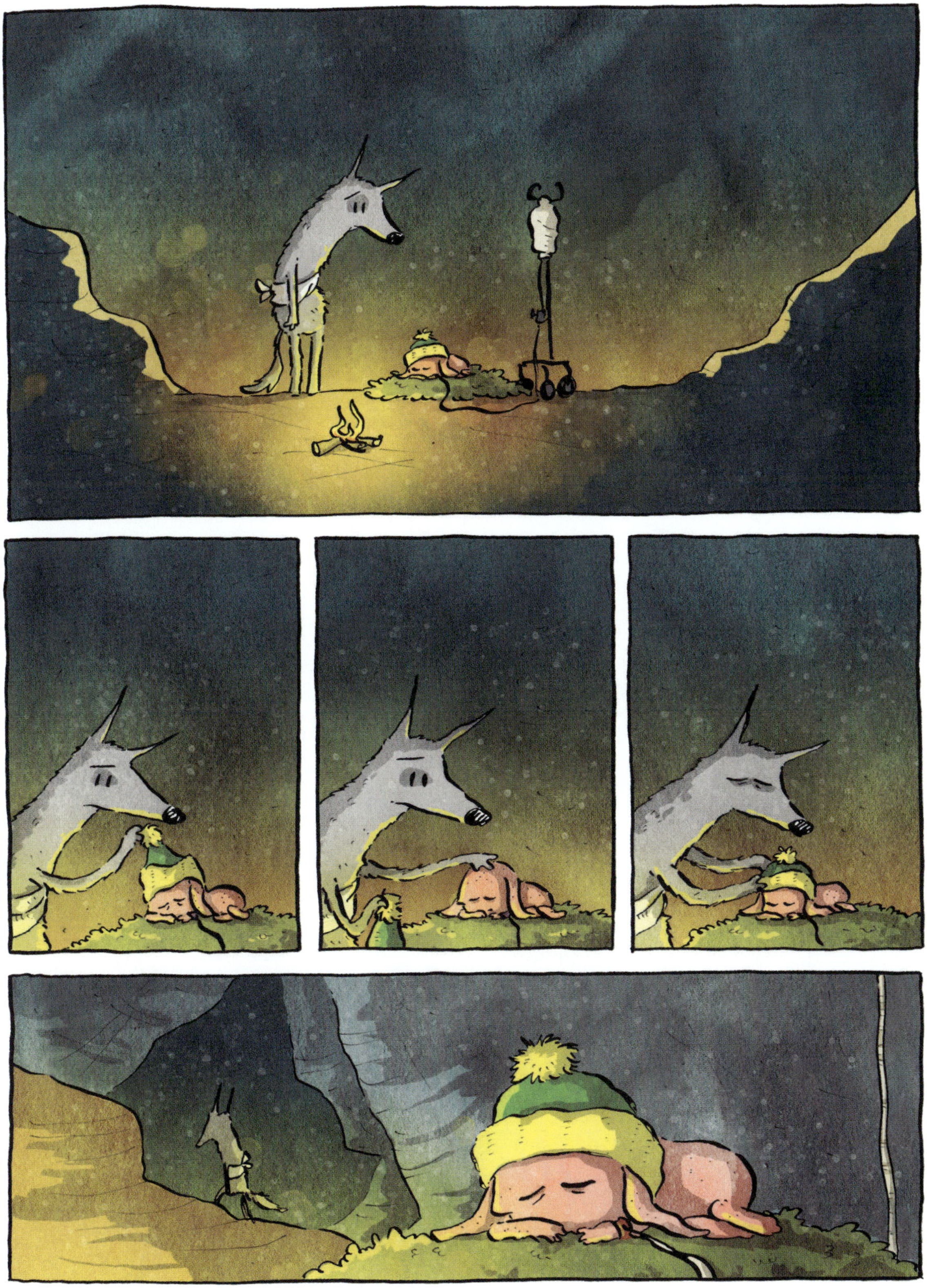

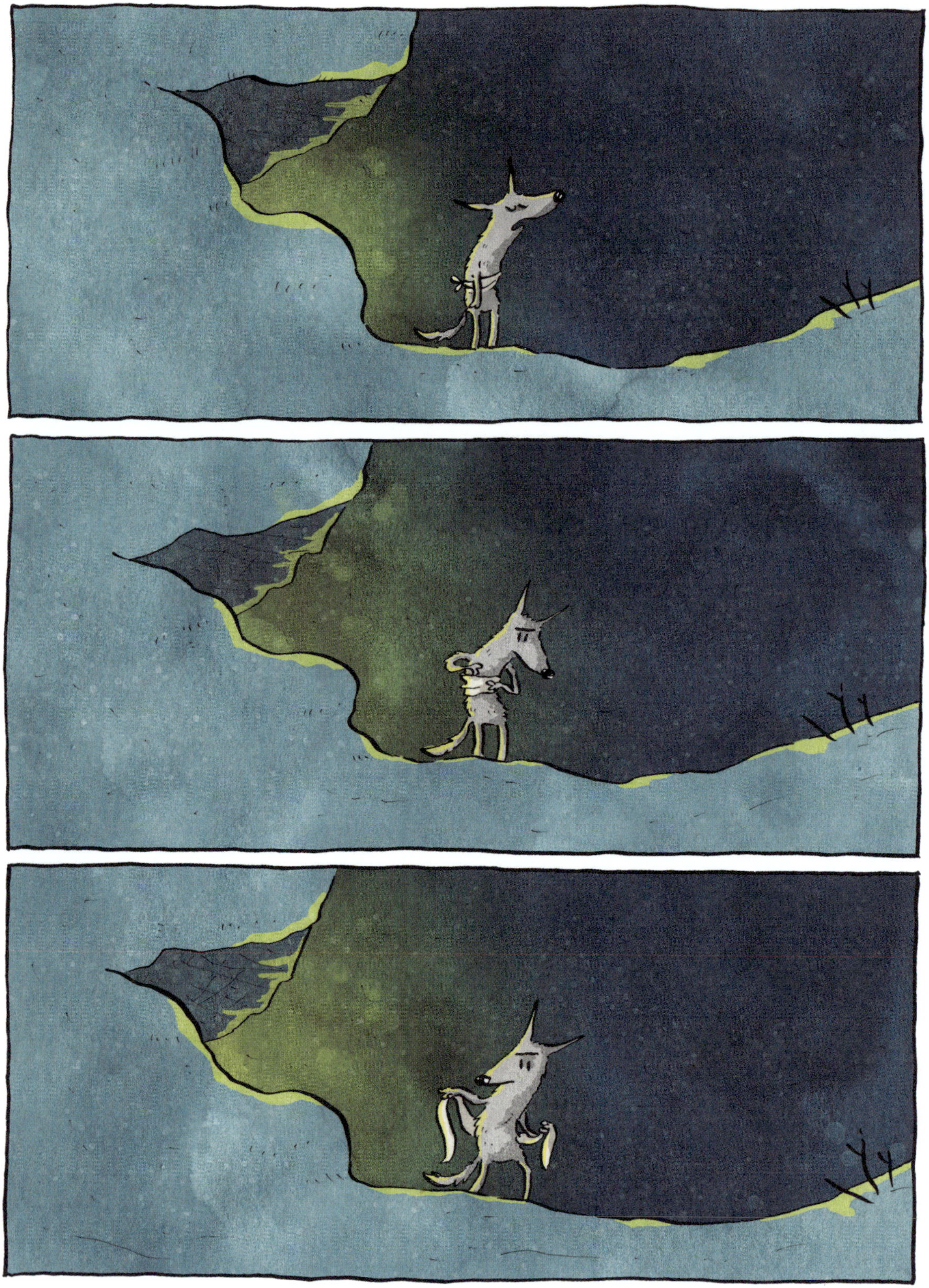

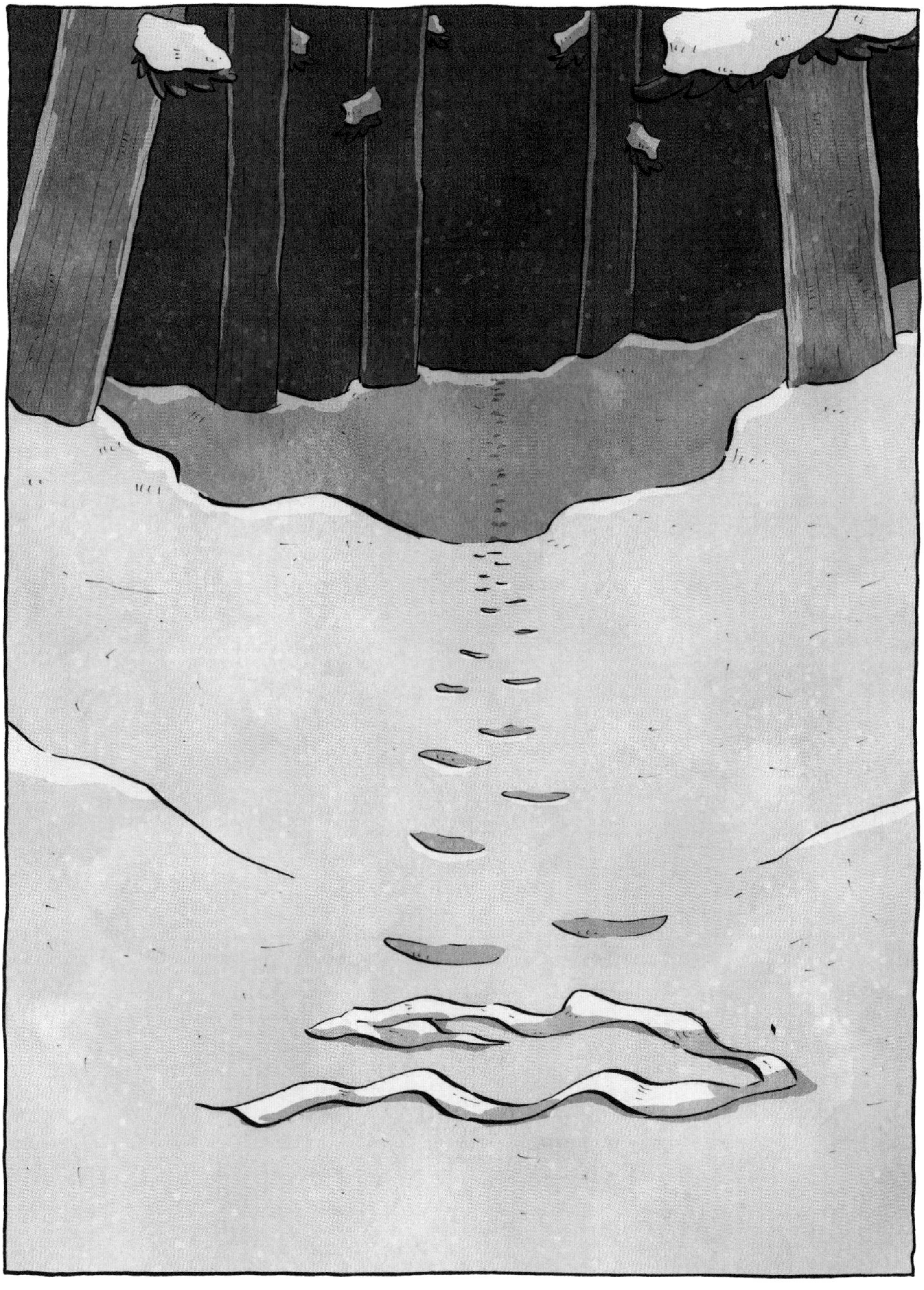

Chapter 5

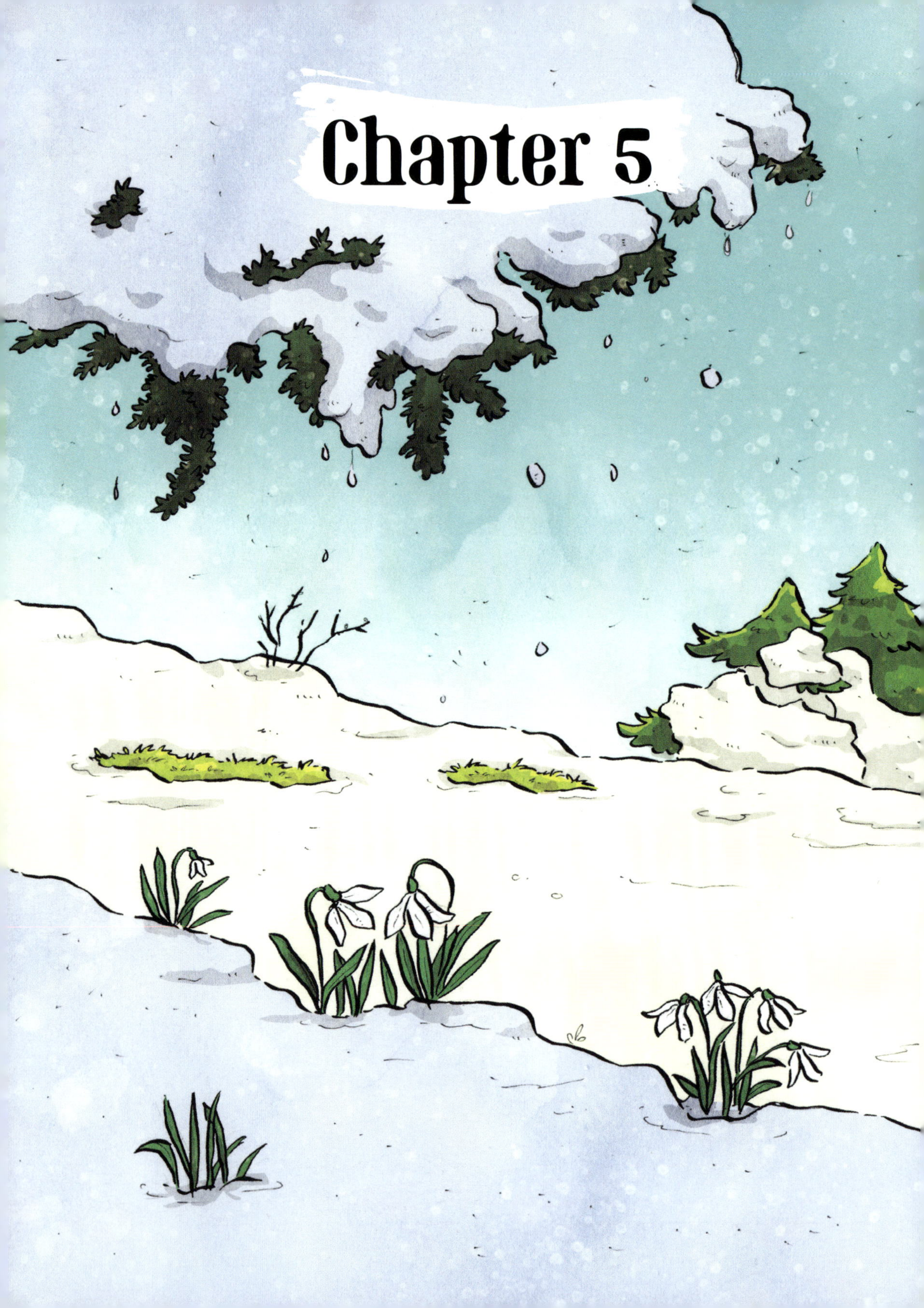

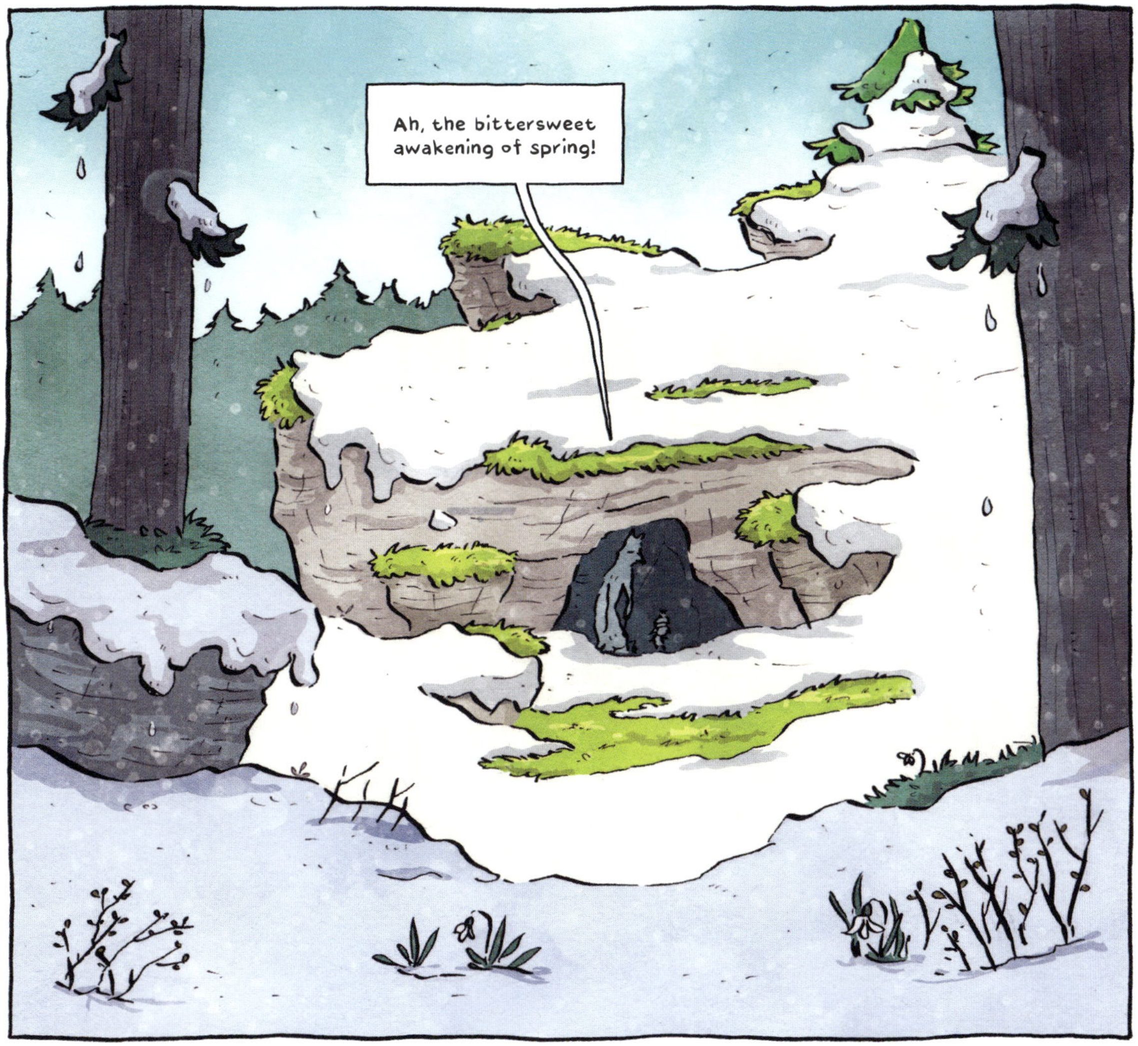
Ah, the bittersweet awakening of spring!

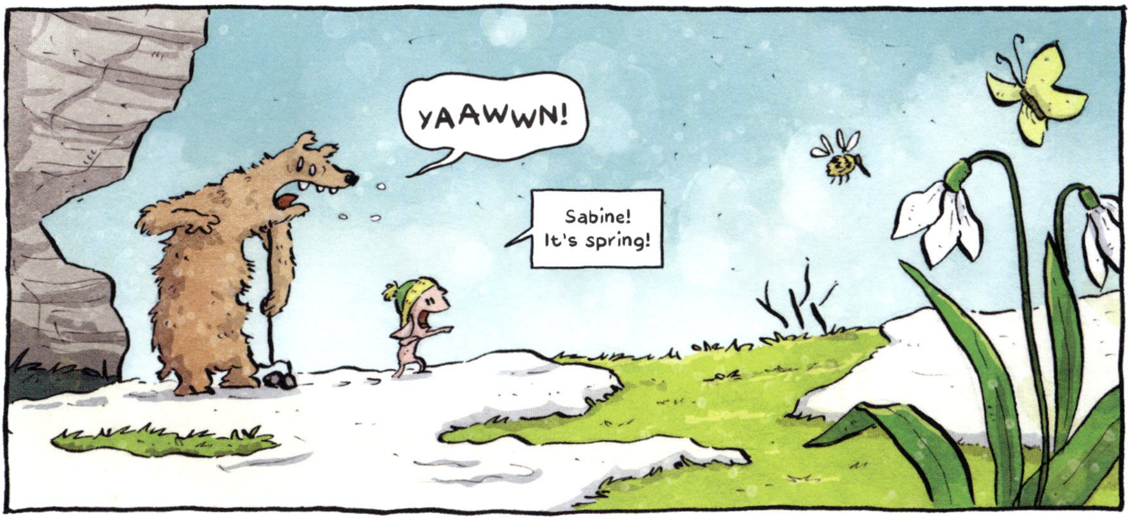
YAAWWN!
Sabine! It's spring!

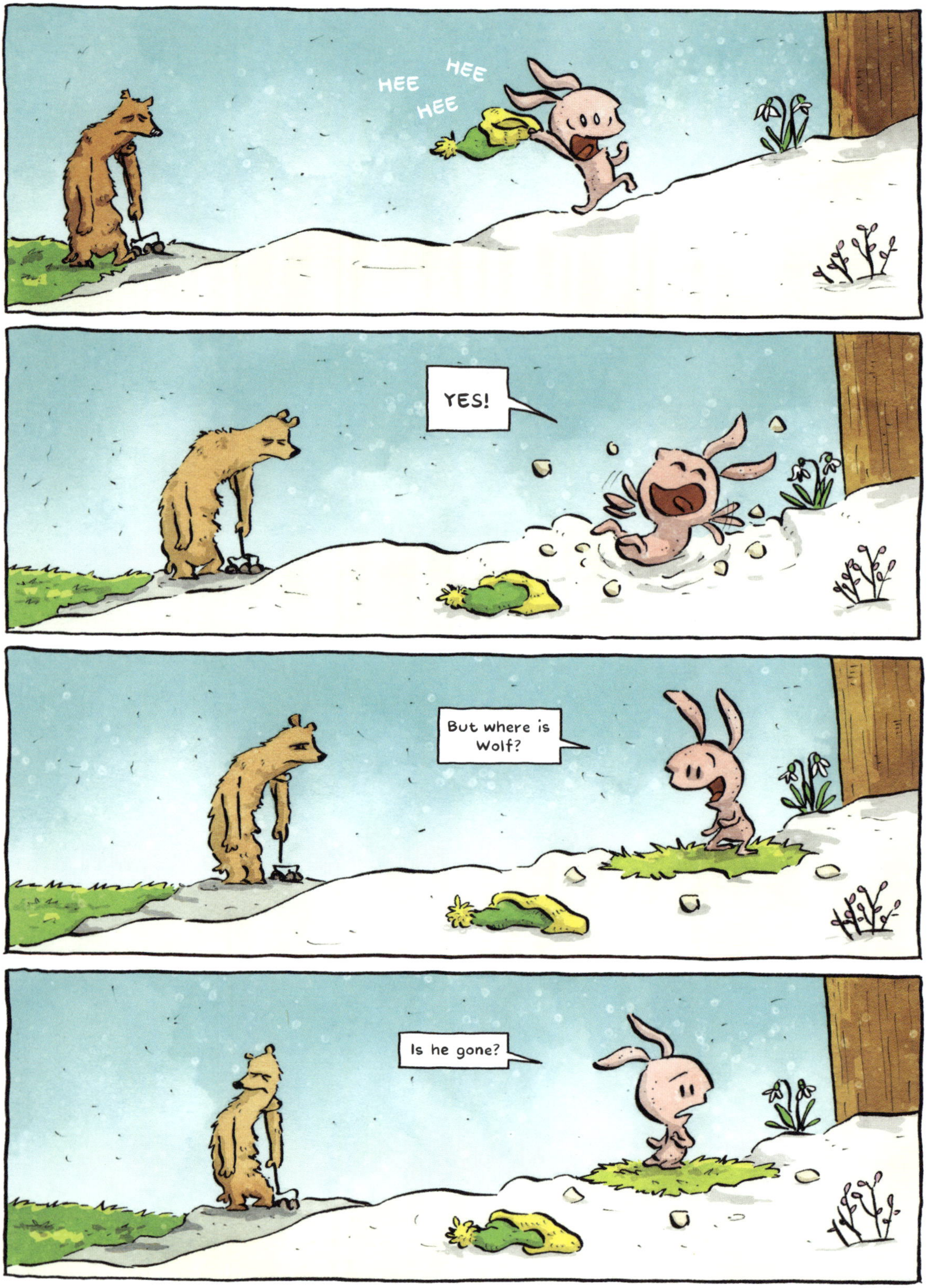
HEE
HEE
HEE
YES!
But where is Wolf?
Is he gone?

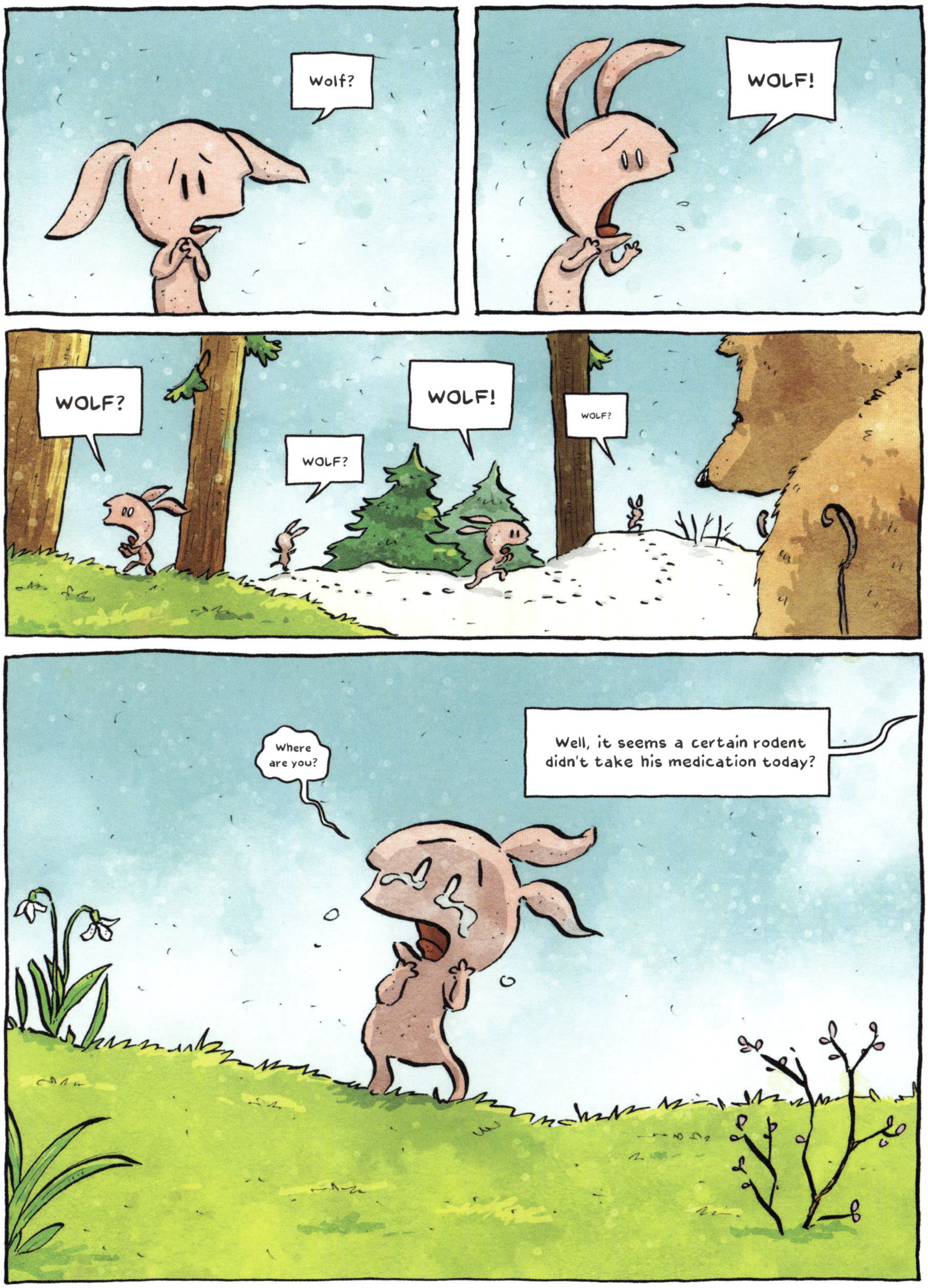
Wolf?
WOLF!
WOLF?
WOLF?
WOLF!
WOLF?
Where are you?
Well, it seems a certain rodent didn't take his medication today?

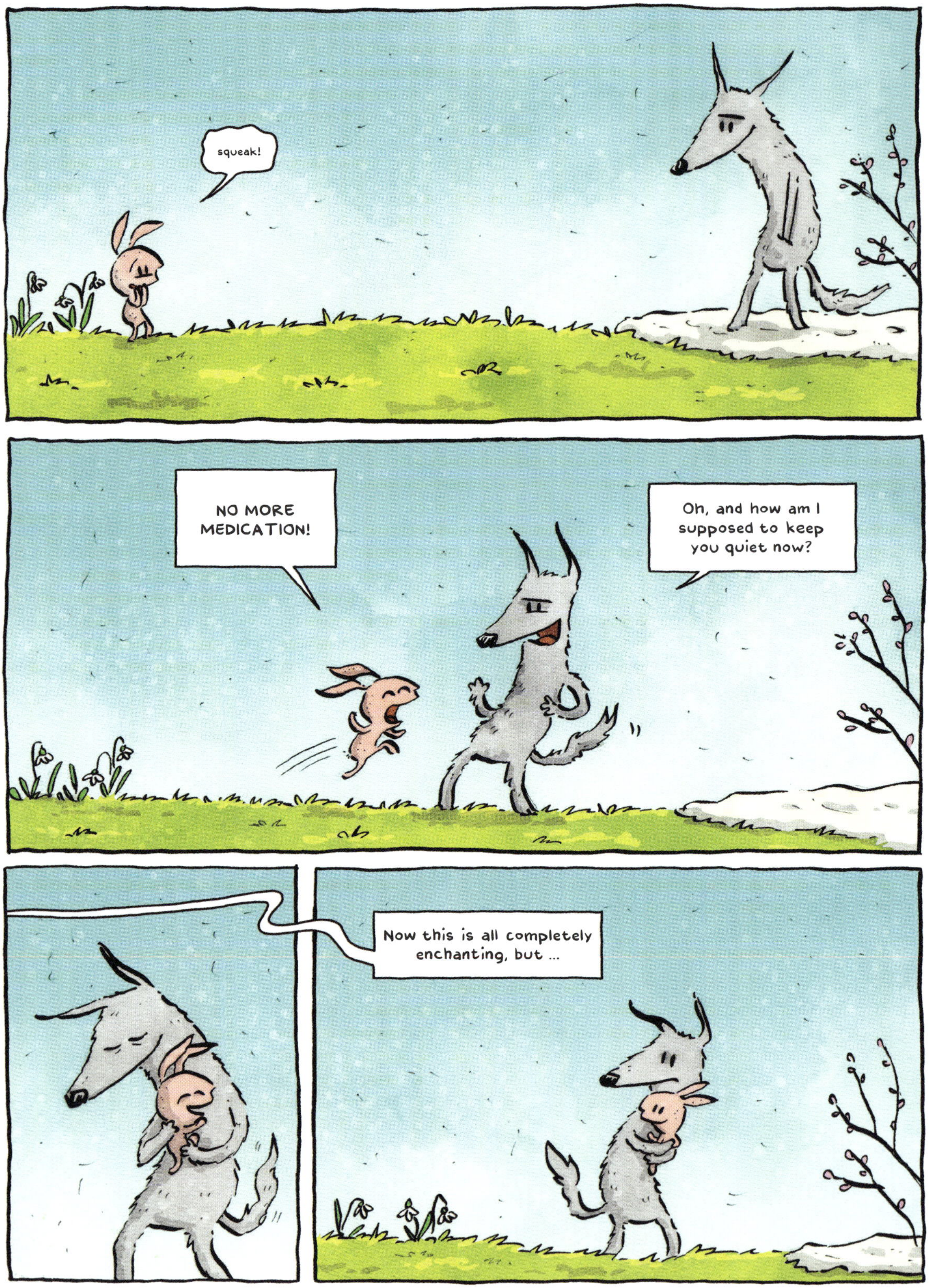
squeak!
NO MORE MEDICATION!
Oh, and how am I supposed to keep you quiet now?
Now this is all completely enchanting, but ...

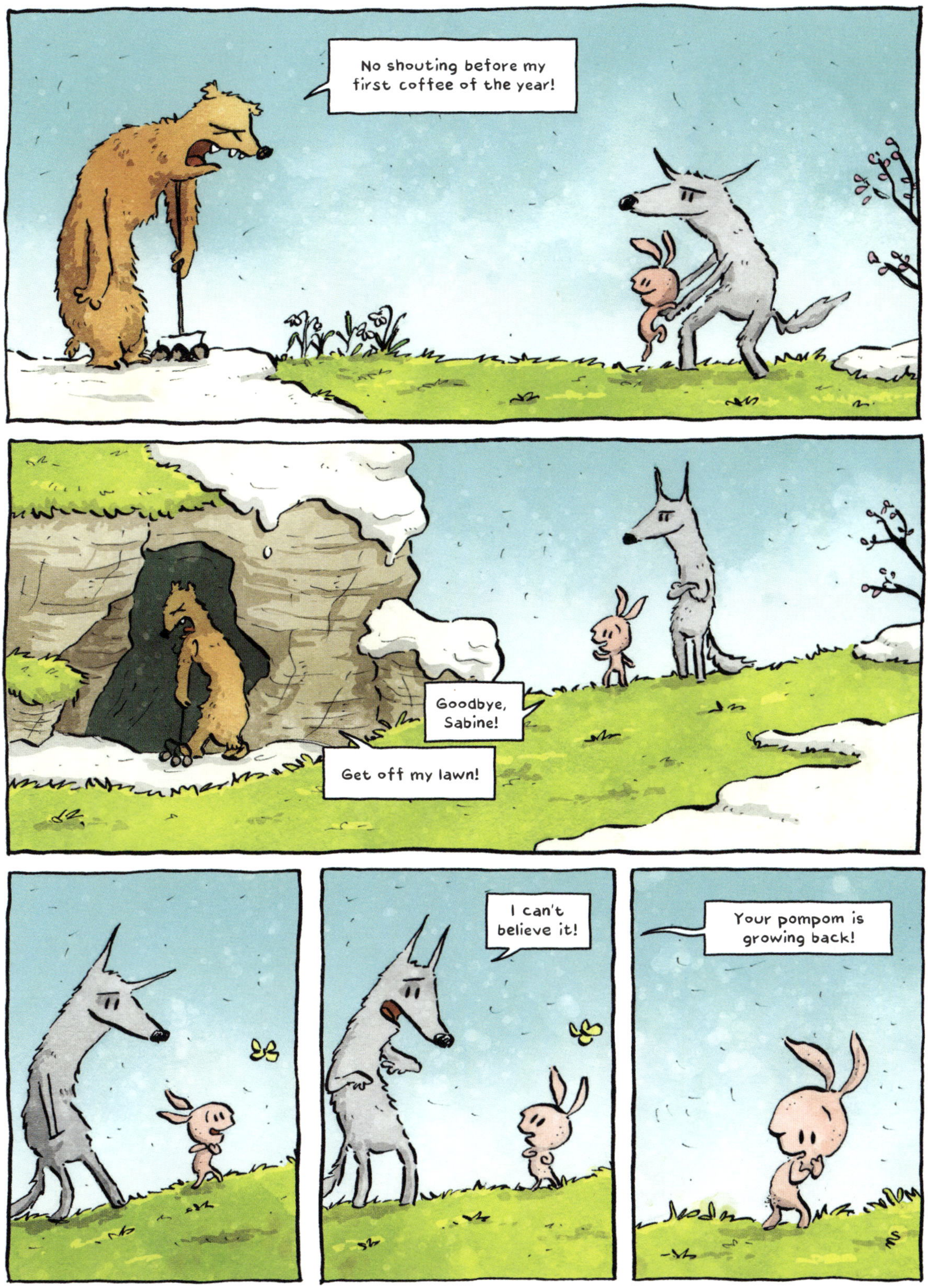
No shouting before my first coffee of the year!
Goodbye, Sabine!
Get off my lawn!
I can't believe it!
Your pompom is growing back!

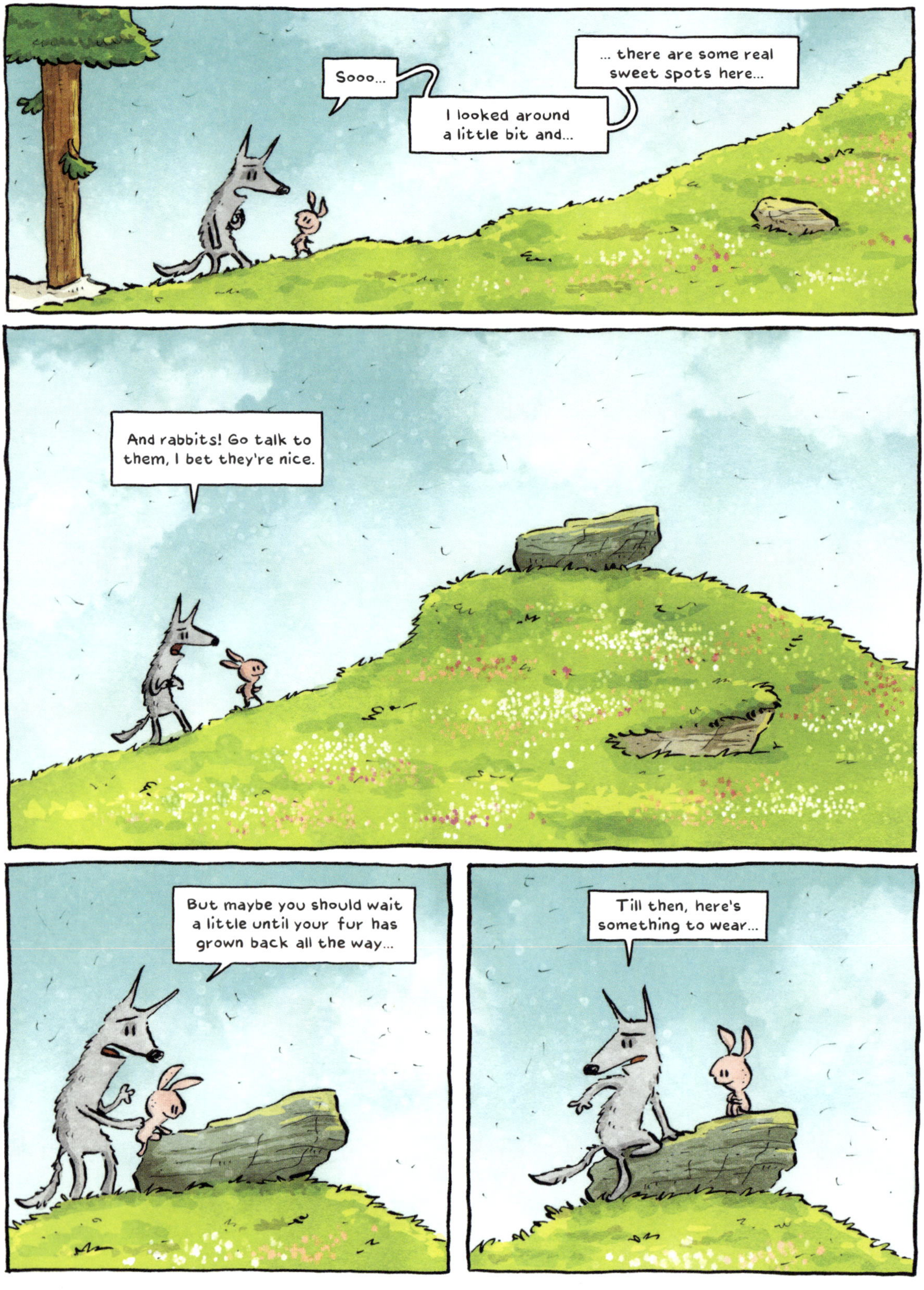
Sooo...
I looked around
a little bit and...
... there are some real
sweet spots here...
And rabbits! Go talk to
them, I bet they're nice.
But maybe you should wait
a little until your fur has
grown back all the way...
Till then, here's
something to wear...

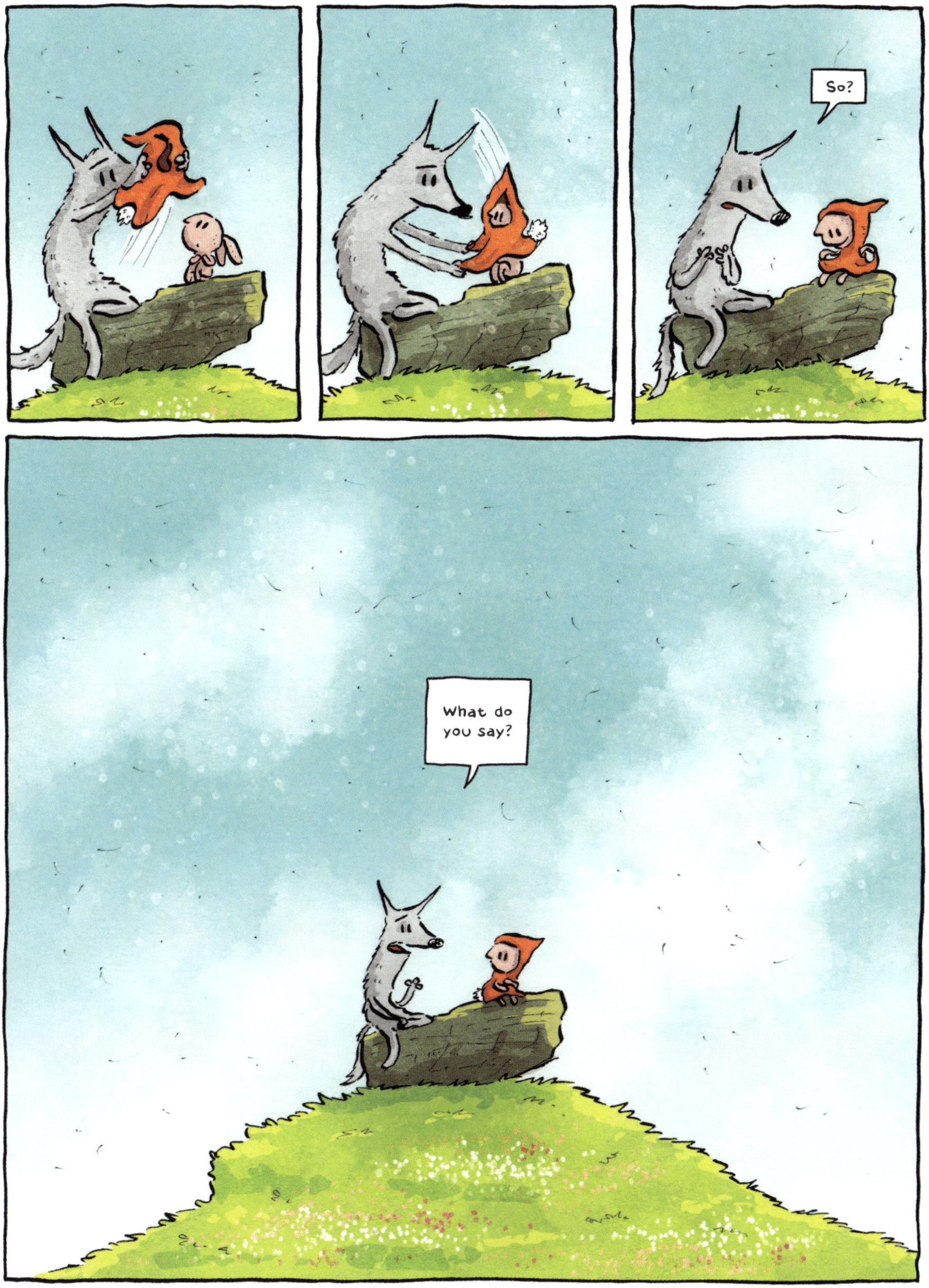
So?
What do you say?

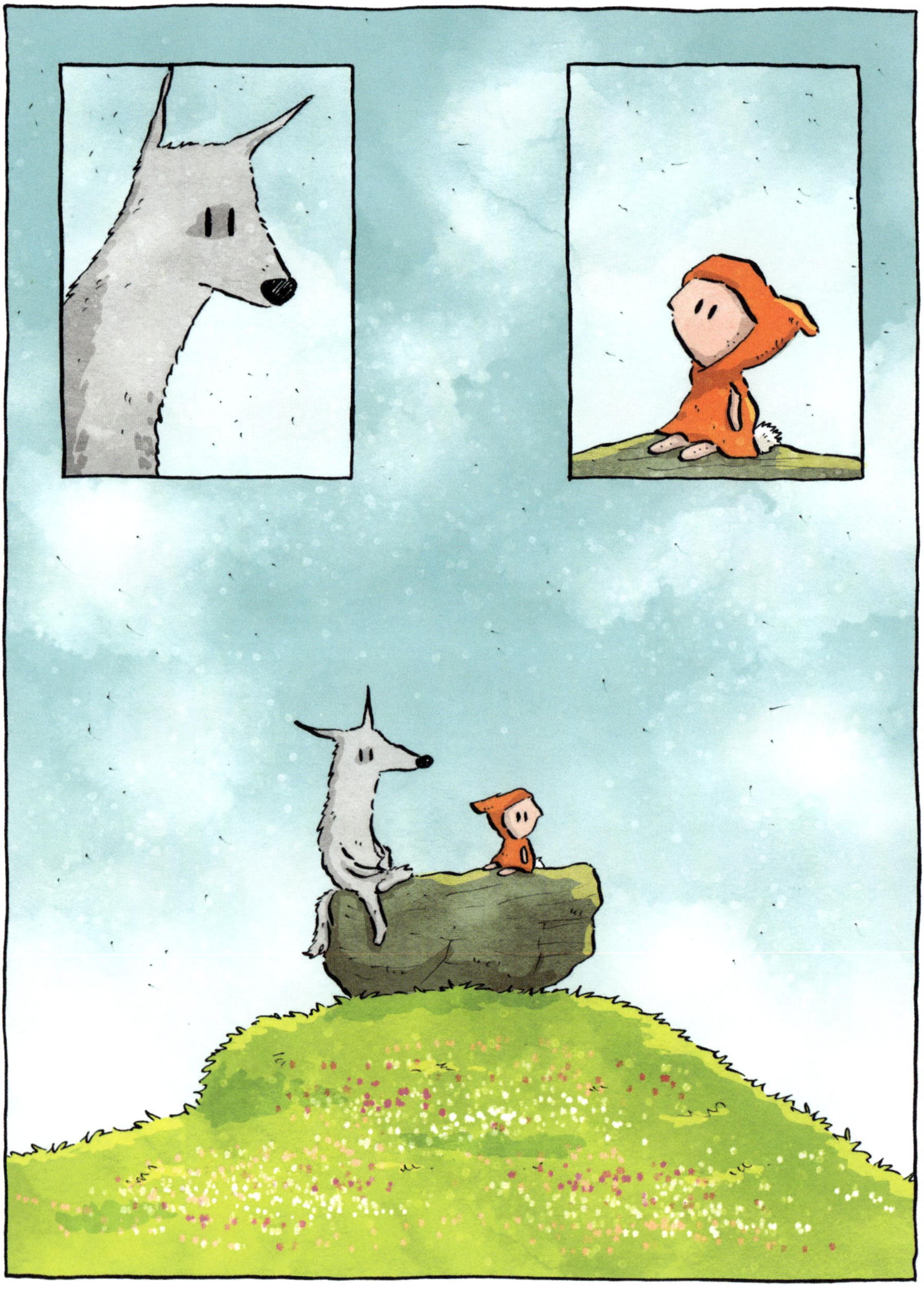

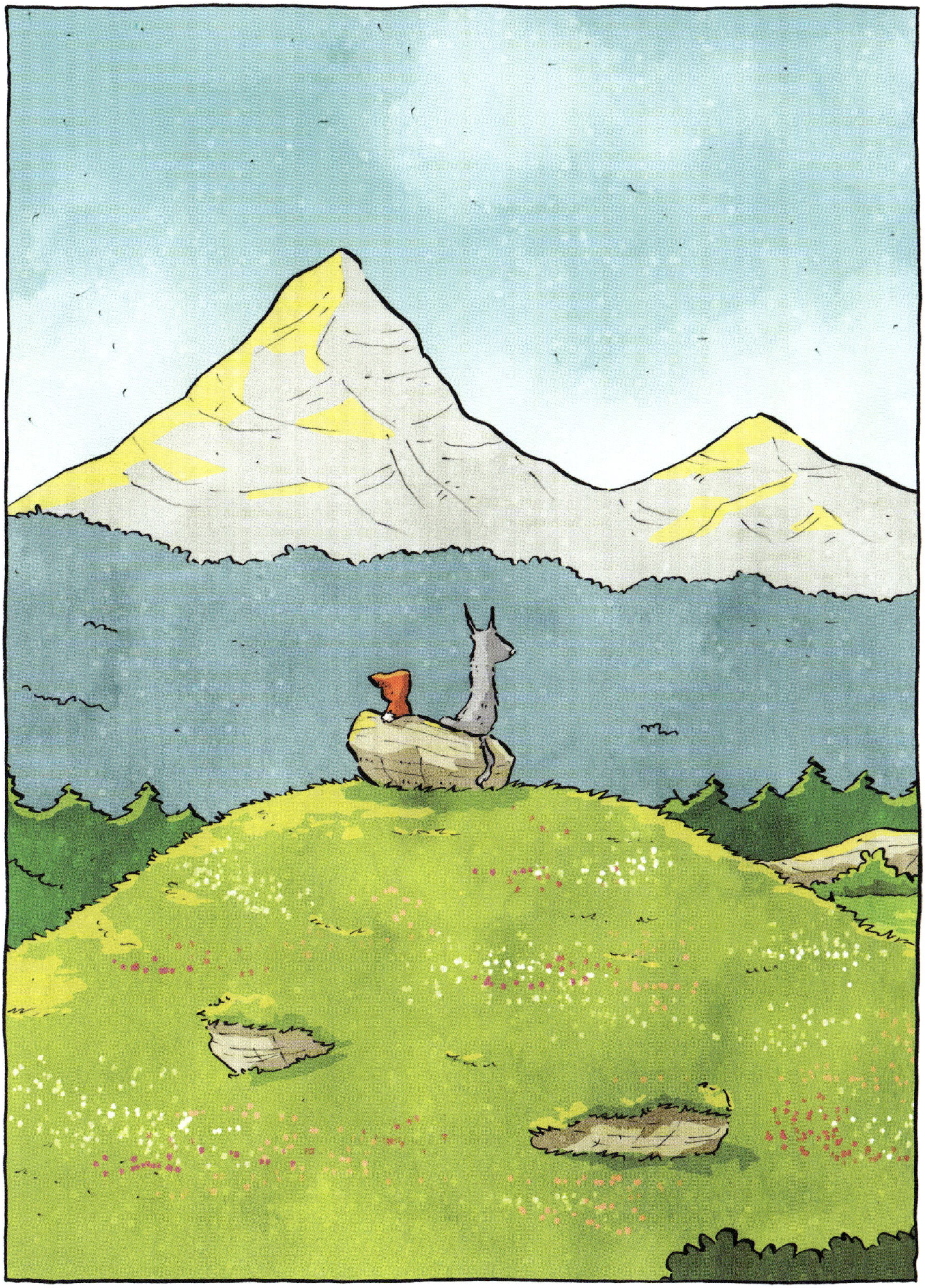

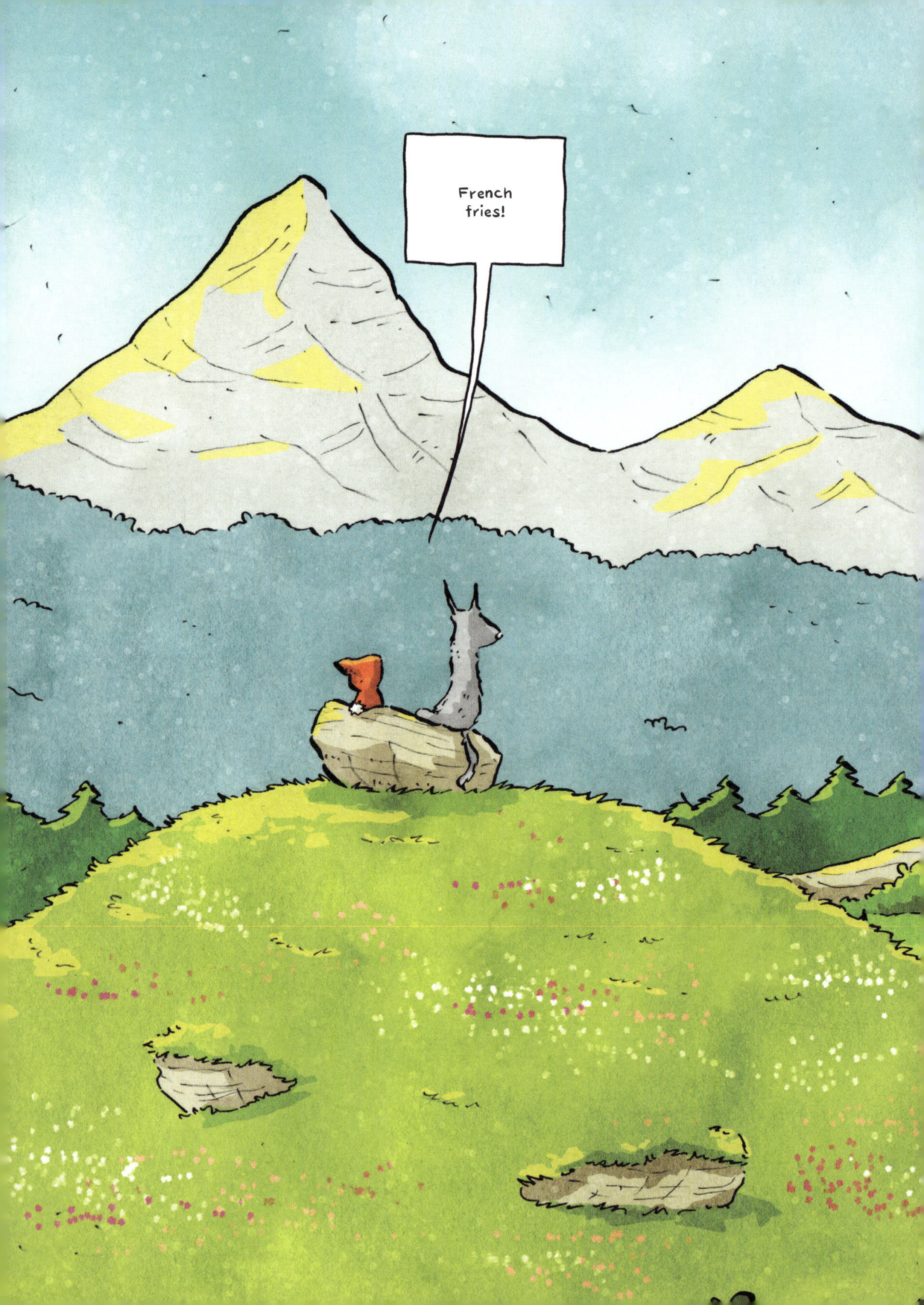
French fries!

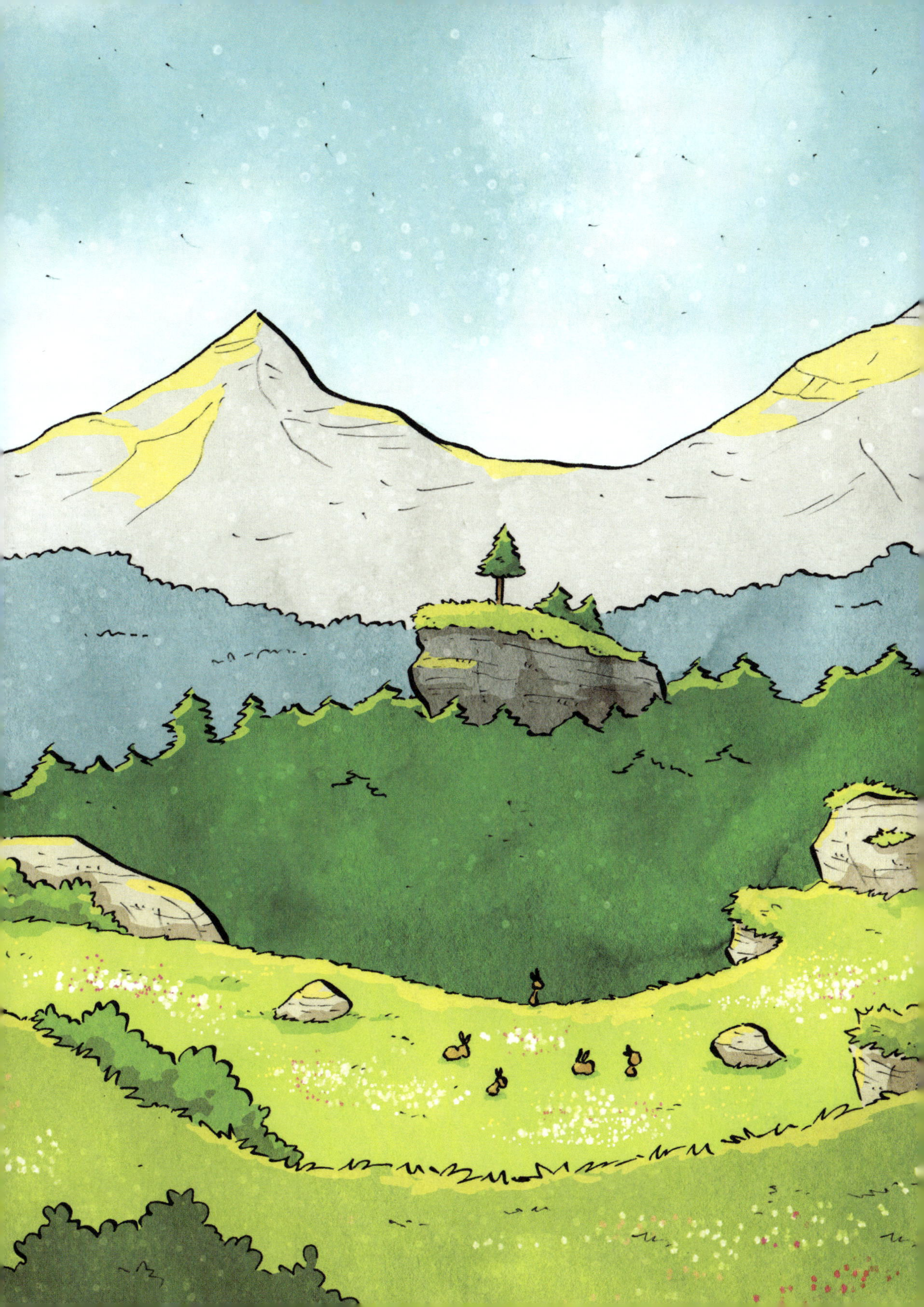

For Thomas, who taught me a lot about wolves.

Thanks!

I would like to thank everyone who accompanied
me on my trip with drip.

Especially

Birgit Weyhe and Ralf König, who motivated me with their enthusiasm for my story and were a great help to me, not only professionally. The team at the comic-drawing seminar in Erlangen, especially Ralf Marczinczik and Katja Rausch. Diana and Philipp for their helpful criticism over the last few meters. Micha and Sebastian for the great support they gave my book. My doctors and nurses at St. Elisabeth Hospital in Leipzig (who, unlike Nurse Erdmute, are all excellent at taking blood samples). And especially my parents.

Josephine Mark

was born in 1981 in Naumburg/Saale and works as an illustrator, comic artist, and graphic designer. She has been publishing comics and cartoons since 2004. *My Trip with Drip* was nominated for the German Children's Book Prize and won the Max and Moritz Award for best graphic novel.

josephinemark.de

Discover Helvetiq's
award-winning graphic novels

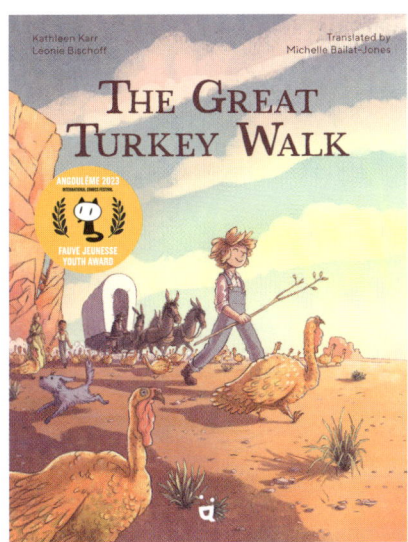

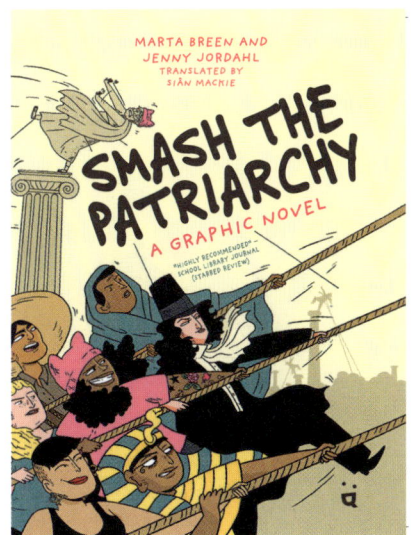

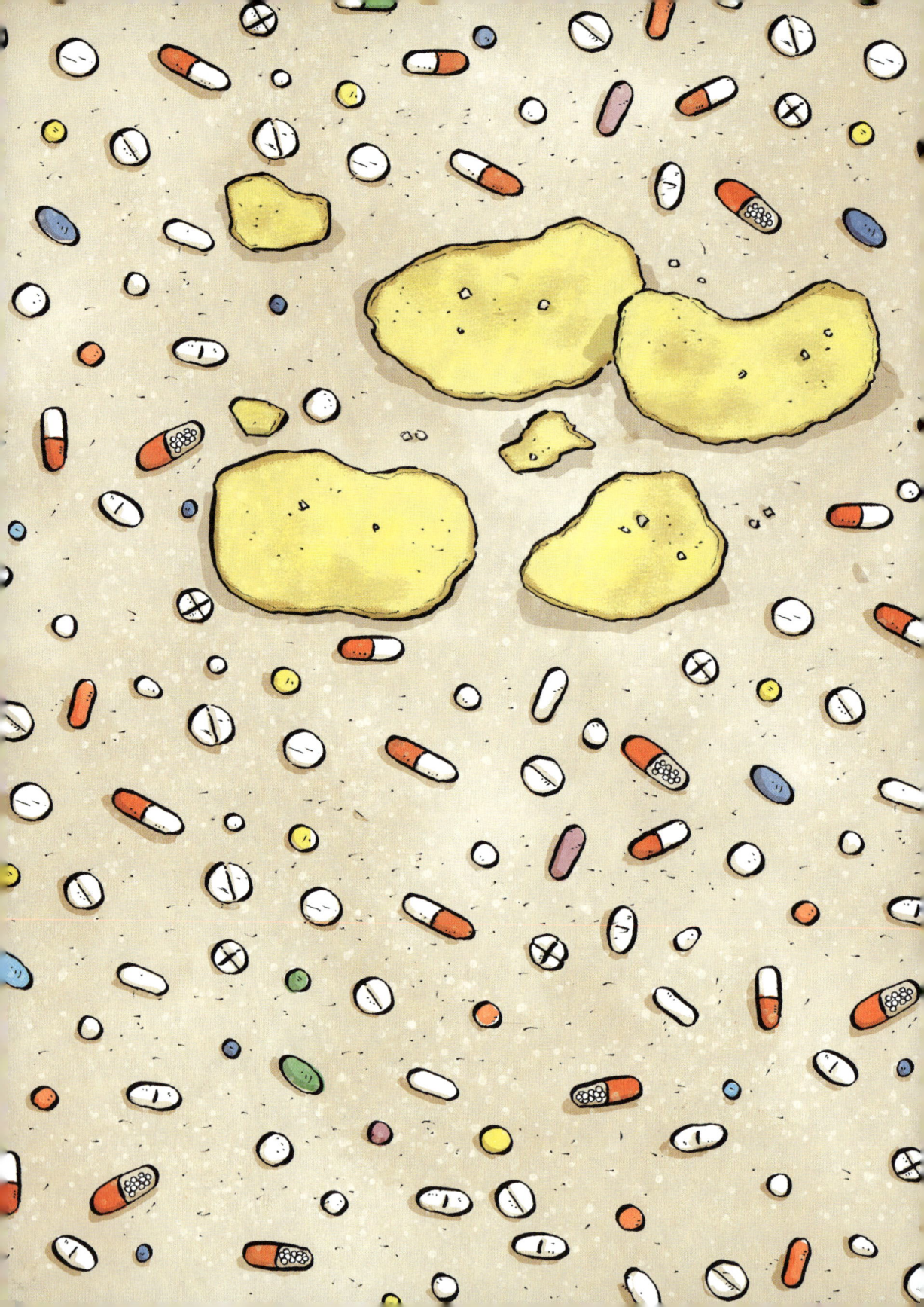